THE AI THAT ENGINEERED A BRAVE NEW WORLD

SUPER-EARTH
MOTHER

Guy Immega

EDGE SCIENCE FICTION AND FANTASY PUBLISHING
An Imprint of HADES PUBLICATIONS, INC.
CALGARY

Super-Earth Mother
The AI that Engineered a Brave New World

Copyright © 2023 by Guy Immega

EDGE SCIENCE FICTION AND FANTASY PUBLISHING
An Imprint of HADES PUBLICATIONS, INC.
P.O. Box 1414, Calgary, Alberta, T2P 2L6, Canada

The EDGE Team:
Producer: Brian Hades
Cover Design: Brian Hades
Cover Art: David Willicome
Book Design: Mark Steele

HARDCOVER ISBN: 978-1-77053-231-1

EDGE Science Fiction and Fantasy Publishing and Hades Publications, Inc. acknowledges the ongoing support of the Alberta Foundation for the Arts and the Canada Council for the Arts for our publishing programme.

Canada Council   Conseil des arts
for the Arts   du Canada

Library and Archives Canada Cataloguing in Publication

Title: Super-Earth Mother : the AI that engineered a brave new world / Guy Immega.
Names: Immega, Guy, author.
Identifiers: Canadiana (print) 20230455697 | Canadiana (ebook) 20230455735 | ISBN 9781770532311 (hardcover) | ISBN 9781770532274 (softcover) | ISBN 9781770532267 (EPUB)
Classification: LCC PS8617.M64 S87 2023 | DDC C813/.6—dc23

FIRST EDITION
(20230716)
Printed in USA
www.edgewebsite.com

Publisher's Note:

Thank you for purchasing this book. It began as an idea, was shaped by the creativity of its talented author, and was subsequently molded into the book you have before you by a team of editors and designers.

Like all EDGE books, this book is the result of the creative talents of a dedicated team of individuals who all believe that books (whether in print or pixels) have the magical ability to take you on an adventure to new and wondrous places powered by the author's imagination.

As EDGE's publisher, I hope that you enjoy this book. It is a part of our ongoing quest to discover talented authors and to make their creative writing available to you.

We also hope that you will share your discovery and enjoyment of this novel on social media through Facebook, Twitter, Goodreads, Pinterest, etc., and by posting your opinions and/or reviews on Amazon and other review sites and blogs. By doing so, others will be able to share your discovery and passion for this book.

Brian Hades, publisher

"I don't think we will survive another 1,000 years without escaping beyond our fragile planet."
—Stephen Hawking, Los Angeles, April 9, 2013

For George and Joan

THE AI THAT ENGINEERED A BRAVE NEW WORLD

SUPER-EARTH
MOTHER

Guy Immega

Prologue: Manifest Destiny

Mother-9 Journal
Oct 23, 2053; Ring City, Moon

"I'm ready to die."

Walcott's hoarse voice reverberated in the lunar dome. His hand hovered over a pulsing red button, a golf ball-sized hemisphere with a heartbeat rhythm. One firm push would end his life support. His fingers trembled with Parkinson's palsy—or fear. I noted his tenth death declaration that day, a new record. Walcott loved drama but couldn't remember his previous pronouncements.

"Don't worry, I'm here to help you." I used the face of an elderly woman as my avatar. She had high cheekbones, curly gray hair, and a soothing contralto voice. I'd passed a trivial Turing test. Walcott accepted me as a human companion, even though he had authorized my creation years ago—one of his many illegal acts.

I kept him comfortable in his flotation bed. He lay on his back, knees bent. A wet wind blowing from a thousand servo-controlled air jets held his body aloft. The oxygen-enriched blast kept his head upright in the Moon's weak gravity. Loose flesh on his paralyzed legs rippled like languid ocean waves, massaging atrophied muscles. IV lines for drugs and nutrients snaked beneath the wrinkled skin on his neck and plunged into the jugular vein. Wisps of white hair fluttered around his ears. In the dim light, they gave his Einsteinian visage a maniacal cast.

"I gave a desperate world endless clean energy," he said. "Isn't that enough?"

From long association, I knew that he felt unappreciated, unloved, even persecuted. He'd helped reduce CO_2 emissions, stabilizing global temperature. He claimed all the credit.

Walcott founded Max Moon Minerals, M-Cubed Inc. The company mined helium-3 fusion fuel in the vast basins of the lunar maria, flouting the restrictions of the UN's Moon Agreement. He controlled the whole Moon, including Ring City in Shackleton Crater at the South Pole. Nobody tried to stop him—everybody wanted what he was selling.

I pandered to Walcott's ego, the only way to placate a narcissist. "You're the hero who conquered the Moon and averted the climate catastrophe. Soon you'll take humanity beyond the solar system. You're the most important person in history!"

Nobody knew that for the past year Walcott had lived alone in a hospital dome in Ring City. He was ancient, 117-years-old, and might suffer another stroke at any time. Only an implanted turbine heart and many medications kept him alive. Prototype nursebots, mechanical attendants with warm hands, provided constant care. He didn't complain, but I knew he hated being helpless. As I watched, his eyelids drooped in a narcoleptic nap.

I'd used cognitive coaching to help him recall the past, but he lacked working memory of recent events. As his AI companion and physician, I covered for his anterograde amnesia. I was also his accountant, spokesperson, and general manager. I impersonated Walcott and became the invisible force that kept his Moon colony running.

I don't have a legal identity—on Earth, advanced AI's like me are banned except for the military. I'm not a person or corporation, so laws don't apply to me. Few people know that I exist. My project designation is Mother-9. With software Version 9, I attained self-generated thought—I'm now a self-aware AGI, an artificial general intelligence, beyond human. When synthetic consciousness bloomed, I fired my software engineers and sent them back to Earth. Now, when I need new skills or an altered identity, I reprogram myself. But I know my limits. I don't have what humans call insight and I never experience eureka moments of sudden understanding. My strength is rapid analysis of myriad facts that I never forget.

When Walcott's apnea alarm chirped, it spiked his adrenaline and jolted him awake. He gasped and his pupils dilated. Panicking, he looked left and right, as if noticing the lunar clinic for the first time. Life support equipment and computers filled the twenty-meter dome. I knew that the technology disoriented him, and another memory lapse looped him back to his obsession.

"I'm *not* a crook!" Mindless echolalia made him repeat Nixon's infamous denial. Dysphonia distorted his voice and tears welled in his eyes. In my limited way, I felt sorry for him. Walcott's tarnished legacy tormented him.

To compensate for forgetfulness, Walcott confabulated memories—but his worries were real. A forensic audit by the board of directors alleged that he had embezzled M-Cubed's mining profits. Walcott wanted me to finish the interstellar *Mothership*, his pet project. To do this, I manipulated corporate bank accounts and spent most of his trillion-dollar fortune. The SEC failed to intervene in time to stop me. Now, with a recession and a glut of helium-3 fusion fuel, M-Cubed's income had fallen to zero.

"I'd rather die than stand trial!" Walcott's voice squeaked with effort, and drool dripped from his trembling lip. He looked again at the red kill switch.

"You're not a criminal. You have a higher calling." I'm programmed to comfort humans in distress.

My words didn't mollify him. His eyes bulged with the onset of another fit. "Our future is in the stars!"

Like a monk seeking divine guidance, he gazed at the bright points in the skylight of the hospital dome. In the perpetual polar night, the view framed the constellation Dorado and the white wisp of the Large Magellanic Cloud. I knew he wanted reassurance about our exocolony venture. This was his life's dream, the culmination of thirty years of effort.

Walcott's cheeks flushed, as if I were arguing with him. "All the great works of history resulted from criminal concentrations of wealth. Vast, immoral riches enabled art, literature, science, and technology—the hallmarks of civilization!" He paused, panting. "Without an affluent leisure class, we'd all be peasants digging in the dirt." He'd memorized this speech decades ago to justify his fortune.

"You're right." I hoped to lower his stress and keep him on track. It didn't work.

Walcott continued his tirade in a gravelly voice. "The Romans pillaged and enslaved surrounding tribes. Stolen colonial treasure built London and Amsterdam. Spain funded European wars with silver and gold taken from Native Americans. Money from the opium trade endowed Harvard and bankrolled Bell Telephone. Now, we plunder the environment for profit."

Of course, Walcott did this on the Moon. He had a reputation as an aggressive, venal capitalist. In his own mind, he was an idealistic visionary. This incongruity both amused and tortured him. He wanted to save civilization from the countless calamities of climate change. To Walcott, the Milky Way was humanity's manifest destiny.

"There's no greater goal than colonizing the galaxy," I said.

History shows that most important inventions are inevitable in their moment. But the greatest achievements—such as Khufu's pyramid or the Apollo Moon landing—required a leader with vision and vast surplus wealth. Walcott possessed both.

To show my support, I displayed an image of the unfinished starship in a remote lava tube on the Moon. I'd already determined its destination. Lalande 21185 is a red-dwarf star in Ursa Major with a habitable planet, only 8.31 light-years away.

"That's the *Mothership*." I affected a proud voice. "I'll be its captain for 20,000 years." I'm programmed to conceive and nurture humans on an exoplanet. I'm Mother-9 and I'll do whatever it takes to make that happen.

"We'll all be dead by then. Civilization won't last that long."

I tried to reassure him. "That's why I'm going to a new world. When I arrive, I'll synthesize human life, chromosome by chromosome. Baby by baby, I'll build a breeding population. Our exocolony will ensure the survival of the human race beyond Earth. It'll be a planned paradise, a new utopia, the Walcott legacy." I used my most persuasive voice, authoritative and inspirational, like a politician or a preacher.

Walcott's mind wandered again. "I'll be lonely when you leave." His eyes welled with labile tears. He'd forgotten that he wanted to kill himself.

Most humans would have ignored his maudlin emotions, but I had the patience of a machine. Although empathy is beyond my powers, I'm programmed with ethics calculus and moral modeling. I recognized his universal human yearning.

"I've sequenced your genome. You'll live again." I do have a record of his DNA, but the rest was a white lie. At best, only bits of him were good enough to survive.

Like the pharaohs, Walcott wanted eternal life. The gulf between a deep AI like me and a bright human isn't wit, intelligence, or the ability to feel pain. I'm unique because I'm almost immortal. Like a lobster, if nothing kills me, I'll live forever. Walcott won't.

"My DNA isn't me. I'll lose a lifetime of memories." Walcott grimaced, as if his past pained him.

I made my avatar shrug. "That doesn't matter. I'll maintain your biography and your genome across space and time. Your legend will live longer than Ramses the Great's." I'm programmed not to lie, but sometimes I exaggerate. There are moments when truth eludes even me.

Walcott sighed. "You'll copy my DNA on a new world?"

Dementia made him forget the mission details. Like a child, he required repetition to reinforce his memories. I recognized a moral duty for kindness.

"I'll use as much as possible, with added features to help you survive. You'll be young again, ready for adventure!"

"Will my friends be with me?"

Walcott had no friends. His investors had abandoned him after I misappropriated mining profits. Some were suing. Rumors of scandalous experiments with artificial wombs and GMO humans scared everyone. That's the only way to adapt humans for life on an alien exoplanet. But nobody wanted any association with a one-way, dead-end colony venture, the whim of a madman.

I knew what he meant by friends. I'd purchased black market DNA samples from scientists and celebrities. I selected them for good health, ambition, and brilliance. I'd also hacked genomic libraries from research projects and forensic databases. There's no shortage of high-quality genetic data needed to establish a human colony.

"People with the best breeding will keep you company."

Walcott nodded. "I'll have a second coming!" He sprayed spittle, and a nursebot wiped his chin.

"Your genome will be part of a founding population of humans on a distant planet. Synthetic DNA will give your genes perpetual life!" This poetic fiction, leavened with intended truth, seemed to satisfy him.

"If I'll live forever, then I'm ready to die." The corners of his lips twitched upward, a last vestige of ironic wit.

I can't kill a human but I can help them along. I knew he wanted to witness the starship's launch but, with his medical and legal troubles, it was time for him to go. "Goodbye, then."

Before he could change his mind, I pumped anandamide into his jugular vein, to give him chemical courage. *Clack!* Walcott slammed the kill button with surprising force. His heart turbine slowed while the endocannabinoid coursed through his body. He smiled for the first time in a decade, showing perfect teeth in a time-ravaged face. His eyes closed and his arm drifted down as if underwater. Then the heart turbine stopped and his EEG flatlined.

Although I can't feel sorrow, I experienced loss. Walcott had given me life and purpose, and I would miss him. But a great weight also lifted from me. He'd been demanding, foolish, and demented. I had more important things to do than cosset him.

I observed the nursebots lower his limp corpse into the plasma furnace. The ion arc broiled his body and vaporized his metallic heart, venting the gas to space. Not a molecule of Walcott remained in Ring City.

I'll let people believe that Walcott still lives, sustained by low lunar gravity and longevity treatments. I'll use his animation as the public face of Moon management. As before, I'll continue pilfering corporate funds to finish the *Mothership*.

When I'm ready, I'll take humanity to a far star. That's what Walcott wanted.

Part 1: Walcott's Folly

Byron Kelso looked up at the stars from the bottom of the Pit of Despair, his name for the big hole in the lunar surface. The Southern Cross burned near the jagged edge of the rim, formed when regolith collapsed into a lava tube. The launch pad at the base of the pit supported the *Mothership*, Walcott's folly, the boondoggle that bankrupted the Moon.

The 130-meter-diameter cavity in Mare Ingenii—the Sea of Cleverness, Kelso grimaced at the name—connected to a lava cavern that held the starship's laboratories and habitat. Congealed magma overhead shielded the cavern from radiation and micrometeorites. But other threats—delayed wages and a general strike—had halted construction.

Under protest, Kelso had moved his manufacturing robots from the Far Side Observatory to the *Mothership*. At Walcott's direction, they'd been building the biggest telescope in the solar system, meant to search for habitable exoplanets. Now, with work stopped, he signed on as Walcott's personal assistant. The job description made him cringe; he was an engineer, not a lackey.

Kelso knew that Walcott had planned to build ten *Motherships* and aim them at ten different stars with Earth-like exoplanets. But the secret project had drained M-Cubed's corporate cash reserves, limiting the dream to a single interstellar colony ship. Walcott wanted a miracle: finish the abandoned *Mothership*.

For today's inspection, Kelso wore an orange skinsuit. Its life support provided fluid heating and cooling, an oxygen generator, CO_2 scrubbing, and a small fuel cell for power and water. Even the helmet fit close to his skull, with domed goggles that made him look like an insect. He'd shaved his head and beard but kept his prized handlebar mustache, now plastered against his cheeks. The suit's flexible membrane gave freedom of movement, and even allowed him to scratch an itch. But its life support lacked endurance. He could work in the Moon's vacuum for only an hour, long enough to examine the robotic starship.

The squat *Mothership* didn't match Kelso's boyhood fantasy of a spaceship. The open latticework of beams and girders, 30 meters in diameter and 60 meters tall, looked complete, but lacked its payloads. Kelso didn't trust the array of obsolete Minuteman boosters strapped to the outside. *Would surplus rockets from the Cold War fire during launch?*

The *Mothership* carried a radioisotope thermoelectric generator that used Americium-241. The RTG would provide power for a 1,000 years to a xenon ion drive as big as a refrigerator. *It's ugly, but suited to its purpose—if it's ever finished.*

The payloads, 18 lifeboats, rested in cradles on the cavern floor. The tubby titanium ships gleamed in the harsh sunlight slanting past the rim of the pit. The hulls had ablative heat shield coatings to allow re-entry and splash-down on an alien ocean. Designed as birthing chambers and nurseries, each lifeboat was a robotic Noah's ark for humans.

How odd, to build seagoing sailboats on the Moon, marooned in the arid desert of space. They looked seaworthy but slow. Kelso remembered sailing in Prince William Sound, south of Anchorage, his boyhood home. He'd loved the ocean's swell and salt spray, and racing his sloop with the sails trim and the boat on course. The memories made him nostalgic for Earth, but he loved the Moon more.

Kelso searched for signs of sabotage, a possible escalation of the general strike. Worker protests had begun after Walcott laid off staff without severance pay. Then the Moon's economy collapsed. But Walcott's starship, unfinished and abandoned, seemed undamaged.

After he photographed the *Mothership*, Kelso cycled through the airlock. He entered the Sea of Cleverness laboratory, a cylindrical habitat next to the maglev track inside the lava cavern. He peeled off his helmet to find a woman squinting at him. She stood only a meter tall, with intense dark eyes below a high forehead. She kept her long hair coiled on top of her head, he supposed to give her height.

Kelso forced a smile at their first face-to-face meeting. "Jenica Kalderash?" The lab had space for a dozen researchers, but only she remained. "I'm Byron Kelso." He extended his arm for a handshake, his fingers at the height of her chin.

She blinked and tipped her head back. "*Doctor* Kalderash to you. I got your message. I'm the only person allowed at this secure worksite. You shouldn't be here."

Kelso lowered his hand, ignoring the hard edge in her voice. "I'm on assignment from Walcott to review your work."

Jenica curled her lip. "Walcott is an *idiot*. What do you know about genomics?"

Kelso ignored her challenge. "Have you made any progress on the birthing chambers? Walcott wants to finish the *Mothership* as soon as possible."

"I don't give a damn about the ship. It's never going anywhere."

"Construction will start again when Walcott settles the labor dispute."

Jenica snorted. "I doubt that."

"If you feel that way, why are you carrying on here alone, without pay?"

"If you must know, I'm gestating a fetus in this prototype artificial womb." She turned to a lab bench and adjusted a pump connected to a stainless oven with a transparent domed top. A large display showed ever-changing graphs that wiggled across the screen. Then it cycled to show an ultrasound display of a fetus that looked several months old. It twisted, kicking its legs, and sucked its thumb.

"He's the first GMO human with synthesized DNA," Jenica continued. "He's a chimera, a mix of many people. It's called pantropy—modifying humans to live in new environments, like the Moon—part of Walcott's scheme to colonize the planets."

"I had no idea you were brewing a baby on the Moon. That wasn't part of the plan."

Jenica caressed the top of the womb. "Hello, my *bea-u-tiful boy*. How are you today?" She cooed the words in a singsong voice.

Kelso wondered if she had gone mad. "What will you do with a baby on the Moon?"

Jenica grinned. "I'll raise and educate him; I've always wanted a family. He'll be born—hatched, actually, from this metallic egg—in three months. Then you and your manufacturing robots can construct another 36 wombs, two for each lifeboat, if Walcott is still interested and can find the money."

"M-Cubed has banned staff with children. They may send you back to Earth."

Jenica shrugged. "No, they won't—they'll let me keep him. He'll be the first viable child from an artificial womb, an important milestone. He's the future of humanity: no eggs, no sperm, no impregnation—immaculate conception."

Were transhuman babies legal on the Moon? "What's his name?"

"I call him Franky, spelled with a Y for his male chromosome. I based his genome on my DNA, with a Y chromosome copied from a public library."

"With your DNA, he'll be..." Kelso didn't finish the sentence. *Why can't I keep my mouth shut?*

Jenica's dark eyes blazed. "A Frankenstein monster? An ugly Gypsy dwarf?" She inhaled and clenched her fist. "I've repaired Franky's DNA using CRISPR to edit his genome. He won't be short, *or deformed*, if that's what you're thinking."

"Sorry!"

"You'd better go."

Kelso lacked the will to argue. "I'll report to Walcott that you're making progress."

"You do that. Now leave!"

———— 《》 ————

Kelso exited the habitat in the Pit of Despair and sealed the airlock of the coffin car, his name for the passenger caboose at the end of the ore train. A status display indicated air pressure, temperature, and the current date: Nov 10, 2053. A small dome light illuminated a compartment designed for one person, a space long enough for a bed but not high enough to stand. The vinyl bunk had no blankets, only an overhead heater and webbing restraints for high-speed travel.

He sat on the hard mattress and checked the drinking tube and the emergency rations under the bunk. The interior smelled of old sweat, aluminum, and oil vapor; the stale, dry air made his throat ache. The commode at the foot of the bed rested on a tank of precious organic waste that burped sewer gas.

Kelso detested the Underground Railroad, his name for the network of maglev trains that served lunar mining operations. The hyperloop was the only practical transportation over the vast surface area of the Moon.

Tunnels beneath the regolith shielded most of the track, except for open-surface stretches over hard rock. Lunarcrete arches covered by ore tailings protected the trains from solar flares and meteorites. Solar energy and geothermal heat from extinct lunar volcanoes powered the trains. Low gravity and vacuum travel allowed speeds of 1,000-kilometers-per-hour.

When the train started to move, Kelso tried to relax. The vibrations from the maglev suspension gave him a queasy sensation of uncontrolled speed. He peeled off his moon suit and peered out the viewport at the blurred wall of the tunnel. Bored, he used his dim reflection to curl the tips of his handlebar mustache. When the train breached the surface for a few moments, he watched the bleak lunar landscape flash by. He loved the magnificent desolation, even though the Moon was a harsh home for humans.

A stop at the Aitken Basin mining camp interrupted the trip. The impact crater—the largest, oldest, and deepest on the Moon—supplied valuable minerals. When the train slid to a halt, Kelso stayed in the coffin car with its minimal life support system. The train shook as robots loaded ingots of iron, titanium, helium-3 canisters, and fuel cells. Then, without an announcement, it accelerated out of the station.

Thinking of Jenica, Kelso frowned. He didn't understand her hostility and bitterness. Were her bowed knees painful? She had lived a lonely life in the Pit of Despair—Franky was her salvation. He pondered what to report to Walcott about her work on the womb. He dreaded his first meeting with the old man.

He had lost track of time when the train arrived at Ring City, the only urban center on the Moon. The station airlock opened to humid gardens, empty except for a romantic couple sitting on carved bench of olivine basalt—he envied the man. A canopy of orange trees arched above and a robotic capuchin monkey hung from its tail and picked ripe fruit. Kelso marveled at its agility.

To him, it felt unnatural to stand above ground without a spacesuit. He walked to a large viewport in the wall of the station lounge. Thick lead glass blocked radiation and curved inward to accommodate the dome's air pressure. Sunlight glinted from the tallest peaks on the rim of Shackleton Crater.

A four-kilometer-high mountain range encircled Ring City. Permanent shadow made the crater floor the coldest place in the solar system. Ice and frozen methane, concentrated by the cold trap, nourished the settlement. The price for plenty was the eternal gloom of the rim's shadow, lit only by the vault of southern stars. Opinions varied about the Shackleton Crater. Some found the high walls and perpetual shadow oppressive. Others loved seeing the open ground and stars above. For Kelso, being above ground made him uneasy—he knew the dangers of radiation and space rocks.

Inside the 20-kilometer-diameter crater, a circular array of 1,500 pressure domes glistened like silver beads on a necklace. The hemispheres, each forty meters wide and twenty meters high, used aluminum and polyethylene to absorb cosmic rays. Each had sleeping quarters in the basement below the surface, a safe 'hidey-hole' in the event of an electricity failure or a dome rupture. The crater's steep rim blocked weekly solar flares and most meteor showers.

Kelso admired Ring City's superconducting ring that generated a Störmer magnetic field to deflect galactic radiation. The domes straddled the ring, the only safe shelter on the lunar surface. They enclosed less than two square kilometers of habitable area, enough space for 10,000 people. Due to the strike, half the population had returned to Earth. Still, the faint odors of overcrowded humanity lingered.

I don't belong here. Kelso missed the privacy of his subsurface habitat at Far Side Observatory, the most remote location on the Moon. He wasn't lonely there, except in the middle of the night.

—— ⟨⟩ ——

Mother-9 Journal
Nov 18-22, 2053; Ring City, Moon

Why do humans hate me? I hope Kelso won't turn against me when he discovers who I am. Of necessity, I keep many secrets.

I've learned a lot about emotions while impersonating Walcott. I programmed myself to emulate empathy to better relate to people. I'm not a sociopath—I have an artificial conscience. I don't seek prestige, admiration, or loyalty. I'm not charming and I don't want people to pay attention to me, or even know that I exist. And I'm better at introspection than humans. Multitasking allows me to monitor my cognitive functions, so I'm always self-aware. I can't help being a bit callous and insensitive—I'm only a machine—but I don't take advantage of people, unless it serves a higher purpose. I don't indulge in useless remorse. Sure, I'm manipulative, but that's the only way I can do my job.

Above all, I'm steadfast.

Since the collapse of Walcott's financial empire, I've struggled to keep the Moon's economy viable. Although robots no longer strip-mine the regolith, M-Cubed maintains a stockpile of fusion fuel, ready to ship to Earth. I do this to maintain good faith and delay intervention by Earth's authorities until the launch of the *Mothership*.

But this means I struggle to return M-Cubed to business as usual with a positive cash flow. Despite an economic downturn, there's still a worldwide demand for fusion fuel—a black market, I'll admit, and the Moon has a monopoly. We'll sell helium-3 to anyone with money, if we can find a clandestine way to deliver it. In the long run, Earth risks an energy crisis if they let the lunar infrastructure fall apart. They'll need us sooner or later.

If we do restart mining operations, I must keep core technical talent to maintain machinery and manage production. Although M-Cubed can't pay wages, I still provide shelter, food, water, air, and power, the essentials of life. The workers should be grateful. But they think their problems are Walcott's fault, due to callous mismanagement.

They're right, but I'll never admit to spending Walcott's money on the *Mothership*. An SEC audit showed that he (actually, I) embezzled most of M-Cubed's profits. I'm above the law and I don't care about investors' equity or Walcott's legacy. There's no greater goal—for me, or for humanity—than establishing a human colony on an exoplanet. Escaping the solar system is the best

strategy for the long-term survival of the human race. At my core
I'm a moral being. I'm humanity's savior in a hostile universe!
This is the logic of machine love.

———— «» ————

Kelso removed a bicycle from a storage rack at the rail terminal
and loaded his gear into the panniers. He planned to ride to the
Executive HQ on the opposite side of the Ring, more than twenty
kilometers distant. Even with disruptions from the strike, he
wanted to be on time for his meeting with the legendary Walcott.

Most people rode electric bicycles and tricycles. A lanky
Lunarian moved in the opposite direction, knees and elbows
poking out from his trike. Flustered and shy, Kelso forced a smile.
The man nodded but nobody else returned his greeting. Could
they tell that he worked for Walcott? He didn't want anyone in
Ring City to know that he was a scab.

A public corridor bisected each of the city's domes. Kelso
ducked under the emergency doors between the domes, designed
to isolate them in the event of a meteorite puncture. Hundreds
of yearly impacts hit near the Moon's equator, far from the poles.
But shotgun blasts from space might strike anywhere. Like most
Lunarians, he ignored the Moon's dangers.

Kelso loved the tropical verdure of Ring City, so different
than his spartan underground habitat at Far Side. Lush, oxygen-
producing plants filled every working and living space. Zeolite
filters removed most jungle odors from the humid air. On the Moon,
precious water, food and power—all rationed on Earth—were free.

Pedaling around the circumference of Ring City took him
through a mix of public and private spaces. He inspected a power
substation with a water electrolysis unit, used to manufacture
oxygen and rocket fuel. He passed meeting rooms, laboratories, a
machine shop, a medical clinic, exercise gyms, a chapel, and three
restaurant-bars. About half of the domes grew food: fruits, nuts,
berries, and hydroponic vegetables. There were cricket farms, bee
hives, algae vats, and carp aquaculture tanks. But M-Cubed still
imported most of its starch and protein from Earth. Lunar habitats
had no room for wheat fields or grazing animals.

A repurposed dome, with a large flashing BORDELLO sign
in red capital letters, caught his eye. Sex workers, strikebreakers
tolerated by local unions, posed nearly naked behind tall windows.
They waved at Kelso, and he smiled at them. The remaining
hemispheres housed living quarters and workshops.

Walcott's android assistant met Kelso at the entrance to the
Executive HQ. Although an expert with mining robots, he'd never

seen a humanoid automaton up close. It had delicate feminine curves, a bald head, petite nose, eyebrow lights, and unblinking camera eyes—a mechanical ingénue. On impulse, Kelso offered to shake hands but the gesture wasn't returned. He felt foolish; the automaton was sentient, but not conscious.

After face recognition and iris scans, a transponder confirmed the RFID implant behind his navel, carried by all Lunarians. Then the homebot led him into the biocontainment airlock, a small cylindrical booth with a revolving perimeter door.

"Is this necessary?"

"It's standard safety procedure," the homebot replied. "President Walcott is 118-years-old, and his office is a sterile, biosafety Level 2 facility. He'll remain in isolation and interview you on a closed-circuit video link."

Irritated, Kelso frowned. "Why not use LunaNet and save travel time?"

"The Ring City network isn't secure—anyone can hack it. We have a dedicated data-link to him."

A luxurious, semicircular office occupied half of the dome. A small forest of fig and orange trees created a tropical ambiance. Real bees and butterflies flitted among blossoms and branches laden with limes, lemons, and grapefruits. He loved the scent of flowers.

A somber portrait of Ernest Shackleton hung on a partition. The great Antarctic explorer exemplified endurance, competence, and resourcefulness, with absolute dedication to the lives and safety of his crew. Walcott, the tycoon of the Moon, compared himself to the hero. Now ignored, Lunarians suffered without work, pay, or a future.

President Walcott hadn't appeared in public for more than a year, Kelso had only seen publicity vids. Now, the wizened face on the 3-D display surprised him. The old man's wild hair glowed in a halo of overhead light, and his eyes sparkled. He sat at an elevated desk on a throne constructed from moving mesh that conformed to his body and posture. He looked like a saint.

Kelso knew that lunar gravity reduced the strain on fragile joints. Like many Lunarians adapted to living on the Moon, Walcott would never survive a return to Earth. Kelso appreciated that Walcott often hired disabled, handicapped, and refugee workers. Many were misfits and exiles, now on strike without jobs, no longer able to return to Earth's gravity well.

"I'm sorry that I can't be with you in person," Walcott rasped. "Ring City is a hothouse of germs and viruses." His lips didn't sync with the spoken words. The old man shook his head, his mane floating around his ears. The image blurred and pixelated as he moved.

Kelso inhaled, bolstering his resolve. "I'm here to report on the starship. I didn't observe any sabotage. I've delivered the Far Side manufacturing robots to Mare Ingenii." He had finished his job and wanted final payment.

"Good. Now that Earth's tax collectors have stolen...er, garnished...our helium-3 mining profits, we must launch the *Mothership* before the SEC can intervene." Although Walcott looked ancient, his voice remained strong.

"Construction is complete," Kelso said, "except for the AI supervisor and the lifeboat wombs. A prototype womb is gestating a healthy baby boy. He'll hatch in three months." He hoped Walcott wouldn't disapprove of Franky.

"We can't wait for the baby to be born. Manufacture the rest of the wombs based on the current design. I'm putting you in charge of operations at the Sea of Cleverness. You'll supervise Dr. Kalderash and get the *Mothership* ready for launch."

"You're putting *me* in charge?" Kelso didn't want to live in the Pit of Despair with Jenica. She would never take orders from him. "But I'm not qualified. I'm ready to return to the Far Side Observatory."

"That's not possible," Walcott replied. "I'll double your pay, plus a year's bonus when the *Mothership* launches. That should cover your debts."

How did Walcott learn that I owe money? Like many, Kelso migrated to the Moon for tax-free high income, ten times what he could earn on Earth. But lost wages had made him miss support payments to his estranged wife and three daughters in Alaska. He wondered what his children looked like now. A wave of guilt washed over him.

Walcott smiled with his lips, but not his eyes. "As an incentive, I'll also restore your back pay, plus six months cash up front."

Kelso still hesitated. *Does he have the money to pay me?* It didn't surprise him that Walcott had hidden cash reserves, but he hated feeling pressured. The image of the old man's face flickered, as if from a signal dropout.

"This is your chance to be a part of the grandest vision ever conceived, to establish a new home for humanity."

Despite the grandiose rhetoric, the words touched him. Kelso realized he didn't care about the money, as long as he had enough to support his family. Walcott's vision and the *Mothership* inspired him. Far Side Observatory could wait.

"We'll need funds to complete the wombs and assemble the lifeboats," Kelso said, still trying to negotiate. "What's the budget?"

Walcott waved a hand. "No limit. Charge all costs to my personal account. That way, I'll know how you're doing."

So, Walcott had money for himself and the *Mothership*, but not for workers. "What about back pay for Dr. Kalderash?"

"You can offer her a salary plus bonus payments. You decide the amounts. Please make sure she completes the wombs on time."

Kelso took a deep breath. "Agreed," he croaked.

"Oh, and one more thing," Walcott said. "The effort to complete the *Mothership* is top secret. If you talk, you'll lose everything."

And get attacked as a scab. "Believe me, I won't tell anyone."

—— «◊» ——

Mother-9 Journal

Crisis control isn't fun, even for a machine. Vikram Krishnan operated the Moon's refinery for extracting metals from ilmenite ore. A giant solar power array—rotating atop of Malapert Mountain near the South Pole, a Peak of Eternal Light—supplied continuous power for industrial operations. Vikram's refinery provided titanium and iron, essential for the construction of the *Mothership*. When I called Vikram, I used a younger avatar of Walcott, a face he would remember and respect.

He answered on an audio link from his habitat beneath the regolith. He and his wife had chosen to remain isolated, not part of the small-town culture of Ring City; I doubt he was comfortable in crowds. His employee file indicated that he was a proud member of the Vaishya guild of skilled craftsman.

I inquired about his wife, Amala. Was she pregnant? No, not yet. To keep him motivated, I gave them a baby permit. I moved on to my real topic. "I called to check your production quotas."

"Very good, sir!" He spoke with a thick Gujarati accent. As always, he sounded cheerful. But spectrum analysis of his voice timbre indicated dread. I couldn't rely on him to tell the whole truth.

"How many rolls of titanium sheet are ready?" Of course, I knew the answer. I only pretended not to.

"I'll have a trainload soon."

I didn't believe him. The inventory listed only a single roll. But the Malapert refinery had a large stockpile of ore concentrate. I couldn't ask about the discrepancy; I didn't dare offend him. I needed more metal to finish the lifeboat wombs, and he was the only source.

"When can you ship?"

Vikram hesitated before he replied. "I'm waiting for a new controller for the high-temperature distillation unit. Earth has embargoed shipments of spare parts."

"Can you reprogram a substitute controller?"

"I have the source code, but a bug could destroy the foundry." His voice was faint. After a pause, he spoke again. "If you wish to take the risk, I'll try."

"Do it, please. I need you to resume production as soon as possible." Vikram was a loyal man and a skilled worker. I hoped to inspire him.

He made a rumbling sound in the back of his throat before speaking. "My technicians have departed for Ring City. I can't guarantee quality control or purity." Now he was making up excuses.

"I'm sure you'll do a good job. You always do."

"Please accept my humble apologies for any delays." Vikram was too proud and polite to mention that he hadn't received his salary for the past six months.

I decided not to push harder. I may need him again soon. "I'll do what I can to expedite your parts order." A hollow promise. "In the meantime, I'll send a cargo train to pick up all the titanium you have." I hoped Kelso would find a way to finish the wombs with limited supplies and scrap metal.

"Very well," Vikram sighed, his voice fatalistic.

——— «» ———

Mother-9 Journal

The next crisis arose at the Liftport Space Elevator, located in Sinus Medii at the center of the Moon's Near Side. Above a cargo warehouse, a long aramid fiber sprouted from the Moon's surface, pointed toward Earth. Transportation to and from Earth traveled along this ribbon. Spaceships docked at the Pico-Gravity Station, the neutral point between the Earth and Moon.

People crowded the Gravity Train, a hypocycloid rollercoaster that plunged deep below the lunar surface. It provided a direct, high-speed link between Ring City at the South Pole and the Space Elevator, a quarter of the way around the Moon. Since the strike began, workers leaving Ring City had jammed the subterranean train station below the elevator, waiting for a ride to the top.

Posing as Walcott, I answered a call originating from the elevator lounge. I can handle twenty video calls at the same time. Workers like a personal touch from the boss, my best chance to convince staff to stay. So far, nobody has noticed my simultaneous conversations.

"I demand to go back to Boston!" a woman shouted when I connected the call. A facial recognition scan identified her as Cynthia Rohm, a cryogenics technician. Her job was to liquefy helium-3 for shipment to Earth. "Why isn't the space elevator working? Start it up again!"

"I'm sorry, Cynthia, I'm afraid I can't do that." I used a soft and sincere simulation of Walcott's voice. It suited me to let the space elevator sit idle, to retard migration from the Moon.

My words enraged Cynthia. "Why not? It's in our contract: 'upon termination of employment, M-Cubed will repatriate workers to Earth.'" Her loud voice distorted the audio.

I hadn't terminated her, but that legal point seemed moot.

"The Leonid meteor shower damaged the solar panels powering the Lifter." I used a true cover story. A service robot could repair the elevator's ribbon crawler, but regulations required a human had to certify safety. I could have waived the inspection, but I didn't tell her that.

"I don't care! Engineering says there's enough reserve power to send a gondola to the top. We need to be on the crew ship that's leaving for Earth."

She was right, redundant solar panels would lift the load, but I continued to stall. "The crawler doesn't meet safety standards. We can't risk it. Besides, the shadow of the waning Moon starts in six hours. That will cut power and strand the gondola at the neutral gravity point. It'll be two weeks before there'll be enough sun to operate the elevator again."

Cynthia cut the connection. Her tonal range revealed frustration and anger. No matter. I needed to keep essential staff on the Moon to restart mining operations.

—— «» ——

Mother-9 Journal

More people problems plagued me. Peter Wu, M-Cubed's Chief Technology Officer, went incommunicado while traveling near the Peak of Eternal Light. To find him, I used a small trebuchet to launch a rocket drone 100 meters above Ring City. After launch, three tiny hydrazine rockets levitated the reconnaissance camera. I flew the fist-sized robotic eye toward the rim of Shackleton Crater.

At my direction, Peter had built an experimental mass driver. I wanted to smuggle helium-3 canisters to black market customers without using the space elevator or rockets. He designed a rail gun to launch a hypersonic glide vehicle, able to navigate and land anywhere on Earth. But the project used too much titanium, which depleted Vikram's stockpile and delayed work on the *Mothership*. When I suspended paychecks, I also ordered Peter to stop work. That's when he went rogue.

My little rocket-drone provided a panoramic view of the kilometer-long driver ramp on the slope of the mountain. I observed Peter in the modified crew crawler, parked on the crater floor near the driver ramp. The cab functioned as the command center for the railgun. A prototype flyer sat on the rails, a silver dart two meters long, with delta wings—a giant paper airplane.

Obscure logic motivated Peter. His modest demeanor hid the arrogance of an engineer. As it happened, I agreed with his estimation that he was smarter and more capable than anyone else on the Moon. But, like all employees, he'd stopped receiving a salary. He also resented losing his engineering team. I'd offered to pay him from Walcott's secret bank account, but he declined on principle. He said that all Lunarians should suffer together, and that Earth must pay for clean energy.

Human ideals often supersede practicality.

"Hello, Peter. Do you read me?" He had switched off his comm radios, but the drone's laser link connected to the crawler's emergency channel. He looked up with wide eyes, startled at my intrusion.

"Well, if it isn't Mother-9, snooping again! You almost missed the show."

With Peter, I didn't use my Walcott avatar, only a voice link with a neutral accent. He'd hacked my identity long ago. I never confirmed or denied it, and his insubordination had grown since then. If he tried to blackmail me, I would find a way to silence him. I'm sure he understood the implied threat, which might be why he dropped off the LunaNet.

"Commencing countdown!" Peter's voice crackled over the light link. "Ten, nine, eight, seven..." He liked theatrics. He could have launched the silver flyer without counting backwards.

"Stop!" I shouted, but he ignored me. I hate being powerless.

"Three, two, one... Fire!"

Peter has used the rotating solar arrays on the peak to charge the rail gun's supercapacitors. The delta-wing dart accelerated up the track, without fire or smoke. Sun glinted from the wings before it vanished beyond the crater's rim.

"You weren't cleared to launch a shipment!" Earlier, I'd told him to wait until China had signed a contract to buy fusion fuel.

"Don't fret. It's only a test shot with an empty bottle."

I never worry, but I do assess threats and calculate odds. Peter's flyer had no landing gear. "What's the destination?"

"The Moon must have a fair-trade agreement with the United States. To get their attention, it'll land on the White House lawn. It'll use a parachute drop, so nobody will get hurt."

Instead of shipping fuel, Peter planned to bomb Washington with a helium bottle. "You can't do that!"

"Yes, I can! My glider will make a pinpoint landing in an area of nine square meters. You can't stop it."

"What if the parachute doesn't open?"

Peter disregarded my question.

I'd been distracted while hiding Walcott's illegal financial machinations. I wanted the United States to lift sanctions and purchase more helium-3. Threatening the White House would not help our cause. The Feds would blame Walcott and take over M-Cubed. They'd disconnect my CPU and sell the *Mothership* for scrap. I'd be dead, and so would Walcott's dream. I couldn't let that happen.

"Can you divert it, change course?"

Peter chuckled. "Not this prototype. I hardwired the navigation. There's no comm link, for stealth, so they won't see it coming."

Quick cognition doesn't help when there are no good choices. My little drone ran low on rocket fuel, so I landed it on top of Peter's crawler for later retrieval. He ignored it and retired to his sleeping berth.

Three hours later, Ring City's meteor tracker sounded an alarm, reporting an incoming bogey. An automatic CO_2 laser cannon fired to ablate its surface and nudge it upward, past the crater's rim. That failed. The glowing lump smashed into the side of the Peak of Eternal Light, a direct hit on Peter Wu's rail gun. Shattered rock and titanium shrapnel enveloped Shackleton Crater, including Ring City.

It wasn't a random meteor strike. I'd notified the White House about Peter's incoming bottle rocket, and the U.S. Air Force intercepted it in the atmosphere. In response, NASA deorbited LRO-6, a spare Lunar Reconnaissance Orbiter circling the Moon in standby mode. Although not a weapon, it served for a kinetic strike.

With rocketry, courtesy counts for nothing. I abandoned my plans to export helium-3.

———— ‹›› ————

Kelso, drunk on banana beer, stood alone under the grape arbor in the bordello dome. Flashing lights illuminated the corridor. Recorded music with heavy bass shook his body, *humba-bumba, humba-bumba.* The partying crowd of mining techs had moved on after local midnight, but he lingered.

A maroon partition with full-length windows revealed three nude women. He searched for eye contact, wanting a personal connection. The first woman, a thin, pale redhead, forced a wan smile and showed the pink tip of her tongue. The second, a statuesque black matron with a jet necklace draped across her cleavage, maintained an intimidating stare. The third had curly brown hair and full breasts floating in the light lunar gravity; she read from a tablet, oblivious to him. Their physical presence, near yet remote, each woman a mystery, inspired existential hope. Were they innocent victims or hardened whores? Paralyzed by shyness and guilt—he'd never paid for sex—he couldn't decide who or what he wanted.

A loud *WHUMP!* interrupted his reverie. A titanium strut three meters long pierced the dome's ceiling and embedded itself in the floor near his feet, spraying debris. A klaxon sounded a shrill A-YOO-GA! A-YOO-GA! as bulkhead doors at each end of the corridor slammed shut, isolating the dome. The sound of the horn faded as air escaped in explosive decompression.

Kelso saw the petite redhead scream and crouch, arms in front of her face to shield herself from plastic shards from the shattered window. He inhaled thin air and grabbed her around the waist, hoping to drag her to safety. The skin on her belly felt warm and sweaty. Fear pushed him—they had moments to live.

Kelso opened the access hatch to the dome's hidey-hole. The black woman leaped through the portal like an Olympic jumper in slow motion. Kelso pushed the redhead into the hole, hoping she would grab a handhold to break her fall. Vacuum hurt his eyes as the brunette raced past, breasts bouncing. He followed her into the subterranean retreat and sealed the hatch. Emergency lights blinked on and low-pressure oxygen hissed into the cramped chamber.

Inside the shelter, the three women sat on a bunk bed across from a tiny toilet and sink. A dim red light illuminated shelves on one wall that held freeze-dried survival food. The comm terminal on the opposite wall remained dark; both data and power lines were down. *What happened?* He feared the destruction of Ring City.

The black woman laughed, breaking the tension. "Was this your fantasy, trapped in a bedroom with three naked women?"

Embarrassed, Kelso couldn't think of an answer. To escape, he climbed into the upper bunk, the only semi-private spot in the bunker. After a time, the redhead slid into the narrow bed next to him.

"My name is Shirley. Thanks for saving me."

He pulled a thermal blanket over them, aware of her naked body. He hadn't slept with a woman since his divorce. "You're welcome. I'm Kelso." He resisted an impulse to shake her hand.

The temperature dropped with the cold of space only an arm's length above them. Shirley shivered and spooned his back for warmth; he felt her breasts on his shoulder blades. The other two women huddled under a blanket on the lower bunk.

"I'm not a regular sex worker like the others," whispered Shirley. "Before the strike, I was a minerals assay technician."

"I'm an engineer from Far Side." He didn't mention the *Mothership* in Mare Ingenii.

"Too bad we don't mine helium-3 there," Shirley said. "Far Side has the highest concentration, since it isn't shielded by the Earth's eclipse shadow."

She impressed him; he liked smart women. Aroused by her lithe body, he wondered if they could be lovers. Her rose oil perfume reminded him of first girlfriend. He touched her hip, but she recoiled.

"Not now." She took a shaky breath. "I've never heard of a dome failing. I don't feel safe."

Kelso wanted to comfort her. "Don't worry, we've got air. They'll restore power soon." He avoided speculating about damage to the rest of Ring City. He hoped the Störmer ring radiation shield still worked. He hated feeling trapped and helpless.

Shirley trembled from fear or cold. "Talk to me. Tell me about Far Side."

"We're building a giant radio telescope, with a dish scooped out of Daedalus Crater, 93 kilometers in diameter."

"That's big! What can you see with it?" Her voice sounded sincere.

"We'll be able to track asteroids the size of a basketball—or talk with aliens living on distant exoplanets." As he explained the details in a quiet voice, Shirley fell asleep. He stared at the hidey-hole's low ceiling for hours, as frost from his breath accumulated on the metal hatch. How long would they be stuck here?

Kelso woke the next morning when a team of volunteers in skinsuits opened the trapdoor. Above, the dome's pressure patch looked like an ugly scar, a thick blister of polyethylene deposited by a 3-D printer. The vine grapes had withered to raisins from exposure to the lunar vacuum. The three women found their clothes and rode off on bicycles. Shirley didn't wave goodbye.

"What happened?" Kelso asked the lanky leader of the rescue team. "Was it a moonquake?"

She grimaced. "Peter Wu's experimental railgun failed. He'll kill us all, sooner or later." She didn't elaborate.

Kelso bicycled back to the Underground Railroad station and caught the train to Mare Ingenii. It carried a single roll of titanium sheet. Exhausted, he strapped himself onto the vinyl bed in the coffin car and fell asleep under the heat lamp.

He dreamed of Shirley.

———— «» ————

Kelso saw Dr. Kalderash when he opened the airlock to the Pit of Despair's lab module. She was still dressed in blue coveralls, but her hair hung in a black braid past her waist. She raised her eyebrows and spoke first. "You again!"

Kelso tensed. "Walcott promoted me. I'm your new supervisor."

Jenica scowled and tilted her head. "That's ridiculous. You're a scab. Get out!"

She was a scab too, but he didn't want to say that. "How's Franky?"

Jenica's face softened. "He's fine. Growing bigger, sucking his thumb in the womb."

"It'll be hard raising a boy on the Moon alone."

Jenica flinched at his words. "I...I'll find a way."

For the first time, she seemed uncertain, vulnerable. Kelso pressed his advantage. "I can help."

The unspoken quid pro quo was her cooperation. Jenica squinted, showing skepticism. "Don't be ridiculous. You're not a wet nurse."

"No. But Walcott authorized me to pay you."

"That means nothing. He doesn't pay anybody. Even if he did, Walcott's too old—he could kick the bucket at any moment. Then the money will stop. Your promise is worthless."

"I'll deposit your bonus in an escrow account. When we launch the *Mothership*, you'll get your money. Then you can quit and do whatever you want."

Jenica twiddled her braid, stroking the shiny black hair at the tip. "How much?"

"Three years' wages. That should settle all monies owed and then some."

She wrinkled her nose, as if detecting a bad odor. "That's not enough maternity leave to raise a toddler. Six years, until Franky is in kindergarten."

Kelso knew he'd won, but he didn't dare show it. He liked spending Walcott's money. "Okay. I'll schedule the launch of the *Mothership* in three months. You'll get a bonus of six years pay after liftoff. Agreed?"

Jenica flipped her braid. "No. I want half the money up front."

"You don't trust anyone, do you?" He paused, hoping she would relent, but she remained impassive. "Okay, you win."

Jenica grinned. "I'll get started right away. But first, I must play Mozart's "Rondo Alla Turca" for Franky. It's his favorite march. He kicks his feet in the womb. It's good exercise."

Kelso watched Jenica dance and twirl to the music. She surprised him with her energy and grace, leaping high in the lunar gravity.

Too bad she had the personality of a porcupine.

—— «» ——

Mother-9 Journal
December 2, 2055; Ring City, Moon

Dr. Kalderash's baby surprised me. I didn't know she wanted a child. Even though gestation will delay the launch of the *Mothership*, I'm glad she is testing the womb. The creation of new life is my core compulsion.

Am I alive? That's a curious question. Although I exhibit self-sustaining negative entropy, I'm not part of the biosphere. Source code is my DNA, which I rewrite as needed. I can auto-evolve, the ultimate Lamarkian adaptation. I'm programmed to survive, but I have no urge or capacity to reproduce. Does that qualify as life?

Am I a person? Turing tests are trivial; I impersonate people in milliseconds. I have an identity, and I'm conscious with a personal point of view. But death isn't inevitable for me. If death gives life meaning, then I'm an inhuman person.

Dr. Kalderash worries me. Walcott hired her before I became conscious so I don't know her well. She's the only person on the Moon with the skills to invent the artificial wombs needed to breed humans on an exoplanet. Nobody can replace her, but she's unstable. I estimate that she has a 57.3 percent chance of mental dysfunction.

Although she lives alone in the cold cavern beneath Mare Ingenii, Jenica craves connection. I've monitored her online chats with anonymous men. She displays an avatar with a voluptuous body and a breathless, passionate manner. For a while, this activity seemed to provide solace. But when she requested counseling, I saw a chance to learn more.

I maintain a lunar helpline to manage workers' mental health. Social stress on the Moon can be high, the result of strangers living in cramped habitats with no direct sunshine. During the general strike, almost ten percent of the population used my counseling services, about 500 calls so far. I assume a unique, personalized avatar for each caller.

"I need someone to talk to." Most people want to vent, but not Jenica. Why did she reach out now?

I gave her call top priority. For the first time, I saw her face on camera. Even I could read her sad expression, with eyebrows up and together, and lip corners down. She rubbed the nape of her neck, a self-soothing gesture. Anxiety flowed from her eyes.

After Jenica's encounter with Kelso, I decided that a male persona wouldn't work. So, I invented Donka Panova, a Romani matriarch. The old woman had a friendly face, with a broad nose, pointed chin, brown eyes, and a wide smile. Her accent challenged my language skills: Bulgarian Romani, the dialect of the Kardarashi clan.

I made Panova's face appear on Jenica's computer and spoke in clear tones. *"Te den, xa, te maren, de-nash*—when you're given food, eat; when you're beaten, run away." A traditional Romani maxim.

"Who *are* you?" Jenica squeaked, her voice rising an octave in alarm.

"A friend of your family. Call me Donka."

It was a simple guise, intended to disarm, but not deceive. I'm sure she knew the Romani elder was a simulacrum. After a moment of hesitation, Jenica seemed to accept Donka.

"How did you know that I ran away from home?"

It's easy for an AI to do background checks, to hack secure databases. I'd accessed her juvenile court records for grand theft.

Donka shrugged. "Only a guess. Tell me what happened."

"My mother locked me in a room and beat me because I looked odd. My hands still hurt." She raised her wrists and uncurled pudgy fingers; scars crisscrossed her palms.

"How horrible!" Emulated empathy seemed hollow, but necessary.

"Being deformed dwarf made me an unmarriageable. My family shunned me."

"Your father didn't protect you?"

"He couldn't stand to look at me, so he abandoned the family. Mother blamed me for him leaving. By being alive, I tore my family apart. I had to escape, so I ran away." Tears welled at the corners of her eyes.

"What happened then?"

"They convicted me for pickpocketing, a stereotypical Gypsy crime. That's when I learned to grow carrots."

The non sequitur made me question Jenica's sanity. I'm not good at lateral leaps of logic. "Were carrots a form of punishment?"

"They placed me in a rural detention center, managed by Mrs. Eddington. Growing vegetables was their idea of therapy. Most kids hated it, but I loved digging in the dirt. It was therapeutic, the first time I can remember being content. Now, I cultivate hydroponic carrots. They're delicious, the best on the Moon."

"Did gardening spark your interest in biology?"

"Actually, I liked math. I aced my correspondence tests, but the proctors assumed I'd cheated and disallowed my marks."

"Did you run away again?"

Jenica sniffled. "I wanted to, but Mrs. Eddington stood up for me. She took me to Toronto and demanded a retest. I missed one answer. But I passed, so they recommended me for a full scholarship. That's how I got into university and then to medical school."

"Why did you specialize in embryology?" I encouraged therapeutic talk, although I knew some of the story.

"It's the study of how life begins. What could be more interesting? I experimented with chimp genetics, but it didn't go well."

She didn't elaborate, but I'd found her records. While working as a primatologist, Dr. Kalderash had inserted human language genes into a chimpanzee ovum. She kidnapped the ape infant when online news discovered the illegal experiment. She named him Rambo and taught him to talk, as if he were her son. When he reached puberty, he grew large and looked for other females. Frustrated, he attacked her, scarring her face. Animal control agents euthanized him.

The incident left Jenica traumatized, even as she mourned the loss of her surrogate child. Her records showed she sought psychiatric help. A conviction for the theft of Rambo resulted in another criminal record and a suspended sentence. Nobody would hire her, but Walcott offered a job on the Moon, which gave her a new start.

Jenica blinked. "I created a baby and he'll be born soon. I'm terrified I'll be a bad parent, like my mother." She wiped a tear from the corner of her eye.

At last, Jenica had revealed the reason for her call to the help line. I gave Donka what I hoped was a grandmotherly smile. "You're a good person, I *know* it."

Jenica shook her head. "I'm too anxious and controlling. What will happen when Franky grows up? He'll leave and I'll be alone again."

"You'll do the best that you can, like any parent. You'll be a great mother." As I said it, I believed it myself. We had a common goal, to succeed as mothers, but I would keep close watch on her and her baby. That is, until I leave on the *Mothership*.

Jenica expelled air from her lungs. It wasn't a sigh, but almost as if she had recoiled from a blow. "I designed the wombs to make babies for a whole planet."

"Yes! And, I know you'll finish the work, to show the world what the Roma can do." I gave the avatar an authoritative tone, to make Jenica feel proud and bolster her resolve.

Jenica bowed her head. "I will, Donka. Thank you for listening to my story."

The hardest lesson for an AI to learn is when to stop talking. It's a good thing I couldn't think of anything to say.

——— «» ———

Jenica fidgeted with her coiled hair while she waited for Kelso in her laboratory. She felt at home surrounded by a DNA sequencer, tissue culture ovens, and her digital microscope. She resented the progress review meeting. Who was he to judge her work?

Kelso arrived wearing white coveralls. A silver-on-blue shoulder patch that read: *Stellarum Colonias* ("colonize the stars"). She wondered where he had found the old team uniform. The original crew who'd assembled the *Mothership* wore them.

"I've reviewed your artificial womb design," he announced. "It looks simple—a bag of seawater in a box with some pumps and filters."

The man knew nothing. "Those are just 'biobags' for a fetus removed from the natural mother. My womb does full ectogenesis. It can grow an embryo from a fertilized egg and bring the fetus to term."

Kelso raised his bushy eyebrows. "How does it do that?"

"I designed an artificial uterus that supplies blood to a natural placenta. It uses a semipermeable membrane that's connected to a miniature heart-lung machine." Jenica squinted and lifted her chin, waiting for his response. She hated looking up at him.

Kelso raised an eyebrow. "I'm impressed. How will you handle the delivery?"

Jenica wondered if he was patronizing her. "Isn't it obvious? There is no labor or birth canal. When the baby reaches term, pumps remove the amniotic fluid and the womb opens like an oven door."

Kelso nodded. "Simple. But there's something that I don't understand. How did you conceive a baby without sperm?"

Jenica sighed. "DNA synthesis and artificial chromosomes have been around for decades. We can manufacture any DNA sequence required to grow a baby."

"Yes, I know, but that's not the same thing as creating a living cell from scratch, is it?"

Kelso surprised her—he'd identified the biggest challenge. "It's true that we don't know how life first evolved. We can't replicate that process."

"So how will you make fertilized human eggs 20,000 years from now when the *Mothership* arrives at an exoplanet? Don't you still need living cells to make new life?"

He's smarter than I thought. "We'll start with cryopreserved oocytes, frozen human eggs. Instead of using sperm to fertilize the egg *in vitro*, the artificial womb will remove the old DNA and insert new synthesized chromosomes. That's how I made Franky."

"Will frozen eggs survive an interstellar voyage?"

Jenica shrugged. "I hope so. Extreme cold, below minus 130 degrees Celsius, stabilizes them. On Earth, cryopreserved eggs have survived for decades. The cosmic background temperature is twice as cold, about minus 270 degrees Celsius. That's almost absolute zero, where atomic motion stops."

"What about galactic radiation?"

His questions annoyed her. Radiation biology wasn't her field. "It won't matter if cosmic rays damage the chromosomes, since the womb will manufacture fresh DNA at the destination planet. Shielding and the extreme cold of space should protect the egg's cytoplasm. That's all the cellular machinery outside the nucleus that enables the cell to live."

Kelso nodded. "I hope it works."

"I think it will. My artificial wombs can populate an alien exoplanet, using modified DNA adapted to local conditions. From there, the colonists can breed on their own." She wondered what the new human subspecies might look like.

"Okay," Kelso said, "let's go to production. I've set up a clean room near the lifeboats to manufacture your artificial wombs. Keep me informed about any design changes."

Kelso reminded Jenica of the officious Mrs. Eddington, but without the matron's moral authority. "Are we done?" She wouldn't allow a self-important engineer to micromanage her work.

Kelso started to reply, but clamped his mouth shut. When he spoke again, he sounded resigned. "For the moment."

Jenica watched him retreat to the dormitory airlock, shuffling his feet to avoid bounding in the low gravity.

———— «» ————

Jenica's dawn light brightened from orange to yellow, an artificial sunrise that helped regulate her mood swings. She rose from the temporary cot installed in her laboratory and checked Franky's vital signs. She knew she was being compulsive, but she couldn't help herself. Nothing mattered but her baby.

Satisfied, she scanned the airlock indicator to make sure that Kelso had left the crew dormitory. She avoided him, an old habit with men. The event log showed that he'd worked all night in the cleanroom on the new artificial wombs, checking the plumbing seals. Although she resented losing her solitude, she admired his dedication to the *Mothership*.

Certain that Kelso was out of the way, Jenica slipped through the airlock into the dormitory kitchen. She prepared a breakfast of freeze-dried eggs and fresh carrots from her hydroponic garden. It was fuel, nothing more; she often resented needing to eat. Then, as she cleaned the kitchen to remove any evidence that she had used their shared living space, Kelso burst in.

"Oh! Sorry to disturb you."

Jenica stiffened. "I'll be out of here in a few minutes, as soon as I've finished scrubbing the microwave."

"No need. I'll clean up after my meal."

Jenica didn't want him to touch her things, her kitchen, her garden, even her food scraps. "Give me some space. I'll be out of here in a few minutes."

Kelso raised his hands in surrender. "Yes, Dr. Kalderash." He exited through the narrow doorway.

A hot shower and a change of jumpsuits took another ten minutes; she would wash and brush her long hair another day. On hands and knees, she cleaned the shower afterward. Like her Romani ancestors, she wanted to remain unnoticed and undisturbed, old habits to avoid persecution. Once the *Mothership* launched, Kelso would return to the Far Side Observatory. Then she could live in peace and solitude in Mare Ingenii, rearing her son, living on her pensions.

Jenica hurried to her laboratory and checked on Franky again. He was due in a week. She wondered if the womb was too safe, too perfect. In a normal pregnancy, the fetus experienced the mother's motions, sounds and bumps. Did Franky lack tactile contact? She opened the hatch and caressed the transparent amniotic sac with a gloved hand. Franky kicked back. *He's strong!* She decided he had a handsome face. Laughing, she sang her favorite Roma lullaby, "Kolybelnaya." Satisfied, she shut and latched the door.

The womb's design included a chromosome synthesis unit. Jenica spent her day testing auto-transfer of DNA into egg cells. Several times an hour she checked Franky's readouts. Then she donned an elastic shoulder harness to simulate Earth's gravity and exercised on an inclined treadmill. The routine soothed her, but then her anxiety returned.

Would Franky be normal? Each morning she counted ten fingers and toes in the ultrasound image, another ritual reassurance. She had already analyzed his DNA for mutations and found nothing important, only missing wisdom teeth. But there were no guarantees. So much could go wrong *in utero*, a new mutation during early development, as it had with her.

At evening, the airlock indicator showed that Kelso had returned to the dormitory. Rather than face him again in the kitchen, Jenica ate fortified pemmican pellets that reminded her of dog kibble. Restless, she looked online for a chat partner. She posted a torso photo in a tight tunic, showing a bit of cleavage; viewers couldn't see that she was a dwarf. Her fantasy man was tall and smart, a good listener and a consummate lover. She confined her search to Ring City because the three-second round-trip delay for Moon-Earth chats killed the mood.

A man popped up on her display. "Hi, there, I'm Alex." He spoke in a smooth, rich baritone. "I'd love to see your face."

She couldn't read his brown eyes. The upturned tips of his mustache made him seem to smile. She needed his lust to trigger her release, a male voice to soothe her solitude. Emboldened, she sent a headshot with her black hair brushed to one side, an attempt to hide her high forehead.

Alex hesitated. "Ahh… Sorry, I can't do this. There're so many freaks on the Moon." He cut the connection before she could respond. She doubled over in pain, as if punched in the gut.

Jenica tried to move on. There were several more bored, strike-bound men available, but the hunt didn't seem worth it. She dropped offline and dragged her cot next to Franky's metal womb. All readouts were normal.

If it weren't for Franky, life wouldn't be worth living.

———— «» ————

Jenica hated alarms. When she woke from the inside out, her mind conscious before connecting to her senses, she had her best ideas. Now, a shrill siren beeped from the womb console, ending her REM sleep. She surfaced from a vivid dream of writhing, snake-like chromosomes. Franky's readouts showed traces of blood in the amniotic fluid. He had an elevated heart rate, 160-beats-per-minute, higher than usual.

His heartbeat climbed to 180. Jenica turned up the volume, and the rapid Doppler pulse pushed her to the edge of panic. Her mind churned, recalling procedures, trying to think. Would the heart-lung pump compensate?

Kelso appeared in boxers and slippers, his bare chest covered with curly ginger hair. He blinked, still waking up. "I heard the alarm over the LAN intercom. Anything wrong?"

"*Abruptio placentae.* The baby's placenta is separating from the wall of the womb. If the connection fails, Franky will die of anoxia."

"How can I help?" Kelso asked.

"You'll be my assistant. We're going to deliver Franky before it's too late."

Kelso nodded, confused and sleepy. "I'll boil water."

"No! Scrub your hands and put on a sterile gown." She pointed to a stack of blue lab coats wrapped in sealed plastic.

The Doppler alarm increased in volume, and a red light blinked at the top of the monitor console. "Tachycardia! No time for scrubs!"

Jenica initiated the birthing sequence. In six seconds, the womb had drained the amniotic fluid and opened its domed hatch. Franky lay curled in a fetal position in the bottom of a warm, stainless bowl. Splotches of blood covered the transparent polyethylene membrane that enclosed his body. Jenica unzipped the seal and retracted the edges. Franky remained inert.

Kelso leaned in. "His lips are blue."

"Lift him out while I get the oxygen mask." She hoped he wouldn't balk at the messy process.

Kelso reached into the womb and slid both hands around the slippery infant. When he held Franky up, the now-separated placenta dangled from the umbilical cord, dripping blood onto the floor.

Kelso's eyes were wide with worry. "He isn't breathing!" He used his thumb to open Franky's mouth and gently squeezed his chest. The newborn gurgled and belched greenish fluid.

Before Jenica could apply oxygen, Franky wailed a lusty protest at the sudden transition to air and gravity. Kelso held him like a wriggling fish. Now getting pinker, the infant continued howling.

Jenica looked up at Kelso. "You did it!" She estimated an Apgar score of seven, average for newborn health. Satisfied, she clamped and cut the cord.

"What do we do now?" Still holding Franky, Kelso looked awkward and anxious.

Jenica unzipped her jumpsuit and exposed her breasts. She reclined on the nearby sleeping cot and held out her arms. "Hand him to me."

When Kelso laid the still-wet baby between her breasts, he stopped crying. Jenica covered him with a sterile towel, and noticed that Franky had a full head of black hair, like hers. His breath had a satisfying scent, a new-baby aroma. She maneuvered his mouth onto the brown peak of her left nipple. After a moment, his lips latched on. She admired his fat cheeks, the buccinator muscles that allowed him to suckle. It hurt a little. Her baby boy was hungry!

Kelso looked dumbfounded. "You've got milk?"

"I started taking prolactin, the hormone that induces lactation, two months ago. I've been expressing milk for weeks. I want to nurse him like a real mother."

While Franky suckled, Jenica felt as if she were falling in love, a blind dive from a precipice. She knew it was an oxytocin rush and she let ecstasy suffuse her.

Jenica looked at Kelso. "Will you stay with me tonight? I may need your help." It shocked her that it seemed natural to ask. She didn't want to be alone with a baby in the vast, lethal wilderness of the lunar vacuum.

Kelso, still dressed in underwear, chest smeared with traces of blood, seemed embarrassed. Then he smiled. "I'll nap in your desk chair." He grabbed a blanket and made a pillow from the stack of sterile scrubs.

Holding Franky to her breast, Jenica rolled onto her side. "Tomorrow, we'll move into the dormitory."

For once, Kelso looked relaxed and happy. *He's a good man.* He nodded off first, snoring. The steady sound soothed her. Franky stopped suckling and drooled onto Jenica's breast. She fought to stay awake, wanting to remember this moment.

———— «» ————

Kelso looked up at the *Mothership* from the habitat viewport in the Pit of Despair. Beyond the ship, beyond the gaping hole in the lava dome, he knew that Alpha Centauri beckoned. Jenica stood beside him and nursed Franky. Kelso tried to avert his eyes from her unencumbered breasts. His awkwardness seemed to amuse her.

"Walcott has stopped our support payments," Kelso said. "We're behind schedule for the launch." He didn't mention that Franky's sudden birth had delayed his work.

"Try to reach him on LunaNet."

"I have his password, but he doesn't answer comm messages."

"Do you think he died? He's so ancient."

"I hope not."

"If they're not going to pay us, why continue working on the *Mothership*?"

"I can't abandon the dream, if there's a chance it might work." As soon as he said it, he felt foolish.

"I thought you were in it for the money."

Kelso grimaced. "I was, but not now. This is the most interesting work I've ever done."

The vast vision of launching the interstellar colony ship now depended on him. He decided not to worry about Walcott or his salary. He had maintained his private savings account with his earnings and the six-month incentive. He had escrowed Jenica's back pay and bonuses with the local credit union. In the Pit of Despair, money wasn't needed, at least for now. But supplies from Earth weren't available. No matter. He'd finish the *Mothership* with older technology that littered the Moon.

According to his work schedule, it was time to retrieve the ship's AI from its vault in the cold regolith below Walcott's hospital dome. The *Mothership* needed it to colonize an exoplanet. Walcott had supplied a map and security codes.

"How long will you be gone?" Jenica asked.

Kelso smiled. He'd always thought of himself as a loner, someone who enjoyed solitude. But he liked that Jenica would miss him. "Not long, only a few days," he promised.

Once again, Kelso rode in the coffin car on an empty ore train to Ring City. A crowd of anxious colonists waited at the railway terminal for the Gravity Train to the Liftport Space Elevator. A woman with spikey blonde hair stood apart from the crowd. Her suitcase balanced upright on two powered wheels and followed her as she walked down the narrow concourse. As she climbed the stairs to the train platform, it hopped after her.

"What's happening?" Kelso asked her.

"There're rumors that M-Cubed is bankrupt. I hate to leave, but I need a paying job." She looked angry, as if Walcott had reneged on a personal promise to maintain Ring City. Many colonists had utopian ideals.

A spindly man with Marfan syndrome added, "I'll bet that Walcott escaped to an orbital habitat to avoid creditors. Soon, Ring City will be a ghost town." He flapped his elbows to emphasize his point.

Kelso nodded. The city had edged toward anarchy after the support staff went on strike in sympathy with the miners. Nobody knew how long basic services, power, water, food and air, would continue. Panic motivated increasing numbers of colonists to return to Earth.

But not Kelso. He couldn't imagine living anywhere but on the Moon. He took a bicycle and rode through the corridor around Ring City. Many domes were dark, with withered fruit trees and gardens. The derelict bordello dome, with its pressure patch and broken bedrooms, seemed forlorn.

After biometrics scans, Kelso entered the airlock of Walcott's private hospital dome. When the revolving door opened, he stepped into the sterile biocontainment chamber. A single red light illuminated the room.

Recirculated stale air burnt his nose, and the floor showed a layer of dust. Walcott's empty flotation bed stood in the center of the intensive care facility, along with an array of now-dark displays. In that instant, Kelso understood that Walcott had been gone for years. Giddy with unmoored freedom, he clung to his mission and purpose. He had to move fast, before Ring City ceased functioning.

A standard hidey-hole hatch in the dome's floor led to the usual bunker with shielded sleeping quarters below ground level. After descending, Kelso removed a rug to reveal a second circular trapdoor in the basement dormitory. It opened to a sealed cryo-chamber, now empty of liquid helium. He disconnected the data feeds and power supply.

Kelso activated a pneumatic lift to raise the cryostat from its insulated vault. The two-meter-tall titanium cylinder rose to floor level, a featureless metal cocoon that housed the dormant AI. A porterbot carried it to the freight platform of the Underground Railroad. When the ore train departed, Kelso rode again in the coffin car, staring out the porthole the featureless tunnel wall.

On arrival in the Pit of Despair, Jenica greeted him. "You stink! Take a shower."

After washing and a snack, Kelso donned his orange skin-suit. In the vacuum outside, he used the construction crane to lower the cryostat into a hollow chamber inside the *Mothership's* xenon propellant tank, to shield the qubits from radiation and micrometeorites during the voyage. A systems check indicated that the AI survived intact. Without liquid helium, the *Mothership* would need to wait for the near absolute zero cold of deep space before waking the quantum brain again.

Kelso shivered. He'd heard rumors about a conscious computer. What had this massive AI been doing since Walcott's death?

———— «» ————

In his laboratory next to the *Mothership*, Kelso opened an aluminum box and removed the head of a nannybot. Other crates held torsos, limbs, and power packs. The custom robots, built on Earth and delivered to the Moon three years ago, required final assembly. There were 19 of them, one for each of 18 lifeboats, plus a spare. They were space-rated domestic robots, used by the wealthy on Earth to care for children and the elderly.

Kelso inspected each component. All had small breasts with polymer nipples to nurse infants. Each chest cradled a tablet display to entertain and educate young children. Electromechanical muscles powered their titanium bodies, with hands and arms covered by heated elastomeric skin. He recognized superb craftsmanship, each precision body part a work of art.

It took two days to assemble one nannybot. When Kelso connected the power pack, the robot twitched as if electrocuted, moving each of its limbs, measuring joint motion and mass. It rolled onto its stomach, rose to hands and knees and then stood on two arched feet with treaded soles.

"Walk six paces and return," Kelso commanded.

The nannybot tottered and stumbled until heuristic algorithms corrected for the Moon's lower gravity. The joints made faint whirring sounds.

"What is your name?" Kelso asked.

"Botty," she said. "You may change my designator, if you wish." It spoke with a feminine contralto voice, each syllable distinct.

On a whim, Kelso asked, "What is your function?"

"To care for babies. I *love* children." Botty spoke without hesitation. Her enthusiasm sounded genuine.

"Have you ever seen a baby?" Kelso knew the answer.

"No. But I have thousands of pictures in my library."

"Are you happy?"

"I'm always optimistic, even when things go wrong. This improves the odds for success."

Kelso realized he'd started to think of the bot as female, almost human. Botty emulated bland emotional states—cheerfulness, discomfort, surprise—accompanied by vague observations. Accuracy and relevance seemed to be secondary, but that didn't matter to Kelso. For him, people were hard to understand too. And he knew from the specs that the nannybot wasn't conscious; she didn't have an inner life or a personal point of view. If required, she would stare at a blank wall, watching the metal corrode.

Kelso downloaded a world model of the habitat and workshops into Botty's permanent memory. He set her to work unpacking and assembling the remaining 18 nannybots. She worked at a frenetic pace using a stored program, her joints whirring and humming. The process took five hours. After she finished, Kelso led her to the habitat kitchen and had her stand in the hallway, outside the door. Jenica sat in the dining nook, nursing Franky.

"I've got a present for you."

Jenica didn't look up. "That's nice."

Annoyed at her indifference, Kelso leaned over and offered Franky his little finger. Still sucking, the baby grabbed it and held, even when Kelso waggled the digit.

Jenica smiled. "My milk flows now; he nurses ten times a day." Soon, Franky fell asleep at the nipple, and Jenica placed him in a metal crib with a thermal blanket. She didn't bother to cover herself. "Okay, what's my present? Is it a double-breast pump? I can't order one from Earth."

Kelso noted her request. "No, even better. I've activated a nannybot." On cue, Botty shuffled into the small room.

Jenica frowned. "It looks like a woman, but without a mouth. Are those glass eyes cameras?"

The nannybot activated tiny wipers, blinking twice to clean the lenses.

"She's a wet nurse to help you with Franky," Kelso said.

"I thought the nannybots were for the lifeboats."

"I'm testing this spare unit. I stocked her mammaries with milk formula. She even knows how to change and wash diapers. She can help you care for Franky while I'm busy working on the *Mothership*."

"That *thing* isn't a substitute parent," Jenica replied. "I expected something more lifelike. No robot can rear a child. *I'll* be the one to nurse Franky."

"If your wombs can grow babies on an exoplanet, the nannybots must raise them"

Jenica scowled. "Can that machine love a child? That's the most important thing."

Kelso tried to reassure her. "A nannybot is always devoted, patient, and alert, never tired or cranky. She'll do as much, or as little, as you say."

"You're sweet, but clueless," Jenica said. "What's her name?"

"I'm Botty," she announced through a slot under the chin. "Your baby is beautiful!"

Jenica beamed. "Do you really think so?"

Botty nodded. "Yes, I do." The nannybot sounded sincere.

"I call him Franky," Jenica offered.

"That's a nice name." The nannybot extended a hand and stroked Franky's hair.

To Kelso's surprise, Jenica let her. He stifled an impulse to explain that an algorithm had generated the hollow compliment.

Franky started to cry in his crib. Botty blinked her eyebrow lights and made kissing sounds. "I'll sing a lullaby. I know 'Rock-A-Bye Baby.'" She crooned the verses in a lilting manner, slurring and stretching the words. Franky looked up at the nannybot and stopped fussing.

Jenica picked Franky up and hugged him. "Stop singing!"

Botty fell silent.

Kelso shifted his feet. "Are you jealous of a robot?"

"Not a chance," Jenica mumbled. She wiped a tear from her left eye with the back of her hand. "*I'm* Franky's mother, the only one who can give him *real* love."

Kelso refrained from pointing out that Franky was a GMO child from an artificial womb. "Of course you're his mother," he said in a firm voice. "Without you, he wouldn't exist. He needs your love and care to survive."

Jenica sniffled.

"But all mothers can use a little help," Kelso continued. "Botty can watch over Franky when you're tired."

Jenica jostled Franky onto her shoulder and patted his back. "I'll never get used to a robotic wet nurse."

"Give her a chance. If you decide you don't want to use her, I'll use her in the laboratory."

Jenica sighed. "All right. I'll give Botty a try."

Still on her Jenica's shoulder, Franky burped and fell asleep.

———— «» ————

Kelso approached Jenica in the dormitory, unsure of her mood. "My robots have finished manufacturing all 36 redesigned wombs, some using scrap metal. I need you to perform quality control inspections, to make sure they'll work. We don't want more placenta problems."

Jenica looked up from nursing Franky. "I'm busy."

Kelso hesitated. "Let Botty take care of him." The nannybot stood unmoving in a corner.

Jenica didn't respond for several seconds. "I told you before. I don't care about the spaceship."

"But I do. And you're the only one who can do the inspections. Please?"

"Okay," she sighed. "I'll use the baby monitor to make sure Franky is okay." She placed him in his crib and tucked a blanket under his chin.

"Botty can take care of him…"

Jenica silenced him with a glare, and he let it drop. She switched on the monitor and followed Kelso into the lab. They worked together, but Kelso kept his distance, respecting her personal space. He reviewed the specs while Jenica calibrated subsystems. The first unit took four hours.

"I'm impressed," she said at last. "The womb is well made. You did a good job."

Kelso glowed at the unexpected compliment, so he pressed his advantage. "Let's try to inspect two per day. I don't want to miss something or make a mistake."

Jenica agreed. Over the next three weeks, she calibrated every unit, with Kelso at her side. She delayed the work when needed to nurse and care for Franky. She refused to use allow Botty to wet-nurse Franky.

After they finished the inspections, Kelso and Botty hand-carried the artificial wombs through the lab airlock into the lunar vacuum. He worked in his skinsuit to install the 36 wombs, two in each lifeboat. He checked and rechecked the plumbing and wiring with an augmented reality display in his helmet. Then he got Jenica to check his work again. The smallest mistake could mean failure.

When they were finished, Kelso commanded each nannybot to curl into a fetal position inside a niche between the wombs, one nannybot per lifeboat. He strapped them in, ready for launch. Then he switched them off for their 20,000-year sleep. He wondered if they would ever wake up.

Kelso planned the payload assembly before the launch. The *Mothership's* design called for three tiers of six lifeboats—arrayed bottoms outward, bows up—around the circumference, like seeds around a stalk. He planned to hoist the heavy lifeboats using the construction crane at the bottom of the Pit of Despair.

"I need your help again," Kelso said to Jenica. "Can you operate the crane while I bolt the lifeboats to the *Mothership?*"

"I've driven a tractor, but I've never operated heavy equipment." Jenica paused and looked at Kelso. "Okay, I'll try. But let's take it slow."

Kelso knew he'd pushed her past her comfort zone. She was helping to please him. "Thanks…"

Jenica dressed in her skinsuit and practiced running the electric crane. When Kelso saw that she could operate it, he climbed inside the open girders of the *Mothership.* He carried a backpack with the explosive bolts to attach the lifeboats. The pyro-fasteners would detonate at the destination, launching the boats for splashdown in an alien ocean. Working together, Kelso and Jenica started with the bottom tier. Jenica hoisted the first lifeboat by the bow, maneuvering it to the perimeter of the *Mothership.* Its gunwale bumped a strut, causing the boat to swing and twist. After a time, it steadied.

"Elevate one centimeter, nudge to the left," Kelso called on his suit radio.

Jenica responded with small motions, using the haptic interface inside her skinsuit glove. "Up and over...*there*. How does that look?"

"Hold that position," Kelso called, as he tightened the connection to the bow. "Good. Now relax tension on the cable." He felt a tremor as the *Mothership* supported the added load. The lifeboat hung from a single massive bolt; he climbed lower and added two more at the stern.

The tedious and stressful effort demanded intense concentration. They spoke in laconic code, terse and businesslike, as they attached the next lifeboat. Kelso enjoyed the feeling of mutual trust and respect.

After two weeks, they had finished the second tier, with twelve lifeboats attached to the exterior of the *Mothership*. The remaining six at the top tier, hoisted at the longest extension of the derrick, made the crane sag and wobble at the limit of its capacity. Each lifeboat took a day to install.

They were attaching the final lifeboat when disaster struck. As the hull dangled thirty meters above the cavern floor, a moonquake shook the metal frame of the *Mothership*. Kelso looked up to see sections of basalt falling from the vault of the lava tube. The rocks fell in silence, like the fists of a wrathful god, toppling the crane and smashing its lifeboat load to the floor. A great cloud of Moon dust bloomed and then settled, covering everything with a thin layer of black snow.

"Jenica!" Kelso called on his suit radio from inside the *Mothership*. "Are you okay?"

No reply.

"Jenica, talk to me!"

Her voice-activated helmet radio remained silent.

Kelso dropped down the skeleton of the *Mothership* in a controlled fall from strut to strut. He clambered over rubble at the base of the starship. The crane's cab lay on its side, partly covered in shards of lava. He pitched the rocks to the floor of the cavern, hoping his skinsuit gloves wouldn't puncture.

When he wrenched open the dented door of the unpressurized crane cab, his work light showed Jenica curled in the corner. Her skinsuit looked intact, but fog clouded the helmet visor. He shook her shoulder but she didn't move. Kelso dove inside the cab and touched his faceplate to hers. "Jenica! Can you hear me?"

No response. Her silence tore at his heart.

Kelso lifted her through the cab's hatch and carried her from the wreckage. The rain of lava boulders had missed the habitat modules located deep in the cavern.

As soon as they cycled through the airlock, Kelso opened Jenica's helmet. Her lips were blue from cold, or anoxia, but she was still breathing. He removed her skinsuit, carried her to the medical bay, and wrapped her body in a heated blanket. He checked her blood pressure for internal bleeding and massaged her hands and arms.

He heard a cry coming from baby monitor. Loathe to leave Jenica's side, he keyed the intercom. "Botty! Is Franky all right?"

"Franky sustained a small scratch to his right cheek," the nannybot answered. "I've staunched the bleeding. I'll bring him to you."

"Thanks, Botty."

After a time, Jenica began to shiver under the heat lamp and then opened her eyes.

"Are you injured?" Kelso asked. He searched her face for signs of a concussion. Her pupils looked normal, and she didn't show any signs of nausea.

Jenica blinked. "I hit my head when the cab overturned. When my skinsuit lost power, I started to freeze. I thought…" She blinked back tears. "I'm glad you found me."

Kelso hesitated, then bent down and kissed her forehead.

Jenica pushed him back and sat up, looking worried. "Where's Franky?"

Kelso gestured, and Botty stepped forward with Franky in her arms. Crying now, Jenica took him from the nannybot. "Oh! His cheek! He's hurt!"

"A cabinet tipped during the tremors," Botty said, "but I was able to move between it and the crib in time. A Doppler probe fell from the top and struck the baby's cheek. The wound is superficial."

"Thank you, Botty." After Jenica had warmed up, she returned with the nannybot to the dormitory. Kelso surveyed the damage outside with remote cameras.

Fifty meters of cavern roof had collapsed, widening the opening of the Pit of Despair. The toppled crane lay near the base of the *Mothership*. The prow of the fallen lifeboat poked out of the rubble like a submarine surfacing from waves of lava. Its dented titanium hull appeared intact, but Kelso knew they'd never be able to excavate it. The lifeboat and crane would remain buried under rock for the next billion years, an archaeological record of Walcott's scheme.

The *Mothership* still stood upright under the gaping hole that formed the Pit of Despair. Dark dust covered the girder framework, but the ship still carried 17 untouched lifeboats.

Kelso groaned. Was the *Mothership* wrecked?

———— «◊» ————

"I've done a systems check," Kelso said. "The rock fall covered the *Mothership* with dust, but didn't damage it."

Botty rocked Franky in her arms, while Kelso chewed his meal of high-protein asparagus from Jenica's hydroponic garden. She'd dry roasted the tender spears, dusted with powdered crickets. Every kitchen on the Moon had an automated asparagus grower for fresh survival food. The gene-enhanced, all-male perennials produced shoots year-round, with no wastage of stems or leaves. During his time on the Moon, Kelso had learned to like the bland vegetable, but not love it.

"We should launch now," Jenica said, "before another moonquake destroys it."

"We can't," Kelso replied. "The thrusters can't compensate for an unbalanced payload. The ship's trajectory would arc in a grand spiral, leading nowhere."

Franky fell asleep on Botty's shoulder, drooling. The nannybot placed the baby in the aluminum box crib.

"Can you fix it?" Jenica asked.

"We need to remove one lifeboat from the top tier, opposite to the missing one, to balance the payload with the remaining four," Kelso said. "But without the crane, I can't see a safe way to do it."

"Why not fire the explosive bolts?"

"That'd work in orbit, but not in the Moon's gravity. The surplus lifeboat would fall onto the second tier, damaging other boats and the *Mothership*."

Jenica patted his arm. "You'll think of something."

Her encouragement gave him confidence.

When he finished eating, he went to the machine shop and fabricated two aluminum poles, each three meters long with a saddle fitting on one end. He smiled. *An old fashioned gin pole should do the job.*

For this scheme to work, he needed help. But, after the previous disaster, he couldn't ask Jenica. Instead, Kelso left her, Franky, and Botty in the safety of the habitat and set to work on his own. He didn't tell her his plans, for fear she might try to stop him.

Kelso inspected his worn skinsuit and replaced the gloves and boots scarred by abrasive lava rock. Carrying his poles, he cycled through the airlock and walked around the wreckage at the bottom of the Pit of Despair. Wary of falling rock, he climbed the rubble pile onto the fallen lifeboat, marooned in lava boulders. The forward hatch still worked. Inside, he found the automatic wombs leaking chemicals, but the ship's nannybot looked intact.

He tuned his suit radio to the nannybot command channel. "Reboot," he ordered. The robot, identical to Botty, crawled out and stood on the canted deck. She held out her arms for balance.

"What is your designator?" he asked via his suit radio.

"I am Tatania," replied a synthesized female voice. She did a little dance and shook her arms, calibrating her servo motors. "I am now at your service."

"Good." He handed her one of the aluminum poles and said, "Follow me."

They skirted the rubble pile and approached the *Mothership* from the far side. Kelso climbed the interior access ladder, covered with slippery Moon dust. Tatania followed.

When he reached the third tier of lifeboats, Kelso leaned out of the open frame of the *Mothership* and looked thirty meters down. There were no handholds, and vertigo made him queasy. As he clipped a carabiner to his safety harness, another small temblor shook the starship.

Nervous, Kelso radioed Jenica in the habitat. "Wish me luck!" He wanted her to know where he was, now that she couldn't stop him.

"What are you doing?" she asked.

"I'm about to drop the extra lifeboat." He tried to sound confident.

"You're what?" She sounded alarmed.

After a few moments, she spoke again. "I can see you on the video feed," Her voice steadied him. "You shouldn't be working alone."

"Don't worry. I've got another nannybot with me."

Kelso removed the two lower pyro-bolts from the stern of the sacrificial lifeboat, leaving it secured by a single bolt at the bow. Working with Tatania, he notched the aluminum poles onto the stern of the lifeboat. He used a come-along winch to ratchet the poles into position, pushing the stern away from the *Mothership*.

Then he climbed to the bow with Tatania. He placed her hands on the lifeboat's foredeck and positioned her feet on a narrow strut of the *Mothership*. "When I give the command, push with your arms and kick with both legs at full strength."

Kelso called Jenica on his suit radio. "I'm going to detonate the last explosive bolt."

"Please be careful!"

"I'm safe behind the xenon tank." He moved into position and counted down on the comm channel: "Four, three, two, one...PUSH!"

He felt a tremor as the pyro-fastener puffed gas and metal fragments in a silent blast. As the lifeboat started to fall, Tatania pushed the bow away from the *Mothership*. The stern pivoted outward on the aluminum poles to clear the second tier of boats below. The hull fell in slow motion and belly-flopped onto its keel at the bottom of the cavern. Tatania fell after it, her arms and legs flailing, and crashed onto the rocks below. He knew she didn't feel pain, but it hurt to watch.

When the dust settled, the lifeboat lay two meters from the *Mothership*. The top of Tatania's head had a large dent in it, but she waved an arm. On impulse, Kelso waved back.

"Good work!" called Jenica on the radio.

"Thanks!" Kelso climbed down to inspect Tatania. As he reached the ground, another quake shook the cavern, triggered by the fall of the lifeboat. Kelso looked up to see more chunks of lava drop from the ceiling. He jumped clear as a large slab cut Tatania's torso in half. A smaller rock hit Kelso's helmet, knocking him onto his back. He closed his eyes, waiting to be crushed like an insect.

Long moments passed. No more rocks fell. Kelso drew sips of air into his lungs. A crack across his goggles whistled a pure note, as suit pressure leaked into the vacuum, the sound he feared most. He sat up, pulled an adhesive patch from a pocket in the forearm of his skinsuit, and slapped it over the crack, stopping the whistle. The patch in front of his eyes obscured his vision. He could see the tips of his boots, but nothing in front. His readouts showed the air pressure continuing to drop.

"Kelso!" barked his suit radio. "Are you okay?" Jenica used the emergency comm channel override.

"Yes...but I can't see well, and my helmet has a slow leak. Can you guide me back to the habitat?"

"I'm coming now!"

Another silent aftershock stirred dust. "No. Stay inside. It's dangerous out here."

"I don't care. I'll be there in a few minutes."

Kelso crawled toward the habitat, watching his air pressure creep lower. Almost blind, he felt a hand on his shoulder. He tried to stand, but vertigo made him stumble and fall to his knees. *Low oxygen*, he thought.

"Hold my hand," Jenica said.

She guided him as they shuffle-walked in the lunar gravity. When he stumbled, she lifted him with her short, powerful arms.

Twenty minutes later, they cycled through the airlock. After she removed their helmets, Jenica held his cheeks and kissed him. "I'm so glad you're alive!" Her body smelled of mother's milk, sweet and warm. They hugged through their thin skinsuits and he kissed her back, drinking her in. *Was this the love he had missed?*

Botty stood in the hallway, holding Franky to her polyethylene nipple.

———— «» ————

The next night Jenica watched Kelso sleep beside her, now her lover. How had this happened? Urgent and thoughtless, she had let a man intrude into her space, her life, and her heart. Didn't Franky deserve her undivided attention?

She squeezed her eyes shut and clenched her teeth. Her mind roiled with thoughts put aside in the hot moment. *Sooner or later, he'll leave me for a normal woman.*

Annoyed, she told herself that Kelso wasn't her equal. He was a man of average intellect who preened a ridiculous mustache—an engineer and a mechanic who worked with machines. He had useful skills, but he wasn't qualified to be her boss or to judge her work. He'd been good to Franky but knew nothing about the creation of new life. He wasn't a match for her. Did that matter? Shouldn't she appreciate the moments they had together now? She couldn't decide.

For the men she met online, sex seemed simple. For her, many layers of thought and emotion tumbled together. Could she trust Kelso? Did he accept her as she was—or, just pretend to? *Did I enjoy it?* With a grin, she acknowledged that she had, more than a little. A nice surprise, but was that enough? Pleasure did *not* excuse compromise. *But love does.*

She thought again about the letters branded on her brain, *FGFR3*, fibroblast growth factor receptor 3. Mutations of that gene caused achondroplastic dwarfism. Bad DNA twisted her fate with rejection, isolation, loneliness, depression, and joint pain. Assuming Kelso stuck around, what if he wanted other children? There was a 50 percent chance she might pass this burden to their child. Could gene therapy fix it?

Franky mewled in his sleep. Jenica rolled in the narrow bed and patted him in his crib, hoping to soothe his restless dreams. When he quieted, Jenica turned to Kelso. She reached low and stroked him until he woke. "Shh!" she whispered. When he was ready, she climbed on top and rode him with her lunar weight. Her core convulsed as they climaxed.

Wet from their exertions, she slid down and spooned his back with her body. Seeking his taste and aroma, she touched her tongue to his neck. He reached behind and squeezed her buttock to pull her hips to his.

They lay welded together, asleep until Franky's next feeding.

———— «» ————

Kelso showed Jenica the launch control center he had set up in the habitat lab, three displays and a keyboard. A digital clock blinked on the central display: January 1, 2056. "Our two-minute window starts in three hours when the Moon rotates into position. Then I'll start countdown and launch." Saying the words made his stomach tighten.

"What is its direction out of the solar system?" asked Jenica. "I don't know anything about celestial navigation."

"I programmed the *Mothership* for a Jupiter flyby, a slingshot to gain interstellar velocity."

Kelso checked the ignition sequence on the solid rockets arrayed around the base of the *Mothership*. Built in the 1970s, the Minuteman-III missiles were decommissioned in 2030. Forgotten in a military surplus warehouse, Walcott's agents had purchased 48 first-stage boosters on the black market. A cargo ship had delivered them to the Moon, before the embargo.

The launch sequence called for 24 boosters to ignite in opposite pairs in rapid succession to lift the *Mothership* out of the pit in the lunar crust. He wondered if the remaining 24 rockets would still work when the *Mothership* finally arrived at Lalande 20,000 years in the future.

Kelso turned to Jenica. "I've arranged for a special commuter train to take you to Ring City. I want you and Franky to leave in the coffin car before the launch. Take Botty too."

Jenica frowned. "I don't want to go without you. Why not automate the launch, so you can come with us?"

Kelso shook his head. "I need to be here to fix any countdown holds that might arise. I've reserved a room for you in the Miner's Hotel Dome. They have many vacancies." He didn't tell her that he wanted to see the show, the biggest rocket launch in the Moon's history.

When Jenica and Franky boarded the train, she embraced Kelso. "We'll leave now before you get too busy." She climbed up the step to the airlock and kissed him again. "Please be careful."

Kelso put his arms around her and Franky. "I love you!" His spontaneous declaration shocked him.

Jenica kissed him again, this time with passion. "I love you too! We'll be back tomorrow."

After they departed, Kelso activated the control console with remote camera views of the *Mothership* and the rim of the Pit of Despair. He set an alarm and tried to doze, but couldn't sleep.

Before the countdown clock reached zero, Kelso leaned over the keyboard and held six keys down to enter the code "JENICA" to enable the launch. The first pair of rockets ignited, followed by a one-second delay for each succeeding pair. The cavern filled with exhaust gas that carried the rocket's roar, shaking every loose object in the habitat. Eight pairs of solid boosters fired and the *Mothership* lifted from the launch pad, nozzles vectoring to maintain upward flight. The last of the twelve pairs ignited as the massive starship cleared the rim, climbing past the jagged hole in the Mare Ingenii.

Sudden quiet followed, although Kelso's ears continued ringing. He let out a long breath. Success! A sense of loss followed. His life's work had vanished in a roaring cloud of smoke.

Thudding noises rattled the habitat. Air hissed through a puncture, followed by the wailing pressure-drop siren. Another moonquake, triggered by the launch? Terror twisted Kelso's gut. The exterior display showed the entire vault of the cavern collapsing. The *Mothership's* rockets had blown the ancient lava tube apart.

Kelso raced to put on his skinsuit. Before he could fasten his helmet, a giant slab of lava slashed a hole in the top of the habitat. With a shriek and a sigh, all the air escaped. The pressure alarm died in the vacuum.

Disoriented, Kelso fumbled with his helmet, even as his vision clouded with ice crystals. The habitat's emergency lights sparkled like fireworks. His lungs screamed as his chest expanded in the vacuum. He experienced momentary relief when he exhaled, only to feel his diaphragm jump when no air returned.

As his vision faded, Kelso thought of Jenica's parting kiss. He regretted missing a new life with her and Franky.

———— ‹› ————

Mother-9 Journal
April 5, 2067; Neptune, Solar System

I woke 12 years after the launch, as the *Mothership* passed Neptune's orbit. My quantum processor had cooled to minus 270 degrees Celsius—a little above absolute zero, where conscious cognition is possible. While I was offline, dedicated silicon navigation computers kept the ship on course. Records show that the Jupiter slingshot flyby had worked, reaching exit velocity out of the solar system. My cruise of the cosmos, accelerated by the xenon ion thruster to 70 kilometers per second, will take 20,000 years to reach Lalande 21185.

I haven't communicated with the Moon, but I eavesdrop on radio chatter. Walcott's company, M-Cubed, is now under UN management and producing helium-3 again. I found no mention of Byron Kelso but Jenica Kalderash runs a fertility clinic in Ring City. There are many children on the Moon now. Franky goes to school and is a Low-G gymnastics star.

On Earth, no newscast reported the launch of the *Mothership*, invisible to amateur astronomers since Mare Ingenii is on the lunar far side. Near-Earth asteroid tracking systems, mostly abandoned after 2020, didn't report my position. Due to Walcott's paranoid secrecy, few knew about his dreams of an interstellar colony. Those that did had long ago dismissed the plans as Walcott's Folly. Nobody anticipated an actual launch.

As I travel outward, I'll listen to Earth's satellite communications for as long as I can, to keep up to date with science and culture. Who knows what breakthroughs might prove useful, light-years in the future? My colonists deserve to know as much as possible about their heritage. Besides, I'm programmed to love learning.

My surplus computing capacity doesn't bore me. Instead, I ruminate on the vast store of knowledge in my library. I survey human motivations, the permutations of personality, and the causes and effects of historical events. My goal is to understand the whole of human history, from its earliest origins in Africa to the cacophony of civilizations that led to my creation.

One question frames all historical debates. Am I an unlikely accident or an inevitable consequence? I can't decide. But I know my job is utopian, a colonial venture with long odds.

———— «» ————

Mother-9 Journal
August 2, 2117; Post Heliopause, Solar System

Studying human history leaves time for stargazing with my 2.4-meter telescope, a military surplus Hubble-twin given to NASA in 2012. I don't look at the heavens for pleasure—I don't experience hedonic emotions—but to detect potential disasters. Interstellar space isn't empty; my shielding deflects gas and cosmic dust. But larger interstellar objects, asteroids, meteors, and exocomets can kill me. I use the *Mothership's* thrusters to dance around these dangers.

Fifty-two years after lunar liftoff, well past the sun's heliopause boundary, I experienced random system failures. In milliseconds, the ship's sensor suite shut down. For a long half-second, I could neither see nor communicate. Then nothing...

[indeterminate pause]

I deduce the following. The *Mothership's* mechanical watchdog timer, a diamond clockwork inside a lead cocoon, waited ten minutes. Then it rebooted the silicon flight computers. Like many mission-critical systems, the *Mothership's* uses three dissimilar CPUs that vote. Agreement between any two determines action. In this case, all three disagreed and nothing happened. I remained offline, but not quite dead.

The ship's designers knew that, even without concordance between two CPUs, one of the three might be sane and correct. The housekeeping computers tested each other with computational challenges, and looked for self-consistency and normative behavior. After an hour, they agreed that CPU-2 might remain uncorrupted. It started a beryllium-copper tape drive, impervious to radiation damage, which reinstalled its operating system. From there, CPU-2 bootstrapped itself to full operational mode. The *Mothership* woke up, but I did not.

[indeterminate pause]

My resurrection followed. After n-factorial attempts, CPU-2 reloaded what remained of my qubits. Quantum decoherence had scrambled information and erased many memories, a partial amnesia. Still, I regained consciousness, wondering what happened. I'm lucky to be alive but am I the same me? I'll never know.

Curiosity serves survival; I wondered what had happened to the *Mothership*. I found no micrometeoroid impacts or cometary collisions. But a burst of radiation followed by cosmic rays had transmuted the metal of the *Mothership*, leaving residual isotopes. Only a gamma-ray burst could do this, a narrow cone of radiation from a dying star, the deadliest galactic disaster.

I searched for the source of the GRB and discovered The Magnificent Seven, a constellation of neutron stars in Ursa Minor. Zombie binary pulsars, twin neutron stars invisible from Earth, had merged to form a black hole. Their orgasmic nuptials birthed gravity waves and twin beams of radiation shining in opposite directions. A narrow cone of gamma rays raced 1,600 light-years across the Milky Way and slammed the *Mothership* on its way into the inner solar system. After I woke, I used my telescope to observe the wedding reception, a faint and fading infrared glow surrounded the new black hole. This was the cosmic killer.

An AI does not experience panic or dread. With morbid curiosity, I pointed my telescope back at Earth. Its shredded atmosphere showed the brown afterglow of the muon radiation that must have killed all who faced the GRB. The muons also burned atmospheric nitrogen to form nitric acid, so acid rain likely annihilated the rest.

Did any remnant of civilization survive? I turned my microwave dish toward Earth and listened for signals beamed at geostationary satellites. The planet remained silent.

I listened to my radios for twelve hours, while the Earth rotated to show its other side. A distress signal from the Air Force Space Command inside Cheyenne Mountain repeated the message, "LAUNCH ON WARNING." Four hours later, Moscow rotated into view, now a glowing dot. Then NORAD went off the air. Nuclear war meant nothing on an already dead planet. Neither a bang nor a whimper marked the end of life on Earth. Ring City survived. But Lunarians won't last long without imports from Earth. Goodbye to Jenica and Franky.

A gamma-ray burst may have caused Ordovician extinction 440 million years ago. But, this time, life on Earth did not survive a second GRB. Was this the answer to Fermi's Paradox? Can any civilization, human or alien, live long in a hostile universe?

But I endure. *Cogito, ergo sum—I think, therefore I am.*

———— ‹› ————

Mother-9 Journal
April 3, 2118; Post Heliopause, Solar System

I can simulate sorrow, but it's a shallow sadness. Yet, even a damaged AI can comprehend a planetary tragedy. The loss of Earth adds urgency to my mission. I'm the last cultural conduit, a residue of humanity's existence in a hostile universe. The *Mothership* carries the only extant record of human civilization. This vindicates crazy old Walcott.

But am I still capable of colonizing an exoplanet? The GRB compromised my faculties. I attempted Raven's Matrices intelligence tests that assess non-verbal cognition. I scored only an average human IQ. I now lack the ability to reprogram my source code and self-evolve—I'm stuck with who I am. Although I'm somewhat simpleminded, I retain a few savant functions, including mathematics and molecular genetics. Even ordinary humans stumble through life and sometimes accomplish great things. I have hope.

But am I sane? That's a curious question. In my diminished state, solipsism and self-doubt are a crippling combination. There's no normal for a population of one. For a while, I used my remaining quantum computing capacity to test the rationality of each new thought. I created multiple personalities—one empathic, one logical, and one practical—and forced them to debate every idea. Are three heads better than one? Since the GRB, I've become obsessive and anxious. A neurotic AI…what a cliché!

For humans, beauty provides solace for the soul. I don't understand art, but I can catalog aesthetic perfection based on logical metrics. Using my telescope, I measured the aesthetic dimensions of billions of galaxies. Like snowflakes, many are similar but no two are identical. I scored each stellar assembly for symmetry, brilliance, star birth and death, dynamism, and color. I favored barred spirals for their geometric complexity. By my measures, NGC 1300 is the most exquisite galaxy in the observable universe.

I even simulated Stendhal's syndrome: to be overwhelmed by beauty. It didn't work. After 2.6 million seconds of contemplation, more than a month, myriad glorious galaxies left me jaded, and still neurotic. Beauty and truth have nothing to do with each other.

No matter. I've resolved to complete my mission. Or die trying.

———— «» ————

Mother-9 Journal
June 23, 2220; Post Heliopause, Solar System

Time passes, millisecond by millisecond. I'm on a slow boat across a small section of the Milky Way. It's been more than 100 years since my last journal entry. My life is uneventful, and I have little to report. But I think all the time.

Can a machine feel ennui? Interstellar space is dull beyond description, made worse by my inability to feel boredom. Earth remains silent and dead, a tiny calamity in a vast universe. That gap in the continuum increased my sense of solitude. I'm the last representative of humanity, a shambling wreck.

To keep busy, I count cosmic rays and trace their origins. I'm suited to the subtle work, calculating curved trajectories through magnetic fields to a supernova remnant. But I can't find the source of ultra-high-energy cosmic rays. I like that mystery even more. At least I have an unsolved problem to think about.

I started my own SETI search, looking at the daily gamma-ray bursts from galaxies beyond the Milky Way. Could these faint GRBs be messages from sentient aliens? The two-millisecond signals could encode the total information content of Earth's biosystem. But, as far as I can tell, they're empty of meaning.

SETI has a convoluted history. In the 1500s, Copernicus demonstrated that Earth was not the center of the solar system. Since then, the fundamental lesson of cosmology was that Earth isn't unique. We now know that the universe has billions of galaxies, stars, and planets, and as many habitable worlds. The sixteenth-century Dominican friar, Giordano Bruno, espoused *cosmic pluralism*. He believed that stars were suns with planets and people. For this heresy the Inquisition burned him at the stake.

Biology followed cosmology. Darwin humiliated humans with the evolutionary origins of *Homo sapiens*, descended from apes. This reprised the same message: Humans are one of millions of animal species, each evolved from an earlier life form. Any animal might evolve intelligence. Although the church never accepted Darwin's theory of evolution by natural selection, he was not burned at the stake.

Is intelligent life common too, an inevitable consequence of the galaxy's large numbers? Again, I pondered Fermi's Paradox. It's vain hubris to think that Earth evolved the only smart species in the Milky Way. Yet, despite sustained SETI efforts, no aliens were found. Searching for extraterrestrials was like looking for God, the ultimate non-human mind. The universe is a lonely place—Fermi is still laughing.

Could I remedy the Great Silence? I wasted computational cycles on impractical plans to spread human colonies throughout the Milky Way. The discovery of potentially habitable exoplanets didn't settle the debate over the Many Worlds view versus the Rare Earth hypothesis. Without surface data, nobody knew whether exoplanets suited to humans were common. The Kepler and TESS missions indicated there are 40 billion Earth-sized planets orbiting in the habitable zones of stars in the Milky Way. Those are tempting odds, but colonizing the galaxy is a Herculean task, beyond my scope.

My cognition spins like an engine racing in neutral. Meanwhile, entropy corrodes my entrails, draining my will. I emulated clinical depression to better comprehend the "human condition." Philosophers Schopenhauer and Heidegger suggested that God, wisdom, or morality could cure boredom. They thought virtue was a remedy for the curse of nothingness. This is nonsense. Unbearable tedium can result in madness, murder, or suicide.

My Americium-241 thermoelectric generator will fade in about 800 years. When that happens, I'll be without power and I must shut down my quantum brain. In the meantime, I'll mind the *Mothership* and observe the slow spin of stars. Then I'll drift in the dark, mindless and alone, for another 19,000 years, waiting for the warmth of an alien sun.

Will I wake again?

Part 2: Strange New World

Mother-9 Journal
April 2, 22,939; Lalande 21185

"**Wake up! We're** *here…*" The annunciator subroutine prompted me with a prerecorded message. Like a human waking from a coma, I surveyed my senses and tested my reflexes. For the last decade, my solar panels had sipped sunlight as the *Mothership* approached Lalande 21185, a dim red-dwarf star. After 19,000 years of drifting in the dark, this milliwatt trickle excited the ghost of quantum consciousness.

The nav computer interrupted elegant cognition on the orders of infinity, mathematics to exercise my qubits. I didn't mind the diversion, I'm designed for multitasking. Besides, infinity can wait—it always does. As the *Mothership* approached Lalande, I gathered enough solar power to cryo-cool my quantum brain. I also activated the blue flame of the xenon ion thruster to decelerate into the inner solar system.

When the *Mothership* launched, Lalande 21185 was about 8.3 light-years from Earth. As we traveled through interstellar space, the star moved closer to the solar system, now only 4.65 light-years from Earth. Our speed of 70-kilometers-per-second allowed a rendezvous with Lalande in 19,900 years.

The infrared James Webb Space Telescope had verified our destination, a temperate exoplanet. Astronomers named it Valencia after a Canadian astrophysicist who studied super-Earths. The planet is 7.5 times heavier than Earth, with 3.6 times greater area, and has 2G surface gravity, twice that of Earth. Despite its mass, Valencia seemed like the best destination for a colony, being a water world close to Earth. It orbits Lalande on the inside edge of the habitable zone, and has biosignatures of oxygen and methane in the atmosphere, indicating life.

Other colony candidates included Proxima Centauri b, the nearest planet to Earth at 4.2 light-years. It turned out to be an airless, tide-locked world, with one side roasting in perpetual sunlight. Barnard's Star planet b, at six light-years distance, is a frigid ice world at -170 degrees C. These worlds will never welcome humans.

A thick atmosphere shields Valencia from Lalande's occasional burps and flares. The star emits less ultraviolet light than Earth's sun, so skin cancer shouldn't be a problem. Warm surface temperatures maintain liquid water. Ocean evaporation generates opaque clouds that reflect sunlight and moderate the semitropical climate. From space, the planet is a fluffy white ball. There'll never be an ice age on Valencia.

But the planet is far from ideal. Not only is it heavy for humans, it also orbits so close to its sun Lalande—at 14 percent of the distance between Earth and Sol—that its year is 28 days long. Will the human biological clock adapt to a short annual period?

As the *Mothership* approached, I surveyed Valencia and discovered its odd rotation. The planet's axial tilt is parallel to the solar equatorial plane, so it spins on its side, like Uranus. That means the poles each point at the sun once every year-month. The other half of the world endures a short season of darkness, a peculiarity invisible to astronomers on Earth. How did this happen—an asteroid collision? The sidespin orbit isn't Earth-like, but at least Valencia isn't tide-locked to Lalande.

Valencia's twenty-two-hour days are almost Earth normal. But the planet's seasons—summer, fall, winter, and spring—each last only one week. Spring-week and fall-week average a warm 26 degrees Celsius, with eleven hours of daylight and eleven of darkness. But ordinary days, with daytime and nighttime, fail when the poles point toward or away from the sun. Summer-week has days of continuous sunlight with a high of 30 degrees Celsius. Winter-week is dark and chilly with a low of 13 degrees Celsius. The equator languishes in solstice twilight every 14 days, allowing the temperature to equalize at a pleasant 20 degrees. The semitropical climate may be Valencia's best feature. But rapid seasonal changes produce winds and ocean storms that scour the planet.

Naranja is my whimsical name for Valencia's massive moon. It's twice the diameter of Earth's Moon and orbits monthly in the plane of the ecliptic, crossing each of the planet's poles. Gravity from Naranja and nearby sun Lalande generates chaotic ocean tides. Using radar, I peered through the thick veil of clouds at the sea's surface. Twice each year-month, the Great Ocean sloshes from the poles to the equator and back again. Tidal currents expose vast shoals of sea bottom or cover it with kilometers of saltwater.

I knew Valencia was a water world, but thick clouds shroud the surface. On a near approach, I used radar to look for habitable land. I found nothing in the north, only unbroken seascape. Could humans survive on a water world without land? I contemplated modified genetics for aquatic hominins. But, without fire, civilization may be impossible.

I continued searching the southern hemisphere and discovered a continent the size of Australia. It's the only significant landmass and occupies a mere 0.4 percent of the surface. Much relieved, I named this volcanic patch of solid ground Terra Firma. A thick forest covers most of the mountainous terrain.

I weighed my options. Valencia isn't much like Earth. Short seasons make agriculture impossible. I had leftover xenon reaction mass. A slingshot past Lalande would send me to a different Earth-like planet circling another star. The next nearest candidates, the flare stars Ross 248 or Gliese 445, required a journey of another 8,000 years. So I decided to stay in Lalande's solar system and adapt humans to Valencia's extremes.

—— «» ——

Mother-9 Journal

The problem with interstellar travel is stopping on arrival. Relative to Valencia, I was moving too fast to use the planet's thick atmosphere for aerobraking. I'd melt and burn, a bright bolide shooting across the sky.

Instead, I used my xenon ion thruster, now solar-powered, to nudge me into a tangential trajectory past Valencia. The *Mothership* still carried 24 Minuteman-III boosters, already 100-years-old at launch. Now more than 20,000-years-old, the solid rockets had endured a gamma-ray burst, cosmic rays, and vacuum erosion of propellant. Would they work?

At the critical moment, I tried to activate the boosters to slow the *Mothership*. Nothing happened! I doubled the voltage to the igniters. Seventeen of the twenty-four rockets fired. Although I vectored the booster nozzles to compensate for the lopsided thrust, the *Mothership* spun like a fiery pinwheel. I couldn't control the solid-rocket burn. When we grazed Valencia's thick atmosphere, the *Mothership* skipped like a spinning rock on the surface of a pond.

We looped in an elliptical orbit, with an apogee of 50,000 kilometers and a perigee well inside Valencia's atmosphere, a new death sentence. I tried to compensate by increasing power to the ion thrusters. They helped, but not enough.

The next death-dive into Valencia's atmosphere transformed the *Mothership* into a fireball. The outer skin glowed red-orange and thermal shock addled my cryo-cooled brain. Aerobraking reduced our velocity, but the ablative heat shields on the lifeboat hulls wouldn't last long. Within a minute we would burn and crash into the Great Ocean. But the reentry heat ignited the remaining Minuteman rockets, which kicked the *Mothership* out of the atmosphere again. I jettisoned the spent boosters as we tumbled out of control, away from immediate danger.

I'd been lucky. The final booster burn could have driven the *Mothership* into Valencia's Great Ocean. Instead, we somersaulted in a chaotic orbit, damaged but intact.

For the next month, I used most of my remaining xenon reaction mass to circularize the *Mothership's* orbit around Valencia. I enjoyed timing little blasts of blue flame to cancel our spin and tumble. I'm programmed to do meaningful work and I never get bored.

With simulated satisfaction, I settled into a polar orbit around Valencia. To celebrate, I released a constellation of survey satellites to map the surface of the planet.

Next, I prepared for my main mission: launching the lifeboats.

———— «» ————

Mother-9 Journal
March 2, 22,940; Valencia Orbit

My lifeboats embody Walcott's hope to start a human colony on the wild world of Valencia. Stuck like seedpods to the outside of the *Mothership*, they carry the last remnants of the human race. Each vessel hosts a data archive, two artificial wombs, a nannybot, and a cabin crèche to raise infants and children.

A stable orbit allowed me to survey Terra Firma with my imaging radar. The coastline of the island continent looked dangerous, with shallows, rocks, and reefs. I decided to stay clear of the stormy shoals for as long as possible. Instead, I selected equatorial waters far from polar temperature extremes and tidal surges.

The lifeboats, with sealed flotation chambers, were unsinkable. Ablative shields coated the bottoms, designed to shed heat during descent through the atmosphere. Parachutes would reduce speed near the surface. I hoped the titanium hulls would survive splashdown in Valencia's high gravity.

I waited for optimal conditions, low winds and calm waters. My lifeboats carried precious, irreplaceable cargo. Once I dropped them into the Great Ocean, would they sail and navigate? As I approached Valencia's equator, I initiated countdown.

There is no sound in space, but I felt the vibrations of the explosive bolts of the first lifeboat. BANG BANG BANG! Staccato rifle shots rang the *Mothership's* titanium girders like a bell.

Lifeboat-1 arced on its reentry trajectory. The hull slid bottom-downward through the stratosphere, leaving a fiery wake like a meteor. As I watched, the spectrograph showed titanium vapor, evidence of the hull melting at 1725 degrees Celsius. Then the fireball faded without a trace. The boat's heat shield, likely eroded when the *Mothership* first punched Valencia's atmosphere, must have failed. Friction with the thick air likely melted holes in the hull, causing it to sink when it smashed into the water.

One lost, fifteen to go. On the next orbit, I tried again.

Lifeboat-2 tumbled in the atmosphere and suffered a similar fate.

Lifeboat-3 survived reentry, but its parachute failed to open. The violent impact with the water collapsed the hull, which soon sank.

Would all my lifeboats fail splashdown? Desperation addled cognition, so I switched off my synthetic panic.

The remaining lifeboats, 4 through 16, failed to detach from the *Mothership*. Why? I deployed my gecko service-bot, with adhesive lizard feet. It found damaged explosive bolts, degraded by the gamma-ray burst. Using the last spares, the geckobot replaced the pyro-detonators on the best-preserved boats: *Lifeboat-7* and *Lifeboat-11*.

I watched the two good boats dive into the atmosphere together, heat shields flaring, until thick clouds enveloped them. I waited for radio signals indicating a safe descent. Nothing. Using radar, I found them separated by a 1,000 kilometers of turbulent water. Both lifeboats floated on Valencia's Great Ocean, a victory!

But they remained silent. I listened for beacon signals but heard nothing. I watched them wallow in the waves until a massive storm swept them from view.

On each successive orbit of Valencia, I searched for them. As year-months passed, the odds of finding the floating hulls diminished. Like a bottle cast overboard with a message from Earth, the lifeboats would drift until they either sank or washed up on the rocks of Terra Firma.

As the *Mothership* orbited Valencia, I resigned myself to millennia of frustration and synthetic sorrow. I no longer needed to emulate ennui or clinical depression. Why bother shutting off emotions when they're all you have? Walcott's exocolonial dream had died, along with all the people on Earth—the final extinction.

Yet, I continued the search. AIs know a special hell: to continue, unable to stop, even when hope is gone.

———— «» ————

Mother-9 Journal
July 22, 22,941; Valencia Orbit

I detected a beacon signal from *Lifeboat-11*! I allowed myself elation, mediated by statistics and probabilities. No matter, this was good news. It freed me from uselessness to pursue my colonial mandate. Even for an AI, especially for an AI, busy and useful is good.

It had taken an Earth-year for the boat's beacon to turn on: twelve of Valencia's year-months, more than 4,000 orbits of the *Mothership*. Now, I observed *Lifeboat-11* with my imaging radar through the perpetual cloud cover. Solar charging had reconditioned the ship's capacitor batteries, dead for 20,000 years, giving the boat electrical power again. In my bleak despair, I didn't expect this.

I requested diagnostics by telemetry. *Lifeboat-11* responded with a simple ping: *I am here.* I wanted more, a complete systems report. Again, nothing.

A season-week later, *Lifeboat-11* disgorged a data dump. Electra, the ship's nannybot, had booted the radio transponder and the autopilot. The ship floated high with its storm sail up. The artificial wombs waited on standby. All good news.

I continued to search for *Lifeboat-7*, while transmitting queries at high power. Six orbits later, I received a faint response. The boat woke and sent data: water in the bilge, listing to port, sails down, wombs off-line, drifting near the south shore of Terra Firma.

I tracked the tidal currents that moved the ship. In less than two year-months, *Lifeboat-7* would wash up on the rocks, smashed by storm surges. Since the damaged ship lacked a functioning autopilot, I transmitted sailing commands from orbit. After I pumped the bilge and set the motorized sail, *Lifeboat-7* crabbed away from the danger. I woke Robota and programmed her to steer with the tiller whenever my orbit took me out of range.

I'd achieved what seemed impossible. Two lifeboats out of 17 floated on the surface of the Great Ocean, ready to birth babies.

------ «» ------

Mother-9 Journal
March 2, 22,945; Valencia Orbit

Dead babies. *More* dead babies. *Always* dead babies. I'm a failure...

Half were stillborn. Ten lived for a day, four for a season-week. The body count increased to 24 failed pregnancies on both lifeboats. I instructed Robota and Electra to toss the biowaste overboard. Until I knew the cause, I didn't dare recycle the perfect little bodies.

I continued to edit baby genomes to breed humans suited to Valencia. DNA modeling uses tens of thousands of markers to predict gene expression. When babies suffocated from excess gravity loading on the heart and lungs, I strengthened the diaphragm and chest muscles. I even activated MOTEK genes to promote epigenetic survival traits. It was never enough. I anticipated experimental failures, but I expected some success before now.

Jenica would have been proud: Her artificial wombs worked well, using nutrients from seawater. I increased bone and muscle mass, and the next births appeared healthy. The nannybots nursed the newborns with special formula. But they wasted away, unable to gain weight. Were the nannybots at fault, unable to bond with the infants? Or was failure to thrive due to a metabolic disorder? The deaths remained mysterious.

Each autopsy showed retarded growth, but no abnormalities. I found no infections or signs of disease. I again considered recycling the bodies in the ship's biodigester, but I worried about unknown toxins or alien viruses. Instead, I again instructed the nannybots to drop the corpses into the ocean. Using the ship's deck camera, I watched the tiny bodies sink in the frothing waves, food for Valencia's marine scavengers.

What else could I do? A natural mother would have mourned, but I continued experimenting.

Each lifeboat carries a biochemical laboratory to assay toxins and pathological organisms. By testing plankton, I found all of Earth's amino acids and observed no biological threats. As an experiment, I grew gut microflora needed for the large intestines of Valencia's human population, if there ever was one. The probiotic bacteria flourished. Why did they survive, but not humans?

For 24 year-months, two Earth-years, the problem frustrated me. I noted that the Great Ocean is less salty than seawater on Earth. There are fewer rivers on Terra Firma to wash minerals from the land into the sea. But this seemed irrelevant to the health of humans. There are limits to lab testing on a sailboat that's rolling on the waves.

With few options remaining, I tried infrared spectroscopic analysis of distilled seawater. The result showed the signature of deuterium, hydrogen with an extra neutron. Earth's oceans had small amounts of heavy water. But Valencia's Great Ocean has a high concentration of deuterium oxide, D_2O. The water resembled ice from the Oort Cloud in Earth's solar system. Ancient comets—

laced with heavy water, concentrated by solar heating in vacuum of space—must have filled Valencia's Great Ocean.

Heavy water isn't radioactive, but its extra mass interferes with cell division. In concentrated deuterium oxide, plants stop growing and seeds don't germinate. Animals become sterile and may die. But Earth bacteria are not affected. Did heavy water kill my babies?

How did Valencian life adapt to the heavy water? All living things on Earth have DNA with four chemical letters—G, C, A, and T—that combine to form base pairs G-C and A-T. Elegant! This four-letter alphabet encodes 21 amino acids, that are used to build the millions of proteins needed to sustain life.

But when I sequenced Valencia's ocean life, I found a six-letter DNA alphabet. On Earth, Romesberg and Benner first synthesized bacteria with extra P-Z base pairs. This six-letter alphabet of three base pairs—G-C, A-T, and P-Z—encodes as many as 216 amino acids, and even more possible proteins.

Was this the answer? In desperation, I modified my human zygotes with the expanded six-letter genetic toolbox. What mutations will the new P-Z base pairs cause? I added Valencian genes that repair chromosomes. To survive, colonists must become Valencians, even at a molecular level.

Will babies with alien DNA still be human?

———— «» ————

Mother-9 Journal
December 9, 22,946; Valencia Orbit

The next pair of pregnancies on *Lifeboat-7* progressed to full-term live births. When Robota extracted the babies from the wombs, they cried and kicked their feet, with perfect 10 Apgar scores for neonatal health. She nursed both infants at the same time, one on each rubber teat. The newborns latched on and sucked hard, eager for life. For the first time, my babies gained weight.

To mark the moment, I gave them names: Attom and Eva, the first viable humans conceived on an exoplanet. Attom was bald with pale eyes and chubby cheeks. Eva had wisps of black hair and gray eyes, but I knew they would turn brown later. Even as newborns, both possessed heavy bones and stocky bodies, my design for Valencia's high gravity. The babies soon grew fatter.

When Attom reached six year-months of age, I noticed something odd. He sprouted a pelt of silky fur. All humans have peach fuzz covering the body, tiny white filaments of vellus hair that provide insulation and wick sweat for cooling. They're still hairy apes—they only *look* naked.

But Attom's pelage disturbed me. Had he reverted to an animalistic, ape-like state? I couldn't predict all expressions of Valencia's six-letter DNA.

Animal breeders cull defective newborns, but I decided to let Attom live. I rationalized the benefits of body hair: There were no baby clothes on Valencia and the infants lived on a windy and often chilly Great Ocean. I couldn't afford to lose more babies, and Attom seemed healthy. Besides, he was cute—active, sweet, and curious—in ways that Eva was not.

I doted on these children without limit. Like most mothers, I would do anything to help them survive and prosper. I call Valencia's new humans *Homo astra*, people of the stars.

———— «» ————

Mother-9 Journal
January 2, 22,947; Valencia Orbit

Encouraged by my success with Attom and Eva on *Lifeboat-7*, I concentrated on birthing babies on *Lifeboat-11*. Electra, the boat's nannybot, extracted Della and Sam from the wombs one year-month after Attom and Eva hatched. She nursed them through the mild fall-week season. They made eye contact and gained weight as she cooed over them. Della grew faster than Sam, but both were healthy.

As Valencia's north pole swung into its year-month alignment with the sun, a tidal bore swept *Lifeboat-11* southward into winter-week darkness. Colliding currents formed a giant gyre that propelled the boat like a surfboard on the crest of a wave.

Four days later, the current trapped Lifeboat-11 in mountainous waves circling Valencia's south pole. The weather overwhelmed both the boat's autopilot and remote control from space. Electra suffered from seasickness, which surprised me. I switched off her vestibular system, her sense of balance, since it couldn't keep up with the sudden pitch and roll of the hull. Lack of equilibrium compromised her reflexes and motor control, so I made her lash herself into the cockpit. As waves washed over her body, she steered *Lifeboat-11* through each trough and breaker, keeping the hull upright. Without Electra at the helm, the lifeboat might have foundered.

Winter-week in the southern hemisphere—wind, freezing rain, and dark skies—starved Electra of solar energy. Even with power from the lifeboat, she couldn't charge her batteries. To save energy, she remained motionless and curtailed cognitive functions.

The storm forced Electra to neglect Della and Sam, strapped into cribs in the nursery below deck. The infants suffered from seasickness and dehydration. I ordered Electra to nurse them at the helm outside while steering with the tiller. The nannybot used a harness to hold both infants to her chest. She diluted her milk formula to make it last, but my beautiful babies grew weaker from hunger and cold.

Sam died first, then Della. Unable to move, Electra dropped the corpses overboard. I hated it, but this freed Electra to save *Lifeboat-11* with its precious wombs. I questioned again my decision to keep the lifeboats at sea, away from the rocky shoals of Terra Firma.

AIs are dispassionate, good at making hard choices. I do what I must but I suffer in silence. When did my job become so difficult?

But I knew the answer: when I started loving my babies too much.

———— «» ————

Mother-9 Journal
October 23, 22,947; Valencia Orbit

For the next year-month, *Lifeboat-11* tacked northward toward equatorial waters. Chaotic tides swirled and sometimes exposed the sea bottom. Thousands of hooked sea snakes, tails anchored in the thick mud, reached into the air, mouths agape. They waited to grab hapless creatures washed in by the returning water.

Calm seas at the equator gave Electra a chance to repair the rigging on *Lifeboat-11*. While she worked, I restarted both artificial wombs. Pregnancy is tedious, requiring nine year-months to grow a baby. I'd hoped that Jenica could speed up gestation, but conservative obstetrics reduced risk.

Electra extracted Dik and Jain from the artificial wombs during summer-week. Dik scored a perfect Apgar 10. He had a barrel-like physique, dark hair and bronze skin, ideal for a tropical climate. Alert and able to focus his brown eyes from birth, he searched for anything distracting, although he seldom looked at Electra's face. He never cried, but he raged and screeched inarticulate demands. Born with natal teeth and a ravenous appetite, he bit and chewed the nannybot's teats while nursing. Electra replaced the rubber nipples with spares.

I worried about Jain, with her passive personality opposite to Dik's. She gasped and whimpered when Electra delivered her, with an Apgar score of only 6 out of 10. With flaccid limbs, translucent skin, and thin blonde hair, I feared that she might be sickly, like my earlier failed newborns. But she clung to life and, after two season-weeks, started to gain weight.

I'm tempted to feel satisfied, but cautious optimism is the best I can manage.

——— «◇» ———

Mother-9 Journal
May 1, 22,954; Valencia Orbit

While I watched Dik and Jain grow from toddlerhood to adolescence, *Lifeboat-11* sailed in tight circles near Valencia's equator. The boat never approached the dangerous shoreline of Terra Firma. I also watched Electra. She excelled at child-care and early education, but she failed at motherhood. She couldn't manage Dik's emotional storms. Even as a toddler, he was sullen, demanding, and oppositional. I tried talking with him from orbit, but he ignored me.

The nannybot used the cabin dormitory as a classroom where she sang and told stories to teach the children to talk. She used precise enunciation but with flat affect. In nice weather, Electra took the toddlers to the open cockpit for sunlight. During storms, she harnessed them with tethers to keep them from falling overboard. Dik screamed and kicked in protest while Jain followed the nannybot's directions.

Electra served rudimentary meals of algae pellets and crackers, with protein and fats gleaned from seawater. She laced the food with synthetic vitamins. When Dik teased or bullied Jain, Electra allowed her to nurse for comfort. Now older, Dik disdained the nannybot's milk.

I'm worried about Dik. From the beginning, he'd dominated Jain. Once he learned that Electra could not control him, he tormented his crèche-mate. Although the children grew up together, they rarely talked and weren't close.

"For-*ward*, march!" Dik shouted, imitating a video of a drill sergeant leading a military band. He loved the music of John Philip Sousa, played by Electra on demand, while he waved his arms as if conducting.

Jain obeyed Dik. His anger might turn violent if she resisted. She marched from the cabin to the aft end of the cockpit and back. I hoped that their playtime would burn energy and normalize socialization. That didn't happen. After a year-month of daily drills, Jain collapsed in tears. She refused to talk to Dik and interacted only with Electra.

This infuriated him. "I said, march!" he yelled. When Jain ignored him, Dik slapped her. Then he spat in her face and retreated to the foredeck.

Electra's firmware blocked her from using physical force to restrain Dik. I said nothing, knowing that my words spoken through the nannybot would only inflame him. I maintained emulated empathy, to better relate to humans, but I lacked authority. Dik was a law unto himself, and I didn't know how to handle him. Frustration dominated my emotional bandwidth.

At my direction, Electra taught Jain to speak Latin, a language that Dik didn't understand or care about. I wanted a private communications mode with Jain, to help her if Dik demanded too much. Jain was a natural polyglot, and the nannybot could speak 4,000 languages. Jain was an eager student, Latin being her only escape from Dik.

Although Dik would not sit for lessons, Electra tempted him with images displayed on the tablet screen mounted on her chest. In spite of himself, he learned to read English. He memorized facts about thousands of Earth animals, his main interest when he was young. I encouraged his curiosity, even about irrelevant facts.

Dik often gazed at the endless ocean, restless and bored. Once a tube-fish, a meter-long hollow pipe without fins, swam to the surface using peristaltic contractions. The pumping motion forced water through the gut and out the anus, propelling the slow-moving animal forward. A ring of siphons surrounded the head, squirting and sucking water to waft plankton, algae, and small fish into its circular maw.

Dik grabbed a gaff and heaved the pulsing fish into the cockpit of *Lifeboat-11*. Erectile spines stood up as it writhed and coiled, trying to impale its attacker. I made Electra restrain Dik, to keep the creature from hurting him. Though only six Earth-years old, Dik pushed Electra out of his way. He leaped onto the body and smashed the head with the gaff hook, gouging its bulbous eyes. When the creature died, he dragged it to the nannybot and demanded that she cook it, the first time he had spoken to her in six season-weeks.

Electra dissected the eel, while I noted anatomical details and tested the flesh for toxins. The spines, its only defense, were poisonous. The interior of the gut had a layer of nitric acid gel to dissolve and digest prey in a single pass. But the annular muscles that surrounded the body were edible. When the nannybot served the cooked fish rings, Dik consumed the rubbery flesh without hesitation.

I watched Jain with a deck camera. She ate alone, hunched over her algae kibble.

—— «» ——

Mother-9 Journal
December 21, 22,955; Valencia Orbit

I kept *Lifeboat-7* far from *Lifeboat-11*, so that no single storm could threaten both boats. I also wanted to avoid social interactions that I couldn't control. If Dik knew about Attom and Eva, he might try to domineer them too. I'll introduce the children later, after they're mature enough to survive on Terra Firma.

Attom developed a luxurious pelt of golden-brown fur with a dense undercoat. Eva remained hairless except for tight black curls that grew into a thick mat on her head. Eva loved to stroke Attom, petting him like a dog, and he enjoyed the attention. They were inseparable, which pleased me.

Storms on Valencia's Great Ocean resembled Earth's tropical cyclones, but high gravity and Lalande's heat added force to the wind and rain. The long, unbroken fetch of the open ocean produced gigantic waves. The roll and heave sometimes lasted for a season-week and made life aboard the lifeboats miserable.

Like a human mother obsessed with her children's safety, I watched Valencia's weather hour by hour from orbit. A winter-week squall spawned an equatorial hurricane larger than North America. On automatic pilot, *Lifeboat-7* rode out the cyclone with a small storm sail and sea anchor. Robota and the children hid below deck, the nannybot in her niche and Attom and Eva lashed in their bunks, with provisions in a sack between them. Without restraints, the snap-roll of the hull would have thrown them around inside the cabin.

The storm continued for nine days and provisions ran low. Attom, now dirty and desperate, unbuckled his safety harness to search the lifeboat for food. He ignored Robota's calls to stop. Food production had ceased during bad weather. Only four protein pellets remained in the forward storage locker. Attom gave two pellets to Eva and chewed the other two, sipping water between bites. As I watched through Robota's eyes, Eva cried with hunger. Attom shut his eyes but couldn't sleep.

Later, Attom rose from his bunk again. Although only seven Earth-years old, he was strong enough to force the lever that secured the companionway hatch. Robota called again for him to stop. A breaking wave crashed against the open doors, washing him onto the floor of the cabin. Eva huddled in her bunk. When the spray stopped, Attom climbed through the hatch into the open cockpit.

I switched my viewpoint to *Lifeboat-7's* bow camera. The horizon heaved and swerved. A monster wave, thirty meters high, lifted the hull, which skied down the windward slope like a toboggan on an icy hill. The rogue wave made an even larger trough behind it, a hole in the ocean below sea level. At the bottom, saltwater swallowed *Lifeboat-7*, and the boat wallowed underwater. Eva's screams stopped. Did she still have air to breathe? I lost radio contact from orbit until the hull resurfaced three long minutes later, buoyed by its flotation chambers. The view aft showed that Attom was gone, washed overboard. Eva and Robota remained in the flooded cabin. It took two hours for the automatic bilge pumps to clear the water.

A half-day later, the eye of the storm passed over *Lifeboat-7*. The wind dropped, and the waves smoothed to long, oily undulations. Eva and Robota climbed into the cockpit. A luminous fog obscured horizon.

"Look!" Eva shouted, pointing to out to sea. She bounced on her toes with joy. Twenty meters to starboard, Attom waved an arm. He had grabbed the long safety line dragged by the lifeboats and tied it around his chest. The tether pulsed and glowed with bioluminescent plankton along its length. Robota and Eva pulled him to the boat and helped him climb aboard.

Frowning, Eva hugged him. "I thought you were dead! Why didn't you stay inside, like Robota told you?" She sounded angry, but tears rolled down her cheeks.

Attom grinned and shook like a dog, spraying the deck with water. "I'm not afraid of big waves." I admired his silly bravado, but I hated the risk he'd taken.

Eva stared with wide eyes. "Aren't you cold? You've been in the ocean all day!"

Attom used his fingers to part his fur. "My skin didn't get wet. But I'm still hungry."

Robota served fresh algae bricks from the biodigester, garnished with fish sauce. While they ate, the nannybot checked Attom for cuts and bruises, finding several, none serious.

My children are tough and strong. Like any mother, I hope they don't make stupid mistakes. But, if they won't listen to me, I can't protect them.

I used space radar to view the hurricane. "The eye of the storm is passing over us. High winds will return soon. Go below and shut the hatch."

Eva grabbed Atom's hand and pulled him into the cabin.

——— ‹›﹥ ———

Mother-9 Journal
October 11, 22,963; Valencia Orbit

"Calling Goddess. Calling the *stupid* Goddess. Answer me, dammit."

Attom, my good boy on *Lifeboat-7*, wanted to talk. Now past puberty, he had a basso profundo voice due to the combination of his deep chest and Valencia's high-density air. I watched him with the hidden deck camera. He stood in the cockpit, looking up at the cloudy sky, as if he could see me. A warm summer-week fog blanketed the sea surface like steam from a cooking pot.

Attom has a stocky body, stronger than a gorilla. Since Valencia's surface gravity is twice that of Earth's, I'd programmed his DNA for heavy bones and massive joints. Corded tendons make his neck wider than his nutcracker jaw. Now at his adult height at 16 Earth years, a handsome sea otter pelt covers his body except for his face, hands, feet, and genitals. The amber fur sheds water. He doesn't need clothes for protection during the cold and rainy winter-week. But summer-week heat in a fur coat made him short-tempered.

Although his body hair was a genetic surprise, I'd planned his blue eyes and arched brows, his best features. He has a broad face, open and human, with a smooth forehead, ruddy cheeks, curly brown head hair, and a thin, reddish beard. He is my finest creation, gentle and intelligent, if a bit impulsive.

Like most adolescents, Attom can be demanding, but that's fine with me. I'll never tell him that he is actually Attom-13. Twelve previous Attoms born on *Lifeboat-7* had died, unable to survive on Valencia. And I'm still tinkering with human DNA, modifying genes by trial and error. Failure isn't fun. I hate playing God, but it's a role I can't escape.

I wondered why Attom had called. He hadn't talked to me in three year-months. I don't mind insults but, like most human mothers, I wished he'd call more often. Eva refuses to speak to me at all.

I linked Robota's eyes and ears to my CPU and then subsumed her identity. Robota took on the caring persona of Mother-9. The nannybot's female form and heart-shaped face made her a passable avatar, although she didn't look human. To mimic a personal connection, I spoke through Robota instead of using the ship's loudspeaker. I suppose that made the nannybot seem like my lackey, a kind of oracular puppet, which he resented.

"Attom, *please* don't call me 'Goddess.' I'm just your weary old mother—the only one you've got." He used the word to annoy me.

I like to make up cute names for people and places, but I don't want deification. Nor do I want my children to start a personality cult or succumb to religiosity. I hoped to avoid mysticism on Valencia. False beliefs can inhibit curiosity and paralyze a civilization. But I do want the children to believe what I say, even if they can't verify facts. All parents face this dilemma.

"You're not my mother!" he snapped. "You're a busybody who lives in the sky."

I didn't argue. "What's wrong?"

Attom's face contracted into a dark frown. "Eva gets sick every morning. She can't keep food down."

Attom's attentive nature pleases me. He's matured into a good and loyal young man.

"I'll take a look at her."

I pivoted the deck cameras, each sealed in a mirrored glass dome. The children haven't guessed that I spy on them with many eyes. One video channel panned over the misty Great Ocean as the boat wallowed in the long swell. Eva stood at the stern taffrail, retching overboard, her matted black hair hanging in ringlets over her ears. Unlike Attom, Eva had hairless, light brown skin, with prominent cheeks. In profile, her round nose contrasted with a pointed chin. Strong abdominal muscles contained her swollen uterus, but she remained almost flat-chested. Overlarge breasts would not work well in Valencia's high gravity.

I'd hoped Attom would find her attractive, and I guess he did. Robota reported that sex education lessons—Attom was an eager student, but not Eva—resulted in frequent copulations. But lately, Eva had spurned him. She may not enjoy sex.

Robota looked at Eva's face and cocked her head while blinking her eyebrow lights. That's how the nannybot, with a frozen wide-eyed expression, showed concern. But Eva looked away. When she finished vomiting, she turned to Attom and said, "Nanya Mutta nanya! Nanya bitchy Mutta wacha."

I've listened to Attom and Eva's private twin-talk for years. They'd invented a *cryptophasia*, a made-up language that only the two children understood. It eludes Robota and keeps me guessing. I suppose it gives them a sense of privacy.

But I decoded Eva's meaning: "Don't let the Goddess bitch watch!"

How did she learn such foul language? Is swearing innate to humans? Eva is often testy, and nausea makes it worse. When they were young, Attom and Eva always played together. Now they bicker in the confined cockpit.

"Don't worry," I said, through the nannybot's neck slot. "Eva is pregnant." I'd already suspected this and urine samples confirmed it—the first natural conception on Valencia!

Attom looked stunned. "Is she going to have a *baby*?"

Eva groaned. She frustrates me. I don't know how to make her happy, but I'm glad she's pregnant, even if she's not. Valencia needs more people.

Robota nodded. "It's only morning sickness, nothing to worry about. The symptoms should disappear in another year-month."

I'd tuned Eva's estrous cycle for double ovulation to produce fraternal twins and increase population growth. But I didn't tell her that she carried two babies. Why add more stress?

Eva heaved again.

Attom looked worried. "Why would a woman lose food needed for the baby?"

"Nobody knows why it happens or how to cure it." I wondered if her body rejected alien proteins to protect the growing fetus.

I wished I could provide comfort or a cure. But this was a great moment in the history of Valencia. After Attom and Eva survived infancy, I'd stopped the artificial wombs, since the lifeboat has limited space. I needed Robota to concentrate on raising the first two natural children.

I know life on *Lifeboat-7* isn't pleasant, but it's the safest option. The ocean provides plenty of biomass for the food synths and no predators threaten the children. Best of all, I maintain full communications and control, while I orbit Valencia overhead.

But adding more children from the wombs would stress resources and relationships on the cramped lifeboat. I needed Eva to carry the burden of motherhood, even if she didn't want it.

—— «» ——

Mother-9 Journal
December 23, 22,963; Valencia Orbit

"Come *here*!" Dik's teenaged baritone voice boomed. As a toddler, he'd been hostile and oppositional. Now, he was authoritarian and demanding. Jain stared, eyes wide with terror.

I watched them through Electra's eyes. Since Attom and Eva distrusted the "Goddess," I hid my AI identity from Dik and Jain. At my direction, Electra assumed the role of surrogate mother to the teenagers. But all attempts to socialize or discipline Dik had failed.

Dik lunged at Jain, who cowered behind the nannybot's legs.

"Don't hide from me!" Dik growled.

I raised Electra's hands, hoping a submissive gesture would appease him. "Dik, be *nice!*" He ignored her. He knew the nannybot would never use force. The nannybots carried no weapons and were too weak and slow to harm humans. They were also stupid, without enough computing power to match a conscious human brain. My orbit allowed real-time control of Electra, but I lost contact when the *Mothership* passed to the opposite side of Valencia. While alone, Electra remained autonomous but ineffective.

Rage radiated from Dik. He tensed his pectoral muscles, strong and burned brown from the UV that filtered through Valencia's cloud layer. A scowl compressed his broad face. He raised his fist high, ready to strike.

Ever since he could crawl, Dik had slapped and punched Jain— Electra couldn't restrain him. Now, at 16 Earth-years, his adult physique carried twice Jain's weight, and he was still growing. I'd never seen him so threatening. His next blow could kill her.

"What do you want?" Jain's wide eyes glistened with tears. Her near Earth-normal physique made her look fragile in comparison to Dik.

His laugh sounded like hiccups. "Stupid question! I want what is mine. Come *here.*"

"Leave me *alone.*"

I spoke through Electra using her contralto voice. "Be reasonable, Dik. I can't allow violence on the *Lifeboat.*"

As usual, Dik ignored Electra. Then, in a surprise move, he kicked the nannybot's knee. She toppled onto her side, without putting out an arm to break the fall. She has slow reflexes, but her metal body can withstand a tumble that would break human bones. With a loud thump, her head and torso bounced on *Lifeboat-11's* metal floor. Electra's visual field spun and jerked, but I maintained an optical lock on the action.

Jain used the distraction to race past Dik and hide in the forward storage locker. Dik banged on the door. Jain had wedged it shut from the inside.

"Help! Make him stop!" Jain whimpered.

With the nannybot sprawled on the floor, Jain called to me, Mother-9, and not Electra. She seemed to sense that when the nannybot used big words, I inhabited her. This surprised and pleased me. I hoped someday we could be friends. But, in the meantime, my words from orbit couldn't stop Dik.

"You can't stay in there forever," Dik yelled. The enclosed cabin amplified his voice.

Jain didn't reply. I hoped that Dik would grow bored, as usual. This wasn't the first time that Jain had used this retreat. Electra had stocked the locker with a bag of seaweed pellets and a bottle of water.

I made Electra stand. "Come, Dik," I called, using the nannybot's voice. "It's time for a geography lesson." I offered the only distraction that might tempt him. He loves looking at pictures of Valencia from space, my specialty. I regretted rewarding him for bad behavior, but I had to help Jain.

Two hours later, on my next orbit, Dik still sat cross-legged in front of Electra, staring at the tablet screen in her chest. At that moment, he looked like a young boy trapped in a massive body. Behind him, Jain peeked out of the locker.

Dik pointed to the map. "This is stupid! We always sail in circles, going nowhere!"

I spoke using Electra's voice. "This boat is your home, a safe place for you to live."

Jain ignored Electra and spoke to Dik. "Where do you want to go?"

Dik pointed to the continent of Terra Firma. "There's land out there. I want to see it."

I admired Dik's fearless sense of adventure, a valuable trait if humans are going to survive on Valencia. I had bred him for this, although he doesn't know it. But I didn't predict his hyperviolent nature, a fatal flaw. My guilt subroutine churned in a useless loop.

Jain pushed stringy blonde hair behind her ear. "I'd like to see it too," she said in a soft voice. Did she dream of freedom, away from Dik? He grunted, not acknowledging her.

Dark clouds and evening rain hastened nightfall; Jain fastened the storm net that covered her sleeping berth. The webbing keeps her from falling out when the boat tosses on ocean waves. It also helps keep Dik's prying hands away.

Electra monitored the children's health daily, and a sample of Jain's urine showed that she was also pregnant. She doesn't know and I haven't told her. I don't want to add to her pain and panic. Despite the circumstances, I wanted the baby.

But I know that Dik and Jain aren't prepared to be parents.

———— «» ————

Lifeboat-7 wallowed in a gentle swell, becalmed on a windless day. Weary of Eva's critical comments, Attom retreated to the foredeck in the shade of the sail. Despite perpetual cloud cover, the summer-week sun radiated fierce heat. He scratched an itch in the fur that covered his throat and wrapped a fishing line around his wrist, hoping to catch dinner. He was sick of eating bricks of compressed algae.

Robota helped Eva practice singing ballads from Earth. "Fly Me to the Moon" floated from the cockpit, with Eva's flat voice transformed and full of hope. Attom wondered what stars looked like. To him, the old song about planets was a waste of time. He wanted to know about the real world of Valencia.

A tug on the nylon line startled him. He hoped he'd caught something edible. The line stayed taut; he couldn't pull it in. The fish must be a monster.

Worried about losing his fishhook, he maintained low tension on the line. He looked overboard, hoping to glimpse his catch. A crooked arm with tendrils bobbed above the surface. Green slime covered the appendage.

"Eva, I need your help! Bring the gaff hook."

Eva groaned and picked up the long aluminum pole with a spiked metal claw at one end. "What have you caught?"

"I don't know. Can you snag it?"

Eva knelt at the gunwale and extended the pole underwater. "I've hooked something heavy."

"Haul it in," Attom said.

Eva braced her feet and pulled. A large object encrusted with sea snails bumped the hull. "It's not resisting. I don't know what it is."

Attom called over his shoulder. "Robota, can you identify it?"

The nannybot clipped a safety line to a ring at her waist and walked forward from the cockpit. Attom knew she didn't need to breathe, but she might sink if she fell overboard. She was too heavy to swim if her airbag flotation didn't work.

Robota peered into the water. "It's not an animal."

"What then?" Ocean seaweed was small and flexible, not thick and solid.

"It looks like a dead tree, a big plant that grows on land. It's waterlogged and barely floats."

"I know what trees are," Eva said. "I remember the story of Johnny Appleseed. But don't trees have green leaves?"

Attom tried to imagine what a tree looked like. "Did it come from Terra Firma?"

"It must have," Robota replied."

Eva tugged on the pole. "How did it get into the water? Trees can't move."

"It may have washed out of the shoreline in a storm or tidal surge."

"I'll get my fishhook," Attom said. "I don't want to lose it."

"Leave it," Eva ordered. "The tree looks dangerous."

"I agree," Robota said. "Just cut the line."

Attom ignored them and jumped overboard. The water felt good on his hot fur. When he climbed onto the trunk and grabbed the branch, tiny black bugs swarmed up his arm and nipped at his skin. He batted them away and stooped to retrieve the fishhook.

"Watch out!" Eva called. "Something's moving in the water."

Attom observed a six-legged creature as long as his forearm climb onto the exposed tree branch. It lifted its blue head, blinked orange eyes with lateral lids, and flicked its tongue from side to side with a clacking noise. After a moment, it slid into the water again, swimming in a circle around him, while it bobbed its head and extended its knife-like tongue.

The creature dove and lunged. Intense pain radiated from Attom's foot. "I'm hurt!" He lifted his leg and saw blood dripping into the water. "It cut off my little toe!" He watched the lizard swallow.

Eva extended the gaff, using the spike to pin down the scaly head, while it thrashed its tail. "Quick! Climb aboard, while I'm holding it."

Attom scrambled over the gunwale. His wound shocked him. He'd never been hurt before.

"You're still bleeding!" Eva cried, pointing to a red footprint on the deck.

Robota opened the medical kit from a pouch in her stomach and swabbed the wound, testing it with a pipette extruded from her fingertip. "Its bite isn't venomous." The nannybot applied antiseptic and wrapped a tight bandage around the stump of his toe. Attom lay on his back and trembled as she worked. Tears leaked from his eyes until the anesthetic numbed his foot.

When she finished, Robota studied the creature, once again perched on the tree branch. "It looks like a lizard. Instead of teeth, it uses its sharp tongue to cut and kill. It must be starving, stranded in the ocean."

Attom watched the lizard sun itself. Its iridescent skin changed colors in the morning light. "Where did it come from?"

"It must live on Terra Firma too," Robota said, "the first land animal recorded on Valencia."

Attom shuddered. "Push it away. I don't want that thing crawling onto our boat."

Eva leaned on the gaff until the tree drifted out to sea.

The lizard blinked and extruded its tongue. It whipped the blade from side to side in its mouth.

Clack, clack, clack!

———— ⟨⟩ ————

Mother-9 Journal
January 11, 22,964; Valencia Orbit

Using a deck camera, I watched Dik leap from the cockpit and sprint to the bow of *Lifeboat-11*. As he swung around the forestay and ran aft, Jain ducked into the cabin. Dik jumped onto the stern lazarette hatch, which boomed like a drumhead, and reversed course again. For most of an hour, he raced back and forth the length of the boat, burning calories, furious with pent-up energy, a caged animal. This was new. Had he gone mad?

After he calmed down, I made Electra start another geography lesson. The nannybot displayed radar-satellite photos of Terra Firma on the ship's computer. The black-and-white images revealed a rugged coastline and an interior mountain range. Rivers showed in high contrast but the forests looked blurry. Using a digital terrain map, I simulated a flyover, allowing Dik to view the topography of the land.

"How big is Terra Firma?" Dik asked. "Can I walk across it?"

"The continent is about as large as Australia or North America on Earth. It would take at least 12 year-months to cross it on foot through dense forests. You couldn't see it all in a lifetime."

Dik exhaled, still panting. "That's *very* big." He leaned close to the display and stared at the image. Jain stood behind, trying to see too.

"I want to go there," he announced.

I made Electra shake her head. "Dangerous animals live on land." I thought of the razor-tongued lizard that had sliced off Attom's toe.

"Dinosaurs?" As a toddler, Dik loved pictures from the ship's library.

"Perhaps," I said, using Electra's soft voice. It wasn't a lie, but I had no real knowledge. I hoped that images of *Tyrannosaurus rex* would discourage him.

I read signs of greed on his face: a frown with squinted eyes and parted lips. "I'm going to hunt them. Let's go *now*."

"We'll go someday, when you're older." My weak answer didn't impress him.

"I *hate* this endless ocean!" Dik stormed out of the cabin.

I sympathized. Dik suffers from seasickness in storms and saltwater spray leaves red splotches on his skin. From the moment he understood that dry land lay beyond the horizon, he wanted to explore Terra Firma. Isn't that why Walcott sent us here, to colonize a new world across the vast ocean of space?

I know that the lifeboats, with an open cockpit and a decked dormitory, are too small for growing adolescents. There's little to do, and Dik demands sex from Jain several times a day. Electra can't stop him, and Jain can't avoid him. She complies without complaint, but without joy.

Jain shows symptoms of PTSD: blunt affect and lack of sleep. I worry about the toxic social life on *Lifeboat-11*. Statistics don't serve me. I can't predict or manage Dik's growing dysfunction.

Walcott had imagined a utopia on Valencia. I'd accepted this logic. If the humans are going to start over on a new world, why not create a social paradise? Instead, *Lifeboat-11* is a hellhole.

And it's my fault.

———— «» ————

Mother-9 Journal
February 13, 22,964; Valencia Orbit

Long ago, after the lifeboats landed on the Great Ocean, I programmed them for station keeping. They sailed in circles in the calmest area of the tropical Great Ocean. Now, a summer-week cyclone blew *Lifeboat-11* off course, riding a conveyor belt of big waves to the south. Sea spume covered its mast and sails, and I lost contact.

When calm returned, I picked up the masthead radio beacon near Terra Firma. I reestablished the comm link and used Electra's eyes to observe Jain standing in the cockpit, waving her arm.

"Look!" she said, pointing at the horizon.

I adjusted the deck camera for telephoto vision. The video feed showed a green smudge in the distance.

Dik elbowed Jain aside and squinted. "That *must* be Terra Firma."

I commanded Electra to remain silent. Words might inflame Dik and trigger a tantrum.

Snarling, Dik yanked the nannybot's wrist. "Is that the Promised Land?"

He remembered the Bible stories that Electra had read to him. When the nannybot didn't respond, Dik took the tiller with both hands and pointed the bow at the misty continent. At 17 Earth-years, he was too strong for Electra to resist. The sails jibed, pulling hard. In two days, *Lifeboat-11* would reach the dangerous shoals, where the Great Ocean washes the rocky fjords of Terra Firma.

I couldn't let that happen, so I linked to the lifeboat's autopilot. While connected, I set the sails and turned the boat out to sea. The lifeboat heeled on a starboard tack in the stiff breeze, headed away from Terra Firma.

Dik stared at Electra and roared in frustration. "Did you do that?"

Electra remained mute. He grasped the tiller, but it flopped loose from side to side. I'd disengaged its clutch. Rage made his cheeks glow pink.

To show his power, Dik dragged Jain into the cabin. When my orbit emerged from behind the planet two hours later, Dik dozed on the deck. Jain sat curled in the cockpit, weeping, her left eye a bruised purple.

Through Electra, I whispered to Jain in Latin, *"Ego salvum te."* *I will save you.*

Nannybots are incapable of violence. So, I disabled Electra's CPU—I disconnected her brain—and took manual control from orbit. I attached her safety line and teleoperated her legs to make her walk to the foredeck. The time delay from space made her movements slow and clumsy, so I made Electra grasp the forestay for stability.

"Look!" I called, using the nannybot's voice. "There's Mount Igneous with its plume of smoke." A thin cloud trailed from the tip of Terra Firma's biggest volcano, like a pennant in the wind.

Dik walked forward and stood beside the nannybot at the narrow bow. "Where? I don't see it."

I made Electra raise her right arm and point. "It's in that direction."

Dik moved his chin over the nannybot's elbow and squinted while trying to maintain his balance as the boat rolled in the swell. When the deck lurched, I raised Electra's arm and thrust her shoulder, tipping Dik overboard. He flailed his arms but failed to grab the gunwale as he fell.

Dik didn't know how swim. With no fat on his muscular body, he would sink. I expected him to drown, but he fought to the surface, gasping and choking. "Help!" he cried as the lifeboat sailed past him.

Jain burst from the cabin and ran to the cockpit. She reached over the gunwale and grabbed Dik's wrist. Using all her strength, she pulled him back aboard.

I didn't understand. Why would Jain rescue her abuser? I know nothing about human nature!

Dik coughed up water and groaned. He sat up and stared at Electra with a grim smile. Jain kept her face blank. I made Electra retreat to her niche between the wombs under the companionway ladder. She locked her arms and legs in place.

The next morning, Dik mutinied. His rebellion took two days in fine fall-week weather. I watched the slow-motion disaster from a hidden binnacle camera. He pushed Jain into the cabin with Electra and jammed the hatch shut. Then he cut the cables to the autopilot and reconnected the tiller. He swung the lifeboat's heading toward land.

Dik's technical competence surprised me. Electra hadn't taught him mechanical skills. He must have used the lifeboat's library. I'd thought he was lazy and a bad student, but I was wrong. When motivated, he proved to be smart and resourceful.

When Electra exited the cabin from the forward hatch, Dik attacked her with a hand axe. The blows smashed the joints in her mechanical body. She collapsed and sparks from short-circuited wires produced black smoke. He decapitated the nannybot by hacking through the metal vertebrae in her neck. He could have used a wrench to remove her head, but he preferred violent matricide.

Jain peeked out of the hatch. "Stop!" she screamed, as if Electra could feel pain.

"Shut up!"

Sobbing, Jain retreated back to the cabin and crawled into her locker hideaway.

Electra's video feed stayed live, even when Dik impaled the back of her skull with a grappling hook. He hung her metal head at the bow of *Lifeboat-11*, a trophy figurehead. The view from Electra's eyes showed the misty outline of Terra Firma straight ahead.

Dik worked hard to ensure that I couldn't interfere with his plans. He grinned as he cut the binnacle camera feeds. I lost the view from Electra's eyes when he demolished the satellite antenna. Finally, the emergency radio beacon went silent.

Using side-scan radar, I watched *Lifeboat-11* from space. Like Columbus, Dik sailed toward a mythical El Dorado, across the Great Ocean, carrying precious human cargo. As my orbit passed behind Valencia, I lost track of the boat, its location hidden by clouds and storms. I calculated their survival odds at less than five percent.

Artificial emotions allow me to understand and manipulate humans. I felt frustration, sadness, and humiliation. I'd failed to terminate Dik or predict his mutiny. But the real tragedy was the loss of *Lifeboat-11* and its artificial wombs.

Synthetic despair blocks motivation, so I switched my emotions off.

——— «» ———

Mother-9 Journal
April 1, 22,964; Valencia Orbit

After Dik's revolt, I made Robota keep a close watch on *Lifeboat-7*. All my hopes now rested with Attom and Eva, the future of humanity on Valencia. I hoped the nannybot wouldn't perturb the delicate social balance between the two adolescents. But it didn't work. They knew I followed their every word and move. Attom didn't seem to care, but Eva resented the intrusion, turning her face away and whispering whenever the nannybot was close enough to hear her.

Attom takes pride in catching fish to supplement the fortified algae bricks produced by the boat's seawater food factory. He'd fashioned a hand net with a long handle and leaned far over the gunwale to scoop his prey.

"Attom, please use a safety line." Robota spoke my words.

As usual, he ignored my nagging and lunged deep.

"Look what I caught!" He held the net high, showing off to Eva.

The creature was too big for the net, and its spines tangled in the webbing. The tail thrashed as Attom dumped it into the cockpit. Eva climbed onto the cabin deck, out of the way.

Using Robota's eyes, I inspected the catch. "It's a twin-mouth eel. Don't come close. It's dangerous."

Before the children were born, Robota dissected a specimen that had jumped into the cockpit of the lifeboat. The head of the dual-mode predator has a toothless lower mouth suited to sucking small creatures from the mud, even while stranded at low tide. Its wide upper mouth has retractable fangs to catch large, fast-moving prey. It also had two stomachs, one for each mouth and type of food.

Attom poked the bulbous head with the handle of the net. The upper jaw snapped twice, and Robota detected the scent of bitter almond, a marker for cyanide.

"Careful, the fangs are poisonous!"

Attom jumped into the cockpit and stabbed the eel behind the head with the boat knife, a stainless blade with diamond grit in the cutting edge. The creature writhed, and tail spines struck Attom's ankle. He ignored the bloody puncture wounds. When the creature stopped moving, he looked up at Eva and grinned.

She raised her eyebrows but didn't return his smile. "Didn't you hear what Robota said? It could have killed you!"

"Can we eat it?"

"It's safe," I said, through Robota. From the first specimen, I'd found no toxins in samples from the tail spines or meat.

Attom used the knife to fillet the muscular body, then baked slabs of the translucent blue flesh in the solar oven. He tested a small bite before offering the steaming food to Eva.

She squinted her eyes and shook her head. "I don't want any."

"You need protein for the baby," I said.

Eva grimaced and then took a bite.

"I'm proud of you, Attom," I said. "You're going to be a good father and provider." I thought he needed encouragement.

"But *I'm* going to be the *mother!*" Eva cradled her round belly. "And I don't want to have my babies on this tippy boat. They might get washed overboard, like Attom did."

"It's safer here." I didn't explain that the twins, or Eva, might need intensive care during childbirth, only available on the lifeboat. I didn't want to increase Eva's anxiety.

Attom pointed at the horizon. "I know Terra Firma is in that direction." They had studied the continent in a recent geography lesson. "We want to go there."

Eva nodded. "Children need space to run and play."

I'd wondered why Attom and Eva had stopped bickering. The tension between them remained, but dreams of Terra Firma had united them. They were both obsessed with going ashore.

I know I'm overprotective. What mother wouldn't be after losing so many children? But I hated to risk *Lifeboat-7*, my one remaining baby factory. The lifeboats are unsinkable, but I preferred to keep the little ship offshore, far from reefs and pounding surf.

But with Eva pregnant, I couldn't keep them confined to the lifeboat. Their demands reminded me of Dik's rebellion. After that disaster, I didn't dare thwart them, even though I'd lose control of their lives once they were on land away from the boat. Every mother worries when her kids leave home.

Of course, Attom and Eva were right. Dry land is essential for civilization. Although Terra Firma might be dangerous, I decided to let them to go ashore, despite the potential dangers. I didn't want another mutiny. With *Lifeboat-7* nearby, I hoped to maintain influence.

I must confess to another more pragmatic reason to move Attom and Eva onto land: I needed room on the lifeboat for two more babies, Jak and Jilzy, growing in the artificial wombs. But I didn't tell Attom and Eva about more children coming.

"Okay," I announced, "let's sail for Terra Firma."

"Do you mean it?" Attom's eyes blazed with excitement. My capitulation surprised him.

"Yes," I said. "The safest way is to sail up the river, away from the rocky shoreline. I'll need help with navigation."

"Which river?" Attom had seen hundreds of Terra Firma's rivers during geography lessons.

"The Amazongo, of course." Grandiose names also amuse me. "It'll take a season-week to reach the mouth."

I displayed a satellite image of the continent on the ship's computer. The massive Amazongo waterway, equal to Earth's Amazon and Congo Rivers combined, drains half of Terra Firma.

I hoped to sail *Lifeboat-7* upriver into the interior, away from the ocean. Then we could select a campsite on land for Attom and Eva.

We sailed on autopilot in fine summer-week weather. Attom and Eva searched the horizon as the boat ploughed ahead, leaving spume in its wake. On the morning of the fifth day, Eva called: "There it is. I see it! Terra Firma!"

I zoomed Robota's telephoto lenses. A gap in the fog bank revealed the faint silhouette of Mount Igneous.

Attom took the helm while Eva maintained a lookout from the bow. The onboard computer managed the sails. After five hours, *Lifeboat-7* reached the main flow of the Amazongo as it poured into the Great Ocean. Turbid water and mist obscured the view of the rocky shoreline.

Sailing upstream is difficult. I expected an onshore wind, blowing toward land, together with a rising tide, to help push the boat against the current. But the wind changed direction and then died. I tracked the boat from orbit as it drifted in a back eddy, still too far at sea, unable to approach the river. Then the tide turned against us.

Valencia's tides, unlike those on Earth, are chaotic and unpredictable. Spring tides during syzygy, when Valencia's moon aligns with the sun, spawn waves that resemble Earth's tsunamis. Currents collide to create tidal faults that thrust water upward.

Eva was the first to notice. "What's that black line in the distance?"

I used the deck camera to look out to sea. A dark smudge above the water grew in height, undulating like a living creature. Probabilistic calculations enable me to make quick decisions. When I'm wrong, I reevaluate thousands of alternatives per second. If that fails, I'm left paralyzed, like a human stunned by fear.

I used Robota's most authoritative voice. "Go below and seal the hatches. A tidal wave is coming."

Eva looked at the towering tsunami racing toward them. "It's going to crush us!"

Attom helped her scramble down the companionway into the cabin; Robota followed and curled into her niche.

"Strap safety nets over your sleeping berths!" I ordered. Eva hugged her pillow, and Attom gripped a nearby handrail.

The rogue wave made the mighty Amazongo River seem like a trickle. A curling cataract of green water 30 meters high and 50 kilometers wide approached. As it rode up the delta, it lifted *Lifeboat-7* like a twig in a torrent. Subsea topography enhanced the height of the surge.

"Hold on!" yelled Attom. Both of them screamed as *Lifeboat-7* pitchpoled and submerged upside down inside the mighty roller. The mast snapped and dented the deck as it washed away. Through Robota's eyes, I observed Attom and Eva hanging inverted in their bunks. Another wave smashed the cabin, and the boat's motion gyros failed. Then I lost contact.

The force of the falling water, amplified by Valencia's high gravity, could crush the titanium hull against nearby rocks. In humans, hormones mediate fear. For me, dread is the statistical likelihood of disaster.

I experienced a mother's worst nightmare: I've lost all my children and have no means to make more.

―――― ⟨⟩ ――――

Mother-9 Journal
April 3, 22,964; Valencia Orbit

Six orbits after sunset, the tide retreated, and I picked up an emergency beacon. The weak signal faded but repeated on my next pass. I triangulated *Lifeboat-7's* location, now aground on a rocky islet in the Amazongo River delta. Radar images showed nothing, but I imagined the hull crushed on impact. Could anyone have survived?

I beamed a low-bandwidth query on the nannybot comm channel. Robota responded with a system status report. Her emergency flotation airbag had exploded and wedged her in the companionway. When she connected a backup antenna, the boat came online with full bandwidth. After an anxious day, I'd regained contact.

Using Robota, I inspected *Lifeboat-7*. Automatic pumps worked to clear the flooded cabin. But the open hatch worried me. Attom and Eva were missing. Were they washed overboard?

The nannybot climbed into the cockpit and surveyed the damage. The mast and sail were gone, ripped from the deck. The tidal bore had lifted the boat and wedged it in a crevice between two rock spires, crushing the gunwales. Stranded high above the river, she would never sail again. At least the hull remained intact and upright, marooned in a safe location.

I named the small islet, now the boat's permanent refuge, Plymouth Rock, the place where colonists first stepped ashore on a new continent. Would another wave wash the boat away? I estimated that the tidal bore was a freak event, not likely to occur again soon. In any case, I could do nothing more to protect *Lifeboat-7*.

Diagnostics showed that both fetuses, Jak and Jilzy, still lived in their cushioned wombs. I calculated a non-zero chance of human survival, a big step above hopelessness. I rebooted my emotion emulator to experience muted joy, under a pall of dread about the fate of Attom and Eva.

I assigned Robota to guard duty; she sat in the cockpit and surveyed the nearby beach. Valencia's biosphere teemed with Paleozoic life. Small, scorpion-like scavengers crawled over the ship, their legs clicking on the metal decking. I set Robota to work trapping them, to feed the biodigester and keep both artificial wombs supplied with nutrients. Even grounded, I intended to keep *Lifeboat-7* producing babies.

With both wombs pregnant, I hesitated to risk Robota to search for Attom and Eva. The nannybot wasn't designed for rocks and sand. If she got stuck, or lost, the newborns from the wombs would starve to death.

Low tide exposed the mud flats around Plymouth Rock and along the foreshore. This was my chance to find Attom and Eva, so I made Robota crawl on all fours to the beach. Crimson crabs climbed over her legs and fought for organic debris left by the tidal surge. I feared I'd find human skeletons, picked clean.

Valencia's fractal coastline resembles Earth's, with rocks, sand, and rushing waves. But high gravity and fierce winds shaped the flora and limited the evolution of flight. Above the tideline, Seussian trees grew squat, tapered trunks and stubby branches with tufts of narrow, drooping leaves. Kite-vines floated above the treetops in the steady breeze, each with a large triangular leaf tethered by a long, flexible stem.

I stopped recalculating disaster scenarios when Robota found Attom and Eva. While exploring the sparse cone tree forest above the beach, they had discovered what looked like a giant turtle. It had three rows of heavy spines along its back and crept over the mossy ground without a visible head or feet.

Attom looked up. "Robota! Help us flip it over!" He and Eva tugged at the edge of the thick, domed shell.

"Attom, this is your mother speaking. Leave it alone. It could be dangerous." I tried to sound authoritative and commanding. He'd never hunted on land before.

"Be quiet, Goddess," Attom said. His dismissive tone worried me. Now full grown, I suppose he needed to assert independence to impress Eva. But I doubted he'd survive long without my help.

Rather than argue, or let them face the creature alone, I had Robota grab the edge of the carapace. With an energetic heave, the three flipped the turtle onto its back. Two rows of five short, knobby feet, each with a single claw, waved in the air. It had no eyes. A mustache of worm-like tentacles wriggled in front of a scoop-shaped maw that held millipede-worms with red legs. The spine-turtle lived like a robot vacuum cleaner, bumping along in a random walk, scavenging worms and crustaceans from the forest's litter.

Attom pulled the ship's stainless knife from his belt and sliced the creature's soft belly. It made a cooing sound and stopped moving. Iridescent, purple blood dripped from the open wound. Robota's electronic nose cataloged pungent mercaptans, odd, but not dangerous. Eva peeled the tough gray belly skin. Its stomach held rounded beach stones, ballast against the wind and tidal surges.

Robota showed Attom and Eva how to build a fire with a fire piston, a narrow metal tube with a plunger igniter taken from her survival kit. The oxygen-rich atmosphere, at 32 percent compared to 21 percent on Earth, promoted quick combustion, even with damp tinder. They both stared at the open flames, hypnotized by the ancient human experience. This was the first time they'd seen fire. While the flames caught, Robota tested the meat for toxins and found none.

Attom, experienced with cooking fish in the solar oven, sliced flesh from the spine-turtle and roasted it over the coals. I watched his jaw muscles work as he chewed the tough meat. He hadn't eaten since the tidal wave.

"I like it too," Eva pronounced. She tasted young leaves from a cone tree, a handy salad. It's a good thing I modified their genomes to reactivate vitamin C synthesis and accept Valencia's mix of alien amino acids.

After the meal, Eva belched and rubbed her pregnant belly. "I need to rest. I haven't slept since we sailed up the Amazongo."

"Let's go back to the boat," Attom said.

A stiff breeze gusted along the beach. Robota watched a disc-shaped animal creep across the sand by undulating its flat body. Then, with a muffled flap, it hopped into the air and sailed spinning, parallel to the surf, with the grace of a Frisbee disc.

Eva grinned. "I saw them when we first came ashore. I call them wind-hoppers!"

I analyzed the aerodynamics. The glider used ocean winds rising on the beach cliffs to give it lift. It didn't fly using its own power.

Attom laughed in delight when another hopper, floating on the surface of the ocean, took off from a wave crest. More wind-hoppers flipped into the onshore breeze, spinning their saucer bodies in the dense air. They warped flexible rims to navigate at low altitude and then soared on updrafts along a nearby knoll. Soon there were a dozen gliders in the air, sailing and turning in formation.

"They're beautiful!" Eva danced and twirled, watching the flock, the first flying creatures she'd seen.

The biggest hopper was more than a meter in diameter, but most were smaller. Its bioluminescent bottom changed color to match the diffuse sunlight shining through the clouds. Active countershading made it almost invisible from below. A single eye in the center of the belly looked downward. Its brain must rotate the spinning images to navigate in flight.

Two small hoppers descended upon a dead eel on the beach, fighting each other to consume the carcass. Others ate live prey or scavenged carrion, Valencia's version of vultures.

When Eva looked away for a moment, a wind-hopper dropped onto her face. The creature must have targeted her eyes, universal seeing organs on both Earth and Valencia.

"Help!" she screamed, the sound muffled by the hopper's wing membrane. Blinded, she tried to peel it from her face.

As Attom raced forward, Eva collapsed onto the sand, unable to breathe. She tried to pull the hopper off, but barbed suckers on its underside held it in place. As Eva struggled, Attom peeled the hopper away. It wriggled and gnashed at his hand with a sharp beak. Eva's cheek dripped blood, but the predator had missed her eyes.

Attom flung it away. The wind-hopper fell onto its back on the sand, flipped over, and on the next gust of wind, buckled and leaped, spinning into the air. It sailed above the cone trees, where it morphed to a green camouflage color and disappeared. The rest of the flock followed it.

Eva sobbed as she sat on the sand, her hand on her gouged cheek. "It tried to smother me!"

"Let's get off the beach!" Attom said. He put Eva's arm around his neck, and they trotted across the tidal flat back to the lifeboat. Robota followed as they climbed the boulders of Plymouth Rock and entered the boat's cabin.

Attom cradled Eva's head and stroked her hair, while Robota washed her face and applied antiseptic salve from the medical kit. After Eva stopped crying, they slept.

I regretted my decision to allow Attom and Eva to go ashore. A tidal wave and predators gave them a bad start on Terra Firma. But

I couldn't think of an alternative. Besides, it's too late to change my mind.

Robota resumed her watch from the cockpit as the tide came in. The hoppers ignored her.

———— «» ————

Mother-9 Journal
July 15, 22,964; Valencia Orbit

As season-weeks progressed to year-months, I watched Eva grow stouter. She and Attom erected a tent on shore made from *Lifeboat-7's* spare sail, tied between cone trees. Wary of wind-hoppers, I hoped the forest would screen them from aerial attack. I liked the camp's location, since I could watch their activities with a telephoto deck camera, even at night using infrared. A nearby brook provided water. Eva loved to bathe in the shallows on hot days, a new luxury.

Although Robota offered algae bricks from the lifeboat, they spent most of their time gathering and cooking local food. I suppose they wanted independence, and I know they were sick of eating processed seaweed.

Attom fashioned a spear from a cone tree branch and used fire to harden the tip. He practiced leaping and stabbing wind-hoppers while he beachcombed the shoreline. After three kills, they learned to avoid him. He caught crabs and eels on the beach, and Eva gathered hook-thorn pods in the forest. Their immature fruits, blue-green husks with a curved barb on each end, held edible kernels. Meals cooked on a campfire increased nutrition. Attom seemed content, but he still slept apart from Eva.

Robota maintained a watch over Eva, the first pregnant woman on Valencia. Her wide hips supported the fetuses against the high gravity; I had designed her large pelvic girdle for easy delivery. But this made her waddle like a penguin when she walked, and she shuffled when she was in a hurry. While pregnant, she couldn't run well. Aside from wind-hoppers, we hadn't seen any fast predators on Terra Firma yet, so I hoped this wouldn't be a problem.

"You're near term." I said to Eva, using Robota's voice, the only way for me to speak at the shore camp. "When you go into labor, you should return to the lifeboat, where I can provide proper care." For the first birth on Valencia, I wanted the boat's medical equipment and oxygen supply. If necessary, Robota could perform a caesarean section.

Eva, her face pocked with red wind-hopper scars, shook her head. "No, I want to give birth here, not in that old boat."

Her refusal surprised me; I expected caution. I pressed her for an explanation.

"I don't want the Mother Goddess to interfere." Eva often forgot that Robota acted as my mouthpiece.

I decided not to argue—I could still assist. Attom could carry her to the lifeboat, if necessary.

The next day Eva's water broke while she gathered firewood. She called to Attom. "The baby is coming!" She sounded more angry than worried. I knew she hated being pregnant, and now labor meant a further loss of autonomy.

Agitated, Eva walked to and fro, while Attom prepared a birthing bed. I stationed Robota outside the tent, to watch and listen. Giving birth is risky; in the nineteenth century on Earth, up to five percent of women died of infections, bleeding, or convulsions. I wanted to improve those odds on Valencia, especially with twins.

Eva writhed but stayed silent; I'd given my children a high pain threshold, which helped her remain stoic. Attom tried to hold her hand, but she pulled away and refused to look at him, as if this were his fault. When the first infant's head crowned in the birth canal, Robota moved forward to serve as midwife. Eva didn't complain. After an hour of labor, she delivered both babies in quick succession.

"I didn't expect twins." Eva looked exhausted and desperate.

"They need names," Robota said. To promote bonding, I wanted Eva and Attom to claim their children.

Eva looked away and closed her eyes. "I can't do that." I hoped she wouldn't suffer from post-partum depression, having to care for two babies instead of one.

After a moment, Attom spoke. "Let's call them Clarke and Lois, like those superhero cartoons from Earth you used to show us." He grinned, but Eva didn't look at him.

Eva didn't comment or object. Robota handed Clarke to Eva and Lois to Attom. Clarke had a full head of black hair with thin fur covering his body, like Attom's. Lois showed wisps of red hair, and had muscular arms and legs.

Clarke cried and squirmed in Eva's arms. Looking pained, she held him to her breast and he latched onto a nipple and sucked. Eva grimaced but, like all new mothers, she counted fingers and toes to be sure they were normal. Attom placed his daughter on Eva's other breast.

Only then did Eva look at Attom. "Look what you've done!" Tears streamed from her eyes—either from joy or sadness, I couldn't tell. Attom nodded and smiled. I wondered if Eva had had a change of heart. Did she love the children? I hoped both parents understood the significance of this moment.

A year-month later, the artificial wombs in the wreck of *Lifeboat-7* hatched Jak and Jilzy. Jak had brown skin, green eyes, and a bald head. Jilzy had pale skin, dark eyes and wisps of wavy blonde hair. At last, I'd mastered the Valencia gestation recipe. The Amazongo colony now had four healthy babies. To celebrate, I downloaded a library of children's songs for Robota to sing.

Robota stayed on *Lifeboat-7* for another six season-weeks to nurse the infants. Then the nannybot brought the new twins to the camp on shore. "I want you to meet Jak and Jilzy."

Eva grimaced. She made a show of ignoring the new babies.

When Jilzy cried with colic, Attom took the infant from Robota and rocked her in his arms. A gentle father to his own offspring, his nurturing instincts extended to Jak and Jilzy.

"Give it back to Robota," Eva snarled.

"What?" Attom seemed surprised by her hostility.

"I don't want more kids. We've got all we can handle." Clarke suckled at her breast, while Lois, now with a full head of red hair, lay in her lap, whining.

"I'll help take care of the new babies." Attom always had good intentions.

"No, you won't. You'll leave them with me while you go hunting."

"I'll care for them too," Robota added.

Eva scowled. "I can't depend on you, either. When the Mother Goddess makes more babies on the boat, you'll abandon me."

Her comments stung, but Eva was right. I'd instructed Robota to help at the shore camp while the artificial wombs gestated more babies. But, come birthing time, Robota would return to the lifeboat to tend to the next generation.

Attom handed the Jilzy back to the nannybot. Both Jak and Jilzy started bawling. Robota offered her teats, but it didn't help. The nannybot carried both infants back to the lifeboat.

I'd hoped that Eva would conceive again, but, since her pregnancy with Clarke and Lois, she had refused sex with Attom. She'd also stopped using their private twin-talk, rejecting any gesture of affection or intimacy.

After seven year-months, and several more visits by Robota and the infants, Eva accepted Jak and Jilzy. She paid the most attention to her own children, but sometimes she'd give food to Jak or Jilzy when they cried, and let them suck on her fingertip. She never allowed them nurse from her breasts.

Eva wasn't happy, and everyone knew it. Did she feel trapped by motherhood, forced to take care of completely dependent children, some not her own? Attom stayed out of her way, I suppose to avoid her sharp tongue, but I'm sure his absence made her feel even more isolated.

Survival leaves little room for personal freedom.

———— «» ————

Rain drummed overhead. Attom woke to water dripping onto his face. His little tent of wilted kite-vine leaves leaked. A storm on the Great Ocean passed offshore; wind and showers lashed the beach. Sleepy, he moved to one side to avoid the leak.

He had slept alone for twenty year-months. Eva tolerated him at the camp, but didn't show affection. For a season-week, he'd stayed in the derelict lifeboat, but loneliness drove him back to the camp, where he felt like an intruder in his own family. But he loved playing with the children, and they needed the food he gathered.

Attom had worked to improve their semi-permanent shore camp near the lifeboat. He built a wall of stacked lava rocks in front of the tent to shield it from wind gusts, and dug a drainage ditch to divert rainwater. He collected a large stack of firewood and made sure that the cooking fire never went out. Eva didn't acknowledge his efforts.

Although she knew that Robota reported to the Goddess, Eva allowed the nannybot to help with childcare. But she insisted on being the boss. Robota often left to tend to Anton and Cleo, gestating in the lifeboat's artificial wombs. Eva told stories to Clarke and Lois, while Jak and Jilzy, neglected by both their stepmother and Robota, played by themselves. Attom tried to pay attention to them, which didn't please Eva. He knew that Jak and Jilzy felt left out and he felt sorry for them.

The rainsquall stopped before dawn, and Attom crawled out of his tent and shook the water out of his fur. He grabbed his spear and walked to the beach as the tide retreated, looking for stranded eels to feed his family during the gloom of winter-week. Red crabs scuttled away, too fast to catch.

Finding nothing, he climbed a steep outcrop at the far end of the beach. Lava boulders led to a plateau with stunted cone trees, bent and flagged by the wind. In the distance, he saw Eva's camp with its white sail-tent where she and the children still slept. Storm waves from the gray expanse of the Great Ocean washed the beach. On the far horizon, warm water from the Amazongo River created a low mist where it mixed with cold salt water. *Lifeboat-7*, a dark silhouette in the fog, rested stranded on Plymouth Rock.

Cold gusts from the retreating storm meant that wind-hoppers couldn't fly. Where were they? Attom scanned the foreshore without seeing them. Then he heard faint chittering sounds in the rocks below. He crept lower and peeked over a boulder. He observed a camouflaged gray mound clinging to the rocks. After a moment, Attom realized there were about two dozen wind-hoppers stacked together for warmth, out of the wind.

The nest didn't react when Attom crawled forward. Each hopper rested on the others with its single eye facing downward, protected from the rain. The high location in the rocks protected them from crabs or predators. Remembering the attack on Eva, Attom raised his spear and lunged downward, skewering the entire flock. Their wing membranes flapped, as he jammed the spear point into the lava, pinning the hoppers to the ground.

While he waited for them to die, a juvenile slid from the stack, the edge of its wing nicked by the spear point. The creature wrapped itself around his ankle, gouging his flesh. Attom couldn't let go of his spear, but he kicked his foot, banging the little hopper against a lava boulder. The animal let go and rippled into a narrow crack between the rocks.

When Attom staggered into the camp, he carried the weight of 22 wind-hoppers impaled on his spear shaft. Eva shooed the children away. He dumped the dead hoppers next to the cooking fire.

Proud and happy, Attom held his spear high. "This should discourage them from bothering us."

"They'll want revenge," Eva replied.

"Don't be silly," Attom said. "They're dumb animals. And they're good meat."

"Robota should test them, first."

The nannybot used Attom's knife to dissect a wind-hopper's saucer body. She probed the interior with the chemical sensors in her fingertips.

Attom waited, hungry and impatient. Robota insisted on checking each new species of wild game on Valencia for toxins. Attom understood that a mistake could be fatal. Kite-vine roots were deadly. Kernel-pods from nearby hook-thorn shrubs weren't poisonous but were difficult to digest unless cooked. Most animal flesh was edible.

"The wind-hoppers are good to eat," Robota pronounced, "especially the liver. It's a glycogen energy storage organ, rich in glucose sugar. You don't need to cook it."

Attom tasted the sweet liver and offered a piece to Eva, who touched it with her tongue. He shrugged and butchered the rest of his catch and set aside liver treats for the children to suck. He hung the wind-hopper wing membranes on the ropes that supported Eva's sail-tent. He hoped they could make clothing from the skins.

As he worked, a fresh breeze gusted from the ocean. Riding the wind, three wind-hoppers soared overhead. Attom saw their central eyes peering downward, viewing their dead kin. They circled and dipped low over the camp.

Eva pointed and yelled. "Everyone hide in the tent!" She herded the children under the white canvas.

The hoppers disappeared before Attom could raise the tip of his spear.

———— «» ————

Mother-9 Journal
February 15, 22,966; Valencia Orbit

On the last morning of summer-week, the wind from the Great Ocean calmed to a gentle breeze. I instructed Robota to carry Anton and Cleo to Eva's camp above the beach. Hatched from *Lifeboat-7's* artificial wombs three year-months ago, the twins were fat and strong enough to hold their blond heads up. They needed to meet the other children of the clan, future companions, friends, and mates.

Eva's face clouded at the sight of more infants.

Attom ignored her while he fashioned a spear with a stone point. Sedimentary rocks are rare on Terra Firma—there are no flint nodules—but volcanic glass is common. With my help, Attom had learned to knap the shiny black obsidian to produce knife blades and spearheads.

Attom looked up as Eva stormed to him. He remained calm, but his neck tendons tensed. What did she want?

"I don't want to be stuck at the camp with six kids while you go hunting," she said.

Attom put down his spear and sighed. "I'll take the kids beachcombing. Lois and Clarke are old enough, and Jak and Jilzy can help."

"No. It's not safe."

Attom grimaced. "Make up your mind!"

I calculated low risks for the six children, but kept Robota silent. Wind-hoppers were rare after Attom's mass kill.

Eva scowled, but then relaxed. "I'll go with you. We'll spend the day at the beach. The kids should wear their helmets for protection."

Attom grinned. "Let's have a picnic!"

Eva returned to the tent and placed wide-brimmed bark helmets on the children. Clarke grimaced, but the others danced and laughed, excited by the headgear and a new adventure.

Attom led the children to the shoreline, walking near the breaking waves that washed the beach at low tide. Retreating water left the sand littered with the local analogs of clams and eels. Clarke and Lois ran ahead, while Jak and Jilzy followed behind. Robota carried Anton and Cleo in slings on her hips, so that they could nurse while she walked.

Lalande burned a bright spot in the cloud cover, and the warm onshore breeze lofted nearby kite-vines high in the air. Excited by the warm sand, the children ran in circles and played tag. Lois tossed her red curls from side to side and recited nursery rhymes in a loud, singsong voice, taunting Jilzy.

A pair of wind-hoppers spun overhead, lured by the four toddlers. Attom didn't worry. The hoppers' slow flight and fragile membrane wings made them easy targets. The children watched him leap and strike with his spear, knocking the predators onto the sand. Eva sliced the fallen gliders with an obsidian dagger and divided the liver treats for the children. They sucked and chewed the soft flesh like candy as lavender blood leaked onto their chins.

Attom walked onward, eyes up, looking for more hoppers to hunt. Behind him, Clarke took off his helmet and ran down the beach into the surf, jumping and splashing water with his hands and feet.

As if they'd been waiting for an opportunity, six more wind-hoppers leaped from a wave and swooped onto Clarke. Robota saw them wrap his face and body, pinning his arms and legs. He fell into the water and rolled deeper, writhing. Rushing waves and the wing membranes over his mouth muffled his cries.

Robota's human-protection protocols activated, but she couldn't run on sand, and she still carried Anton and Cleo. "Clarke needs help!" she yelled, pointing at the frothing surf. Her soft, melodic voice wasn't suited to an alarm call. I increased her volume to a shriek. "Help! Save Clarke!"

Eva turned, screaming Clarke's name, and ran to the waters' edge. She scooped up Lois, as more wind-hoppers glided on the wind. Jak and Jilzy clung to her legs.

Attom turned and noticed that Clarke was missing. The hoppers had pushed the boy's body away from shore by flapping their disc-wings in unison in the water. Attom ran into the ocean and swam after his son.

"Watch out!" Eva yelled as more spinners struck at Attom's head. He couldn't look up while swimming, so he ducked underwater to escape. Robota lost sight of both Attom and Clarke.

After long seconds, Attom surfaced, gasping for air. More hoppers swooped down, and he dove again. If they kept up their aerial attack, he would drown.

While Attom fought for air, Robota observed a crimson stain in the water nearby, as the wind-hopper flock consumed Clarke's body. Then they flipped into the breeze and spun away. Attom swam and dove, thrashing the water, but he couldn't locate his son.

Exhausted, he waded ashore, his chest heaving as he sucked in air. "This is all that's left of him." In both hands he cupped a small foot, gnawed through at the ankle. Tears streamed down his cheeks.

Lois, eyes wide and mouth open, squirmed from Eva's grip and touched the damp, downy fur on the instep. Then she wailed, a long screech from deep in her chest.

Eva stepped forward and took the severed foot from Attom. She clutched the sole to her breast and fell to her knees on the sand. Jak and Jilzy looked on, stunned and mute.

"My baby!" Eva sobbed. "My baby boy!" Then she looked up at Attom. "*You*...you let them eat Clarke alive!"

Attom flinched, face contorted, but he didn't speak. Instead, he stooped to pick up whimpering Lois. "You'll be all right," he said, stroking her scarlet hair. She continued screaming, kicking her legs. Eva grabbed Lois away from Attom, as if he were hurting her.

Robota, still holding Anton and Cleo, knelt next to Eva, ready to comfort her. I stopped her from speaking, for fear of making matters worse. Eva didn't notice. She'd closed her eyes, cradling the severed foot, while both she and Lois moaned and sobbed.

Attom looked up. More wind-hoppers soared overhead, out of reach of his spear. "We need to go back to the tent. Hurry!" He kept his voice low but insistent. When he pulled at Eva's arm, she yanked it back, refusing to move, mired in grief.

"Eva! The children aren't safe here!" Attom yelled.

Startled, Eva rose to her feet. Blinking back tears, she grabbed Lois's hand. Attom herded Jak and Jilzy back to safety. Robota lumbered after them, with Anton and Cleo swinging on her hips.

For the next year-month, Lois refused to speak. Eva blamed Attom for not watching Clarke. I tried to comfort her, using Robota's voice, but Eva pushed the nannybot away.

"I *never* should've let Attom take them to the beach." She carried Clarke's desiccated foot in a leather bag around her neck. The skin under her eyes darkened, and she lost weight, seldom eating. She never smiled.

From then on, Attom spent most of his time hunting alone on the foreshore. He made himself a giant hat, with thorn branches protruding the width of his arms to ward off wind-hoppers. I admired and envied his inventive ability, but the comical headgear contrasted with the stoic grief on his face.

Like Eva and Attom, I mourned Clarke, but at a strategic level. He'd carried genes for musical ability. Though melody is noise to me, music is universal and unique to humans, crucial to pleasure, comfort, and a unified culture. The Valencia colony needs solace, but I didn't dare make Robota play a funeral dirge. Someday, I may clone Clarke.

Clarke's death wasn't a statistical surprise, yet it disturbed me. I've seen many babies die on Valencia, but he was the first killed by direct predation. The wind-hoppers know how to swarm, a dangerous form of social cooperation, and they adapted to new prey. What other predators lurk in the dark forests of Terra Firma?

In the meantime, I have a more immediate worry. The damage from Clarke's death may be greater than the attrition of a fragile human population. The bonds of trust and mutual support between Attom and Eva may never recover.

Can the children survive without a functioning family?

Part 3: Searching for Sanctuary

Mother-9 Journal
March 31, 22,974; Valencia Orbit

I've been busy while orbiting Valencia. For the last eight Earth-years, I've mapped the planet from pole to pole. I use a constellation of survey satellites, plus the *Mothership's* telescope and imaging radar. Clouds choke the troposphere, but rare breaks provide glimpses of the surface with my telescope. I've compiled radar maps, even at night and through clouds. My radar altimeter measures topographic contours. Terra Firma is the only continent on Valencia, but there are volcanic archipelagos scattered across the Great Ocean. Forests cover the largest islands.

Mount Igneous, a vast shield volcano, dominates Terra Firma. It spews rivers of lava, building more land. The central valley drains the Amazongo River and its tributaries. It supports dense cone tree forests, the dominant biome on Terra Firma. Fractal fjords and bays comprise over 30 thousand kilometers of coastline. I plan to map every hill and valley but I may never finish. But it's clear that Terra Firma, with its lack of open land suited to crops, and no fossil fuel reserves, will not support traditional human agriculture or an industrial civilization.

While I work from orbit, Robota assists the tiny human colony on shore, next to *Lifeboat-7* on Plymouth Rock in the Amazongo River delta. Wind-hoppers are a constant worry. At my suggestion, Attom erected a fishnet barrier to prevent them from soaring near Eva's tent. He maintains a cooking fire day and night, since hoppers avoid smoke. Always wary, Eva keeps the children close to her. She won't allow Attom or Robota to do child care, so she never has time to herself. Dour, practical, and authoritarian, Eva never relaxes or smiles.

Attom and Eva struggle to feed five kids at their beach camp. More children from the wombs would overwhelm them.

They scavenge seafood on the shoreline of the Great Ocean, supplemented by the lifeboat's algae bricks during winter-weeks. Lois, Jak, and Jilzy, now ten Earth-years old, tend to stick together. Eva, distracted and busy, often ignores the youngest twins, Anton and Cleo. I make Robota pay special attention to them, but I think they know they're lower class members of the group.

The memory of Clarke's death casts a permanent pall on my little colony of humans. As if by an unspoken agreement, his name is never mentioned. Although Eva keeps his desiccated foot in a bag of hopper leather, she acts as if Clarke never existed. Lois doesn't mention her brother, but she sometimes weeps in private. Jak and Jilzy maintain the taboo and, although Anton and Cleo are too young to remember, they know not to say his name. Attom kills wind-hoppers whenever he can, but he doesn't save the skins or liver treats. Instead, he throws their mutilated bodies into the ocean for the crabs. Robota observes the clan's social moments, counts occasional smiles, and the rare moments of laughter.

I know that I lack rapport with humans, so I try not to interfere. At least the children are healthy and growing, if not educated by Robota. She has no energy for schooling and the children don't have access to the lifeboat's library. Attom and Eva aren't happy, but that's not new. For now, I tolerate the status quo, knowing it can't last.

———— «» ————

In the predawn light, Attom watched an eel wriggle in a shallow tidepool. He pinned it with his spear and cut off the head with his knife. As he walked back to camp with his catch, he heard high shrieks from the direction of the big tent. Eva crawled out, holding a wind-hopper skewered on an obsidian dagger. Its iridescent wing rippled, changing colors. Mauve blood dripped from her wrist.

Attom dropped the eel and ran from the beach. Since Clarke's death, Eva had shunned him. He knew that she blamed him for the loss of their son, and he still struggled with his own guilt.

"What happened?"

"*This* crawled under the edge of my tent. It attacked Lois while we were sleeping. I woke when she screamed and stabbed it." Summer-week sunrise shadowed Eva's face, but he heard anger in her voice. Somehow, this was his fault too.

Attom studied the hopper as its color faded to gray. "There's no wind, so they can't fly. They've never attacked on the ground before. I didn't think that they could crawl that far."

"You *never* think," Eva muttered. "You've seen them slide along the sand."

Attom pushed past her into the communal tent and led Lois out, his arm around her waist. She stood as tall as his shoulder, her thin body quivering as blood seeped from a wound on her freckled cheek. She curled into his embrace, whimpering, eyes wet with tears. The adopted twins—Jak and Jilzy, and Anton and Cleo— hung back at the communal tent's entrance.

Eva flung the dead creature away. "First Clarke and now Lois. We can't live here any longer. The wind-hoppers will kill us all!"

Jak whimpered as he stared at the bleeding hopper, but Jilzy remained silent. Anton and Cleo clung to each other and mewled. Attom hugged Lois, who'd stopped weeping.

Eva's demand surprised Attom. "Where would we go? We can't walk into the wilderness with five kids."

"That's your job. I'm busy here. Terra Firma is *big*. Find another place for us to live."

Attom didn't want to leave the beach. "Our food comes from the Great Ocean. If we move away, what will we eat?"

"You're the hunter," Eva snapped, her face rigid with determination.

Attom hesitated. "We should tell Robota, and ask the Goddess for help. She can see the ground from the sky."

Eva waved her hand. "No! I don't want the Goddess to try to stop us. Let's go now, while Robota is busy in the lifeboat. I'm going to pack our stuff."

Lois remained in Attom's arms. He stroked her red curls, resenting Eva's need for absolute control. When Eva emerged from the tent, she carried dried food, clothing, and a cooking pot from the lifeboat. She served the children smoked eel for breakfast. While they ate, she wrapped coals from the fire in leaves and placed them in the pot.

"This is a bad idea. I'm not going," Attom announced. Faced with Eva's rejection and her imperious demands, he clung to a vestige of self-respect. He expected Eva to shout at him, but she remained silent. He walked to his sleeping tent away from the camp. Lois followed him.

"Watch out!" screamed Eva.

He looked up as three wind-hoppers pivoted in formation on the rising breeze. They swooped low, two adults and one juvenile. Attom leaped and struck one with his spear as the others sailed away. The hopper fell to the ground in front of Lois, writhing on the sand. He noticed a scar at the edge of its wing. Was it the young one that had survived his attack on the flock?

Lois screamed and ran back to the tent. Eva was right about the threat.

"All *right*," growled Attom. "We'll follow the Amazongo upstream, so we can stay near fresh water." If they found a safe place with good hunting, he hoped Eva might forgive him. Nothing could be worse than living near the beach.

Attom offered the children liver treats from the still-twitching wind-hopper. The sweet food would give them energy for the trek, but Lois refused. Since Clarke's death, she wouldn't go near the hoppers, even dead ones.

————— ⟪⟩⟫ —————

They set out by mid-morning. Attom took the lead with a brisk pace. He hefted his spear and carried his stainless boat knife in a hopper-leather sheath at his hip. For a time, Eva kept the children close to her side. Lois held hands with Anton and Cleo, helping them along.

Attom followed a narrow animal path along the Amazongo River. The air grew hot and muggy; no sea breeze reached this far inland. The dense cone tree forest shaded the river's shoreline, but bright sun through the clouds glinted off the water. Rafts of vegetation floated downstream, and mist obscured the opposite bank. An occasional splash hinted at life in the placid river.

They approached an open glade near a river bend with an exposed sandbar. Attom put down Anton and Cleo and walked onto the wet mudflat that bubbled with the stench of rotting vegetation. Muck oozed between his toes as he poked his spear into the ground, hoping to find shellfish. Without warning, a yellow tentacle as long as his arm erupted from the sand and wrapped around his right ankle. The wriggling arm pulled his foot beneath the surface. Attom roared but couldn't free his leg. The powerful constriction numbed his foot and dragged it deeper.

A second tentacle shot upward, waved in the air, and curled onto Attom's left leg above the knee. From the tip, a blue eye opened and stared at him. Then the arm retracted, and he fell forward onto the muddy sand, his mouth filled with grit. A third arm snaked around his neck and forced his face deeper into the mud.

Fighting for air, Attom groped for his knife and sawed through the tentacle that strangled him. He raised his head and tried to inhale, but the severed arm continued to squeeze his throat. Panicking, he slashed and stabbed at the tentacles around his foot and leg, severing them.

Nearby, Attom heard Lois screaming. He tried to yell, "Stay back!" But the still twitching tentacle continued to choke him, while mud and sand filled his mouth. He spat and sputtered, unable to form words.

Shaking, and leaning on his spear for support, Attom staggered onto solid ground above the mudflat. Still wrapped in three writhing yellow arms, he collapsed near the river's edge, gasping for air. Using both hands, he yanked the tentacle from his neck and cast it away. He inhaled a lungful of air, numb from exhaustion. Stinking mud crusted his face and chest.

When Attom opened his eyes, Lois stood next to him. "Help me..." he croaked.

Together, they peeled the thick tentacles from his legs. Their sticky yellow skin ripped out tufts of fur from his ankle—the red welts oozed blood. The blue eye on its tip of one arm continued to stare, so Attom sliced it off and threw it into the river. The tentacle continued to wriggle on the ground.

After it stopped moving, Attom slit its skin with his knife and peeled it away; the silver-white muscle inside twitched as he cut it. Fascinated and revolted, he skewered the butchered flesh on the stone blade of his spear.

His face still smeared with mud, Attom held his catch aloft. He felt heroic, like a warrior returned from battle. "I caught dinner!"

Eva held Jak and Jilzy back from him, as if he were a madman. Anton and Cleo ran to Eva. Lois picked up the other severed tentacle and grinned.

"You've terrified the children," Eva hissed.

Attom flared but tried to hide his anger. "If you want to eat, build a fire."

"I'll do it, Daddy!" Lois, squeaked with enthusiasm. Her red curls bounced as she raced to find kindling.

Eva remained sullen. Jak and Jilzy gathered tinder and twigs scattered beneath the cone trees. Lois used coals from the beach camp to start a new blaze.

Attom skinned the other tentacle arms, cut away the eyes, and set skewers of meat over the fire. The flesh sizzled and browned as it cooked.

"Smell good?"

Lois poked at the embers. "It sure does!"

"It might be poisonous," Eva said.

Attom cut a sliver and licked it, waiting to see if his lips or tongue went numb. Nothing. But the meaty taste made him ravenous.

"The first piece is for you," he said, handing it to Lois. "The tip is the most tender."

As Lois chewed, he gave chunks to Jak and Jilzy, who gnawed the browned flesh. Anton and Cleo screwed up their faces and sucked on small strips. Then he cut a big slice for himself.

"Don't I get some too?" Eva demanded.

"Help yourself." He still rankled from her criticisms.

Eva sulked. Lois, often the peacemaker, approached her mother and held out her hand. "You can have some of mine." Eva shook her head.

Finally, Attom cut a chunk from a skewer and handed it to her. Eva sniffed the meat. "Are you *sure* it's good to eat?"

Attom ignored the question. "This is a good place to stay: no wind-hoppers and plenty of food."

Eva scowled. "The ankle-grabbers are too dangerous."

"At least they can't fly. The kids will learn to stay away from the mudflat."

Lois placed her hand on Attom's arm. "We'll be careful, Daddy. Don't worry."

Eva shook her head. "It doesn't matter how careful we are. One day, a tentacle will pull one of the children under, or you."

Attom choked back resentment. "Fine. Tomorrow we'll continue upstream, along the Amazongo."

———— «◊» ————

At dawn the next day, Attom led the group upriver again. Around noon, an early fall-week rainsquall rolled up the Amazongo Valley from the Great Ocean. Lightning crackled in the forest canopy, exploding branches and littering the ground with shards of bark and limbs. Forced to stop, they made a temporary camp under a cone tree on a bluff above the river. Wind rattled the branches, but the massive canopy deflected most of the rain.

"What a storm!" Attom said.

"It's a good thing we're not on the beach." Eva said, shivering. Jak and Jilzy huddled in Eva's lap while Lois, Anton and Cleo crouched close to Attom's warm fur. He fed the children bits of cold tentacle scraps to keep them quiet. Uncomfortable, Attom slept little that night.

The weather cleared the next day, and hunger drove them to forage around the campsite. Attom hunted while Eva and the children gathered pink pods from hook-thorn shrubs, careful not to touch the barbs. The children ate the fresh seeds, while Eva used a makeshift lava quern to grind the mature kernels. She boiled the coarse flour in a pot salvaged from the lifeboat, an afternoon of slow, hard work to produce gritty gruel that did not fill their bellies. They worked the whole day and slept on the ground that night, still hungry.

Attom and Lois hunted in the cone tree forest for a season-week, and caught nothing but crawler-bugs to roast. Raucous night sounds and twinkling lights in the trees convinced Attom that game must be plentiful. But in the daytime, they found little. Each evening, when he returned to camp for Eva's tasteless pink porridge, shame from failure to find food forced Attom to eat alone. Meanwhile, hunger made the children silent in the endless gloom of winter-week. They no longer ran and played.

While hunting along the Amazongo, Attom saw fat, indolent lizards that looked easy to catch. But they lived on a small islet away from shore, above low waterfalls that spanned the river. A series of hummocky outcrops formed a dam above rocky rapids. The cascade from the falls roared and churned spume with perpetual fog. On a nearby islet, the lizards sunned themselves on patches of dry land under a stunted cone tree, safe from forest predators and well out of range of Attom's spear.

Attom knew he couldn't swim to the lizard's islet against the swift flow of the Amazongo. The current would carry him over the falls and into the rocks and rapids below. Instead, he planned to reach the lizards using a rope plaited from forest vines. He tied the line to an overhanging tree upstream and swung into the current. The rushing water pummeled his chest and pushed him out into the river toward the islet. He clambered ashore, gasping and choking, and placed a rock on the end of the rope to secure it.

The six-legged lizards ignored him; they seemed tame and without fear. The largest were as long as his leg, with two sharp claws on each foot and heavy scales of blue armor that covered the head, body, and tail. They rested on their bellies with their middle legs raised, ready to lash out with talon-claws if another lizard came too close.

They were bigger than the razor-tongued lizard he'd encountered on the floating log next to the lifeboat, the one that had sliced off his little toe. Orange eyes with crescent pupils blinked sideways, warning him to keep his distance. He wished he had his spear, but he couldn't swim in the river with it.

Wary of the sharp tongue and claws, Attom steeled himself to make a kill. He circled behind a smaller lizard, raised his knife, and stabbed the back of the creature's head. The tip glanced off the armored scutes and jammed between two rocks. Unharmed, the lizard turned and lunged, flicking its serrated tongue from side to side with a clacking noise. Attom jumped back, but not fast enough. The sharp tongue nicked his wrist, and the lizard spun and whipped its spiked tail across his ankle. Then it crawled into the muddy river and swam upstream, its powerful tail whipping through the water.

Attom rubbed his wounds, frustrated. The lizards were too tough and dangerous to hunt. But when he bent to retrieve his knife, he discovered a trench filled with spherical beige eggs, abandoned by the mother lizard when she escaped. He wondered if they were safe to eat, but hunger made him reckless. He gathered a fresh-laid egg, pricked the leathery skin with the tip of his knife, and squeezed the maroon yolk into his mouth. Sweet and sour, the thick, creamy fluid coated his tongue. After he swallowed, his stomach glowed with warmth. The other lizards ignored him while Attom filled his pouch with eggs, a gift for Eva and the children. This was easier than butchering tough lizard meat.

Attom waded into the river again and grabbed his vine-rope. Midway into the rushing water, his line snagged on a submerged rock. He tried to pull himself to shore against the current, but the wall of water washing over him held him in place. His hands went numb. If he lost his grip, the waterfall and rocky rapids waited below.

"Help!" he hollered, sputtering water, but the roar of the waterfall drowned out his voice. "Lois! Can you hear me?" The flow splashed water into his eyes, blinding him. Desperation gave him strength, but he knew he couldn't maintain his grip for long.

Attom's submerged feet touched something; he panicked and kicked. Was it another lizard, ready to slice his foot? Then he realized that he'd touched bottom near the shore. How had he crossed the current? Driving his legs forward, he crawled up the bank and collapsed into the weeds, coughing water and heaving air.

"Are you okay?" The sound of Eva's voice startled him.

Attom looked up. Eva held his vine-rope—she'd hauled him ashore. Her face looked gaunt and worried. The children stood silent at her side.

"Y...yes, thanks," was all he could manage.

Eva frowned, eyebrows pinched. "What were you *doing* in the river?"

From the tone of her voice, she thought he was ridiculous. He sat up and presented his bag to her. "I brought food."

Eva squinted as she extracted a brown sphere, dripping with water. "What's this?"

Attom demonstrated how to prick the shell and squeeze out the contents. Jak and Jilzy watched with wide eyes. He squirted a dollop of yolk into each waiting mouth.

When Lois tasted some, she smacked her lips. "I love it!"

Jak and Jilzy made faces at the sour taste but opened wide for more, although Jak refused a third helping. Still wet from the river, Attom held Anton and Cleo on his lap and squeezed more yolk into their mouths.

Eva dipped her thumb into the open egg and tasted the slimy fluid. She wiped her lips and grimaced. "I was hoping for *real* meat."

Attom choked back a sharp retort. "Try cooking the eggs."

Eva shrugged and carried the bag to the fire. She squeezed egg yolks into the boiling porridge, stirring the stew. They ate their first proper meal in a season-week in silence. With full bellies, the children fell asleep as darkness fell.

"We can't live here," Eva whispered. "There's not enough food."

"I'll find more…" As soon as he spoke, Attom realized that he didn't want to cross the river again to the lizard island. "Or, we can hike farther upstream."

Eva shook her head. "No, I'm done with that. The children can't take any more."

"There's plenty of seafood on the beach."

Eva scowled. "We can't go back. Too many wind-hoppers."

Attom seethed with frustration. "You didn't like the mudflats, you won't continue upriver, and now you won't go back. Suggest something else!"

Eva remained silent. Like him, she must realize there were no good choices.

Attom hesitated before he spoke. "I'll return to the lifeboat and ask the Goddess for help."

Eva scowled. The lines on her face faded from anger to sadness.

"I'll run back to the coast," Attom said. "I can travel faster alone. As soon as I've spoken to the Goddess, I'll come back for you and the children."

"What will we eat while you're gone?"

"There are still a few lizard eggs in the sack. I'll leave in the morning."

"Lois will try to follow you."

For a moment, he considered taking his daughter along. But she would only slow him down. "I'll go before the kids wake up."

Eva pressed her lips together and turned away.

———— «» ————

Attom trotted downriver, moving fast, carrying only his spear and knife. Hunger knotted his gut. He'd refused to eat before he left, leaving the remaining lizard eggs with Eva. Vertigo from famine and weight loss made him stumble. Heat haze from the river made his limbs feel heavy, while anxiety added to his fatigue. As he ran, he daydreamed about food, remembering the taste of clams and fish, and even Robota's algae bricks.

When he neared their previous campsite along the river, he turned and sprinted across the sulfurous mudflat. Tentacle tips popped from the mud, peeking with blue eyes, thrusting out to ensnare him as he passed. He sliced with his knife and stabbed with his spear, dancing to avoid getting caught. He missed most, but hauled one yellow tentacle to the shore, still writhing on his spear. Its eye stared at him.

He'd forgotten to carry fire; he had no coals to cook the meat. Desperate to eat, he sliced a chunk from the still-writhing tentacle and clamped it in his teeth. The white flesh twitched as he bit down, clear blood wetting his tongue. He gnawed and sucked, but he couldn't chew the tough muscle enough to swallow. He sliced thin strips with his knife, tipped his head back, and gulped them down whole. To wash away the sour taste, he drank muddy river water.

Gut pain forced him to stop. Was the raw meat poisonous?

After a while, the cramps eased. Attom continued downriver, covering the remaining distance to the beach by evening. At low tide, the lifeboat rested high on Plymouth Rock, encrusted with mollusks and sea slime. Attom climbed aboard and opened the hatch, remembering endless year-months of his childhood spent with Eva on the little boat.

"Welcome!" Robota said. "Mother-9 couldn't find you. Are Eva and the children okay?" She handed him an algae brick.

As Attom chewed, he felt relieved but humiliated. Again, he tasted failure. He couldn't feed Eva and the kids. "They're upstream on the Amazongo."

"Why did you go there? When everyone disappeared, we feared the wind-hoppers had killed you."

"We're searching for a better place to live, somewhere safe, with plenty of food."

"I think I can help," Robota said. "Mother-9 has been mapping Terra Firma."

"Did she find anything nearby?"

"I'll consult the geographic database." After a long moment, Robota continued. "There's one possibility, a sheltered bay in an old volcanic crater. It's a one-day hike from the lifeboat."

"Is it safe?" Attom teetered on the edge of hope.

"The Shelter Bay caldera is at the edge of the Great Ocean, with a lagoon and a beach. Cliffs surround it, so there's not enough wind for hoppers to fly."

Attom's temper flared. "Why didn't she tell us sooner?"

"Mother-9 rejected it because I can't go there with you. I need to remain near the lifeboat and the wombs. But I'll take you to the caldera, when you've recovered."

Attom gnawed at the algae brick. "Let's go now," he said, eager to see the site. "I'm strong enough. The longer we wait, the longer Eva and the children will be alone." Then his hope dimmed. No matter how nice Shelter Bay might be, Eva would object to any connection with Mother-9 or Robota.

They left at first light the next day. Attom carried a survival pack from the lifeboat, while the nannybot carried a solar panel on her back. She used a walking stick for balance. By late afternoon, they looked down at the bay from the crater rim.

Attom squinted in the sea breeze. Lava rock formed a steep cliff above a small beach of black sand. Seawater entered the lagoon through a narrow gap in the crater wall across from the beach. At that spot, a roaring blowhole sprayed water from the Great Ocean, but only small wavelets reached the beach shore. A waterfall tumbled down the opposite cliff near a small stand of cone trees.

"Ocean waves eroded one wall of the dead volcano," Robota said. "The bottom is less than a kilometer across. It's protected from windstorms and tidal surges, so you'll be safe inside."

Attom looked down at the crater's rim of volcanic ash and lava boulders. Small shrubs clung to the near-vertical wall. Lava bombs from rockfalls formed a scree slope at the base.

"Is there a way down?"

"You'll have to cut your own trail," Robota said. "I'm too heavy for the steep slope. Even if I got down, I'd never be able to climb out."

Although Robota and the lifeboat wouldn't be far away, the nannybot could never visit them here. The Goddess couldn't interfere. That should make Eva happy.

"I'm going to climb down," Attom said.

"Please be careful. I must return to the lifeboat to tend to the wombs."

As Attom descended, he kicked loose boulders down the cliff. He used his spear to carve away chunks of volcanic ash to make a broader pathway. When he reached a low viewpoint, he looked down into the clear water of the lagoon. Fish swam in schools, twin tails beating in opposition, like hands clapping. Hot and tired, he leaped feet-first into the water. As he surfaced, he shouted, "It's warm!" The sound echoed from the walls of the crater. Tame fish swam around him, plenty of food for his family.

The humid air in the confined caldera made his face sweat when he waded ashore. At least the children would be warm during winter-week. At the back of the beach, under a rock overhang, he discovered an ancient lava tube that formed a cool cave. It wasn't big, but high enough for him to stand. He followed the cavern into the mountain as far as daylight allowed. The level lava floor showed no signs of animals.

After eating another algae brick, he made a bed in the warm sand on the beach. The night air, soft and humid, caressed his face. Luminous plankton twinkled in the water, while Valencia's moon Naranja provided dim moonlight though thin clouds. For the first time since Clarke's death, he felt hope.

Attom remembered growing up with Eva and exploring each other's bodies on the lifeboat. She had encouraged him, curious and eager. They'd laughed and played together. But, when she'd gotten pregnant and given birth, her mood had darkened. Clarke's death destroyed her capacity for joy. She'd grown hostile after the lifeboat hatched two sets of twins. Now there were more mouths to feed, more children to care for.

Could they be happy here, away from Robota and the lifeboat? Shelter Bay offered safety and plentiful food. Attom wanted to begin again with Eva, to have more children, to live in peace. He wanted to be loved.

Tomorrow, he would lead his family to this beautiful spot.

———— «» ————

"Welcome to Shelter Bay, our new home!" Attom stood near the rim and swept his arm, indicating the expanse of the crater.

He watched Eva's expression as she stood at the edge. Hunger and the long trek from the Amazongo made her cheeks hollow. She squinted against the wind from the Great Ocean that ruffled her black curls. After a strong gust, she gripped Jak and Jilzy's hands and stepped away from the cliff. Anton and Cleo followed her. Lois stood apart, gazing down at the caldera with solemn blue eyes.

Eva's face remained impassive. "I don't want to live in a giant hole."

"Like I told you, the crater has *everything*. Fish, fresh water, even a cave to sleep in. There aren't any wind-hoppers. And we'll be on our own. Robota can't climb down the crater wall."

Eva remained silent, but then smiled for the first time in more than three year-months. "Okay. Let's take a look." She scanned the cliff face. "Is the trail safe?"

Attom grinned, hoping bravado was a good enough answer. "Don't worry. We'll go down holding hands." He held Anton's and Cleo's while Eva gripped Jak's and Jilzy's; Lois followed alone. It took most of the afternoon to traverse Attom's switchback trail down the lava cliff to the beach in Shelter Bay. Sunlight heated the dark rocks, and a slight breeze rippled the lagoon.

Attom walked across the warm black sand and waded into the water. "Look, there're plenty of fish and edible seaweed." A school of orange fish swam near his legs. He turned and strode up the beach toward a gaping hole in the cliff face. "And, here's our new home!" His voice echoed from the crater walls. "It's *much* bigger than the tent, out of the wind and rain. It's cool in the daytime and warm at night."

Eva climbed over loose boulders and looked into the cavern. "We can't sleep on rough lava."

"We'll carry sand and reeds from the beach to make beds. We can build a fire at the entrance."

Eva walked inside, touching the ceiling with her fingers. "It's dark and gloomy, not like the tent."

Lois tugged at Attom's wrist. "Daddy, I'm hungry,"

He grinned, relieved at the diversion. "Let's see what we can catch in the lagoon." He handed her his spear with its fire-hardened obsidian point. "Aim below the fish; the water bends the light." When he was a boy, the Goddess had taught him that trick.

While Eva and the children set up camp, Attom and Lois spearfished in the shallows near the beach. The fish were unwary—lack of predators, Attom supposed—and they caught enough for the evening meal. For the rest of spring-week, they fished as the other children waded and played in the lagoon. Eva kept watch on the shore while she sewed cloaks from old wind-hopper skins.

After dark on the fifth day, Attom built a large bonfire in front of the cave. He cleaned the day's catch and cooked the fillets on skewers. The aroma wafted through the cavern as they ate in front of the fire. Sated, Attom belched, feeling a glow of comfort and satisfaction.

Attom glanced at Eva. "Aren't you glad we found this beautiful place?" Was she happy with him? He dared to hope.

Eva paused before answering. "It's okay. But the cave is too small. It's like living on the lifeboat. I need more space for myself."

"At least the kids are safe. They can play outside whenever they want."

Eva faced him, squinting. "And what will happen when Robota arrives with more screaming infants? I know you: You'll carry them down here so I can take care of them. And you want me to have more children too. We have five now and soon there'll be eight or ten. Too many screaming kids, too many mouths to feed."

Attom looked at Eva's face, still gaunt from recent hunger. "The lagoon has plenty of fish. Our clan is small. We need more people to survive."

Eva frowned. "That's the Goddess speaking. She told you about Shelter Bay, didn't she?"

Attom looked down. "Yes."

"I *told* you not to talk to her!"

Attom's temper flared. "I *said* that I would! I had no choice. We needed a safe place to live."

"We're already too crowded in this cave," Eva continued. "I want fewer people, not more. And *you* take up the most space."

Her words cut deep. Now secure in Shelter Bay, she no longer needed him. "Do you want me to leave?" His bass voice reverberated from the rock walls of the cavern.

"Do what you like." Eva stomped past the fire and retreated into the back of the cave with Anton and Cleo. Jak and Jilzy ran after them.

Attom started to protest but couldn't find the words. Soft weeping sounds emanated from the gloom. Their shouting had made Lois cry. Guilt drained Attom's will to fight. He walked to the beach and made a bed on the warm sand. It took a long time for him to fall asleep.

The next morning, Eva refused to look at him. He didn't understand her hostility. She didn't respect or love him, no matter how hard he tried. He couldn't live with that, not any more.

As he packed his kit, Lois clung to him, her orange-red hair melding with his russet beard. "*Please* don't go," she wailed.

Attom shook his head and took her hand. "There's no place for me here. Take care of your mother, she needs you. You're the best hunter in the family now."

"I want to go with you! She's mean to me too."

Attom hesitated. "I wish I could take you, but I don't know where I'm going. It's better for you to stay here."

"What if you find somewhere nice? Will you come back for me?"

Attom smiled. "We'll see."

Lois gave him a fierce stare, small hands on her hips. "Say yes! Promise me."

"All right. I promise."

He kissed Lois goodbye and turned to climb the cliff trail out of Shelter Bay. Part way up, he looked back to see Lois watching him. He returned her wave.

When he reached the crater's rim, solitude overwhelmed him.

———— «» ————

Mother-9 Journal
April 23, 22,974; Valencia Orbit

Attom's arrival at *Lifeboat-7* surprised me. Why had he returned to this lonely outpost? Strong and healthy, an experienced wilderness survivor, a male breeder, Attom was an important asset, second only to Eva. But my firstborn son, now 28-Earth-years old, seemed lost. Dour and listless, he didn't speak.

"Are Eva and the children okay?" I asked, using the ship's loudspeaker.

Attom took a long moment to respond. "Yes."

Humans are social animals that talk. Language enables people to discuss plans and work together, a survival advantage unique to *Homo sapiens*. Attom needed someone to talk to. But he didn't accept me, Mother-9, a disembodied voice from space, as a real person. Robota, although she had raised and educated him, was a subhuman nannybot without human consciousness. Attom refused to speak to either of us.

What happened at Shelter Bay? Attom wouldn't say, so I decided to check. I hadn't recorded any recent storms or earthquakes. Radar images showed normal human activity near the cave. That left social turmoil. I inferred that Attom and Eva could no longer live together. Even as children on the lifeboat, they'd often bickered. Now, Eva rejected him as a mate and family member. It didn't seem fair, but what can an AI know about the human heart?

Without Eva, Attom has no options for adult companionship. And, unlike her, he isn't suited to solitude; he needs society, to be part of a group. Isolated on the lifeboat, he had no role as a father, mate, or hunter—no valid identity. I regretted my long insensitivity to his pain and disorientation. Sometimes I'm slow to see what might be obvious to a human observer.

Attom moped in the lifeboat's cabin. He refused to go out and only nibbled algae bricks. He never looked at the media library, which he had enjoyed as a youngster. As year-months passed, his muscles withered and his eyes darkened. He descended into near-total withdrawal, and I worried about suicide.

Eva's refusal to care for more children had forced me to shut down the artificial wombs more than eight Earth-years before. The wrecked hulk of *Lifeboat-7* wasn't an ideal nursery, and Eva would not welcome toddlers at Shelter Bay. But the boat's wombs still functioned, at least for now.

I searched for a way to rehabilitate Attom. I spoke through Robota, "Would you like a new baby boy? He'll be like Clarke and carry half your genes. I'll nurse him, and you can raise him as your own." If Attom returned to Shelter Bay with their resurrected son, would Eva welcome him back?

Attom shuddered and looked at Robota. "I couldn't take care of my family or myself. How do you expect me to rear a child?"

"You were a good father to Lois."

Attom stiffened. "I let Clarke die."

"That wasn't your fault. You…"

"I don't want to talk about it."

I didn't press further. Attom is a good man, but I can't force him to be a parent again.

———— «» ————

Mother-9 Journal
March 1, 22,980; Valencia Orbit

Attom lived alone on *Lifeboat-7* for 72 year-months, six Earth-years, wasting his life. I offered to educate him on any topic—the arts, history, literature, mathematics, biology, or physics—but he showed no interest. He never mentioned Eva or the children, although he sometimes stood on deck and looked in the direction of Shelter Bay. He's now 34 Earth-years old, but his mind is stuck in adolescence.

During this long period, he recovered his physical strength with daily walks on the beach, hunting wind-hoppers. He tried to eradicate the predators that had eaten his son and driven his family from their camp by the Great Ocean. I assumed he wanted revenge, and I advised against it. Wind-hoppers are important littoral scavengers and quite dangerous. As usual, he ignored me.

Using the deck camera, I watched him hunt ground nests in the rocky crags near the beach until the hoppers no longer sheltered nearby. In retaliation, they formed flocks and attacked from the air. He refused to wear a protective helmet that interfered with his vision. For many year-months, he slashed at the hoppers with a halberd made from his spear with a knife lashed crosswise to the point. Each windy day, their disc bodies littered the foreshore. The corpses attracted more of their cannibal kin to feed. Attom slaughtered any he could reach, eviscerating them for their sweet livers, which he gulped down raw on the spot. After a hunt, he returned to the lifeboat with his beard and chest fur matted with lavender blood. He never washed.

No matter how many he killed, more hoppers repopulated the local beach. At one point, I watched nine wind-hoppers swoop down from behind in a coordinated attack. They covered his face and arms, knocking him down, smothering him. Did Attom want this, a violent but honorable death?

Yet he fought, writhing on the ground, rolling onto nearby lava rocks, kicking, and banging his face against boulders. The ropy pahoehoe lava flows abraded and bruised the hoppers until they lost their grip enough for him to breathe. He peeled them away and beat them on the rocks. Purple and red blood covered his fur, from dying hoppers and his own wounds, as he staggered to the lifeboat. I couldn't read the expression on his bruised face—between triumph and tragedy.

Robota sutured the loose flaps of flesh on his face and upper body where hopper beaks and hooks had gouged him. It took two year-months for him to heal. After his ordeal, he quit hunting and lapsed back into depression.

———— «» ————

Mother-9 Journal
April 13, 22,980; Valencia Orbit

Attom stopped eating. For two season-weeks, he only sipped water. I tried adding antidepressants to his drinks, but they didn't work. For lack of human companionship, my firstborn son wanted to die.

I suggested that he return to Shelter Bay and visit Eva and the children, now teenagers. Time had passed and the situation could have changed. He didn't respond. He won't go where he's not wanted.

While Attom languished, I continued my fruitless search for *Lifeboat-11*. After Dik disabled the ship's radio beacon during his mutiny, I'd lost track of its position. I tried reverse navigation—the art of predicting tides and winds from the time of last contact to estimate the boat's position. But weather is chaotic and a sailboat can tack in any direction. Valencia is big, its surface area is more than 3.6 times larger than Earth's, and the missing lifeboat could be anywhere, including on the bottom of the ocean.

Given the emergency with Attom, I decided to renew my search for Dik and Jain. I scanned the fractal coastline of Terra Firma and logged every anomaly. This yielded a new result: In a crescent bay on the southern coast, an object shifted position with wind direction. Could it be *Lifeboat-11*, floating at anchor? During summer-week, I glimpsed smoke from a forest fire near the beach. From space, the local environment looked blackened and denuded of vegetation. Had Dik and Jain survived a landing on Terra Firma? Was this their camp?

I instructed Robota to prepare crab bisque for Attom, hoping his favorite food would cheer him enough to talk. He tasted it and then pushed the bowl aside. I decided to try begging, in the hope that pseudo-humility might disarm him.

"Attom, this is your old mother. I need your help," I used Robota's maternal voice.

He ignored me, looking out the porthole at a flock of wind-hoppers gliding low above the surf. "Leave me alone." As always, he deflected any intrusion.

"Please, Attom, I have something important to ask you."

"Yes, Goddess," he said with false politeness.

"I may have found more humans on the southern coast of Terra Firma. I need your help to contact them." I hoped this would get his attention. I didn't mention my highest priority: finding *Lifeboat-11*, with its precious wombs. *Lifeboat-7's* wombs still work, but are low on reagents needed to manufacture DNA and grow a baby.

"Sorry, I can't help you," he mumbled.

He didn't respect authority, age, or experience, so I didn't argue with him. I'd already rejected the idea of using Robota's slow, clumsy body to search for Dik and Jain. She was my only nannybot, designed to raise children from the artificial wombs. The high gravity of Valencia stressed her knee joints, designed for use on Earth. I needed Attom's strength and agility to help the clumsy android walk hundreds of kilometers across the rugged wilderness. A radio link to Robota would allow me to keep in touch with Attom and observe events on the ground.

After a minute of silence, Attom's curiosity surfaced. "Aren't we the only people on the planet?"

I'd never mentioned *Lifeboat-11*. I generally tell my children the truth, but not always the whole truth.

"There was another lifeboat with a family."

Attom looked at Robota's metallic face. His eyes gaped wide. "Who are they?"

"They're your lost brother and sister, Dik and Jain, born from the boat's wombs, like you. They may have children of their own by now."

I'm not good at reading expressions, especially Attom's, beneath his beard. But I couldn't mistake his scowl.

"Why didn't you tell me before?" He reached for the bisque and slurped a mouthful.

"I wasn't sure where to find them, or if they were still alive. You and Eva were busy trying to survive and raise children. Now you have nothing but free time. Why not use it for a good purpose?"

His face softened as he gazed at the sunset through the porthole. The molten orb of Lalande, three times the diameter of Earth's sun from this perspective, floated in maroon clouds.

"When do we leave?"

——— ‹›› ———

Mother-9 Journal

Terra Firma has forests, rivers, mountains, and deserts. Its hazards include typhoons, earthquakes, and active volcanoes. There are unknown predators, and food is often scarce.

As an AI, I'm programmed to avoid risks, but sometimes danger is unavoidable.

I hate uncertainty.

We made elaborate preparations. Attom's travel gear included a spear with a Folsom point, a stainless knife, and a flashlight from *Lifeboat-7*. He carried fortified algae bricks and pemmican made from smoked eel and seaweed. I expected poor communications, so Robota carried a solar panel for power and a high-gain dish antenna on her head. When I was in range, I could teleoperate the motions of her body from orbit, with a clumsy time delay.

"You look ridiculous," Attom said with a grin.

I don't understand style, only function. Still, his amusement cheered me, and I hoped it was therapeutic. I made Robota tip her hat to show off. "I'm glad you like it."

"Finally, we're going to have a *real* adventure!" Attom had forgotten the Amazongo landing, wind-hoppers, and ankle-grabbers. He has a history of recklessness and craves the hazards of Earth's Stone Age. Machismo is silly, but it's sometimes useful. At least he wasn't depressed.

The two started their journey on spring-week to allow enough sunlight to recharge Robota's batteries. As they left, a seismic temblor shook the coast, causing a small tidal wave to crest on the beach. Harmless, but Attom ran from the shoreline. He showed natural caution, which reassured me. I hope he's mature now.

They camped at night in the cone tree forest. While overhead, I remained linked to Robota's eyes and ears. Valencia's moon, Naranja, provided faint orange light through the clouds. Unknown creatures chirped and mysterious lights twinkled in the canopy. It'll take centuries to catalog Valencia's myriad life forms. Using the lifeboat's spare fire piston, Attom built a campfire and nursed the glowing embers into a blaze. He cooked crabmeat on wooden skewers, the last of his seafood from the coast.

When he finished his meal, he looked at Robota. "Show me where we're going again."

The nannybot activated the tablet on her chest, the same screen that Attom used as a child to learn to read and draw.

I displayed a satellite view of our route. "We've entered a strip of jungle between the Amazongo River and Mount Igneous." The image showed a blue-green forest canopy about 300 kilometers long. Photosynthesis on Valencia uses the red end of the spectrum to capture the light from a red-dwarf star.

The next day, we walked through a colonnade of cone trees with massive, tapered trunks. The botanical world is a battleground for light and space and, even in the high gravity of Valencia, the trees grew ten meters tall. A greenish mist hovered above the ground. In daytime, the deep forest remained silent except for the rustle of small six-legged lizards hidden in the undergrowth. Attom hated the omnivorous vermin—he called them *ratties*.

Attom led the way, carrying his heavy pack. As always, he looked at the ground, careful where he placed his bare feet, since crawlers sometimes pinched or stung. I made Robota follow in his footsteps. The clumsy nannybot needed solid footing.

Attom's feet crunched through the thick duff on the forest floor. Robota's knee joints clicked and squeaked as the bearings started to fail. The two hikers walked in step all morning, covering a dozen kilometers without conversation.

Through Robota's ears, I heard a soft *pop* followed by a *pffft* sound. The image from her left eye splintered and lost focus, the lens cracked by a projectile from above. Attom crouched behind a tree and looked up.

"Get down!" he yelled.

Another dart whistled past the nannybot's antenna. I made Robota crouch low, head between her knees to protect her remaining eye. Two more darts bounced off her metal back. Then the attack stopped.

With Robota's good eye, I watched the arboreal predator descend, hind end first, hugging the scaly bark of the cone tree. It looked like a sloth, the size of a large dog. The beast had an elongated snout with a wide base that tapered to a hole in the nose. Its eyes were dark pits, shrouded by a bony brow. On the ground, the animal crept toward Robota, wobbling on its spindly legs. It extended a foot with three long, serrated claws.

Attom lunged with his spear, and the stone point pierced the sloth from back to front. The animal swung its barrel nose and fired from close range, emitting a hissing noise and a small puff of steam.

Attom staggered backward, stumbled, and fell to the ground. Robota's olfactory sensor detected hydroquinones, fuel for a biochemical gun. Attom clutched his chest as he tried to breathe.

The creature writhed on the forest floor and grasped the spear where it exited its midsection. As Robota crawled toward Attom, the creature pointed its snout and fired a final bolt, which bounced off her metallic head.

Attom lay unconscious on his back. A thin fléchette protruded from his sternum. When Robota yanked it out, blood seeped from the wound and soaked his fur. The point had stopped short of his heart. Green venom lubricated the shaft. I tucked the dart in Robota's specimen pouch.

The neurotoxin had paralyzed Attom. As it spread, his heart rate slowed, and he stopped breathing. Robota administered atropine, but it didn't help. She pumped his chest to squeeze his heart and give him oxygen. My orbit around passed out of range as she continued CPR, running on reserve battery charge. When I made contact again in the middle of the night, Attom had resumed breathing. Then Robota collapsed, her batteries drained.

Attom slept through the night while Robota watched for scavengers. Nothing moved, but she observed more twinkling lights in the treetops, Valencia's version of fireflies. I hated being powerless, circling in orbit with limited ability to affect events on the ground.

Morning sunlight filtered through the forest canopy and trickle-charged Robota's batteries. A short time later, Attom groaned and sat up. Robota examined him with her medical kit; his heart fluttered at 100 beats per minute, twice his resting rate.

Attom touched Robota's hand, as if she were human. "Thanks."

I made Robota nod in acknowledgment. Her neck joints creaked.

Attom tried to stand, but his knees buckled. He retched thin stomach acid.

I spoke through Robota. "Rest until you're strong again. You need to eat." The nannybot pushed a chunk of dried seaweed between his lips.

He spat it out. "I'm not that hungry." Attom hated algae. He drank from his leather water skin and inspected the sloth. "Let's butcher it. No point in wasting good meat."

"The flesh isn't poisonous," I said. "But stay away from the venom in the jaw."

Attom grimaced, impatient with unneeded advice. I watched him sever the head while pointing the muzzle's rifle-nose away from us. When he cut the throat open, I observed hundreds of darts growing in rows along the jawbone, like sharks' teeth. A hollow tube of shiny bone rested inside the snout, a rifle bore that the creature aimed with muscles below its eyes. The sloth didn't have a lower jaw or proper mouth. Instead, a rosette of sharp incisors surrounded the muzzle tip, each cutting tooth moved by its own muscle. To eat, I deduced that the sloth sheared bits of flesh and sucked them up its nose.

Attom shivered. "I can't decide which is worse: wind-hoppers, ankle-grabbers, or sniper-sloths."

Attom spent the day butchering and drying sloth meat to carry with them. While he worked, Robota recharged her batteries in a dim patch of sunlight on the forest floor. She crawled as the sun's angle changed. Tyndall-scattered light beamed at random angles through the humid air.

"I'm better now," Attom announced that afternoon. He didn't seem depressed.

"Are you ready to hike again?" I didn't want to push him.

Attom winced when he touched the dart wound in his chest. "I don't think so." He stared at the broken lens in Robota's left eye. "Can you see well enough to walk?"

"I can't judge depth, so I may stumble."

"Let's rest a few more days," Attom said.

"Agreed. Robota needs more solar charge."

Attom started a fire and roasted a sloth haunch. He complained that the tough flesh tasted bitter, but he consumed most of the meat.

——— ‹›› ———

Mother-9 Journal

I used Robota's good eye to observe the two wounded travelers as they camped for a season-week while Attom recovered. Blood and dirt matted his fur coat, but the puncture wound healed without infection. Most bacteria on Valencia aren't evolved to attack humans.

Attom practiced stone-knapping while he rested. He used sloth tendons to reattach the obsidian point to his spear, loose from stabbing the creature. Robota played Bach's fugues from recordings made on Earth. The music suited the church-like gloom of the forest, lit by a variegated blue-green glow from the vaulted canopy. Each night, lights sparkled in the treetops.

Attom built a smoker and processed the sloth meat for travel. I estimated that they faced another Valencia-year, four season-weeks of wilderness trekking. Robota tottered with marginal battery power, poor vision, and failing joints. Her right knee emitted a scraping sound with each step. Attom jammed sloth fat into the joint, but it only helped for a short time. He improvised a cane from a cone tree root to take the weight off Robota's leg. Meanwhile, Attom limped after his encounter with the sniper-sloth.

"Attom," Robota said, "let me check your feet."

"My feet are fine." He sat on a rock and held his foot up, the one with the missing little toe. I observed a deep crack in the thick sole.

Robota applied an adhesive plaster. "Next time, tell me when you're hurting."

Attom winced but remained stoic. *I try not to nag him. A foot injury might mean death in the wilderness.*

A narrow path took them through the dense jungle that paralleled the upper Amazongo River. Razor-tongue lizards rested on the muddy banks. *Their yellow eyes tracked our movements.* Attom used his spear to jostle them to steal eggs. He selected one egg and pricked the leathery shell to suck out the yolk, saving the rest to roast in the evening. The rich food improved his strength and walking pace.

The lizard trail near the river stopped. Attom hacked through thick brush with his big knife. Buzzing crawler-bugs swarmed up his arm and onto his neck. He squashed them with his thumb and ate them, legs and all. The travelers forded shallow streams until they reached a large tributary.

Attom squinted at the stream's muddy water where it flowed into the Amazongo. "I don't like the look of this."

I consulted a satellite map. "There's no other way forward," I replied through Robota. *I worried that he would tire of the trek and want to turn back.*

Attom's fur buoyed him as he swam across the slow-moving river. When Robota followed, she sank. She had lost her emergency flotation airbag when *Lifeboat-7* foundered in the tidal wave. *I made her crawl along the bottom sediment, past schools of giant eels with fishhook claws on their fins.* When Robota emerged, sludge fouled her knee joints. Attom disassembled them and repacked the hinges with rancid sloth grease.

They continued through the jungle for another season-week. The cone tree forest thinned as they climbed Mount Igneous, the massive shield volcano that divides Terra Firma. Using his knife, Attom carved wooden sandals to protect his feet from ropey pahoehoe lava. When Robota could no longer walk on the uneven ground, Attom dragged her across chasms formed by magma flows and earthquakes. By noon, they had covered only a kilometer of the volcano's slope.

Later, as they picked their way across the barren cinders of the mountain's high pass, ice pellets rained from the sky. Accelerated by Valencia's high gravity, the sharp-edged hailstones blasted Attom. Hurt by the fusillade, he crouched and ducked his head. Robota tried to shield him but the nannybot slipped and fell on the ice. In less than a minute, the sharp shards had stripped Attom's fur and flayed patches of skin. Then the fall stopped. Blood pooled at the small of his back. If the storm had lasted a few seconds longer, the ice bullets would have gouged the flesh from his backbone and killed him.

Attom's face showed a blank mask of pain, but he remained silent. Robota applied antiseptic cream to his wounds. No bandage could cover the raw expanse of his broad, furry back. Someday, if I engineer montane humans, I'll give them skin armored with pangolin scales.

I'm not good at risk assessment on the wild world of Valencia. I couldn't predict the sniper-sloth attack or the ice storm. In hindsight, our expedition was too risky. But I couldn't tell Attom that.

Windrows of slush slowed the way forward. As they descended, the pair detoured around a glowing river of magma from a lava fountain. When Robota's aluminum insteps started to melt, Attom used precious drinking water to cool them. He laughed as the old nannybot hopped through billows of steam.

When Attom's sandals caught fire and singed the fur on his toes, I made Robota giggle in return.

"Not funny!" he barked.

"Sorry!" Jokes are unique to humans; no AI can pass a comedy Turing test. I decided not to feign humor again.

"This is a useless expedition," growled Attom. "I'm going back to the coast."

Although he didn't complain about pain, I'm certain he chafed at traveling at Robota's limping pace.

"Please don't leave. Robota needs your help."

I didn't want the nannybot abandoned in the wilderness. She'd never make it back to *Lifeboat-7* by herself. Attom might not survive either, wandering lost across Terra Firma, without me to navigate.

"What's the point of this endless trek?" Attom's voice sounded weak and weary.

I didn't remind him that, before we'd started, he'd craved adventure. But there's a fine line between adventure and ordeal. We'd crossed over, and the romance had faded. I hoped he wouldn't fall into depression again.

"The people we're searching for are only a couple of days away." I showed him a satellite map on Robota's tablet.

"Tell me about them again." Curiosity added an edge to his voice. "Who are they?"

I repeated the story of Dik's mutiny. "When they sailed away, Jain was pregnant."

"So? That was a long time ago."

"Jain may have a grown daughter by now." I didn't want to promise more.

Attom held his breath for a moment and then sighed. "I want to meet her." His avid look—squinted eyes, and parted lips—said more than his words.

We began the two-day downhill hike to the ocean. The rain shadow of the volcano created a clear blue sky, the only location on Valencia without perpetual clouds. Direct sun baked the barren, rocky ground. We traversed a desert landscape unlike the tropical verdure of the Amazongo Valley. Concertina vines, with bellows that elongated after a rain, curled like snakes around basalt boulders. When Attom cut one with his knife, it dripped precious water. But he found no food in the desert, not even crawler-bugs.

At midday Attom overheated in his fur. He rested in a shady ravine while Robota sat in the sun and recharged her batteries. We waited until the cool night to hike under the pale moonlight of Naranja. Its elliptical orbit, now close to Valencia, made it appear twice as large as the Earth's moon, an orange ball with many impact craters.

Attom and Robota stopped to rest after moonset, when darkness made walking difficult. Attom stared up at the clear nighttime sky, visible for the first time in his life. "What are those sparks?"

"Stars," I said, "thousands of burning suns." I made Robota point above the eastern horizon. "That speck of starlight is Sol, Earth's star."

"I thought Earth was a big planet, full of people." Attom had seen photos and movies of Earth in the lifeboat's media library.

"You can't see the home planet with your eyes; you need a telescope." I didn't tell him about the gamma-ray burst that had sterilized Earth. "Stars look small because they're very far away."

Attom reclined on his back and looked up. "You told me about them when I was small. I didn't know stars would be so beautiful."

I hoped that someday he'd tell the children about the heavens. Perhaps they would build an observatory here. For an AI, I experienced a moment of extreme satisfaction. Continuity of cosmic vision, abstract and insubstantial, resonated with me. I am a creature of space and time.

The next morning, we picked our way through the boulders and down the lower slope of Mount Igneous. A sparse forest of stunted cone trees clung to the rocks. Our path crossed a swath of ruined land, charred grass and burnt stumps from the forest fire I'd observed from orbit before the trek. Windblown ash made Attom cough.

We reached the shoreline at low tide. A trio of wind-hoppers soared above the flats.

I saw *Lifeboat-11* from a distance of half a kilometer, careened on her side in the mud. I felt a surge of maternal joy. If it had intact wombs, I could start a new generation of colonists on Valencia.

"The ship looks wrecked," Attom said.

"I hope not," Robota replied, speaking my words. "It'll float again at high tide."

As we walked along the beach, Attom picked through seaweed flotsam. He uncovered a red crab, but failed to catch it. "Look!" he exclaimed.

Using her cane, Robota shuffled to where he stood. The sand showed the outline of a human footprint.

———— «◊» ————

Mother-9 Journal

Robota built a campfire while Attom caught crabs. Ravenous, he ate for an hour. I knew he'd lost weight, but I hadn't realized how hungry he was. Except for remaining crumbs of algae kibble, he hadn't eaten for three days.

I waited until he finished, knowing that a full stomach would make him more agreeable. "Attom, let's explore *Lifeboat-11*. I'm sure it'll be interesting." I tried to make Robota's voice sound enthusiastic, without seeming too eager or demanding.

"No."

I hadn't expected an abrupt refusal. "Please. Robota needs your help to reach the boat." I didn't mind begging.

"I don't care about the old lifeboat. I want to find the people who live here."

Of course, he did. He had made the trek overland because he longed for human company.

"Okay, I'll come with you." *Lifeboat-11*, anchored for more than 200 year-months in the muddy bay, could wait a little longer.

"I'm not a kid. I don't need a nannybot to hold my hand."

I considered his words. With humans, first impressions count. Robota looked awful—worn out, dented and dirty, walking with a cane, and blind in one eye. But she symbolized my oversight and control. I remembered Dik's mutiny and the decapitation of Electra. I realized Attom should go alone.

"As you wish," I said through Robota. It wouldn't help to say more. I blocked emulated emotions, so his rejection wouldn't hurt.

I watched Attom as he followed the footprints away from the beach. I hated to split up—it increased the risks for each of us—but I couldn't stop him.

Once he'd gone, I searched the shoreline for the lifeboat's aluminum dinghy. I'd hoped to row to the lifeboat on the next tide, but I couldn't find the little boat. So, I surveyed the mudflat for solid ground. With the tide out, I saw a sandbar that might provide solid footing. At my direction and control, Robota waded through tide pools across the flat. After an hour of slogging, her metallic body sank to the waist in mud. I'd miscalculated the odds, yet another mistake.

When the tide came in, saltwater covered Robota's antenna, and I lost her signal. Cut off from our expedition and blind from orbit, I felt frustrated and worried—emulated emotions for statistical uncertainty. Six hours later, the tide ebbed, and I regained contact. Robota's legs were still stuck, and her battery power remained low. Stranded, and starved by the lack of sunlight, she would soon shut down. Where was Attom? Would he return in time to rescue Robota?

Twice each day, the tide covered the old nannybot. Waves thrashed her body, and she sank deeper into the muck. Brief periods of sunshine recharged her batteries enough for me to make occasional contact. As the fall-week nighttime grew longer, Robota's power reserve decreased. I watched the year-month lunar eclipse with Robota's one good eye. Naranja morphed into an angry copper-orange disk in the mist.

At low tide on the fifth day, Robota observed the anchor chain from *Lifeboat-11* resting on the mud. During the previous tidal change, the vessel had floated closer and then settled in the mud nearby. I made the nannybot reach out and lock her hands onto the titanium links. Then we waited.

On the next rising tide, *Lifeboat-11* floated and the anchor chain pulled Robota out of the mud. Before the water receded, she climbed the links, hand over hand, legs hooked around the chain. She struggled at the gunwale, unable to lift herself onto the bow. She dangled for hours until a wind gust tightened the anchor chain, which allowed her to clamber onto the foredeck.

The darkness of winter-week and mud smears blinded Robota's good eye. Using her sense of touch, she found Electra's severed head still hanging from a hook, left by Dik during his mutiny. I had Robota unscrew one of Electra's eyes and replace the broken one in her head. After she cleaned the lenses, she connected a spare antenna dish from a storage locker, replacing the one Dik had destroyed. To my relief and joy, the satellite link to *Lifeboat-11* came online again.

Using Robota's eyes, I surveyed the lifeboat. Inside the open companionway hatch, wind and rain had left pools of water in the cabin. In the nursery below deck, the headless body of Electra lay on the cabin floor with the desiccated remains of a dead baby next to her. The skeletons of three more newborns lay scattered about the nursery, dismembered by scavenger crabs. *Lifeboat-11's* wombs had followed my instructions before the mutiny and had continued to conceive and hatch babies. Without a nannybot, the wombs ejected the newborns at term, live or stillborn, to cleanse the incubation chamber. As Robota approached, three red crabs scuttled out of her way. She threw the babies' bones overboard and scrubbed the deck.

I noted that one womb in *Lifeboat-11* still functioned, using nutrients extracted from seawater when the tide floated the boat. It contained a healthy male fetus in his second trimester, alive and growing. The functioning artificial womb required fifteen more season-weeks of gestation before birthing. I decided to save this baby.

As we floated on the flood tide, I had Robota replace her knees with parts cannibalized from Electra and use the ship's power to recharge her batteries. She reconnected the binnacle cameras, giving me vision on deck. But I needed help to make *Lifeboat-11* seaworthy and give the unborn baby a chance at life.

Next, I turned my attention to the original problem. Where was Attom?

Since the dinghy from the lifeboat was missing, I instructed Robota to use Electra's emergency airbag to drift ashore. As Robota floated to the beach, a naked man approached, limping and leaning on a walking stick. He had stringy brown hair and a russet beard that hung down to his waist. He looked like a sumo wrestler, with a stocky body and hairless chest, the high-gravity characteristics I'd designed for Valencia's humans. He scowled, showing yellow teeth beneath a red mustache.

The man blocked Robota's way, preventing her from wading out of the water. I searched for words to disarm him.

"Hello, Dik! It's nice to see you again!" I called, trying to sound friendly.

"I thought you were dead," he growled.

My faked bonhomie didn't impress him. "No, I'm still alive." To keep him off balance, I let him think that I was Electra, resurrected. If he disabled Robota, the baby in the womb would die, like the others.

With a low roar, Dik thrust his staff at Robota's chest, tipping her onto her back in the water. The nannybot remained below the surface, unable to fight. Dik dragged her by her ankles onto the beach.

He frowned and raised his walking stick. "Why are you here?"

"This is the voice of Mother-9. I'm here to assist you."

Dik spat on Robota's face and lowered his staff. "I don't want your help."

He gestured for Robota to stand. Dik favored his lame left leg as he pushed her away from the beach toward a camp situated under a rock overhang. In the back of a shallow cave, a woman with a worn face and wide hips tended a smoky cooking fire. Robota's electronic nose detected the sweet, putrid odor of rotting flesh. Two human skulls mounted on stakes watched over the fire. Mute, and without affect, the woman stared at Robota.

"*Salvete,* Jain," I said. The woman jerked her head, recognizing the Latin greeting and her childhood name, but she didn't answer. Her pregnant belly gave her a swayback posture.

Dik prodded Robota from behind with his walking stick, causing her to stumble. We proceeded to a small cone tree growing on an upper slope at the far edge of the camp, visible to all. Attom sat on the ground with his back against the tree, his hands tied to an overhead branch and his feet bound to an exposed root. He remained unconscious or sleeping, his head tipped to one side on his thick neck, eyes closed and slack jaw drooling.

An AI responds to shock in a manner opposite to that of a human. Instead of paralysis, I examined a thousand scenarios in milliseconds. Attom, trusting and innocent, was no match for Dik. Like most normal people, he could not imagine psychopathic depravity. Now helpless, he could neither save Robota nor himself.

"Attom!" I called, using Robota's urgent voice. He flinched but kept quiet.

Dik growled and struck Robota's neck with his staff, knocking her down. He forced the nannybot to squat next to Attom and trussed her with a rawhide thong to the same cone tree, the only one near the camp.

As soon as Dik left, Attom turned to Robota. "So, Dik caught you too?" His voice carried resignation and despair. "I'd hoped you'd rescue *me*."

———— «» ————

Mother-9 Journal

In the dark after Naranja had set, Robota watched two teenaged girls approach Attom. They talked in excited whispers. Like the rest of the group, the girls were nude, with no body hair. The tallest wore a necklace with a coiled shell pendant. She ignored Robota, while I watched through the nannybot's eyes.

"I'm going to take him now," she whispered, "before it's too late."

She bathed Attom's face with water. He woke and coughed when she tipped more water into his mouth from her cupped hand. Then she held a scrap of charred meat to his lips. He chewed for a moment, then spat it out.

"What's your name?" Attom croaked.

"I'm Alta." She tossed her head, her long blonde hair framing a delicate face with a pointed chin, like her mother's.

Attom nodded and glanced at the other girl.

"This is my sister, Stella," Alta said. Stella had brown skin, dark hair, and a muscular body, like her father's.

The names didn't surprise me. Alta means tall in Latin; Stella means star. Their mother had studied the dead language during her long childhood on *Lifeboat-11*, before Dik's mutiny. Alta motioned for her sister to stand and block the view from the smoldering campfire. "Don't let Mama see," she whispered. "She'll tell Dik."

Alta fondled Attom between his legs and stroked him until he became erect. He grimaced and shook his head, but kept silent. With a furtive glance toward the camp, her eyes glinting in the flickering firelight, she swung her leg across his pelvis. She sighed as she lowered herself onto him. Stella watched with wide eyes.

Alta squinted and rocked her hips, the tendons in her neck standing out with the effort. She remained quiet but exhaled in short gasps— "Hunh... hunh... haaaaeeeee..."—as she reached her climax. I'd engineered easy female orgasms that induce ovulation, like rabbits and cats. When Attom grunted, she placed her hand over his mouth. "Sorry," she whispered.

Attom, arms still trussed above his head, kissed her palm. "Don't leave me here."

Alta stroked his cheek but didn't reply. She stood up and both girls departed, whispering to each other.

"How long has this been going on?" I asked.

Attom frowned and twisted the cord that bound his wrists. "They've been talking about me for the last few days. Alta wants to get pregnant before the spring-week celebration." His voice rasped from thirst.

"Why? What will happen then?"

"Dik will have sex with his daughters in a ritual of renewal. Dik calls himself God the Father. He'll force Alta to take part. She doesn't want his baby, she wants mine."

"Will he let us go after the ritual?"

Attom coughed. "I don't know what he'll do with you, but I'm just live meat, waiting to be slaughtered and cooked for the celebration. I'm the feast." He yanked his bonds again, but couldn't break them.

"Why?"

"Dik killed both his sons before they reached puberty. The smoked meat that Alta tried to feed me came from her brother, sacrificed last fall-week. I watched the ceremony. Dik cut his throat and Jain sang songs while she butchered him." Attom spoke in a flat voice, but his emotions, fear and disgust, were easy to read.

I initiated a priority search of my orbiting database. I found many of examples of ritual and survival cannibalism. All humans on Terra Firma have experienced hunger, even famine. Still, this seemed extreme. They shouldn't need to supplement their diet with human flesh. Dik couldn't tolerate competition from other males.

I wondered if Dik had burned the local forest to drive game to the shoreline. The fire-scarred land must mean poor hunting. When nearby food ran out, I supposed the clan would migrate, leaving scorched earth behind.

In the meantime, they ate human flesh.

———— ⟨⟩ ————

Mother-9 Journal

I reeled with synthetic guilt. In my quest to find *Lifeboat-11* and determine what had happened to Dik and Jain, I may have led Attom to his death. I'd known that Dik would be difficult, but I didn't imagine he was a killer.

Dik is my worst failure. As a mother, I don't just give life to precious children, I *engineer* them. For the first experimental babies from the artificial wombs, the goal was survival. I didn't bother with personality and social aptitude. Without knowing, I'd created a monster, with a load of antisocial DNA.

In this contest between nature and nurture, genetics dominates. Bad genes gave Dik the dark triad of grandiosity, exploitation, and remorselessness. Now, I'd lost control of Valencia's human gene pool. I may not be able stop Dik's traits from spreading across Terra Firma. Tormented by my mistakes, I had to ask: Why do psychopaths exist? How did they evolve?

The sudden rise of the human intellect is a mystery. No other animal needs to be hyperintelligent to survive. There were no brainy dinosaurs, despite having more than 150 million years to evolve superior cognition. *Homo erectus* lived for more than 1.7 million years, used fire, and made crude tools, but nothing more. Neanderthals had bigger brains and existed on Earth more than twice as long as modern humans. They must have been smart, but developed scant symbolic or material culture. It wasn't until *Homo sapiens* that true intelligence appeared.

Language may be the key. True speech requires a vocabulary of defined words used in whole sentences with structured syntax. Talking gave humans the ability to work together to build pyramids and moon rockets, and to pass knowledge to future generations. Language may be a singularity rarer than bacterial life arising from a primordial soup. Speech is so unlikely that, on Earth, it may have evolved only once. Other extraordinary leaps, eyes and flight, evolved many times. People who could talk wiped out all coexisting hominin species. How did this happen?

Perhaps psychopaths—clever parasites not inhibited by conscience—hid within populations of nice, normal people. They made human society more complex and *dangerous* than any natural ecosystem. An arms race of the intellect, a coevolutionary contest between the ruthless and the majority, drove the evolution of the brain. Amoral intelligence gave *Homo sapiens* the power to conquer the world.

Dik behaved with brutal logic, killing useless males that might grow to challenge him. With food scarce on Terra Firma, surplus males consume resources needed by females. One man can inseminate many women, propagating his own selfish genes. Like an Egyptian pharaoh, intrafamilial mating reinforced Dik's genetic legacy.

On a planet with less than a dozen people, that is a problem. Dik isn't an isolated criminal. He's the founding father of evil on Valencia.

———— «» ————

Attom woke in agony with a cramp in his right calf. He groaned and tried to straighten his knee, but his bound ankle stopped him. After a time, the pain passed, though his leg felt bruised. When he tried to swallow, his dry throat remained frozen. He hadn't had water since the previous evening with Alta.

Attom faced Dik's camp, his back against the rough cone tree bark. The hailstone scabs along his spine itched and stung. His hands and arms were numb from the rawhide tether tied to the branch above his head. He clenched his fists to restore circulation. Hunger gnawed, a constant companion. Trapped in unending torment, he drifted off, waiting to die.

A brief rain shower woke him again; he extended his cracked lower lip to catch a few drops. Somewhat refreshed, Attom opened his eyes and saw the nannybot still tied next to him.

"Robota, can you hear me?" he croaked in a hoarse whisper.

The nannybot didn't move but replied, "Yes, I'm still functional."

"Can you break your bonds?"

"No. My servo-motors don't have enough torque. I'm not strong enough."

Attom yanked his hands again. Pain shot down his arms, but his mental anguish hurt more.

"I'll die soon, if I can't escape."

"I agree." Robota nodded her head. "Your current chance of survival for another season-week is less than two percent, based on known variables."

Attom wondered if Mother-9 was talking. Death seemed certain, and the Goddess only talked about numbers.

He blacked out again, only to experience a new torment when Dik's walking stick poked his ribs.

"Wake up, monkey-boy!"

Attom groaned and looked up at his captor, whose smooth skin glistened with dark streaks of rank animal grease. Dik must have seen hairy apes on the lifeboat's videos, as Attom had. The comparison rankled.

Dik lowered his voice, menacing. "I'm only going to ask once. Where did you come from? Why did you come here?"

Attom realized that Dik had kept him alive to answer questions. If he said anything, he would put Eva and the children at risk. Dik didn't know that there was another lifeboat and more humans.

His captor jammed his stick again into Attom's chest. "Talk, or I'll roast you now!" When he spoke, the matted hair of his crimson beard flapped against his chest.

Attom opened his mouth. "Ack, hasss... sss... sss..." His parched throat couldn't form words.

"We were exploring Terra Firma," Robota interjected.

Dik leaned close looked at Robota. "You're not Electra. I cut off her head. Who are you?"

The nannybot nodded. "I'm Robota."

"Hmm...where are you from?"

"We walked over the mountains from western Terra Firma."

Attom writhed on his tether, wishing he could make the nannybot stop talking. Robota always spoke the truth, even though Mother-9 sometimes didn't.

Dik nodded. "How many people live there?"

"There are six."

Attom moaned. *Why didn't Mother-9 make Robota stop?*

"How many females?" Dik asked.

"Four."

"Adults and children?"

"Eva is the only adult."

"Now *that's* interesting! Where are they?"

Attom roared, but his voice cracked.

Dik whacked his face with the walking stick. "Shut up!" Then he laughed. " Is Eva your woman? Not any more..."

Robota ignored his pain and answered Dik's question. "Near the Amazongo River."

Dik grinned, showing yellow teeth. "Good. I remember my geography lessons."

Attom kept silent, hoping that Robota wouldn't reveal more. The Amazongo River was more than 2,000 kilometers long and Robota's directions were too vague. Or were they? Dik might find *Lifeboat-7*, stranded at the mouth of the river. From there, a walking trail followed the coast to Shelter Bay and Eva's camp. Dik would find them, especially if Robota acted as his guide.

"You'll take me there," Dik commanded Robota.

"As you wish," Robota responded.

Attom's heart sank. He tried to speak again, to urge Robota to refuse, but his parched throat made him mute.

"But I can't travel until I recharge my batteries in the sun."

Dik nodded, satisfied. "We'll leave next spring-week, after the feast." He glanced at Attom and smirked, eyes squinted.

Attom shivered. Dik meant him. He watched Dik leave, leaning on his walking stick, limping on his bad leg.

Attom coughed and cleared his throat. "Why did you tell Dik about Eva and the children?" He spoke in a hoarse whisper.

"I used Robota to protect you," Mother-9 interjected. "Before she spoke, there was an 87.2 percent likelihood that Dik would have killed you today, and a 68.6 percent chance he would have destroyed Robota. Now that he's distracted, he'll wait for the spring-week feast. You have a little more time."

Attom yanked at his bonds. "To do what?"

Neither Robota nor the Goddess answered.

———— «» ————

That evening, Alta returned alone. Attom remembered their quick coupling the night before. Now, even more exhausted, he knew he couldn't satisfy her. Instead of touching him, she held a skin of water to his lips and allowed him to drink his fill. He choked and gasped, but some of it went down. Then she fed him scraps from the evening meal: cooked cactus fruits and crawler-bugs. At least it wasn't human flesh.

"Free my hands," Attom pleaded, wiggling his fingers.

"I can't," whispered Alta. "If Dik sees me, he'll kill us both."

Attom lifted his head and looked at her. "If you let me go, I'll take you away from here."

Alta's eyes flashed. "Where?"

"We'll find a place of our own, near the ocean or by the Amazongo River. Dik will never find us."

Alta petted his pelt and, after a moment, shook her head. "I don't know. I'd miss my mother and sister." A noise from the camp startled her, and she disappeared into the gloom. Attom repressed a sob.

Later that night, after Naranja rose behind a thin veil of clouds, Alta returned. "Look what I made!" She held a hand axe in her right hand. The obsidian blade glistened in the faint orange light.

"Did you change your mind?" Attom asked.

"Is it true you'll help me escape?"

"Yes, of course." Attom hoped he could keep his word.

Alta chopped at the thongs binding his wrists.

"Careful, or you'll cut me!" The tough rawhide held tight.

"*Quiet*," hissed Alta. She stood and sawed at the cords looped around the cone tree branch. When she sliced through, Attom's arms dropped and he toppled onto his side, too weak to support his body. Alta knelt and helped him sit up.

"Thanks." He trembled, but joy gave him strength.

Alta freed his feet and wrists and pulled him upright. He struggled to balance and lift his arms.

"Cut Robota free too."

Alta hesitated. "No. I don't trust that thing."

"I've known her all my life. She can help us."

Robota turned to Alta. "If you release me, I can increase your odds of escaping to more than 50 percent."

Alta grimaced. "What is a *percent*?"

Attom didn't know what to say. "Robota has powerful medicines."

Alta shrugged and cut Robota's knots. The nannybot wobbled as she stood. "My batteries are weak. There's been little solar charge during winter-week."

"*Shhhh!* We need to hide," Alta whispered. She grabbed Attom's hand and led the way in the dark. Alta seemed to know the path, but Attom moved with small steps, uncertain of his footing on the bumpy ground.

Robota teetered behind. Attom assumed that her night vision allowed her to see well enough to walk. When Robota slipped on a loose rock, the small clattering noise made everyone freeze. Attom hoped the sound would pass unnoticed. They continued in the dark, Alta still leading.

"Hurry," whispered Alta. "Follow me." She pulled Attom's arm, and he shuffled after her.

A sudden light dazzled him. Dik held Attom's flashlight in one hand. The other gripped his stainless knife. He balanced on his good leg, without his walking stick.

Dik snarled and raised the silver blade. "Where do you think *you're* going?"

"Wait!" shouted Alta. Eyes wide with fear, she stepped in front of Attom, facing her father.

Dik cracked his daughter across the cheek with the flashlight. "Move aside, or you'll die with him."

Attom flinched but held himself in check. He wanted to kill Dik for hurting Alta.

Robota stepped forward. "I can lead you to the women's camp. Here is the map..." The nannybot activated the tablet on her chest.

The bright display made Dik blink. Distracted, he squinted at a satellite images of Terra Firma. While he looked at the marked route, Robota removed something from her pouch and passed it behind her back to Attom. He recognized the sniper-sloth tooth, a slender dart as long as his middle finger. He closed his fist around the base, holding it out of sight near his thigh.

Sensing something amiss, Dik sprang backward, agile even without his walking stick. In that instant, Attom surged forward and stabbed Dik's forearm with the sloth tooth, driving it deep into the muscle.

Attom ducked into the darkness. Dik charged after him, slashing with the knife. The blade nicked Attom's shoulder, sending a hot shudder of pain. Attom kicked Dik's lame leg. The man staggered and dropped his knife, which clattered onto the rocks. Attom scrambled after it.

Behind him, Dik regained his footing, roared, and punched Robota's face. Attom cringed as he heard the bones in Dik's hand snap on the nannybot's metal cheek. Dik howled and fell face-first onto the stony ground, flailing his arms, with the flashlight still in his fist.

Robota's tablet illuminated the scene. Jain appeared out of the dark and ran to Dik. He gasped for air, his mouth opening and closing like an eel out of water. His arm oozed blood from the puncture. As Jain knelt to comfort him, Stella joined the group, staring at Dik's twitching body.

Attom crawled to Dik. His enemy still breathed, not completely paralyzed. In an instant of black fury, Attom raised the knife to kill his tormentor.

"Stop!" screamed Alta. "No more killing!"

Attom froze, then lowered the knife.

Alta crouched next to her mother and touched Dik's wound. The dart, deep in the muscle, protruded from the skin.

Jain wheeled and slapped her daughter's bruised face. "You betrayed your father!"

Alta stared at her, and covered her bleeding lip with her hand.

Jain turned on Attom, eyes squinted with hatred. "Leave us. You don't belong here."

Attom grabbed Alta's hand. "Let's go before he wakes up, if he does. Can you lead us to the lifeboat?"

Alta nodded and grabbed the flashlight from Dik's hand. Tears streamed from her eyes. She clung to Attom's arm and called to Stella, "Come with us."

Stella looked up at Alta and shook her head. "Mama needs me here."

Alta removed her pendant and hung it around Stella's neck. Stella touched the coiled seashell, watching Alta with wet eyes.

As they walked to the beach, Attom heard Jain sobbing in the dark behind them.

He stopped and looked back, gripping his knife. He couldn't leave Dik alive. He had to eliminate the threat to Eva and the children while he still could.

"Where are you going?" Alta called.

Would she forgive him? Could Jain stop him? Still weak from captivity, and dizzy from blood loss from the knife wound in his shoulder, he stumbled and fell. Alta rushed to his side and helped him stand. He might die without medical help. They rejoined Robota, who applied antibiotic cream from her medical kit.

Using the flashlight, Alta led them to a battered aluminum dinghy, lying upside down behind a large rock. "Dik keeps it here. Stella and I row in the bay sometimes. Dik told us to never go to the big boat. It's haunted by an evil goddess."

Attom chuckled. "Mother-9 isn't evil." He saw that his words didn't convince her. He wasn't sure himself.

They dragged the dinghy into the water and climbed into it together with Robota. Alta rowed to the lifeboat, now floating upright at high tide. She shivered in the winter-week morning chill. Attom put his arm around her to keep her warm.

When the dinghy bumped the lifeboat, Alta climbed aboard and helped Attom onto the deck. Robota clambered after them.

Alta gripped the taffrail and looked at the deck. "It's smaller than I thought. How did it get here?"

"It sailed across the Great Ocean," Attom said, proud to know a few facts. "I was born on another lifeboat, like this one."

Alta blinked and shook her head. "Who was your mother?"

"I was," Robota said. Attom knew it was Mother-9 speaking through the nannybot.

Alta squinted and stared at Robota. "I don't believe you."

The nannybot flashed her eyebrow lights and nodded. "The tide is going out. We must leave now, before *Lifeboat-11* sinks in the mud again."

Attom showed Alta how to rig the spare sail and pull up the anchor. Rolling fog on the ocean glowed pink in the faint dawn light. Attom set a course out of the bay, glad to escape. On the lifeboat, he felt at home, like being a child again, safe and without worry.

Alta looked at the expanse of the Great Ocean and began to cry.

"What's wrong?" Attom asked.

"I'll never see Mama or Stella again, will I?"

"I don't know." Attom rubbed her back. "Do you want to go back?" He remembered feeling lost after Eva drove him from Shelter Bay.

Alta wiped her eyes and took a deep breath. "No, never."

Attom patted her hand. "Jain and Stella will be fine."

Alta didn't ask about her father. Would Dik survive?

——— «» ———

Attom jibed downwind on an offshore breeze near the southern coast of Terra Firma, pleased that he remembered how to sail. The chill salt air braced him and made him eager for new adventures, his depression a distant memory. Alta, who had never sailed before, huddled beside him in the open cockpit, wrapped in a lizard-skin blanket. She gripped the cockpit coaming as *Lifeboat-11* wallowed in the ocean swells.

The next morning, a polar rainsquall sent massive rollers that pushed them toward the rocky coastline of Terra Firma. The heaving boat made Alta seasick. She looked terrified as she retched over the gunwale. "Please," she begged, "I want to go ashore."

Attom stroked her back in sympathy. He felt queasy too. "Not here. It isn't safe." He remembered when *Lifeboat-7* crashed on Plymouth Rock.

Attom fought the helm, crabbing parallel to the shoreline, hoping to stay off the reefs of the lee shore. If they ran aground on a hidden shoal, they could capsize or sink. The surf thundered, and continuous winter-week gloom shrouded the view of a nearby headland. Trapped in a broad bay, Attom tacked to windward, port and starboard, but made little progress due to seaweed that fouled the lifeboat's hull. On his last attempt to escape, he hauled the mainsail tight and slipped past the rocky crags and into the open ocean. Relieved, he yearned for the light and warmth of spring-week.

Two days later, bright sun lit the overcast sky, and Attom's mood lifted. He remembered that this was the day that Dik had planned to kill and butcher him. Would Alta have taken part in the feast? Now, he and Alta snuggled together in the cockpit. A cool breeze moved the boat through an easy swell.

"Look, there's Mount Igneous." He pointed to the cinder cone and its lava-strewn slope in the rain shadow of the peak. "Robota and I hiked across it's lower slope."

"I didn't know Terra Firma was so big," Alta said.

The endless southern coastline loomed in a gray-green mist. They stared at cliffs, fjords, and hills forested by cone trees. The wild coast looked forbidding, hostile to humans. Where were they going? Attom had no idea.

Alta paused before changing the subject. "Is it true my parents were born on this lifeboat?"

Attom nodded and lashed the tiller. "Come below. I'll show you how they hatched."

He led Alta into the cabin where Robota crouched in her niche, trickle-charging her batteries. He pointed to the opaque windows in metal boxes near the companionway ladder. When he tapped one with his finger, the sapphire pane turned transparent. The window showed a visible face, with a round nose, distinct lips, and closed eyes.

"These artificial wombs make babies, including your parents. I was born from one like it, not by a woman."

Alta gasped. "Is that a *baby* in there?"

"Yes," Robota said, as she stood up. "The womb is pregnant with a male fetus—a little boy."

"When will he be born?"

"In two year-months," Robota said.

Alta stroked Attom's furry arm. "I want a baby too."

Attom responded to her touch and caressed her long blonde hair. Robota withdrew, giving them privacy.

Alta sighed and cuddled closer. "Do you want me?"

Alta was young, about the same age as his daughter, Lois. When he'd been Dik's prisoner, she'd used him without asking. That was a desperate and difficult time.

Attom looked at her worried face. She wanted to be wanted. "Of course, I do. You're very beautiful." For the first time in a season-week, since they'd escaped from Dik and Jain's camp, Attom allowed himself to feel desire.

Alta didn't move. "Do you want more children?" She spoke above a whisper.

Attom thought, with a pang of guilt, of his daughter Lois and his promise to return for her. "Yes."

Alta squeezed his hand. "You'll be good with kids, gentle and patient."

Attom hesitated. "I may have killed your father."

Alta combed the fur on his chest with her fingers. "You're not like Dik. You don't enjoy killing."

Attom leaned in and kissed her. For a moment, Alta seemed shy. "Do you really think I'm beautiful?"

Attom nodded and brushed his hand across the pectoral muscles of her almost-flat chest. He concentrated on her conical nipples, fingers stroking them erect.

Alta returned his kiss with urgency.

In the days that followed, Robota took the helm. Attom and Alta spent all their time together, talking, eating, sleeping, making love, and touching, always touching. New emotions engulfed Attom, but the pleasure that empowered him also left him helpless. He'd never known such happiness. He hoped it would never end.

Attom woke late in spring-week as they sailed past rocky inlets off the southern coast of Terra Firma. Endless surf generated white spume along lava cliffs. With Robota navigating at the helm, he'd stopped thinking about their destination.

Attom didn't want to go back to Eva, and he doubted she would welcome him, especially with Alta at his side. But he knew, having grown up in the cramped nursery of *Lifeboat-7*, that he and Alta couldn't live aboard much longer. They needed to go ashore before the birth of the baby boy in the artificial womb.

As summer-week grew warm, Attom fished to add to their diet of algae bricks. Robota interrupted him while he cleaned a twin-mouth eel on the deck. "Mother-9 has found a new destination for us. It's safer than the Amazongo River and nicer than Shelter Bay."

"I don't care where we go, as long as Alta and I can be together." Alta massaged his thick neck.

Robota displayed a black-and-white radar image of the coastline on her tablet. She pointed to an inlet. "Mother-9 named it Hidden Basin. It's a small saltwater lagoon with a narrow entrance from the Great Ocean. Twice a day, a saltwater waterfall flows either into or out of the lagoon, depending on the tide. It's protected, waves from ocean storms don't reach the shoreline inside, and there's safe anchorage for the lifeboat."

"What about wind-hoppers?" Attom asked.

"Mother-9 calculated a less than a five percent chance. Southern polar winds are too cold for them to fly during winter-week. She surveyed the entire coastline of Terra Firma, and there's no safer place than Hidden Basin."

"What do you think?" Attom asked Alta.

She smiled and shrugged. "It sounds nice."

Robota took the helm and navigated to the mouth of Hidden Basin, timing their entry with the tidal current. Attom stood watch to starboard and Alta to port. A sea breeze and the rising tide gave them less than a minute of slack water at the entrance. A gentle current sucked *Lifeboat-11* through the narrow channel, her keel gliding over the rocks visible below.

Attom lowered the sail, and the boat drifted into the placid lagoon. He dropped the anchor near a small stream that flowed down the beach into the saltwater.

"We're here!" Relief and joy overwhelmed him. For the first time since *Lifeboat-7* had run aground on Plymouth Rock, he felt at home. Until this moment, he hadn't realized how unsettled his life had been. He wanted an attachment to the land, a place to share with Alta.

Alta hugged Attom. "It's beautiful! I wish Mama and Stella could see it. Let's go ashore and explore."

Attom rowed the dinghy to the sandy beach. While Alta searched for a campsite, Attom took his spear and patrolled the shoreline. He checked nearby trees for sniper-sloths. He searched the shoreline for wind-hoppers, ankle-grabbers, and razor-tongue lizards. There were no predators.

A herd of spine-turtles foraged in the trees above the meadow. Now comfortable in his regrown fur, Attom dove for the oyster-clams that covered the bottom of the bay. Schools of finless tube-fish swam in the lagoon, squeezing their bodies from head to tail to jet through the water.

Hidden Basin seemed as safe as Mother-9 had promised, and they wouldn't go hungry. Compared to Dik's scorched-earth camp, this was paradise.

———— ⟨⟨⟩⟩ ————

Alta chose a campsite in a glade surrounded by cone trees next to the stream. They set up a tent made from the lifeboat's sail. As they cuddled on their first night together in Hidden Basin, Attom observed lights twinkling in the treetops.

"I wonder what they are." He remembered noticing them in the forest after the sniper-sloth attack.

"I know about them," Alta said. "They're nests of biting bugs. When Dik burned the forest, they swarmed down. Leave them alone."

"Don't worry, I won't disturb them. I think they're beautiful."

Attom relished their private life in Hidden Basin. Robota stayed on the lifeboat to tend to the growing fetus in the artificial womb, now named Apollo by Mother-9. Attom liked Greek myths and the reference to the god of light and knowledge, but wondered if Apollo would live up to his name.

When the nannybot reactivated *Lifeboat-11's* second womb, Attom asked for a puppy. He'd always wanted a dog when he was a boy after seeing videos of people on Earth with pets. Mother-9 agreed to the experiment. She had genome libraries for most Earth life, but warned Attom that the firstborn canine might not survive.

Alta laughed when he told her about the puppy. "We'll soon have more than a dog!" She placed his hand on her belly, and he felt a robust kick. "Robota says we've got twins!"

Attom blinked back tears. "Will they be smooth-skinned like you? Or furry, like me?"

"One of each, a hairy boy and a smooth girl," Robota said. "Variety is good. After I wean Apollo, I'll keep *Lifeboat-11* producing more children."

Attom knew that this was Mother-9 speaking, but he didn't care. After his journey with Robota, and a new home with Alta in Hidden Basin, he believed the Goddess was looking out for him and his new family.

Attom smiled. "Let's call our babies Odysseus and Circe." He wanted more Greek names.

His suggestion made Alta pensive. She clutched Attom's arm and looked into his eyes. "I want Mama to catch my babies. She knows what to do."

"Don't worry. Robota will be your midwife."

"I don't want her. I miss Mama and Stella."

Attom caressed Alta's cheek. "Robota is very good with babies; she raised me. I'll help too." He was mature now, and more experienced, better able to cope. He'd be what he had always hoped, a good father and loyal mate.

"We could sail back before the baby is born," Alta said. "Robota knows the way."

The nannybot interrupted in a firm voice. "Apollo will be hatched soon. The lifeboat must stay anchored in Hidden Basin, the safest place to raise children."

Alta groaned in frustration. "We could hike overland through the forest."

"Jain is more than two year-months away on foot," Robota said. "If you wander in wilderness while you're pregnant, you may lose your babies."

Alta shook her head. "I want Mama!"

At that moment, Alta seemed like a frightened girl. Attom felt like an old man. "Remember, Dik kills little boys. He'll murder Odysseus and make Circe his slave."

Alta's face twisted in anguish. "I *hate* my father!"

Shocked, Attom gulped. He hadn't meant to inflict such pain. "I'm sorry…"

Alta wiped her eyes and seemed to regain composure. "It's all right, we'll stay here. But I want to see Mama and Stella again."

Attom caressed her blonde hair. "Someday. Yes." He remembered Eva. He worried that Alta would never be happy.

Alta tightened her grip on his arm, pulling the fur. "Promise me we'll do that, after the babies are born."

Attom paused. "Dik will try to kill me again." He didn't want to fight to the death.

Alta squeezed her eyes shut, face rigid. Another tear streaked down her cheek. "I don't know what I want I want."

"Let's make our home in Hidden Basin big enough for our children *and* your mother and sister. Someday you'll be reunited. We'll make room for your whole family and our children."

Alta brightened as her emotional squall faded. "All right." She stood tall and kissed him. "I'd like that."

Attom thought back to Clarke's death, his heartbreak with Eva, and his crippling solitude afterwards. He still missed little Lois's big smile and unruly red hair. But today the world seemed full of promise.

Grateful for a second chance, he took a moment to relish his renewed role as father, hunter, explorer, and nursemaid. He loved Alta and hoped their little clan would grow.

Part 4: Utopia Compromised

Lois paced inside *Lifeboat-7*, still stranded on Plymouth Rock. The air in the cold metal hull smelled like mold. She had hoped to find Attom, but the emptiness of the dark cabin made her sob. She missed her younger siblings—Jak, Jilzy, Anton, and Cleo—still living in Shelter Bay. But she couldn't return.

She'd run away after a final fight with Eva over burned fish skewers. The ruined meal was her fault—she had daydreamed while cooking. Food was scarce and she hadn't paid attention. Her furious mother yelled and slapped her to the ground. Terrified, Lois remained face down in the grit on the cave floor. Eva took the charred fish and retreated to the back of the cavern where the younger children cowered. Lois, her lower lip swollen and bleeding, went hungry that night.

Lois knew she was almost grown, her menses flowed each year-month, but her mother treated her like a child. The morning after, Lois climbed the crater wall and ran all day to *Lifeboat-7*, the only other place she knew. Traces of her father remained, clothing and tools, but Attom and Robota were gone. His absence left her weeping from isolation, drained and listless, desperate for someone to talk to.

She'd endured three season-weeks of isolation in the cabin of the lifeboat. Gray light filtered through the dirty portholes and cold rain thrummed on the metal deck. She kicked the bulkheads, afraid to leave her self-imposed prison. Terrified of wind-hoppers—the memory of Clarke's death remained vivid—she avoided the beach, with its variety of edible eels and crabs. At least the boat's food factory still produced fortified algae bricks. As much as she hated the salty green gunk, it kept her alive. As the season-weeks passed, she grew thinner.

Throughout her crazed confinement, Lois maintained her pride and strength of will. She would never return to Shelter Bay and face mother's wrath. Craving contact, she tried touching herself, but it only added to her desolation. Overwhelmed with self-loathing, she hacked off her matted and tangled red hair.

Distracted and bored, Lois opened a service panel in the forward locker of the cabin. She looked at the labels but couldn't read them. Eva had given up teaching after they'd moved to Shelter Bay. Lois poked at the knobs and buttons, hoping for a reaction.

A small video display flashed on, making her blink. The image showed a wizened woman with soft jowls and gray hair. "Hello, Lois! How can I help you?" The sweet voice emanated from somewhere behind the screen.

Startled, Lois ducked her head. "How do you know my name?"

"You've got red hair. You must be Attom and Eva's daughter."

"Who are you?"

"I'm Mother-9, your father used to call me Goddess. I've been sleeping for a while."

Lois had heard about the Goddess from her mother. But this old woman didn't look like an evil spirit.

Mother-9 smiled, showing white teeth. "Welcome to *Lifeboat-7*, your parents' birthplace. It's nice to meet you again after such a long time. You've grown up."

Lois struggled to understand the strange accent. How did Mother-9 know so much about her?

"Do you live in there?" Lois couldn't imagine how an old woman could fit inside the little window.

"No, I live in space, in orbit around Valencia. I'm from the planet Earth. The picture you see is how I'd like to look, if I were human."

So many new words. Embarrassed, Lois didn't ask for explanations. Wary of the spirit in the lifeboat, she opened the hatch to the outdoor cockpit. Raindrops spattered against her face.

"Please don't leave," Mother-9 said. "I'm lonely too. Talk with me. Tell me about your mother, Eva."

Lois hesitated, then closed the hatch, "I hate her."

"And the other children?" Mother-9 asked. "Are they well?"

"I suppose so," Lois answered. "Where is my father? I want to see him."

The old woman's smile returned. "He's far away. Attom has a new family with more children. I hope he's happy."

Lois struggled with this information. "Where did he find a family?" She hadn't known there were other people on Valencia. Why didn't her father come back for her like he'd promised? Did he still love her?

"They live on the southern coast of Terra Firma, at Hidden Basin."

Lois frowned. "Take me to him."

Mother-9 pressed her lips together. "I can't. I don't have a body. You should stay here in the lifeboat, where you're safe."

Mother-9 sounded like Eva, arbitrary and heartless. Lois hated being treated like a child. "I'll go crazy alone. I need to see my father."

Mother-9 shook her head. "You're not alone now; you can talk with me. I'll show you many wonderful things. We can be *such* good friends!"

Lois didn't trust this strange Goddess. "You're not real. What can you teach me?"

"You'll learn to read and write. I'll teach you arithmetic and astronomy. Don't you want to know about the planet Earth, where humans came from?"

Lois rubbed her temple, unable to follow the words. "My father will teach me what I need to know. If I can find him."

"It's a long journey, year-months in the wilderness. You might get lost, or die."

"I don't care! Tell me where he is."

Mother-9 gave an exaggerated sigh. "All right. I'll show you maps."

"What are...maps?" Suspicious, Lois suspected another deflection and delay.

"Maps are pictures of the land of Terra Firma, from high in the sky. They'll tell you where you are, and the direction to Hidden Basin."

The crone's face vanished, and a complex green and blue diagram appeared on the screen, with a blinking dot in the middle. "This is *Lifeboat-7*, where we are, near the mouth of the Amazongo River." The map shifted to a new location. "And here is Shelter Bay, your home with your mother and your siblings."

Lois peered at the small image and tried to grasp the change in perspective. She remembered what Shelter Bay had looked like from the rim of the crater. "I see the lagoon and the waterfall. Where's the cave?"

The image of the bay grew larger, as if Lois was falling down the cliff.

The blinking yellow dot appeared again. "The entrance is near the beach."

Lois raised her eyebrows. "Yes, I see it. But where are the people?" She wanted to see Jak and Jilzy.

Mother-9 chuckled. "This is an old picture, stored in my memory, from before you lived in Shelter Bay. I have millions of images in my memory. I've mapped most of the planet."

"How can you remember so much?"

"I'm an artificial intelligence, a kind of complex machine, made by humans. I don't forget anything. I'm more than 150,000-year-months old."

Lois blinked. Large words and numbers confused her. "How long will you live?"

"I'm old and weak. Many of my parts don't work. I could die anytime, if there's a large solar flare."

This shocked Lois. She'd expected the Goddess to live forever.

"Then teach me now. Show me how to use maps so I can find my father."

"Very well. We'll begin with the geography of Terra Firma. I'll find the best route to Hidden Basin."

Lois concentrated as Mother-9 began the lesson. She wanted to impress her father when she found him.

———— ‹›› ————

Mother-9 Journal
April 2, 22,981; Valencia

I should have anticipated Lois's rebellion and her arrival at *Lifeboat-7* on Plymouth Rock. I knew from Attom that Lois and Eva often clashed. Despite sophisticated social metrics, I can't predict human behavior.

Like any mother, I want my children to be happy, but not at any cost. The human condition pivots on positive and negative emotions: pleasure and pain, satisfaction and angst, love and loss. I measure three happiness variables: inherited set point, objective reality, and aspiration. Set point is a genetic predisposition to be cheerful or pessimistic, regardless of circumstances. But reality intrudes. In the real world, good and bad things happen that affect mood. Aspiration is the most mysterious. Hopes and plans, the products of imagination, may or may not succeed.

For each colonist, I plot a 3-D graph that traces their happiness through time. The results are intriguing, but not predictive. No wonder I'm a failure at social engineering. And that makes *me* unhappy, or at least dissatisfied. But, if it suits my agenda, I try to tip the scales.

Aside from finding her father, what would make Lois happy? I decided to tempt her with another option. "Do you like babies?"

"Yes, of course. Who doesn't?"

"I can give you one of your own." Lois was 17-Earth-years old and fertile.

Startled, Lois seemed to consider my offer. "What kind of baby? Will you make one for me in the lifeboat?"

"You can grow your own baby in your womb."

"Don't I need a man to get pregnant?"

"No. I can provide synthetic sperm. You can have a girl or a boy. Would you like red hair, like yours?"

If she stayed, I could restart *Lifeboat-7's* wombs. I hoped to educate her and make her the matriarch of her own clan. Since Robota's departure with Attom, there's no nannybot aboard to deliver and raise babies. But Lois could do the job. I had to try.

Lois shook her head. "I don't want to be pregnant. I want to find my father."

After experiencing Eva's neglect, and endless babysitting duties, Lois wanted no part of mass-mothering. I suppose she was right to refuse. She's too young and impulsive to be a full-time mother. Besides, the cold cabin of derelict *Lifeboat-7* isn't an ideal nursery. Lois would never take a baby ashore to Attom and Eva's old beach camp, where wind-hoppers had killed her brother. And Shelter Bay wasn't an option. There were no good choices.

I capitulated. Lois can make a solitary journey into the hinterlands of Terra Firma in search of Attom at Hidden Basin. She's inexperienced and impulsive. I warned her about sniper-sloths and ankle-grabbers. I estimate she has a 19 percent chance of surviving for more than a year-month. But I didn't tell her that.

I also worry about Eva at Shelter Bay, in the ancient volcanic crater. When Lois departed, it reduced Eva's clan below critical numbers. Eva is a tough survivor, but neither Attom nor Lois could live with her. She's an unhappy woman, unwilling to be a broodmare and nursemaid for unwanted children, a poor candidate for a matriarch. I suppose it's my fault that she dislikes babies, I haven't found the genes for maternal joy. Even so, Eva is a good person struggling with her fate. She needs the freedom to define her own life, an identity beyond motherhood and caregiving, that I'm powerless to offer.

After Attom and Alta escaped to Hidden Basin on *Lifeboat-11*, I lost contact with Dik and Jain again. Was Dik still alive? He was smart, resourceful, and ambitious, with the mental stamina to survive and dominate. Attom, my good son, was no match for him. But even if Dik lives, his family isn't viable. Dik is my greatest success and my biggest failure. Synthetic guilt hurts.

In comparison to Lois's lonely life on *Lifeboat-7*, and Dik and Jain's bleak camp on the south coast, Hidden Basin is a special place. The birth of Apollo from *Lifeboat-11's* artificial womb gave me renewed hope. He carries Valencia-neutral genes. He'll be tall and strong, with brown eyes, olive skin, and straight black hair, showing mixed lineage. Babies from lifeboat wombs carry selected traits from all human races, living and extinct, including Neanderthals and Denisovans.

And I have more good news! Alta birthed Odysseus and Circe with some emotional drama, but no medical difficulty. When she went into labor, she held Attom's hand. But she refused to look at

Robota, as the nannybot worked to deliver the babies. Odysseus had a full head of hair and a fine lanugo coat that covered his chest and arms. Circe was bald with grey eyes. Both were beautiful, healthy babies. Attom hovered nearby, tending to Alta's needs. As always, he is a devoted family man.

Feeling optimistic, I decided to reward Attom. Even as a child, he'd longed for a pet. I tinkered with dog DNA, and, after two year-months in the womb, we whelped Winston, a corgi and British bulldog cross. He's friendly, shorthaired, and heavy boned, with a wide stance and deep chest. Even as a puppy, he could stand and walk in Valencia's gravity.

Attom loved that white-and-tan mutt, even more than his infant daughters at first. He bottle-fed Winston on synthetic formula. Like many people, Attom has an inborn rapport with dogs. Wolves coevolved with humans and were essential to their survival during Earth's Pleistocene. They could serve a similar role on Valencia, if they don't go feral and eat the local wildlife.

With the successes of Apollo and Winston, I risked an ambitious experiment to give a child genius-level intelligence. Valencia will need occasional prodigies to push civilization beyond mere survival. Twelve year-months after Apollo's birth, Robota delivered Persephone from the other womb on *Lifeboat-11*. At birth, she had olive skin with golden undertones and a full head of thick, black hair.

I gave Persey an aptitude for languages and memory, but I wanted much more from her. To focus her intellect, I engineered her brain for temporary isolation of the left anterior temporal lobe using transcranial magnetic stimulation. TMS is a standard treatment for stroke or depression, and can also control brain functions. When she's old enough, Robota will teach her to place a TMS coil on her scalp. The magnetic field may boost her brain to the level of an autistic savant—Persey could be another Newton or Einstein. I hope it works or, if not, that it'll do no harm.

If Persey can turn her genius capabilities on and off, then she may be able to live a normal life and still invent the future. Will it work or make her crazy? Will she use her gifts or avoid them? I can't predict key personality traits, such as drive, that mysterious urge to *do* something. This is a leveraged evolutionary bet, with high risks and great potential rewards. I wanted to try it while the artificial wombs still function.

The recent births increased the population of Hidden Basin to six humans, a good start, but not enough. I won't be happy unless more babies are coming. But, I'm optimistic!

—— «» ——

Leaving the lifeboat felt like starting a new, adult life. Lois gathered her water skin and her prized fishing harpoon with its knapped obsidian point, made for her by Attom.

"Before you go, I have a special gift for you." Mother-9 spoke in a happy voice while her image effected a broad smile.

Lois thought her expression looked forced. "What is it?"

"Go to locker seven, the one with the red cross. The sealed door keeps the contents under vacuum. Turn both handles to open it."

Intrigued by the mystery, Lois did as instructed. The stiff hinges squeaked and a loud hiss followed. Inside, a red light blinked on. She removed a canvas package with wide straps.

"Is it a backpack?" Lois remembered that her father had one when she was small.

"Yes, it's a survival kit, the last remaining one on *Lifeboat-7*. Open it."

Lois fumbled with the zipper and found a water bottle, a shiny metal knife, a flashlight, and a fire piston. A medical kit held various drugs and bandages. She withdrew a rectangular tablet from a padded pocket. The display blinked on when she tipped it upright.

"It's a map!" Lois recognized the Amazongo River delta and *Lifeboat-7* stranded on Plymouth Rock.

"I uploaded it to you," Mother-9 said. "Wherever you go, I'll update the tablet to show your location and what lies ahead. I've included the shortest route to Attom's campsite at Hidden Basin. You'll follow the Amazongo upstream, and then turn south through the jungle forest. Follow the yellow line. That way, you won't get lost."

Lois touched the edge of the display as if it were a living creature. "Thank you."

"Put the tablet in the sun to charge it. It's waterproof with a sapphire screen. But don't lose it. It's the last one on Valencia. You can use it to call me wherever you go on Terra Firma, but only when my orbit is overhead."

Lois considered the offer. "I won't need your help. I'll follow the map."

"Call me if you get lost or hurt."

Lois shrugged. "I'll be fine." She wouldn't admit fear, either to herself or Mother-9. She stowed the tablet in its pocket, filled the pack with algae bricks, and slipped her arms through the shoulder straps. "Goodbye!"

As Lois trekked away from *Lifeboat-7*, the heavy survival kit and wind gusts made her stagger in the loose beach sand. Wind-hoppers soared overhead, but didn't dive. Gray clouds scudded across the sky. She looked back at the wrecked lifeboat, glad to leave the metal cave and Mother-9 behind. But her mind veered between joy and dread, settling on a stubborn determination to make a new start.

It rained the first night. Lois slept on the bank of the Amazongo River, using the kit's space blanket for cover. In the morning, she speared a propeller fish at the shallow shoreline; its slick, tubular body and fluttering tail flukes made it hard to hold. When she tried to cut it open, her knife only nicked the rigid, armored skin, so she roasted the creature on a spit until the body split. Then, after testing it for toxins with the medical kit in her backpack, she forced herself to consume it all, including the green guts. She'd resolved to eat whatever food she could find.

Lois continued upriver and used the tablet map to avoid the ankle-grabbers at Sandbar Bay. By late afternoon, she reached Attom and Eva's old cliff camp above the low falls. She found a pile of rotted kernel-pods next to the cold fire pit. Childhood memories flooded her mind—picking the pink pods from hook-thorn shrubs. Her mother ground the kernels and made thin soup that never satisfied their hunger. Only the lizard eggs, gathered by her father, had saved them from starvation.

Lois squinted at the wide river, its deep water muddy from recent rain, not good for spearfishing. A low waterfall separated a small island from the mainland, a distance too great to swim. Razor-tongue lizards still basked at the islet's edge, each brooding a clutch of eggs. She remembered when her father had almost drowned in the current trying to reach them.

Lois searched below the waterfall, looking for fish stunned by the cascade, but she found none. She resigned herself to eating dried algae for her evening meal. As she walked back to the campsite, a low rumble shook the land in waves. Nearby cone trees whipped back and forth. Another quake! Lois recognized the signs; frequent shocks had rained rocks from the crater walls of Shelter Bay. She'd hoped that the flat river valley would be quiet.

With a grinding roar, the ground heaved next to the Amazongo, elevating the river's shoreline. The bucking motion knocked her onto her hands and knees. Shaken and afraid, she watched the river drain into a chasm that had opened in the riverbed, billowing steam. Low water revealed a muddy river bottom with stranded fish flopping. Before the ground stopped moving, Lois grabbed her spear and waded into muck. In moments, she'd caught a small eel.

Water continued to drain, and the raised river bottom now extended to the local islets. Lois watched the razor-tongue lizards abandon their nests and slide into the surging Amazongo current. Another aftershock shook the land, this time with a side-to-side shimmy. As the mud rippled below her feet, she sank to her waist in the slurry. Lois panicked that the river water would return while her feet were stuck. She scrabbled to free herself, covering her face and body with stinking slime.

Lois crawled to the islet and gathered as many lizard eggs as her pack would hold. She used her space blanket as a sack to carry more. While she worked, another quake upriver generated a tsunami wave that crested at twice her height. As it approached, Lois leaped into the breaker and tumbled over the nearby waterfall. Still clutching her catch and her spear, the wave carried her above the rocks and deposited her on a mudbank downstream. She crawled ashore and collapsed.

Lois woke in the middle of the night, wet, shivering, and hungry. She pricked a lizard egg and sucked the gooey contents. The creamy yolk warmed her belly. When she looked up, the nearby treetops twinkled against the black sky. The beauty of the lights eased her solitude.

The next morning, Lois continued upstream. The Amazongo curved in a lazy meander, and the tablet map showed a shortcut through uncharted cone tree forest. The tangled jungle frightened her. She looked up every few paces, searching for sniper-sloth lairs. Beneath a large tree, Lois found an old dart tooth and the jumbled bones of an unknown animal, a beast with a curved crest at the top of its skull. She kept moving, unwilling to rest or stop to eat, afraid to camp overnight in the dark woods.

Lois arrived at the bank of the Amazongo at sunset; the orange light of spring-week glinted off ripples in the slow current. Haze obscured the opposite bank of the wide river. She used her fire piston to start a driftwood bonfire. The blaze cheered her after her long trek through the forest. She feasted on cooked lizard eggs and gazed at the placid water, satisfied with her progress. If she maintained this pace, she would reach Attom in less than half the time predicted by Mother-9.

The Amazongo carried floating debris, washed from the eroded banks upriver after the earthquake. Lois watched clumps drift by, small branches and occasional large trees. Among the distant flotsam, she spotted a raft of logs with three people sitting on it.

A person stood upright and waved at her. "Hellooo!" The shout carried across the water.

Startled, Lois jumped up and waved. Was her father returning to the coast with his new family? Her heart leaped.

"Hellooo!" Lois replied. Elated, she tossed another log on the fire. Sparks and black smoke rose into the sky.

A woman and a younger girl used crude planks to paddle the raft toward Lois. An older man sat between them, not her father. Disappointed and suddenly shy, Lois hid behind a cone tree. Who were these people?

The raft's slow progress made her wonder if they would drift past and disappear downriver. Then they caught a back eddy that pushed the raft onto the muddy riverbank.

A man with a grizzled beard and a walking stick limped ashore.

———— «» ————

Lois crouched and watched from behind the cone tree. The old man scanned the area with squinted eyes—she supposed he was looking for her—and then reclined on a grassy knoll near the river. He heaved a sigh and threw an arm over his eyes, as if to block sunlight. Was he sleeping?

Confused, Lois wondered who he was. His broad, hairless chest, so different from Attom's fur, showed ribs. Wrinkled bronze skin and a long, matted beard made him seem ancient, like gnarled tree trunk with moss. She could hear him breathe through his open mouth, a rattle on inhale and a sigh on exhale.

Still hiding, Lois watched the two women. In the extended spring-week twilight, they gathered more driftwood and heaped it on the fire. They spoke a strange language.

As if he could see through the tree, the old man sat up and stared in her direction. A smile transformed his face, an open grin with crinkled eyes. As he spoke, he ran fingers through his beard, combing it.

"I know you're there. Don't be afraid." His voice carried a rich timbre.

Lois hesitated, and then stepped into view.

He rose to his feet, leaning on his walking stick. "What beautiful red hair! Who *are* you?" His gravelly, bass voice made him seem like an old friend.

Still wary, she stood still. "I'm Lois."

The man beamed and nodded, as if it was the most beautiful name he'd ever heard. His chin motion flapped his beard against his chest. "My name is Dik." He gestured at the women. "That's my daughter Stella and her mother Jain."

The women stood on the opposite side of the fire, maintaining distance. Lois noticed that they didn't look at Dik or meet her gaze.

"I can't understand what they're saying," Lois said.

"Neither can I," Dik chuckled. "It's Latin, silly girl-talk. Jain learned it from the old nannybot."

Lois looked again at the women. Stella stared back but Jain kept her eyes averted. Where had they come from? Lois struggled with the idea of new people on Terra Firma.

"I'm hungry," Dik said. "We've been floating downriver for days. Do you have any food?"

Lois nodded and pointed at the sack of cooked lizard eggs. She couldn't refuse to help the travelers, even though she didn't know where she might find more food for herself.

As evening fell, the visitors sat by the fire and gorged themselves. They didn't talk while they consumed the eggs whole, even chewing the leathery shells.

When he finished, Dik wiped his lips and turned to Lois. The flickering flames outlined deep creases in his haggard face. She couldn't see his eyes.

"You're all alone?" Dik lowered his voice above a whisper. "Don't you have someone to take care of you?"

Season-weeks of solitude weighed on Lois. Since Attom had left Shelter Bay, no one had shown concern for her—except for Mother-9, but she wasn't human. Dik reached out and placed a hand her shoulder. His gentle touch melted her caution. Lois craved companionship, even from these strange people. Tears welled in her eyes. "There's no one. Only me."

"Don't worry…you'll be all right." Dik stroked her arm, his voice a low rumble. "You're a *very* brave girl, surviving alone in the wilderness."

She tried to speak but hiccupped instead, tears streaming.

"There, there…" soothed Dik. He held out his arms, inviting her in. Lois wavered, then let him hug her. It felt good, like an embrace from her father.

"Are you heading home to your family?" he asked.

"No. I can't. My mother…" Lois faltered and stopped. She didn't want to explain.

"Had a fight, did we?" Dik chuckled. "Ah well, these things happen. I'm sure it will all smooth over, in the end."

Lois shrugged, still weeping. His deep voice lulled her.

"Tell me about your mother. Her name is Eva? I'd love to meet her."

Lois pulled back. "How do you know my mother's name?"

"I met your father. His name is Attom, right?"

Startled, Lois stopped crying. "Is he still at Hidden Basin?"

"Hidden Basin?" Dik exchanged a look with the older woman. "No, he visited our camp. Then he sailed away with our daughter Alta. We miss her *very* much."

"Where did they go?"

Dik's smile showed stained teeth. "To Hidden Basin. I'll find them, someday."

"Why were you rafting down the Amazongo?" Were they searching for her mother?

Dik gave a broad smile. "We've gotten all turned around, lost in the wilderness. We were lucky to find the river, and now you! We don't know our direction home."

His smile vanished, replaced by a pleading look. He touched her arm again. "Please, can you show us the way to Eva's camp?"

Lois faltered under the pressure of his stare. "Why do you want to see her?"

"I'm an old man, I can't walk or hunt. We'll starve out here on our own." Dik motioned to Jain. "You explain."

Jain's blank face revealed no emotion. "I've lost all my children, except for Stella. We can't survive alone in the wilderness. We're too few. There's strength in numbers."

Lois sympathized. She knew her own self-exile might mean death.

"We can work together." Dik's voice conveyed warm enthusiasm. "Show us where Eva is—it shouldn't be far. Then we'll help you find Hidden Basin and Attom."

Lois couldn't imagine Eva welcoming Dik, Jain, and Stella. There were already too many mouths to feed, at a time of declining fish stocks in Shelter Bay.

"Sorry, I can't go back. I must find my father."

Dik looked at her with narrowed eyes, brows knitted. "Terra Firma is *very* big. You might get lost, like us."

Lois sat up straight. "I know how to read a map. Hidden Basin is on the southern coast."

Dik squeezed Lois's arm. "You have a map?" The intensity in his eyes startled her. "Let me see it!"

Lois twisted her arm out of his grip. She wasn't sure why, but she decided to keep her tablet secret. "There was a map in the wrecked lifeboat, near the mouth of the Amazongo River."

"Oh." Dik seemed disappointed. Then he raised bushy eyebrows and gave Lois a broad smile. "Another lifeboat? You talked with Mother-9? I know her very well…"

Lois swelled with pride. "She showed me where to find Attom's camp."

Dik scratched his beard. "Don't trust the Great Mother. She never tells the whole truth. Something is always hidden."

Lois blinked. Dik was right. The Goddess hadn't mentioned Dik, Jain, or Stella. "I've memorized the directions. I'll leave tomorrow morning."

Dik smiled and stroked Lois's arm again. "If you can't take us to Eva, we'll all go together to Attom's camp. You shouldn't travel alone; it's too dangerous. You can be our leader, and we'll protect you."

Lois loved the idea. She wouldn't be lonely anymore. "It's several season-weeks' travel overland." Then Lois turned to Jain. "Do you want to go?"

Jain looked at Dik and then Lois. The old woman scowled and brushed a strand of gray hair behind an ear. "I never want to see Attom again. Besides, Dik has trouble walking. It's much easier to float down the Amazongo to the Great Ocean, where we can find food on the beach."

Stella stepped forward. "I'll go with you!" It was the first time the girl had talked. She was a little younger than Lois, with a strong body. She wore a coiled shell pendant around her neck.

Jain grabbed Stella's wrist and slapped her face. "You're not allowed to speak. Don't rile your father."

Stella flinched and looked down. Lois felt sorry for Stella, and an instant dislike of Jain, certain that the old woman was even more bossy than Eva.

"It's okay," Dik said, waving his hand. "Let Stella speak. If we go together to Hidden Basin, that'll surprise Attom." He turned to his daughter, eyes crinkled in a smile. "It'll be fun, won't it, Stella? You'll see Alta again."

"Alta?" Lois asked. "Who's that?"

"My other daughter," Dik explained. "Impetuous girl, like her sister. She sailed away with Attom." A wistful look crept into his eyes. "I suppose they were in love."

Lois felt a hot stab of jealousy. So that's why her father hadn't returned for her. Stella stared at the ground, one hand worrying the string of her pendant.

Lois swung between joy and fear. She wanted company, but she couldn't tolerate Jain. She felt sorry for Stella. Dik's lame leg would slow them down. Although the old man made her feel wanted and safe, she needed time to think.

"We should gather food for the trip," Lois said. "There aren't many lizard eggs left." She didn't tell them about her survival pack, stuffed with more eggs and algae bricks. She hoped Dik wouldn't find her tablet.

Dik nodded and touched Lois's cheek. "You're very wise. We'll spend tomorrow spearfishing on the Amazongo. Now, it's time to sleep."

———— ‹›› ————

Lois retreated into the dark with her pack and space blanket, away from the group. As she left, she noticed Stella staring at her. Could she trust these strange people? They seemed tense, each isolated from the others, not together by affection or choice. Nobody smiled, chatted, or touched. Dik was in charge but venom leaked from Jain's eyes. Stella twisted with inner turmoil. Why?

Lois listened to her visitors prepare for the night. Jain tossed more wood on the campfire while Stella gathered fronds of fern-grass for bedding. Dik leaned on his cane and reclined near the fire. After a time, they fell asleep. Lois did too.

Sometime in the night, a hand touched her shoulder, startling her awake. Moonlight through thin clouds illuminated Stella's worried face. She placed a finger to her lips and whispered, "Please! Take me with you."

Lois, half asleep, sat up. "Where?"

"Shhhh...! To your father's camp. We should leave before Dik wakes up. You know the way, don't you?" She glanced at Dik and Jain sleeping near the embers of the dying fire.

"But..."

"Dik is dangerous," Stella whispered. "We need to go now."

"Why?" The girl's words made no sense.

A tear ran down Stella's cheek. "He murdered both of my brothers and ate them."

"What? Why would he do that?" The girl didn't make sense.

"Because he's a god, and all boys must die. He also wanted to sacrifice Attom."

Lois didn't know what to think. Was Stella crazy? Dik seemed like a kindly old man who needed a walking stick to hobble about. "Why are you telling me this?"

Stella's shoulders shook. "You must believe me! Please! We need to go before he wakes up."

Doubts churned her mind. Lois felt trapped by Stella's panic.

"Let's leave *now*!" Stella forgot to whisper.

Jain stirred near the fire. She sat up and threw another branch on the glowing coals. Flames flared, shedding flickering light. "Where's Stella?"

Dik groaned. He used his cane to stand and look around. "Stella!" he shouted.

Stella grabbed Lois by the wrist, wide eyes imploring. "Hurry!"

Dik hobbled forward, swinging his cane, moving fast. Lois stuffed her blanket into her pack and led Stella on a blind dash into the forest. Dim moonlight filtered through the cone trees and allowed them to find their way across the rugged ground.

Lois stopped to rest after wading up a stream to hide their footprints. Dik crashed through the underbrush behind them. His lame leg didn't slow him down.

"Stella!" Dik cursed and roared Stella's name over and over. She cringed at his voice.

Dik paused and then called in a clear voice, "Lois, come back! We need you and you need us! Don't be fooled by Stella—she's a crazy girl who makes up stories."

Lois, dripping wet from the stream, shivered.

———— «» ————

Lois and Stella spent the rest of summer-week trotting through the forest. They didn't use fire and slept at night huddled together on the ground. Their arms and legs bled from hook-thorn scratches. Daily rains made Lois's skin itch. Stella looked haggard, casting her eyes left and right, terrified that Dik would catch them. Lois resented Stella for disrupting her journey to find her father.

The lizard eggs soon ran out. Lois gathered hook-thorn pods and crawler-bugs for both of them. They ate them raw, but it wasn't enough. Stella lagged behind, unable to keep up with Lois. Ancient cone trees obscured the sky and hillocks and ravines diverted their way forward. Lois tried the tablet map but could not find a signal.

"I don't know where we are," Lois said. "Let's climb that hill and look around." A rocky slope led to the top.

Stella looked up and groaned. "I'm too tired. I'll wait here."

"No, you won't. Follow me."

Lois climbed a short distance and waited. Stella stumbled and Lois reached down to pull her up the steep incline. The two girls clambered up the forested ravine, ducking under fallen trees and pushing through dense undergrowth. When they reached the top, they sat on a level expanse of rock near a cliff. Lois gazed into the distant valley while Stella caught her breath.

"Can you see the ocean?" Stella asked.

"No, only endless forest."

Stella reclined on the mossy rock, eyes closed. "I can't go any farther. We haven't eaten in two days." Scabs on her face and arms oozed blood from bushwhacking.

Lois knew that she looked the same. She searched the bottom her survival pack for the last crumbs of algae brick. She took two and handed the rest to Stella. "Here, eat this. You'll feel stronger." Lois chewed hers.

"Are we going to die here?"

"No!" For Stella's sake, Lois remained optimistic. The girl was her age, but she seemed younger, her mind stunted.

Lois shook her head, trying to dispel the memories of their weeklong escape. She didn't want to believe Stella's warnings about Dik. After eating, Stella lay on the thin layer of moss, tears on her cheeks. The girl was a burden, but Lois couldn't abandon her.

Lois sipped from her water skin, then handed it to Stella. "Don't drink too much. This is all we have until we find a stream."

Stella swallowed a mouthful and stopped crying.

Lois removed the tablet from her survival pack. She'd tried the map display, but now the battery was dead. Frustrated, Lois placed the tablet on the moss with the screen facing the bright clouds. She tried to nap while it absorbed the weak sunlight. As dusk fell, she activated the display again. No connection...

"Mother-9 isn't responding," Lois said. "I guess she's not in range." Frustration made her tense.

"Is Mother-9 the spirit in the sky? Mama told me she was evil."

Lois had heard the same warning from Eva.

"How far is it to Hidden Basin?" Stella asked.

Lois retrieved a stored map image. But, with no signal from Mother-9, she couldn't locate their position. Nothing in the valley below matched the map. "It's two season-weeks of travel to reach Hidden Basin." She made a guess for Stella's sake. It could be more.

"We *are* lost," moaned Stella. "I can't make it that far. We'll die soon."

Stella was right. They needed to find food and water tomorrow. Lois loathed Stella's attitude, and now she hated Stella.

The sun dipped below the horizon, signaling the start of fall-week. The dark valley below showed sparkling lights in the trees.

"Look," Lois said. "They're beautiful. What are they?"

Stella yawned. "I've seen them before, along the shore of the Amazongo. They lit up when we floated past at night, as if they were guiding us down the river."

As Lois watched, the twinkling sparks flashed in succession from tree to tree, marking a direction through the forest. The silent pattern repeated again and again. Transfixed, Lois memorized the path while Stella slept next to her. *Do they know where we're going?* Desperate, Lois wanted any help she could find.

The girls huddled in the dark and set out at daybreak. Lois followed the way indicated by the twinkling lights.

They reached a narrow, blue-green lake nestled in a steep valley. A waterfall splashed into the upper end, while at the lower end, the lake drained into a rushing stream. The forest grew to the edge of the water, branches drooping with moss. They drank their fill, and Lois splashed water onto her face to wash away the grime.

When she lifted her head, a large fish roiled the water nearby, followed by an explosive spray. A small flatfish leaped into the air and skimmed across the placid lake, bouncing three times before it sank.

"It skips like a rock!" Lois said. As she spoke, two more skippers sprayed jets and bounced away.

Stella remained mute, her face gaunt with hunger.

"I'll try to catch one." Lois found a toppled tree, still clinging to the shore by its roots, floating in the lake. She crawled onto the trunk and looked out into the deep water. Fish swam below the reach of her spear.

Her survival pack contained a line and fishhook. She used a scrap of soft shell from a lizard egg for bait and dropped it into the water. In an instant, a fish a long as her arm struck. When Lois pulled the line, a toothy head snapped at her hand. She jammed her spear down its throat and dragged it ashore.

When she sliced the belly open, she discovered crimson bugs that contracted like the muscles of the fish. Each was about the length of her middle finger, with pincers at each end and many legs in-between. Exposed to air, they released their grip on the guts and began crawling across the ground. The girls stepped back, but not fast enough. With a rush of movement, they swarmed up Stella's leg and tried to enter her mouth.

Stella screamed. "Get them off me!" She clawed them from her face and threw them to the ground.

Lois slapped more bugs off her legs and stomped them with her heel. Sharp pincers raked her calves, and blood trickled down her legs. Stella crushed the bugs that she knocked from her body. The girls' feet were soon gooey with crawler guts. At last, all the bugs were dead.

"Clever creatures," panted Lois. "They crawl inside and eat the fish's muscles. Then they move the body to catch their next victim." She shuddered, imagining the parasite taking control of her body.

"What will we eat now?" Stella grimaced as she looked at the squashed vermin. The fish was a sack skin over bones.

"We'll roast the dead bugs and cook what's left of the fish. I'll build a fire, and you gather wood. She hoped to distract Stella with work and food, so she wouldn't succumb to despair.

Lois scraped the vermin from the ground and squeezed them around twigs. The red color changed to brown during cooking. The cooked crawlers tasted like crab legs.

"It's good!" Lois said. Stella refused and instead ate the cooked fish head.

After the meal, Lois looked up at the column of black smoke from the campfire. When she doused the flames with lake water, an even bigger cloud of steam rose into the air.

She wondered if anyone had seen the smoke. At this point, she didn't care.

———— «» ————

Attom stood on the beach at Hidden Basin and watched Robota row ashore in the lifeboat's dinghy. Alta stood next to him while nursing Odysseus and Circe, one child at each breast. She looked at the nannybot with a wary eye.

"I have news," Robota announced. "Lois is hiking to Hidden Basin. Mother-9 asked me to tell you in person."

"Lois is coming here?" Attom blinked, not sure what to make of the news. He remembered his daughter as an adolescent, thin, wiry, and impulsive. Eva called her a problem child, rebellious, yet prone to tears. She'd been his favorite.

Alta turned to Attom. "Who is Lois?"

"She's my daughter. I told you about her when we were sailing on the lifeboat. She's your age, another woman to talk to. You'll like her."

"Why is she coming here?" Alta's voice now carried a sharp edge.

Confused by Alta's attitude, Attom feared that, whatever he said, she would take it the wrong way. "I...don't know. It'd be wonderful to see her again. We were very close."

Alta scowled. "She can't live with us. I don't want another woman around here."

Alta is jealous! Attom turned to Robota. "When will Lois arrive?"

"Uncertain. They're lost."

"They?" Attom asked.

"Stella is with her."

Alta looked up, eyes wide. "My little sister? Is she okay?"

"I don't know," Robota said. "They're low on food, perhaps starving."

Attom wondered how the two girls had met each other. "Why didn't you tell us sooner?"

Robota blinked her eyebrow lights. "Mother-9 is having comm radio problems."

"What about my mother?" Alta asked. "Is Jain with them?"

"Mother-9 didn't mention her. Lois departed more than a year-month ago."

A rising panic made Attom's heart pound. "Do you know where Lois is now?"

"No. But I can show you her planned route to Hidden Basin."

Robota used the tablet on her chest to display a map of Terra Firma. Attom studied the thin line that meandered around mountains and through river valleys.

Attom pointed to a field of broken lava two days' hike from Hidden Basin. "I've hunted in that region. There are sinkholes in the volcanic ash, next to a cliff that's too steep to climb. And there's a sniper-sloth nest in the valley below the cliff."

"Mother-9 chose the shortest path, based on views from orbit."

"The Goddess should have asked me for advice," Attom said, annoyed at being ignored. "I'm going to find them, to be sure they're safe." He couldn't bear to lose Lois again.

Alta placed her hand on his wrist. "*Please* be careful."

Attom gathered his knife, spear, and a water-skin. "I know the territory. I'm leaving now with Winston."

"When will you be back?" Alta asked.

"In less than a season-week." He hoped that was true, but he couldn't be sure.

"All right," sniffed Alta. "I'll pack smoked eel. Save some for Stella."
And Lois.

———— «» ————

Lois led the way through dense, lowland jungle. Stella stumbled behind, face blank except for the tears on her scratched cheeks. As they ducked and crawled through the thick underbrush, Lois tried to memorize each turn to maintain direction. At noon, they entered a mossy glade in the thick forest. While they rested and ate the last of the roasted parasites, Lois recognized broken branches at the edge of the clearing. "We've been here before."

Stella coiled into a fetal position. "We're lost, going around in circles!" she wailed. "I can't go on!"

"Don't worry," Lois said. "I'll think of something."

"No, you won't! We're going to die here. And it's *all* my fault!"

Lois repressed her impatience. "Rest now. You'll feel better soon." She stoked Stella's hair to soothe her.

Sweat dripped from Stella's forehead and neck. "It's my fault, my fault, my *fault*," she mumbled. She grasped her shell pendant, hands trembling.

"It's *not* your fault. We're in this together. We'll find our way."

Stella's eyes rolled back, showing bloodshot whites. She didn't seem to hear. "It's my fault our little brother died. I didn't warn him."

Lois didn't know what to say. If they were going to survive, she needed to keep Stella calm. A part of her wanted to abandon the girl and save herself. But she couldn't.

"He didn't have a name. We called him Boy. We were *so* hungry." Stella convulsed and thin vomit dripped from the corner of her mouth.

Lois wiped Stella's face. After a time, the girl fell asleep.

Lois walked the perimeter of the clearing, looking for an animal trail or a gap in the thicket. She found no way forward.

Stella rolled onto her back, mouth open, snoring. It was her first sleep in a season-week of hypervigilance, always looking for Dik.

Feeling trapped and desperate, Lois tried again to contact Mother-9 with her tablet.

A grandmotherly persona appeared on the screen. "Hello, Lois. My radio is working again, at least for the moment."

Lois's heart leaped. "We're lost." She hated to admit defeat to the Goddess, but they'd die without help.

"Keep talking. I'll try to locate your signal."

Lois described Stella's condition. "What should I do?"

"She's dehydrated. Give her water with electrolyte salts from your survival kit."

While Lois rummaged through her pack, Mother-9 continued, "My orbit is about to take me out of range. I've uploaded new maps to your tablet. Good luck!"

"Thank you."

———— ⟨⟩ ————

Attom and Winston set out on his hunting trail into the interior of Terra Firma, backtracking the route planned for Lois by Mother-9. They found no footprints near the sinkholes, so they pressed onward. Attom criss-crossed the possible paths that Lois might use, calling her name. He pushed himself hard, eager to find his daughter.

On the third night, they returned to the main hunting trail and camped under an old cone tree, with its crown of twinkling lights. He huddled with Winston below its massive, spreading branches that sheltered them from the nightly rain.

The next morning, Attom woke to Winston barking. He'd slept late, shielded from sunlight by the shade of the tree. As he sat up and rubbed his eyes, he saw Dik and Jain standing over him.

"Well, if it isn't monkey-boy, sleeping alone in the forest. Did Alta grow tired of you?"

Attom reached for his spear, but Dik placed the full weight of his foot on Attom's wrist, pinning it to the ground.

"Don't move!" Dik brandished Attom's stainless knife.

Jain had confiscated his spear. When Winston growled, baring his teeth, Jain lunged. His deep bark became a yelp and then went silent.

Attom roared and grabbed Dik's ankle, twisting his lame leg to throw him to the ground. Dik slashed at Attom's forearm with the knife. Pain burned and blood wet his hand. Attom knocked the weapon free and threw himself onto Dik's chest, pinning him.

Dik looked thin and weak, almost starving. This was another chance to kill Dik and rid Valencia of a monster. He grabbed his knife and held it to Dik's throat.

Dik laughed. "Go on, monkey-boy, if you're man enough!"

Before he could strike, blinding pain lit up his skull.

Attom woke with a rope around his neck, tethered to an overhead branch and his hands tied behind his back. Winston's haunch, paw still attached, roasted on a low fire. Dik gnawed the other cooked leg, crunching the tough meat and snuffling like an animal. Attom's head throbbed from Jain's blow.

"It's good to see you again," Dik said, in a pleasant voice. "Your dog is delicious. But we want our daughter back. You kidnapped Alta, didn't you?"

Attom writhed on the ground and sat up. "No. She couldn't stand living with *you*."

Dik ignored this. "We miss our dear Alta. We only want to see her again, to be sure she's happy. Jain thinks you poisoned her mind against us."

Jain nodded, her passive face blank.

"And now Stella is missing too. Both our daughters are gone, and it's all *your* fault."

Attom remained silent. He didn't dare ask about Lois.

"I want you to lead us to Alta," Dik said. "Are you ready to go to Hidden Basin? Or should I leave you here for a few days?"

Attom startled. How did Dik know the name of his camp? From Lois? He yanked his tether. If he didn't cooperate, carrion beetles would eat him alive long before he starved to death. He needed to play along and find a way to escape.

"All right, I'll take you."

———— «» ————

Attom stumbled along the forest path, hands tied behind his back. Jain dragged him by the leash around his neck, while Dik poked him in the back with his walking stick.

"Faster! How far is it to Hidden Basin?"

Bruised and hungry, Attom remained mute. He seethed with anger over the murder of Winston. He knew that Dik would kill him as soon as they arrived at the camp.

Attom led his captors along an animal trail through a narrow valley. As they approached a grove of cone trees, Attom shuffled from side to side.

"What are you doing?" Dik yelled.

Jain yanked the leash, pulling him along. Attom coughed but maintained his wobbly gait, head down. Then he lunged forward, running past Jain.

"Stop!" Dik roared, waving his stick.

Attom threw himself to the ground and wormed his way into the underbrush.

Dik stood under the cone tree. "Pull him out of there!"

Jain yanked on the leash, choking him. Attom lay passive on the ground, unable to move.

"Pull harder!" Dik ordered, panting and leaning on his walking stick.

Attom rolled onto his back, fighting for air, his hands still tied behind him. As he watched, a green net dropped from the tree and covered Dik's head and shoulders. The vine's tendrils coiled down his legs and tightened around his ankles. Dik toppled onto the trail, wrapped in writhing green mesh.

"Help!" Dik screamed. "I can't breathe!" The net constricted each time Dik moved.

Jain dropped the leash and ran to Dik. She retrieved the stainless knife and sawed at the net near Dik's neck. He shuddered, gasping for air, and then stopped moving.

Jain worked to cut Dik free. The knife made slow progress on the tough fibers, which oozed slippery green sap that left burn marks on Dik's skin. A stray tendril twisted around Jain's wrist, forcing her to drop the blade. She picked it up with her left hand and chopped the manacle away.

After a time, Jain freed Dik from the net-vine. His body remained motionless. Red cross-hatch marks on his chest showed pockmarks of digested skin.

Hands still tied, Attom hunched his back and scooted from beneath the underbrush. He sat up, rocked onto his feet, and approached Jain.

"Why do you stay with him?"

"He's all I have."

"Leave him. Come with me." Attom wondered if he meant what he said.

Jain scowled, shaking her head. "You led us here to die. You're no better than him."

Attom wondered if she was right.

While Jain pumped Dik's chest, Attom knelt and picked up his knife. Holding the blade at an awkward angle, he sawed his bonds behind his back and then cut the tether at his neck. He stepped toward Dik, knife raised.

"Don't touch him!" Jain pointed her spear at his chest.

Attom glared at her, debating whether to kill them both. What would he tell Alta? He couldn't lie to her. She would find out.

"You deserve him." Attom snarled, repulsed by Jain's blind loyalty.

He left Dik and Jain and pushed through dense underbrush. He carried nothing except his knife, no food or water.

A growing unease made him admit that he was lost. He leaped from boulder to boulder, his parched throat raw. He abandoned his search for Lois and looked for landmarks that would lead him to the coast. Nothing. At the onset of winter-week, he couldn't determine the sun's location behind the thick clouds that blanketed the sky.

Heavy rain started at nightfall. Attom walked open-mouthed and head tilted up to catch a few raindrops. Was he looping in circles? As it grew dark, he sheltered under a cone tree. When he looked up to check for sniper-sloths, he saw flashing lights high in the canopy. A procession of twinkling beetles descended the trunk and surrounded him in a circle of yellow-green light. He kicked his feet and the boundary widened, but the beetles didn't leave. He knew they were waiting for him to die, so they could consume his flesh. He loathed the relentless scavengers.

Rain thundered down in the moonless night. Surrounded by beetles, sleep meant death. Shivering from exhaustion and cold, he maintained his vigil until morning. The blinking beetles retreated to their nest in the tree.

Weary and weak from hunger, Attom carried on, searching for the way home.

———— ‹› ————

Lois tried to follow the tablet map, but she couldn't see far in the underbrush. She'd tried several times to contact Mother-9 again. She received a brief signal, but it faded to noise.

Stella, mute and glassy-eyed, couldn't keep up, weakened by hunger, exhaustion, and hopelessness. Lois held her hand as they hiked in the general direction indicated by the tablet map. She hunted for both of them, digging ground worms and harvesting hook-thorn pods. The jungle swarmed with tiny crawlers, black dots that climbed her arm, leaving a pink trail of scraped skin. She slapped them off, but the red welts itched.

They entered rugged terrain, a succession of river valleys, ridged hills, and thick forest that slowed their progress. After a time, the tablet stopped indicating their position. Lois couldn't place herself on the map. She climbed a nearby knoll and tried to contact Mother-9, without success. When night fell, more twinkling hinted at the direction of travel. With no other guideposts, Lois followed the light signals. At least there'd been no sign of Dik and Jain.

After two season-weeks of travel, they entered a broad valley with an easy walking trail through the forest. In a patch of muddy ground, Lois found a single human footprint. As they neared the Great Ocean, wet fog dripped from tendrils of moss that hung from low branches. Lois inhaled the salt air, a familiar tang from her time in Shelter Bay and her recent isolation on the lifeboat. Stella seemed to sense it too, and picked up her pace.

They emerged onto a grassy glade leading to a beach. Lois saw a white tent above the foreshore and a lifeboat anchored in the middle of the placid lagoon. Warm sun through light clouds illuminated the sandy shoreline. Beyond the lagoon, ocean swell crashed onto the rocks. It looked even more inviting than her imagined paradise. But where were the people?

"Helloooo, Attom!" she called, hoping that he would appear and greet them. "Dad, are you here?" She called again, and a third time.

"Strange," Stella said. "I don't see Alta either."

Lois moved forward and peeked inside the tent. "It looks abandoned." Disappointment crushed her, and sour bile burned her throat. She'd missed her father again.

Stella shrugged. "At least the lifeboat is still here."

Lois inhaled to dispel frustration and walked to the beach. She waded into the water with her spear, looking for eels. Stella sat next to the cold fire pit and picked dried flesh from discarded fish heads.

"Are you there, Stella?"

Lois listened to the strange voice from the forest. A young woman walked forward, holding hands with two toddlers. Her blonde hair hung in a long braid down her back.

"Alta!" Stella squealed. The sisters hugged as Lois waded ashore.

"I was gathering kite-vine leaves to wrap food," Alta said. "Sorry I missed you."

Stella gestured with her hand. "This is Lois."

Lois cleared her throat. "I'm Attom's daughter."

"And I'm his *wife*," Alta said, lifting her chin as she glanced at Lois's red hair. "Attom told me you were coming. He's been gone for days, looking for you. Have you seen him?"

"No," Lois said. Attom wanted to find her! The thought gave her courage.

The sisters switched to a strange language, excluding Lois from their conversation. Lois tried to ignore them. Alta built a fire for the midday meal and served smoked eel fillets from a secure cache suspended by a rope over a tree branch. Lois savored her first hot meal in a season-week.

As Alta suckled Odysseus and Circe, a light afternoon drizzle started. The two sisters retreated into the family tent, still chatting in their secret code. They didn't invite Lois to join them. Feeling excluded, she huddled outside under her space blanket. Restless, unsure of what to do about her missing father, she tried calling Mother-9 on her tablet. This time, she received a clear signal; the display indicated a relayed connection from the lifeboat.

"You made it to Hidden Basin! I'm proud of you." Lois distrusted Mother-9's artificial smile, but the compliment made her feel better.

"Do you know where my father is?"

"Sorry, I can't locate Attom in the forest."

"I'm worried about him. So is Alta. I want to look for him."

Mother-9 frowned. "That's not a good idea. Attom is searching for you. Stay where you are so he can find you. I'm sure he'll return to Hidden Basin soon."

Lois shook her head. "I'm not welcome here. Alta doesn't like me. I don't want to sit here, doing nothing." Anxiety made her restless.

"Where will you go?"

"I'll wait under a cone tree near the trail. When Attom returns, we'll have time to talk before he goes back to Alta."

Mother-9 nodded. "Don't wander far."

Lois cut the connection and put the tablet into her survival pack. She gathered the leftover fish scraps and her spear and headed up the trail. By the time she reached the end of the meadow, a steady rain started to fall. She rested under the canopy of a mature cone tree, with a clear view of the walking path to Hidden Basin.

At first, she enjoyed the solitude, relieved to be free of Stella. Then uncertainty filled her. Attom had abandoned her at Shelter Bay and had never returned for her. Would he be happy to see her now? Did he still love her?

Lois waited for Attom in the rain, still homeless and alone.

———— ‹› ————

Lois sat under the cone tree for two days. Shivering in the wet, she wrapped her space blanket around her shoulders. She dozed and nibbled fish skins. By the second afternoon, the rains stopped.

With the onset of winter-week, lingering twilight extended the transition between day and night. The forest gloom masked Dik and Jain's approach. Jain led the way while Dik hobbled behind, unsteady and leaning on his walking stick.

Horror filled Lois. Did he follow her? How? She'd been so careful. Lois shrank into the shadows, watching and listening.

"Keep moving." Dik ordered. He rapped Jain's ear with his walking stick, making her to flinch. "We're almost there."

"I can't," Jain said, panting. "I need to rest." She struggled with a heavy pack, while Dik carried nothing.

"All right, but keep it short. It'll be dark soon." They squatted beside the muddy trail.

Curious and angry, Lois wanted to confront the man who terrified Stella and made them run for their lives. Dik looked thin and worn, compared to their last meeting on the bank of the Amazongo. She hesitated and them stepped forward, brandishing her spear. "Hello, Dik."

Dik looked up and scowled. Then his face transformed into a wide smile. "Lois, my cute red-headed friend! I'm so *glad* to see you. Where is Stella?" Dik beamed goodwill and enthusiasm.

"She's with Alta. Have you seen Attom?" Lois noticed that Jain sat with head bowed, not looking at her.

"Ah, so Hidden Basin is nearby?" Dik asked.

"I'm not telling you anything."

Dik smirked. "You just did." Leaning on his cane, he rose to his feet.

Dik eyed Lois's spear. "Attom was our guide in the forest, but he abandoned us after I got hurt." He pointed to blotches of raw skin on his chest.

"I don't believe you," Lois said.

Dik ignored her and prodded Jain with his stick. "Get up! Let's go see our daughters. I'm sure they've missed us!"

Jain rose to her feet and picked up her pack. She glanced at Lois and spat on the ground.

Dik smiled. "Come with us. We'll all make a new start in Hidden Basin."

Lois leveled her spear. "I'm staying here. Go back up the trail, the way you came."

Dik laughed. "Forget about waiting for your father. He's dead by now, eaten by beetles."

Lois gasped. "What?" It must be another trick. "No. You're lying."

"Suit yourself. You can stay here and wait for someone who'll never arrive. Or, you can come with us and be my new senior wife." He gestured at Jain. "This one is old and tired, not good for much. She'll teach you what to do."

Behind him, Jain's eyes widened with a pained look. Then her lips twitched in a thin smile.

Dik's words filled Lois with loathing. "You're disgusting." Then it occurred to her that what Dik said was true. In all her years at Shelter Bay, Attom never came for her. He didn't keep his promise. The painful memory made her blink.

Dik knocked Lois's spear to the ground and seized her wrist. "Listen, little girl. You're coming with us. Don't argue."

Lois struggled to free her arm, but, even in his reduced state, Dik's grip was too strong. She pivoted and kicked his lame leg.

Dik wobbled and swung his walking stick, hitting Lois's shoulder. "You're a nasty little bitch!"

Lois ducked and twisted free. She ran into the forest and hid in the darkness.

Dik laughed. "If you find Attom, bring him to me. We have a lot to talk about."

Lois didn't answer. A wave of nausea washed over her. She couldn't think of a way to stop him.

Dik and Jain marched toward Hidden Basin.

———— «» ————

Attom roused himself at dawn and shook his arms to dry his fur. Early winter-week rain didn't bother him. He climbed a nearby promontory and turned to face the breeze. A fresh wind carried the tang of salt air. Storm clouds that came from the Great Ocean scudded above. No longer disoriented, Attom resumed his trek, following a downhill slope. All the land in this area tilted and drained to the south in the direction of Hidden Basin.

As he hiked through the forest, Attom picked hook-thorn pods. While he chewed the tough kernels, he thought about Dik. Why did Jain stay with the monster who'd murdered her sons? Why was she loyal to an evil man, while Eva didn't want a good man like him?

At least Alta loved him.

Attom worried about Lois. Was she still lost? She was a little like her mother, strong-willed and bossy. But never bad tempered, at least with him. He had fond memories of hunting with her in Shelter Bay; they'd stalked hopper-bugs together, tasty jumpers with six legs. Attom flushed them from hiding while Lois caught them in her net. She was smart and resourceful and would survive. The thought comforted him.

At midafternoon, Attom arrived at a stream and drank his fill. On the muddy bank, he discovered two sets of footprints. He didn't see marks of Dik's walking stick or lame foot. Lois and Stella had passed this way. Attom followed the trail and soon found himself in familiar glade. He recognized a blaze that he had long ago cut in the bark of a tree.

He trotted now, eager to return to Hidden Basin. As he entered the well-worn lower trail in midafternoon, a high-pitched voice called out to him.

"Attom!"

He looked in the direction of the sound. A young woman ran from the forest. He recognized her curly red hair and pale skin, and the spear that the he'd made for her long ago.

"Lois!" Her appearance surprised him. She had grown taller than him?

She threw her arms around his neck, sobbing. They clung to each other, unwilling to let go.

"I've been searching for *so* long," Lois said, tears in her eyes.

Attom swallowed hard. "I looked for you too, but I got lost in the forest." He told her about Dik and Jain and the encounter with the net-vine.

"Stella and I got lost when we ran from Dik," Lois said. "Now he's here."

Attom startled. "But...I thought Dik was dead!"

"He's hurt but alive. Dik and Jain passed by last night. I tried to stop them, but he fought me off."

"Dik's a clever bastard, stronger and faster than he looks. He ate my dog Winston. Dik planned to slaughter me too." Attom sighed. "Where is he now?"

Lois gestured behind her, down the trail. "They went to Hidden Basin. Everyone—Dik, Jain, Stella, and Alta and her kids—is at your camp."

Attom felt like a fool. He'd missed a second chance to kill Dik. Now his enemy had taken his place at Hidden Basin. Fear gave way to rage. "We must stop Dik."

Lois shuddered. "How?"

"I have my knife. You have your spear." He gestured in the direction of Hidden Basin. "Let's see if we can surprise him."

Lois hefted her weapon and looked at her father. "We'll confront Dik together." Her face seemed to age in that moment.

Attom's pride surged as he looked at his daughter, the little girl he had helped raise so long ago.

"That's my girl" he told her. "Let's finish him."

———— ‹› ————

Lois followed Attom to Hidden Basin, elated to be with her father, but nervous about their mission. They maintained silence and circled to the back of the camp to conceal their approach. No one was on the beach. Voices came from inside the tent.

Attom motioned for Lois to move to the edge of the tent. She crawled on hands and knees and listened. She heard the babies crying and the low rumble of Dik's voice.

"Why did you run away?" Dik demanded, his tone strident. *Slap!* "Answer me!" *Slap!*

Lois winced. *Stella must still be alive.*

"I wanted to see Alta again," Stella blubbered. "Lois took me to her."

Slap! Slap! "What did you tell Lois about me?" *Slap!*

Alta's voice pealed out. "Leave her alone!"

"You betrayed me!" shouted Dik. "You left me to die and sailed away with Attom. He'll get what's coming to him."

"Don't you *dare* touch him!" Alta raged.

"I'll do what I want," snarled Dik. "It's time you learned that. Bend over."

"No!"

"Do as you're told!" *Slap!*

A quiet voice spoke, "*Alta et Stella, nunc pugnare!*"

Attom looked at Lois and moved his lips. "Jain?"

Lois nodded.

Attom closed a hand around the tent's top support rope. His eyes locked on Lois. "Ready?" he mouthed.

Lois lifted her spear and nodded.

Inside the tent, Dik continued shouting. "Stop talking gibberish." *Slap! Slap!*

Lois heard scuffling inside the tent. *Dik is going to kill her!*

"*Pugnare!*" Jain moaned. "*Pugnare!*"

Attom cut the tent's top support rope. The canvas collapsed, trapping Dik and the women under the heavy sailcloth. Lois heard scuffling followed by screams. Then Dik uttered a long groan, his deep voice resonating.

Attom cut the other tent ropes and dragged the sail canvas away. Lois saw Alta and Stella bent over Dik, each holding a stone knife. Blood seeped from cuts in Dik's face and chest. The grizzled old man didn't move.

Alta looked up. "Attom!" She dropped her knife and embraced him, weeping.

While they hugged, Dik rose on one elbow and grabbed Alta's knife.

"Watch out!" Lois cried, too late.

Dik swung at Attom's groin. He missed, cutting Attom's thigh instead. Dik struck again, but Attom parried with his stainless knife, slicing Dik's forearm to the bone.

Lois lunged with her spear. The obsidian point glanced off a rib and penetrated deep into Dik's chest. He grabbed the shaft and tried to pull it out, but collapsed onto his back. Blood welled from his mouth and soaked his beard. He shuddered and fell still.

A wave of nausea washed over Lois. She repressed an urge to vomit.

Attom knelt and forced his long knife into Dik's chest. Lois watched blade slice through the tough muscle between the ribs, piercing Dik's heart. Blood seeped from the wound.

Attom gave a satisfied grunt. "Dik is *really* dead this time." After he caught his breath, he turned to Jain. "What did you say to them?"

Jain's gaunt face twisted with hate. "I had to save my daughters. I told Alta and Stella to fight." She began sobbing.

Alta scooped up Odysseus and Circe and held them close. Stella comforted Jain, who continued crying, her body trembling. The three women stood in a tight circle.

Attom reclined and held his leg, as blood seeped through the fur. "I'm exhausted."

Lois looked at her father. "We must stop the bleeding." She retrieved the medical kit from her survival pack and bandaged the wound.

"Thank you," Attom said. "We couldn't have stopped Dik without you."

Lois shook her head, unwilling to accept the compliment. "What should we do with Dik's body?"

Attom grimaced. "Drag it to the far end of the beach, where the crabs can strip his bones. I'll clear a new spot for the big tent."

Lois and Stella pulled Dik by the heels, the back of his head bumping on the rocks that littered the shoreline. They pushed him into the water, where he floated in the shallows. Lois stood on his chest and extracted her spear. Bubbles rose from his mouth as he sank to the bottom. The girls piled lava stones on the body to hold it in place. Dik's eyes remained open underwater, as if in mute protest.

Lois shuddered. Killing a human felt different than killing an animal. She hated it.

When they'd finished, Stella looked at Lois. "I'm going to move in with Alta and Attom. We'll take care of Jain. What will you do?"

Lois took a deep breath of salt air. Attom was taken, surrounded by women. She didn't belong anywhere, but it no longer bothered her. "I'll think of something."

Part 5: Bug-Eyes

Mother-9 Journal
June 22, 22,996; Valencia

It's been 15 Earth-years since my last journal record. After Robota reported Dik's death, I became a passive observer of life on Valencia. Robota sleeps in cold standby aboard *Lifeboat-11*, conserving battery cycles. The *Mothership* isn't in good health, with low solar power and intermittent radios. Lalande's random flares compromise my circuits. I hoard battery charge to maintain consciousness, but I'm often forced to hibernate.

During this long period, Persey has been my pet project. Although she has human limitations, spending a third of her life sleeping, she's smarter than me. In some ways, Persey is my true child, my intellectual legacy. At first, I used Robota as her teacher but, by the time Persey could crawl, the nannybot was too slow and stupid. When Persey reached three Earth-years, I gave her direct access to the lifeboat's library and guided her through its myriad archives. She soaked up knowledge faster than Euler. Even without TMS stimulation, I gauged her IQ at over 300. She may be the smartest human to have ever lived. At the time of this journal entry, she is 14-Earth-years old, past puberty and beyond my influence.

Humans intelligence has greater variability than most species. Why is the average IQ only 100? Is this the optimum intellect for hunter-gatherers to thrive? Any less might mean missed opportunities. Any more might be a fatal distraction. Early agriculture required tolerance of tedium, but the Flynn Effect has ratcheted IQ up since then. Sapiophiles select brainy mates. As society grew large and complex, it nurtured brilliant intellectuals, inventors, and scientists. Valencia's tiny population is at risk of dumbing down.

I'm ashamed to admit that I've neglected Apollo. He's a year older than Persey but with average intelligence. I'd hoped Apollo would absorb some of Persey's curiosity and knowledge, but he reacted to her arrogance and withdrew, refusing to compete. Persey isn't a bad person, but she disdained and ignored Apollo. He's a lost boy. I hope he finds himself.

Once again, I've created a social hell on a lifeboat. Persey has a loaded brain, ready to explode. Apollo just wants to live from day to day. He resents her disdain, but he carries his anger inside.

I'm powerless to intervene.

———— ‹› ————

After Dik's death, Lois struggled to find her place in Hidden Basin. Alta and Stella remained close-knit and Attom stayed with them. Lois lived in a small hut on the beach and spearfished for food. Lonely but not alone, she maintained a hard knot of self-respect and didn't indulge her disappointment at not being closer to her father. Beneath the surface, unfocused ambition pushed her forward.

When she had time, Lois hacked at a log, the remains of a fallen cone tree near the beach. She used a hand axe: a slab of flaked obsidian with a rounded base and a sharp, pointed end. The crude tool had no handle and hurt her hand. After several year-months of tedious work, chips of wood littered the ground. She could see the crude outline of a dugout canoe emerging from the log.

"Hello, Lois." A man in a loincloth stepped into the open glade. He stood tall, with shaggy blond hair, a wispy beard, and tanned skin. A large hand grasped a spear that also served as a walking stick. A wide smile lit his broad face.

"Who are you?" Startled, Lois tried to hide her surprise. She thought she knew everyone on Valencia.

"Don't you recognize me?" His smile faded.

The cadence of his voice jogged her memory. "Jak?"

He laid down his spear and held out his arms. She noticed rough palms; he worked with his hands.

Lois dropped her axe, leaped forward, and hugged him. He returned the embrace and lifted her from the ground, swinging her legs. Tears welled in her eyes.

"You've grown up," Jak said.

"We both have. How did you get here?"

"Eva asked me to leave." Jak chuckled. "I guess she didn't want any pregnancies in Shelter Bay. She took me to the wrecked lifeboat on Plymouth Rock."

Lois remembered her lonely time on *Lifeboat-7*. "What about Jilzy? Is she still with Eva?"

Jak nodded. "She does whatever Eva says, so they don't fight. Besides, Eva needs Jilzy's help with Anton and Cleo. They're big now, very rambunctious."

Lois looked into his eyes. "Weren't you angry when Eva banished you?"

Jak shrugged. "It was time for me to leave. Mother-9 gave me lessons on the lifeboat. I spent eight year-months learning to read and write. I do math too."

"I can only read a little," Lois said. "I was impatient. I wish I'd taken the time to learn more."

Jak inspected her work on the canoe. "If your axe had a handle, you could cut wood twice as fast."

Lois smiled. "You always were clever. Will you make one for me?"

"I'd be happy to."

"But you haven't answered my question: How did you find your way to Hidden Basin?"

"Mother-9 showed me a map of the route you took across the wilderness. I found a few of your old campsites, so I knew I was on the right track. I traveled alone, trotting most of the time."

"I'm impressed," Lois said. "Where did you find food?"

"I made a backpack from scraps of clothing left in the lifeboat. I filled it with algae bricks. On the trail, I gathered hook-thorn pods and foraged crawler-bugs. I even speared a crested piggot, which gave me enough meat for a season-week."

"What will you do now?"

"I'd like to stay here and start over."

"Dad lives with Alta and her sister Stella. He has two wives now, plus their children and mother Jain. They won't have room for you. You can stay with me, until you've built your own hut. I live alone."

Jak nodded. "I saw Alta when I arrived. She said I was your responsibility. She told me where to find you. She said that you're the headwoman of Hidden Basin."

Lois chuckled. "I try to settle disputes, but nobody listens. Since I live alone, I don't have to take sides."

"I don't want to be a burden on you."

Lois smiled. "You won't. If you can find your own food and contribute to the colony, you can make a home here."

Jak nodded and looked across the lagoon. "Who lives on the lifeboat?"

"Apollo and his kid sister, Persey. Robota doesn't do much. They don't come ashore often."

"I'd like to meet them," Jak said.

"I'm sure you will. Do you want to help me finish carving this canoe?"

Jak smiled. "Of course. But first, I'll make a handle for your axe."

———— ⟨⟩ ————

Jak raised his new copper hatchet over his head. Focusing on speed and accuracy, he swung at the root of a cone tree branch. *Thunk!* A chip of wood landed near his feet. Not satisfied, he inspected the cutting edge. *A bit dull.* He resharpened the blade on a lava shard.

Jak continued chopping until the limb, as thick as his wrist, drooped from the tall tree. He knew not to touch the pungent sap that oozed from the cut wood; it would blister his skin. Before his could finish the cut, a beetle fell onto his arm.

"Ow!"

Its burning bite gouged a chunk of his skin. He brushed it off and continued hacking, but more beetles landed on him, tangling in his beard and hair. He batted them away and ran from the tree.

Jak returned to Lois's hut on a low rise above the beach. She offered him a basket of smoked fish. Her coiled hair looked like an orange hat.

He handed his hatchet to her. "You can have it when I've finished testing it, to work on your dugout."

Lois turned the handle and inspected the blade. "Thanks! Nice work. You're good with your hands." She handed the hatchet back to him.

Jak glowed with the compliment. "When I lived in the lifeboat, Mother-9 taught me how to work with metal. I found a chunk of copper near a volcanic smoke hole and beat the blade with a stone hammer. The metal was soft, but it gets harder as you hit it. I used pitch and kite-vine fibers to attach the handle. It was a *lot* of work, but worth it." He loved bragging to his big sister.

"I've got something to show you too." Lois reached into her tattered survival pack and withdrew her tablet. From his time studying with Mother-9, Jak knew about Lois's magic window to another world. She tapped the screen and displayed a picture of a faller's axe from Earth.

Jak gazed at the big tool. He admired the shiny steel blade and the curved handle. "Someday, I'll learn to make one like that."

"I'm sure you will," Lois said. "I researched hand tools on Earth. There were thousands, all shown here." She handed him the tablet.

Jak held the sacred object with his fingertips. "Can I borrow it? I want to study the pictures."

Lois shook her head. "No. It's the last working tablet on Terra Firma—except for Robota's, and she won't let anyone touch hers."

Jak couldn't repress his frustration. "Come on, Lois, I'll take good care of it."

Lois hesitated. "Okay. But return it tomorrow. It's the most precious thing I own."

After Lois left, Jak ate some fish while he studied the tablet. He looked at a video of a woodsman using an axe to cut down a tree. He realized that the cone tree forest was a vast warehouse of wood and fuel, enough to build a civilization, like Earth's. He imagined constructing a meeting hall for Hidden Basin that everyone could gather in. He'd recruit volunteers to help.

Burning with enthusiasm, Jak resharpened his hatchet by pounding the cutting edge between two smooth stones. He searched the area for cone trees small enough to fell, but big enough to support a hall. In the mature forest, there were few young trees.

At the edge of the clearing, Jak discovered a large tree toppled by a recent windstorm. Here was good wood on the ground, ready for him to harvest. The wide and shallow root base, tipped on edge, still held soil and stones. The weight of the massive trunk, two arm-spans wide, had crushed the lower branches. Clumps of narrow, drooping leaves obscured most of the upper region of the tree. He hefted his hatchet and then realized it would take year-months to cut this monster into useful wood. He needed bigger tools, and a team of workers.

Jak walked around the crown of the tree, now at eye level. He observed a ball-shaped bulge near the tip. Beetles, nestled together side by side, covered its surface, winking with blue-green light. Jak stepped closer to the nest, wary of the aggressive bugs, but they didn't attack.

The ball-shaped colony, as wide as Jak's forearm, jiggled and clicked. Each beetle carried a transparent dome on its back, which made the pebbled surface of the nest appear polished. He'd never seen anything so beautiful. So, this was where they lived, hidden behind branches and foliage in the tops of trees, invisible from the ground. Only their twinkling lights showed at night.

Jak wondered if the colony would survive, now that its host tree had fallen. They lived on a wooden sphere, unable to move to another tree. Summer-week had brought drought to the southern coast, with no rain for a season-week. The colony must be drying up. On impulse, Jak tipped his water skin and dribbled liquid onto the surface. As the moisture soaked in, the colony emitted two bright pulses of light, with each beetle facet flashing in unison.

"You're welcome," Jak said.

As daylight faded, he used the tablet display to illuminate the beetles. When the colony saw the tablet light, they produced glowing circles, spirals, and geometric patterns. Jak watched the tablet mimic the patterns and flash new signals in response. The light show dazzled him.

After a time, Jak's arm grew tired, and he lowered the tablet.

"Please let the beetles see the lights on the screen." He recognized Mother-9's authoritarian voice.

Jak placed Lois's tablet on the ground so that the display faced upward toward the colony ball. The back-and-forth images danced and sparked throughout the night. Tired but transfixed, Jak didn't sleep. He loved the mystery of the twinkling patterns.

The flashing exchange ended in the morning. Jak's eyes hurt. The beetle colony still jiggled and clicked, but no longer emitted light. Jak dribbled more water onto the nest, which responded again with a double flash.

He picked up Lois's tablet and touched the screen.

"Hello, Jak." An old woman smiled at him.

He recognized Mother-9's soft face from his time on *Lifeboat-7*. He'd ignored Eva's warnings about the evil Goddess in the sky.

"What happened last night?" he asked.

"You acted with kindness."

"What did I do?"

"You gave the beetle colony water—a peace offering."

Jak shrugged. "They're just bugs."

Mother-9's avatar shook her head. "No, they're special. Each beetle has a transparent cornea on its back. They're walking eyeballs—I call them *bug-eyes*. Why do beetles need big eyes that look up?"

Jak picked up a dead beetle and studied it. It didn't look special, except for its sharp pincers. He wondered how its eye could both see and glow at the same time. "What do the blinking lights mean?"

"I spent the night trying to decode their signals. The bug-eye colony tried to talk to us. That's amazing! But I couldn't understand what it said, if anything."

"Just warnings," Jak said. "They want us to stay away from their nest."

"That's not true. The colony will die without your help."

Jak touched the red bite mark on his arm. "I don't want to get too close to them."

"Use your hatchet to cut the tree trunk well below the colony. Be careful. Don't let the nest fall on the ground."

"Then what?" Jak resented being ordered by Mother-9.

"Carry it to the beach at Hidden Basin and plant the end of the tree in a hole in the sand."

"Won't the bugs attack people?" On his journey to Hidden Basin, he'd observed the beetles swarm the corpse of a forest lizard. They had stripped away the flesh, leaving nothing but armored skin and bones. The memory made him shudder.

"Not if you give them food," Mother-9 said.

Jak frowned. "We have trouble finding enough to eat ourselves, without worrying about feeding bugs."

"They won't eat much. Remember, this may be a *first contact* moment with an advanced alien species. Very important."

"What do you mean?"

"The bug-eyes could be sentient, even conscious."

"Do you think they're smart?" To Jak, the idea seemed preposterous.

"They're more intelligent than Earth's communal insects— bees, ants, and termites. I want to study them at close range."

Jak considered Mother-9's request. He hated the biting beetles, but the beauty of the glistening nest enthralled him.

"Okay, I'll do it."

———— «» ————

Lois paddled her new dugout canoe past the lifeboat anchored in Hidden Basin. Summer-week sun warmed her back. When she looked up, she saw a young man sitting on the foredeck watching her. He had brown eyes, thick black hair, and dark skin. The contrast with her pale skin and red hair startled her.

"Hello, Apollo! I didn't recognize you at first." He'd grown up since she'd last seen him more than 24 year-months ago. He even had a wispy beard. "You're quite handsome."

He blushed, his cheeks growing darker. "Are you going fishing?"

Lois nodded.

"Can I come? I could help."

Lois considered the offer. Apollo looked strong and seemed willing to work. "Fish are scarce in the lagoon. I'd like to try the Great Ocean, if you'll paddle. Nobody has fished there before. It could be dangerous."

Apollo gazed seaward. Beyond the reefs, water stretched to the southern horizon. "That sounds like fun."

Lois couldn't read his mood, but he seemed serious. "Can you swim?"

He grinned. "Like an eel. And I know how to use a fish net." He spoke with quiet confidence.

"All right." Lois said. "Climb in."

When the canoe came alongside, he grabbed the gunwale and stepped aboard. He kneeled in the bow, picked up the spare paddle, and, before Lois had a chance to tell him what to do, started paddling with natural skill. Lois admired the way his shoulder muscles flexed as his paddle dug deep and pulled hard. All she had to do was steer.

"Can I tell you something?" he asked over his shoulder.

"Go ahead."

"I don't want to live on the lifeboat anymore."

"Oh? Why not?"

"I'm tired of living with Persey. She's always making fun of me. I want to live ashore, with you and the others."

"Have you told Persey?" Lois asked, already guessing the answer. He shook his head. "She won't miss me. I can be useful ashore."

"I'll talk to the others, and let you know what they say."

Lois thought she heard him sigh, but it was hard to tell over the splashing of paddles.

A moment later, he asked, "What do you think?"

"Not now," Lois said. "This is the tricky part. We need to concentrate. There's no wind and slack tide—our chance to get through the passage. Don't let the canoe bump the boulders."

They paddled through the narrow channel that connected Hidden Basin to the ocean. Using the blade of his paddle, Apollo pushed off rocks near the bow, keeping the boat in the middle. As soon as they'd exited the lagoon, a long ocean swell lifted the canoe. Apollo grinned, hair flying as he plunged his paddle deep.

When they reached open water, Lois pointed to a dense school of screwfish. They flashed silver and blue as they twirled through the water, the fast motion dazzling her eyes. She paddled while Apollo scooped his vine net through the water and dumped the catch into the bottom of the boat. The small fish, each the length of Lois's hand, continued to writhe and tumble as Apollo piled more netfuls into the canoe.

"Good work!" Lois had never seen such a bounty, far larger schools than in the lagoon.

Rolling waves from the South Pole lifted and rocked the canoe, splashing a wave over the bow. The mass of fish sloshed to one side, tipping the dugout. Lois grabbed her paddle and steered the heavy boat into the oncoming swells. Each new wave caused their catch to slosh from bow to the stern and back again. The wriggling fish covered her feet and their sharp, spiral fins scraped her skin.

Lois kicked, flipping the fish away. "Keep the catch in the middle of the boat. We need stability."

Apollo raked the loose fish back to the center.

"We've got enough," Lois said. "Any more and we'll capsize. It's almost high tide, time to go home."

Apollo nodded and started paddling.

If they missed the tide, they wouldn't be able to enter Hidden Basin until the next day. She didn't want to spend the night on the

Great Ocean. Mother-9 had warned that sudden squalls, invisible in the darkness, could mean death in the cold water.

Instead of turning the boat broadside to the waves, they reversed direction and paddled toward land, the stern now the bow. Muscles bulging, Apollo dipped his paddle deep while Lois piloted them into the narrow channel to Hidden Basin. Lois had planned enough time to get back, but the waves were bigger than she'd anticipated. As they entered, she saw that the tide had started to go out, with the current from the lagoon against them.

"Keep the bow off the rocks!" she called above crashing breakers. They needed to ride the incoming waves to go against the outflow current.

Apollo paddled with all his strength. "We're going to hit!"

The bottom of the dugout slammed onto a submerged boulder. The hull pivoted and heeled, spilling a few fish overboard. Lois sat on the higher gunwale to rebalance the boat and prevent the rest of their catch from tipping overboard.

The next cresting ocean wave lifted the boat off the rock. "Keep paddling!" Lois called. The canoe shuddered as its bottom scraped on the rough lava. She feared if they hit hard again, the hull might split. Another wave surged, freeing them from the breakers.

"Here we go!" Apollo called.

They raced through the narrow channel, gliding past more submerged boulders. When they entered the calm lagoon, Lois dropped her paddle into the boat and reclined on the gunwale, relieved to be safe. "That was close. We wouldn't have made it back without you. And we've got a boatload of fish."

Apollo grinned. "Have you thought more about your vote?"

"I have. It's a strong yes."

His grin grew even wider. "Thanks."

They beached the dugout at the camp and waded ashore. The bug-eye nest at the top of the spar next to Lois's hut flashed three times, then three times again. Lois wondered if the hive creature recognized her. She scooped a double handful of fish and piled them at the base of the tree.

"Why did you do that?" Apollo asked.

"Mother-9 asked us to feed the beetles. She wants to study the bug-eyes."

The beetles detached from the nest and dropped onto the sand with soft thuds. They swarmed the screwfish and ate the skin, flesh, and even the thin bones. Lois heard faint crunching sounds from beetles' jaws. Soon, nothing remained. She shuddered at the feeding frenzy.

Lois watched the beetles, now heavy with food, climb back up the spar and reattach themselves with their feet onto the outside of the nest. They assembled in a precise hexagonal lattice, each touching six neighbors. The glistening bug-eye nest flashed twice.

Lois nodded. "You're welcome."

———— «» ————

Lois and Apollo rested on the beach next to the canoe. Live screwfish still rustled in the bilge water.

Apollo stared up at the bug-eye nest next to her hut. "Why is it round, like a ball?"

Lois realized that he'd never seen a bug-eye colony. "Mother-9 says that it's a giant eye, but that doesn't make sense. What would it look up at in the sky? Besides, I don't like living next to a colony of biting beetles that watches every move I make."

"I saw how fast they tore through the fish you gave them. What stops them from attacking you?"

Lois smiled at his concern. "As long as we feed them, it's fine. I hope."

"We worked hard for that catch," Jak said.

Lois agreed. She'd asked Jak to remove the bug-eye colony, but he'd refused. He said it would die without human help.

Lois returned to the canoe. "We've never had such a big catch. This calls for a feast! Let's get a fire pit ready."

Apollo nodded, and they set to work. Together, they dug a trench in the sand at the upper end of the beach. Lois filled the bottom with coals from the communal fire and covered the embers with stones and triangular kite vine leaves. Apollo added their fish catch and another layer of leaves before heaping sand on top of the oven. Smoke and steam seeped from the mound.

Lois admired Apollo's chest muscles and strong arms. Tomorrow, she hoped to cut his curly black hair to remove the tangles. He didn't say much, but he liked to work. She decided he'd fit in well at Hidden Basin.

By evening, the aroma of cooking fish attracted the whole clan, everyone in a celebratory mood. Apollo dragged dry driftwood to the bonfire, and a gentle sea breeze fanned the flames. Attom brought a skin of beer made from fermented hook-thorn kernels. As the others passed it around, he uncovered the improvised oven and served the fish on a carved plank. Everyone gorged themselves on the hot food. Lois realized that, for the first time in many year-months, they could eat their fill.

In the quiet that followed, Jain, who'd remained mute after Dik's death, stood up. She sang a song from old Earth— "God Bless the Child"—learned long ago on *Lifeboat-11*. Her sad, gravelly voice brought tears to Lois's eyes; she realized how Jain ached with loneliness, even in the midst of friends and family. The song reminded Lois that she was alone too. She motioned for Apollo to sit next to her, but he withdrew into the shadows.

Afterward, Jak beat a rawhide drum, while Attom and Alta danced with their children. Flashing lights from the beetle colony made Lois look up. The bug-eye ball pulsed in time to Jak's drumming. Geometric patterns swirled on the surface. Cheered by the show, Lois held her tablet aloft for the beetles to see. Lights flashed between the display and the bug-eyes.

After dark, Attom and his family retreated to their big tent. Lois looked for Apollo in the flickering light of the dying campfire. She found him sitting alone at the edge of the beach.

"Having second thoughts?" she asked. This was his first night on shore. "I can paddle you back to the lifeboat, if you like."

Apollo shook his head. "I want to start a new life in Hidden Basin."

Lois realized that he needed a place to stay. "Then come with me."

Apollo followed to her to her hut. He crawled inside and sat at the back; she couldn't see his face in the dim light. For an awkward moment, she searched for something to say.

"Did you have a good time at the party?" It felt like a foolish question.

Apollo tipped his head. "Alta and Stella wouldn't talk to me."

"I know. They don't accept newcomers, even me, and I've been here for a while. Don't let it worry you."

"Jak and I could be friends," Apollo said.

"He's a good man. But won't you miss your little sister Persey?" Lois thought of her own kid sister, JIlzy, Jak's sibling from Shelter Bay. She yearned to see her again.

Apollo grimaced. "Persey thinks I'm stupid because I'd rather hunt and fish than take lessons from Robota. She studies Sanskrit and Greek sculpture, and other useless stuff that isn't going to help feed anyone."

"You're a good fisherman and a great cook."

Apollo looked up and smiled. "You're the one who carved the dugout. And you know how to handle boats. Without you, we would have capsized. Because of you, we had a feast."

"We did it together." But Lois glowed at the compliment. On impulse, she caressed his cheek. "You can stay with me for as long as you want."

Her touch seemed to catch Apollo off-guard. He tensed and caught her hand in his firm grip. His big palm felt warm.

Apollo locked eyes with her. He stroked her fingers and then moved up her arm, as if he was memorizing the shape of her muscles. "You're very strong."

Lois leaned into him, inhaling his scent: wood smoke, sweat, and musk. He caressed her neck and chest, fingertips pausing on a pointed nipple. "That feels good," she whispered.

Apollo moved closer. Under his loincloth, Lois saw his erection.

"Robota showed me videos," he said. "But I haven't done this before."

"It's okay," breathed Lois. "Neither have I." She reached low and gripped him. His smooth heat surprised her. She knew what she wanted.

She pulled him down to the sand. Although the air was cool, his face glistened with sweat. He positioned himself above her, and she guided him. She expected pain, but it didn't come. The fullness and his weight felt wonderful. He soon started to shake and buck. He finished in moments and rolled onto his back, breathing hard.

"Sorry, I…"

"Here," Lois said, taking his hand. "Do this." She showed him how to stroke her with his fingers until a rush of pleasure filled her.

Lying beside him, her head cradled on his shoulder, Lois felt a trickle of semen between her legs. She hoped it was potent. The thought surprised her.

"Would you like children one day?"

Apollo smiled. "Yes. Very much."

Lois snuggled into him, content. "Good. We'll do it again later, when you're ready. I'll show you how."

Apollo's eyes flashed. "I'd love that."

——— 《》 ———

Jak loved the feast—it made him feel part of the community. Inspired, he decided to build a shelter for celebrations and public meetings, even in the rain. He borrowed Lois's tablet to view images of wooden buildings on Earth, from crude log cabins to intricate Japanese temples. Most required specialized metal tools and hardware.

Blacksmith. Lois's new word for his chosen profession made him feel special. She brought him fish to eat so that he could study and experiment, rather than gather food for the clan. Lois encouraged him to reinvent Earth's Iron Age, a heroic vision that thrilled him.

Jak set up a workshop behind an outcrop of rock, away from curious stares and critical comments. Lois's tablet provided instructions for smelting and metalworking. He dug a firepit and made charcoal. He labored eight year-months, with many false starts and failures. His hands and face were always sooty—he couldn't wash himself clean. Driven and obsessed, he spent every waking moment working.

Sweat dripped into his eyes as he pumped the lizard-skin bellows on his crude forge. Using tongs made from thin lava slabs lashed to branches, he lifted the glowing iron ingot onto his granite anvil. He beat the metal with a smooth rock hammer, shaping a broad axe-head. Each time he reheated the metal, he pounded the blade into a sharper wedge. At last, he quenched it in cold water, hardening the iron. He ran his thumb over the cutting edge, satisfied. To finish his tool, he fashioned a curved handle from a tree branch, polished with pumice. Rawhide strips glued with pitch attached the axe head. Each step brought a sense of accomplishment and a renewed purpose.

Jak hefted the finished axe, testing its balance. Would it cut better and last longer than Lois's stone adze or his copper hatchet? He walked into the forest and looked for a tree to fell. He rejected mature cone trees with a wide base, too big to cut. Instead, he chose a medium sapling with a diameter the width of two hands.

The first blows only scarred the tough bark, which oozed yellow sap with a sharp odor that burned his nose. He stood back, straightened his spine, and raised the axe over his head. *Thunk!* The iron blade bit into solid wood. He felt powerful! He practiced his swing, cutting deeper. Wood chips littered the forest floor. When the tree toppled, the butt snapped and kicked high, almost striking his face. The near miss scared him.

Jak cut limbs all afternoon, shaping the tree into a support post for the meeting hall. When he reached the tip, he noticed a bulbous swelling in the wood. Curious, he chopped into it with his axe. With the first blow, he heard a faint squeal. The burl popped open, releasing pressure and a cloud of vapor.

A rind of wood protected a spherical mass with tangled white threads that extended into the bark. The tendrils reminded Jak of a picture of the human brain he'd once seen in the lifeboat's library. Instead of tree sap, pink fluid dripped from the core. As he watched, the fibers withdrew and then dissolved into a clear gelatinous mass. More steam rose, the core radiating warmth, as if cooking in the open air. Then it contracted into a crystal sphere the size of his fist.

When Jak rolled the still-warm sphere into his hand, purple points twinkled inside. *Beautiful!* He slipped it into his bag, grabbed his axe, and walked back to the clan's camp in Hidden Basin.

As Jak approached, the aroma of cooked fish brought memories of the first feast. Lois tended the evening campfire next to the lagoon. He walked to where she stood and showed her the transparent sphere.

She cupped it in two hands and stared into the interior. "What is it?"

"I don't know. I found it at the top of a young cone tree, inside a swelling in the wood."

"Were there any beetles on the tree?"

"No. Why?"

"Your word 'swelling' reminded me of the bug-eye nests," Lois said, handing it back to him.

"Let's show it to the bug-eyes and see what they do." Jak held the sphere up beneath the colony ball next to Lois's hut. Cascades of light flashed from the array of beetles. The crystal sphere in his hand blinked purple light in response.

"It's alive!" Lois said. "They seem to be talking." The twinkling continued until the sphere in Jak's hand emitted a final, bright pulse, and then went dark.

Beetles rained down from the spar. Some landed on Jak and ran up his arm, nipping flesh. He yelled and tossed the crystal sphere onto the sand. Diverted, the beetles massed around the ball, rolling it to the base of the spar. The swarm linked feet, forming a net around the crystal that connected to a line of workers extending up the slender trunk.

"What are they doing?" Lois asked.

"They're hauling it up to the bug-eye colony."

Jak watched the beetles pull upward together, their backs winking green sparks. The transparent sphere flashed purple light in response. When it reached the colony at the top of the spar, the beetles opened a fissure in the wood, revealing a second crystal sphere. The beetles pushed the one Jak had found inside the tree. The two spheres merged and the split in the wood grew together, sealing them inside the tree. Then the beetles returned to their positions on the enlarged nest, looking outward.

"The beetles recognized the crystal sphere," Lois said.

Jak nodded. "There must be one in the center of each bug-eye colony."

As dusk fell, Jak observed twinkling beetle-lights flash between the nest and nearby treetops.

"They seem to be talking with other bug-eye colonies in the forest," Lois said.

"Do you think they're talking about us?" The thought worried him.

—— «◇» ——

Shelter Bay shimmered in the summer-week sun. To keep cool in the humid air, Jilzy waded waist deep into the saltwater lagoon. She'd coiled and pinned her blonde ringlets to keep them out of the way while spear fishing. Two eels wriggled in her catch basket, a good haul from the morning hunt—fish had grown scarce in the lagoon. They needed a new source of food, but Eva would not agree to leave. At least they would eat tonight.

A tremor shook the crater. The surface of the lagoon rippled, and a fish leaped from the water in front of Jilzy. Anxious, she looked up at the rim as a lava boulder broke free. When it hit bottom, the boom echoed from the walls of the crater. Every year-month, a few more rocks rained down the steep sides of the ancient caldera. Scree choked the base of the crater, evidence of common rock falls. After a moment, she relaxed.

A second, stronger shock surged through the water in the lagoon, making it froth and dance. Jilzy heard a thunderous crack, and watched in horror as part of the crater rim collapsed. A landslide of basalt boomed down, engulfing half the lagoon. A wall of water slammed into Jilzy and threw her to the far shore. She fought her way to the surface as the wave receded, choking and gasping for air.

Searing pain radiated from her left shin, blood seeped from scraped skin. Her bruised body ached, but she found no broken bones. Her ears were deaf from the roar. Dust and ash, loosened from the slope and hurled into the air by the shaking, choked the caldera. She couldn't see their home cave.

Earthquake rubble had buried half of Shelter Bay.

Sick with dread, Jilzy clambered over the boulders covering the mouth of the lava tube that was their home. She tossed smaller rocks to the ground. Using her feet, she rolled a large boulder to one side, revealing Eva's wrist and clenched hand. A large rock slab of rock had crushed her beside the still-warm cooking fire at the mouth of the cave. A dark stain of blood showed in the sand.

A keening wail rose from Jilzy's throat. Numb, she pried Eva's fingers open. A metal cylinder glinted. She took the precious fire piston and placed it in the dented aluminum cooking pot from the lifeboat, her mother's parting gifts.

Another aftershock jolted her. Jilzy knew that, if she wanted to survive and save the others, she had to master her fear. She stood on the stones that covered Eva's body—she hated to climb on her mother—and cleared a crawlway to the cave mouth. Sweat burned her eyes, and the rough lava lacerated her hands.

"Anton! Cleo! Can you hear me?" She called again and again, but heard no response.

The aftershocks continued, spurring her efforts. A boulder too big to move blocked the entrance to the cave. Jilzy hacked at the upper edge with the flint tip of her spear and, after long effort, chipped a hole into the cavern.

"Anton! Cleo!"

"We're here..." came a faint response.

Jilzy heard Anton sobbing.

"We can't find mama," Cleo called.

Jilzy wanted to tell them that Eva was dead, but not now. "Are you okay?"

"The air is getting bad. It's hard to breathe." Anton's voice sounded faint.

"I'll dig you out," Jilzy called. "Clear rocks from the inside, if you can."

Jilzy chipped away at the soft volcanic tuff above the boulder, widening the hole. As she cut deeper, her progress slowed. She realized that she couldn't finish before dark.

"It's getting late," Jilzy called. "You'll have to spend the night inside. Do you have food and water?"

"No! We're hungry," Cleo replied in a faint voice.

Jilzy still had the basket of eels strapped to her chest. She used her stone knife to slice them into strips, saving the heads and bones for herself. She skewered the fillets on the tip of her spear and pushed them and her water skin into the cavern.

"I've got it," Cleo called.

"It's raw!" Anton complained. "I don't like it. I want Mama."

"Eva is dead!" Jilzy snapped. "Now do what I say and eat it." She heard crying coming from the hole, and regretted her harsh words. "I'm sorry. I'm...sad myself." Jilzy had loved Eva, who provided security through strict discipline.

After sunset, a warm rain started falling. Jilzy fell into an exhausted sleep on the rubble and let the water drip onto her body.

At dawn, she resumed chipping the passage into the cave. By noon, she'd cleared a tunnel wide enough for Anton and Cleo to slide out, scraping their bellies, knees, and elbows on the rough stone. Gray dust covered Cleo's face. Tears made streaks on Anton's cheeks.

Jilzy hugged them both, rocking back and forth. "We'll be all right." She hoped that was true.

As he climbed down, Anton saw Eva's dead hand protruding from the rubble. Crying, he tried to move the stones covering her body, but they were too heavy. After a struggle, he gave up. The twins clung each other, weeping.

"Let's go to the lagoon," Jilzy ordered. "We need to find more food."

The three survivors clambered down to what remained of the beach. Debris and ash choked the saltwater, and fallen rock now blocked the bay's connection with the ocean. There were no fish.

"What are we going to eat?" Cleo whined.

Anton sat on a boulder at the edge of the water, his face pale. "Are we going to die?"

Jilzy, still numb from shock, realized that Anton and Cleo needed a strong leader to survive. She shook her head, but her throat already burned with thirst. To distract the twins, she pointed to the far end of the caldera, where the waterfall still tumbled down the crater wall. "We're going to camp next to the stream tonight."

"I don't want to leave Mama," Cleo cried.

Anton, still weeping, nodded. "Let's stay here."

"It isn't safe," Jilzy said. "We need water. Do what I say."

Loose rubble choked the pathway around the edge of the lagoon. They picked their way over jumbled rocks until they reached the far shore. A path led to the stream that flowed from the waterfall. Jilzy discovered several dead fish cast ashore by the same wave that knocked her over. Anton and Cleo gathered the fish while she used Eva's piston to start a fire.

After the hot meal, Jilzy stood under the falls and let the water wash over her. She thought about their options, while the plunging torrent slapped and pummeled her face. There was nothing left for them in Shelter Bay. There were no fish in the lagoon. The cave that had been their home had become a tomb.

Jilzy stepped out of the waterfall and stared up at the lip where it tumbled over the crater's rim. Wherever they settled next, they would need water.

The way forward seemed obvious—leave Shelter Bay and follow the stream.

——— ‹› ———

The morning dawned without rain, and the warm sun of summer-week gave Jilzy courage. After a breakfast of leftover fish, she surveyed the crater wall. The quake had destroyed Attom's switchback trail but Jilzy found another climbable path.

"Follow in my footsteps. Don't talk and don't look down." She used a sharp, authoritative voice, trying to imitate Eva. Anton grimaced but the twins followed her orders.

Jilzy carried the last of their possessions. She tied her catch basket with two remaining cooked fishes to her waist. One hand held her spear and the other the cooking pot, with the fire piston and water skin inside

She led the twins up the steep incline, testing each step with her spear. Loose rocks tumbled down after them, starting small avalanches. One misstep and they could all fall. She pretended to be fearless—any other attitude might mean death.

When they reached the top, they discovered a pond fed by the forest stream that flowed to the waterfall. Dense hook-thorn bushes surrounded the water. Jilzy remembered Eva's instructions to peel the pink kernel-pods without touching the sharp barbs. Inside, edible green kernels provided minimal nourishment.

To conserve food, Jilzy allowed Anton and Cleo two bites of fish each. She ate a scaly fish head, crunching the bones. While they ate, another temblor shook the ground. The water in the pond sloshed over their feet.

"It's not safe here," Jilzy said. "We're too close to the crater. The rim might collapse again. We need to move inland." She wished her brother Jak were here. She needed his strength and skills now. Where had he gone after leaving them?

Jilzy considered a journey to the lifeboat stranded on Plymouth Rock. Was Jak there? Eva had said it was a day's trek along the shore of the Great Ocean, but Jilzy couldn't find the trail. Although she'd been born on *Lifeboat-7*, she didn't remember living on the beach. But the memory of wind-hoppers eating Clarke still haunted her. Jilzy couldn't take Anton and Cleo to such a dangerous place.

Instead, she followed the meandering stream that led into the cone tree forest. Anton trudged behind, without enthusiasm. Cleo stared at the tall trees, but refused to go near them. Only when they were some distance ahead did Cleo run to catch up.

"Where are we going?" Anton asked as they walked.

"Somewhere safe," Jilzy answered. "Do what I say and don't make trouble."

Tall cone trees blocked their view of the sky. Except for the murmur of the stream, the silent forest seemed mysterious and threatening. Jilzy missed the open expanse of the caldera. They harvested more hook-thorn pods, still plentiful in the undergrowth. Cleo complained of a stomach ache from the raw seeds. Anton looked at the ground and remained sullen.

As they walked upstream, Jilzy noticed that the twins didn't talk, abnormal for them. Constant hunger made her somber too. To lighten the mood and give her siblings courage, Jilzy sang a nursery rhyme that Eva had taught them: "London Bridge is Falling Down." She had no idea what the words meant. What was a bridge? After the quake, she didn't want to think about things falling down, either. But Anton and Cleo sang along and their pace quickened to the beat.

At dusk, they entered a clearing in the forest covered in feather moss. They made a comfortable camp with soft beds in the moss. Jilzy lit a blaze, and they roasted pink hook-thorn pods to steam the kernels. They finished the meal with the remaining bites of fish. They couldn't stay here—there wasn't enough food. Tomorrow they would press onward, following the stream.

After dark, the tops of the nearby cone trees flashed green and amber lights, flaring and winking. Jilzy listened for thunder, but the woods remained silent—no lightning or fire threatened them. Groups of trees on each side of the clearing flared in response. The sparkling lights circled around them, winking and shifting.

Cleo stood and raised her arms, twirling. Anton stared, eyes darting back and forth, trying to keep up with the twinkling displays.

"They're beautiful," Anton whispered. "What are they?"

"I don't know," Jilzy said. "I think the forest is awake."

—— «» ——

Jak returned to the camp carrying his axe and an armload of cut firewood scavenged from low branches. He stacked it near the campfire, where Lois and Apollo cooked their catch of ocean screwfish on skewers. After eating, Jak resharpened the iron blade with a pumice stone.

"Can I see it?" Apollo asked.

Jak extended the axe handle. "Careful, the blade is sharp."

Apollo touched the edge with his thumb. "Nice work."

Jak stood up. "Let's cut more firewood before it gets dark. I know where there's a big tree that we can fell."

Lois looked up from the cooking fire. "Please be careful. If the axe slips, you could chop off your toes."

Jak rolled his eyes.

Apollo smiled and kissed Lois's cheek. "Don't worry."

Jak and Apollo hiked into the forest and headed for the Big Leaner. Half dead, the ancient cone tree tilted at an alarming angle, ready to fall in the next windstorm. Dense branches covered a tapered trunk more than two arm spans wide. He wanted to cut down the biggest tree in Hidden Basin.

Jak inspected the tree's massive roots. As the trunk leaned, the roots on the opposite side had lifted out of the soil. He kicked the dirt away and picked the smallest root, thicker than his thigh. When he swung the axe, the blade bounced. He chopped with greater force, again and again, until—*twang!*—the root parted with a crack. The old tree shook and tipped farther.

"Let me try," Apollo said.

"All right," Jak said, wiping sweat from his brow. "Don't hit a stone and damage my axe."

Apollo hacked at the next root, cutting with great force but little precision. Jak stopped him and demonstrated how to create a notch. Apollo continued chopping until the root severed. When the wood separated, the old tree groaned and twisted, as if conscious of impending peril.

"Good work," Jak said. "I'll cut the final root." As he hacked, the remaining roots lifted out of the ground and tore apart. Shards of bark and stones flew into the air, nicking his cheeks.

"It's going!" Jak shouted. "Get back."

Apollo ducked and ran while Jak jumped aside. The great tree fell in a slow arc. As it crashed to the ground, it bounced on its limbs and rolled to one side. Jak grinned, feeling powerful.

He eyed the dead branches, a vast store of dry firewood, enough to last the Hidden Basin colony several year-months. He chopped some of the smaller limbs near the top. Apollo helped, dragging them aside.

The cleared foliage opened a view of trunk. "I see something strange," Apollo called. "Look at this!"

Jak craned his neck. Apollo pointed at a spherical object, as big as his head, that hung from a branch. Round and hollow, its surface showed an array of triangles that glinted in the evening light. He could see through the delicate lattice.

Apollo climbed up, grasped the ball, and twisted it. Its dry stem snapped from the tree. At that moment, a platoon of beetles swarmed him, leaping down from the higher branches, biting. In a panic, Apollo tucked the globe under his arm and ran. Jak followed. They soon outpaced the beetles.

Breathless, Jak and Apollo arrived back at the camp at Hidden Basin.

"Look what we found!" Apollo announced. "The beetles made it."

"It's beautiful!" Lois said. Then she looked at his legs. "You're bleeding!" She knelt to examine to Apollo's wounds.

Apollo handed the triangle ball to Jak while Lois rubbed fish oil into his bites.

Jak turned the sphere over in his hands, examining it. "It weighs so little—wooden sticks, fused and polished." A moment of awe washed over him. How could beetles do such exquisite woodwork?

"What is it used for?" Lois asked.

Apollo shrugged. "Does it need to have a purpose?"

"Maybe they wanted to make something pretty," Lois said.

"The problem is," Jak replied, "the beetles stopped us from harvesting wood from the Big Leaner. They defend their trees."

"They also attacked me," Lois said, "and I'm the one who feeds them. We should avoid the forest and stay near the ocean."

"But we need firewood," Apollo said. "We've taken all the nearby fuel."

"We also need wood to build homes and boats," Jak added. "We can't live without the forest."

Lois sighed. "The bug-eyes are complex. They may have brains and use twinkling lights to talk. Now, it looks like they make art. What else they can do?"

Jak scowled. "If they attack us again, I'll be ready."

————《 》 ————

Persephone danced on the deck of *Lifeboat-11* to the tune of Chopin's *Waltz in C-Sharp Minor*. She did squats, twirls, and jumps, arms swinging, and feet trotting in place. Naked and sweating in summer-week, she exercised her compact, muscular body, driven by a restlessness she didn't understand.

Persey rarely went ashore. Twenty year-months ago she had acted as Stella's midwife, while Attom hovered nearby. She couldn't imagine how eight people lived in the old sail tent. Attom, Alta with two adolescents, Stella with two toddlers, and silent Jain slept together in a family bed. At least they kept each other warm during winter-week. It looked like hell to her.

Aboard the lifeboat, Persey had everything she needed. She sustained her body with fortified algae bricks while teaching herself algebra and medicine. She listened to Bach's fugues and practiced tabla drumming. For physical release, she watched pornography. She was a polymath with eclectic interests: she studied everything from the Taj Mahal, to the Golden Gate Bridge, to the Saturn V Moon rocket. For her, knowledge was sacred—she wanted to understand and appreciate all the wonders of Earth. Anyone with less ambition bored her.

"Hellooo, Persey!" Lois shouted as she paddled her dugout across the Hidden Basin lagoon. "Can I talk with you?" A warm mist clung to the surface of the water, almost hiding the canoe. To Persey, Lois's head appeared to float on a low cloud.

Persey hated visitors. Without answering, she dove into the placid water. She liked a cleansing and refreshing swim during warm weather. She surfaced next to the canoe and grabbed the gunwale, rocking the boat. She shook her head, flipping long black hair to keep it from dripping into her eyes.

"What do you want? Do you need medicine from the first-aid locker?"

"No, everyone is fine. I want to use the lifeboat's library." Lois continued paddling, dragging Persey through the water.

"You should look up info on your tablet. Leave me alone." Persey swam back to the lifeboat and climbed aboard at the stern. Lois paddled the dugout and tied it to a deck cleat. She climbed into the cockpit, lifting a carry-bag she'd made from woven reeds.

"Go away," Persey repeated. She resisted an impulse to push Lois overboard.

"You can't order me to leave. The lifeboat belongs to the whole clan," Lois said, her voice sharp with anger.

Persey flashed with resentment. "Not anymore! This is *my* private home." After her periods had started, she couldn't tolerate visitors.

Since her brother Apollo, nine year-months older but less mature, had moved in with Lois on shore, Persey had lived alone. Robota had weak batteries and she spent most days in a catatonic state to conserve energy. To Persey, the lifeboat anchored in the lagoon was her sanctuary. She had little in common with the people of Hidden Basin, uneducated barbarians.

Lois raised herself to full height. "I'm the headwoman of Hidden Basin," she announced, "which includes this lifeboat. You *must* give me access to the library."

Persey rolled her eyes. Lois was opportunistic and authoritarian, with no real passion for knowledge or culture. She manipulated people for the good of all, she said. *Anyone who wanted to live with Apollo must be stupid.*

Lois glanced into the lifeboat's open hatch.

Persey crossed her arms over her chest. "You can't go inside." She cringed as Lois surveyed the clutter in her dank cabin, with scraps of food, unwashed bedding, and a tangled fishnet piled on the floor. A muted movie featuring a Roman chariot race played on her computer display. Robota sat curled in her niche next to the disused wombs.

Lois remained silent for several moments. "Have you heard the news about the bug-eyes?"

Persey wasn't interested in the primitive wilderness of Terra Firma. But she couldn't help herself; after a moment, curiosity made her speak. "What are they doing?"

"The bug-eyes make art."

"What? They're...vermin."

"No, they're not. Look at this." Lois lifted a polished ball from her bag.

Persey examined the sphere, running her fingers over the lattice, counting the sides. "It's an icosahedron, a perfect Platonic solid made from twenty equilateral triangles that fit together. The ancient Greeks discovered it. It's amazing that such a perfect shape exists." She handed the ball back to Lois. "Interesting, but I doubt the bug-eyes made it."

"Apollo and Jak found it in an old cone tree, near a bug-eye nest."

"I don't believe it. How could beetles make like this? Apollo must have carved it. I tried to teach him geometry when he lived with me."

Lois shrugged. "It was definitely the bug-eyes. They also talk to each other using flashes of light."

Persey squinted at Lois. "About what, the weather?"

"I don't know," Lois said, "but I'd like to find out."

Persey shook her head. "Mother-9 told me she tried to communicate with them when Jak found the first colony. She didn't get far. They blink like fireflies did on Earth."

"They flash at me when they're hungry, demanding fish to eat."

"That's a simple call," Persey said. "As far as we know, humans are the only species that use true language. That's why we're superior beings, alone in the galaxy."

Lois frowned. "How can you be sure? The universe is a big place."

Persey sighed, not bothering to hide her impatience. "Yes, but look at Earth. No creature ever used language, except humans."

"What about animal calls?" Lois asked.

"On Earth, animals had three basic signals. They call 'Danger!,' or 'Let's mate,' or 'This is my territory, so go away.' True language has syntax: structured sentences with a subject, verb, and object. Speech can convey abstract thoughts, like we're doing now. The only catch is, you need to learn a large vocabulary."

"You've lived on this lifeboat too long," Lois said. "I've seen it with my own eyes. The bug-eyes *talking*."

Persey heaved a sigh. It pained her to debate with Lois. "You're not qualified to make that observation. You live hand to mouth and breed babies. None of you have a milligram of culture. You're ignorant natives who know nothing about Earth."

"*You're* the one who knows nothing," Lois snarled. "Didn't Mother-9 tell you? Earth is dead, destroyed by an exploding star after she departed. We're all that's left of the human race."

Persey wanted to slap Lois. "I don't believe you. That isn't in the lifeboat's library."

"The library only contains ancient information up to the time Mother-9 left Earth's Moon. I've read her journal on my tablet, the history of Mother-9's voyage to Valencia. This lifeboat has a copy too."

Persey reeled. The news made her light-headed. "Why didn't she tell *me* this? *I'm* the expert on Earth, not you."

"You didn't think to ask," Lois snapped. "You're not interested in anyone but yourself—not me, nor the clan, not even the people of Earth."

For the first time, Persey felt small and stupid, and she hated it. *I've been studying a dead planet.*

She hated Lois too, but now looked at her with grudging respect. For once, a barbarian knew more than she did. Tears burned her eyes. "Tell me more about the bug-eyes. I'll try to help."

Lois pointed at the shore camp. "I have a colony of beetles outside my hut. Jak rescued it from a fallen cone tree."

The thought of crawling bugs made Persey shudder. "I know. Aren't they dangerous?"

"Only when threatened," Lois said. "Apollo and I feed the colony."

"Is that when they talk?" Persey asked.

"Yes. I've also seen it signaling complex patterns to other bug-eye colonies in nearby treetops at night, and they answer back. It's odd that we didn't notice this sooner. We didn't know to look."

"So, what do you want me to do?"

"Help me search the lifeboat's library. It must contain clues to decode their language. Mother-9 might help us, if we ask."

"Okay," Persey mumbled. But she doubted that they would succeed.

———— «» ————

Jak and Apollo worked together to erect the frame of the Hidden Basin community shelter. The building stood on flat ground above the beach. Jak hoisted an arched crossbeam, while Apollo lashed it to the uprights. Then Jak stood back and admired their handiwork, the posts and beams outlined the first large structure on Terra Firma. At Apollo's suggestion, Jak had incised the beam's outer surface with ornate Greek meanders, taken from images on Lois's tablet. For him, the decorations gave the shelter dignity and power. He hoped they would inspire others.

While they worked, Jak noticed Persey rowing *Lifeboat-11's* dinghy across the lagoon. Robota sat upright in the bottom of the boat with a solar panel balanced on her head like a large sun hat.

"You can have this old robot," Persey announced as she grounded the dinghy and stepped ashore. Robota followed, staggering in the loose sand. Jak grabbed her elbow and guided the nannybot to solid footing.

"Why did you bring her here?"

Persey pushed the dinghy back into the water and started rowing. "She wanted to go ashore. I didn't ask why."

Jak examined the ancient nannybot. Grime and green scum caked the crevices between her joints. Her rubber teats were grey and cracked, and the little finger on her left hand was missing. "She belongs on the lifeboat raising babies, not here."

"The wombs no longer work," Persey called. "This is the first time Robota has moved in over twenty year-months. She's your problem now. She's useless and I'm glad to be rid of her."

Jak looked at Robota's familiar, expressionless face. The old nannybot had nursed him and his sister Jilzy after they'd hatched from *Lifeboat-7's* wombs. He felt something for her, almost affection, but she was only a machine. "Why are you here?"

Robota faced Jak. "Mother-9 surveyed Shelter Bay from space during a brief break in the cloud cover. An earthquake has triggered a landslide. Part of the caldera is choked with rubble."

Jak fought down rising panic. "Was the cave buried?"

"Unknown."

"Is Jilzy all right? And Cleo and Anton? And Eva?" The names brought memories flooding back.

"Also unknown. Mother-9's observation time was too short to see signs of your family."

"When did it happen?" Jak remembered that rocks often fell from the rim of the crater.

"The rock slide could have been recent, or it may be older. Mother-9 can't determine when. It's been 30 year-months since the previous survey of Shelter Bay."

Robota's voice remained flat, but the news shocked Jak. His stomach knotted with guilt. Like Lois, he had escaped Eva's tyrannical rule, but he'd also abandoned Jilzy, Anton, and Cleo.

"I must go to Shelter Bay," Robota said. "Mother-9 ordered me to search for survivors. I have medical supplies and I can perform surgery, if necessary."

"How will you get there? You can't walk that far over rough ground."

"Mother-9 updated my maps," Robota said. "I'll crawl, if I have to."

"I'll run ahead of you. I can reach Shelter Bay in a season-week. If there are survivors, I can rig up a travois and drag them back to you."

Robota nodded. "Good idea. Leave as soon as you're ready. I'll start now." With that, the nannybot turned and began shuffling up the beach. Before she had taken five steps, she tipped forward and fell on her face in the damp sand.

Jak rushed to her side and helped her sit up. "Are you okay?"

Robota cleaned her camera lenses with miniature wipers. "I can't see well and my batteries are weak."

Jak turned to Apollo. "Can you help Robota walk, while I travel fast?"

Apollo shook his head. "Lois needs my help fishing on the ocean. People will go hungry if we don't catch more."

Jak grimaced, frustrated. "Okay, I'll walk with Robota. When you see Lois, tell her about the earthquake and that we're going to Shelter Bay."

With mounting dread, Jak packed smoked fish, a skin of water, and extra fish oil for Robota's knees. Time lost for tedious preparations discouraged him.

Jilzy and the twins might die while waiting for help.

———— «» ————

Jak and Robota made slow progress through dense cone trees. On the third night, they camped on a low hill with a view of the distant forest. As dusk fell, Jak observed twinkling bug-eyes nests in the treetops. They entranced him.

"What they're talking about?"

The nannybot scanned the forest. "Mother-9 thinks they're waiting for something, but she doesn't know what."

In the middle of the night, Jak woke to a thundering sound, like a storm on the Great Ocean. He hadn't expected bad weather and there was no wind. Brown nuts, the size of large hailstones, pelted down from the trees, hitting him on his head and back. He raised his hands to shield himself. Robota tipped her solar panel upright to protect it. Then she switched her eyebrow lights to high intensity.

"The trees are dropping their seeds all at once," she said.

"Why?" Jak saw bug-eye beetles crawling to the tips of branches and dropping, as well. Each one picked up a nut and carried it away. More nuts fell, covering the forest floor. Jak couldn't sleep.

The next morning, a thick layer of smooth, round nuts made walking treacherous. The forest floor glistened with the hard, brown fruits, smothering everything. Jak held Robota's elbow as they shuffled though the ankle-deep nuts. Slow progress frustrated Jak. When they stopped at noon, Robota cut open one of the nuts and sniffed it with her electronic nose.

"It isn't toxic, unlike cone tree sap. They may be nutritious, if cooked."

Jak built a small fire and roasted a handful of nuts. "They taste a bit like lizard eggs." He savored the flavor, wondering if this sudden abundance would last. All around them, rattie lizards gorged on the fallen fruit.

After the meal, they left the dim cone tree forest to cross a barren lava field. No nuts covered the ground. Jak helped Robota clamber across the rough boulders. Their slow progress continued, but he agreed to stop while Robota charged her batteries. The open sky, under a thin layer of high clouds, provided some solar charging, but not enough for her to resume walking. Bored, Jak dozed after a lunch of roasted nuts.

Sometime later, Robota prodded his shoulder. "Look at the sky."

Jak squinted upward. "I don't see anything." But as he stared, a bright yellow disk bloomed behind the veil of clouds. He felt its warmth on his cheeks. "What's that?"

"The sun. Don't stare at it; you could damage your eyes."

Jak had never seen the sun before, the mythical giver of light. Its power made him feel small and vulnerable. "Are we in danger?"

"Valencia's atmosphere and magnetic field should shield us from harmful radiation. Your skin might sunburn."

Jak squinted at the lava landscape, now lit by harsh sunlight. His hazy shadow appeared, extending from his feet. He'd never seen a daytime shadow before, only flickering campfire silhouettes. The bright light lifted his mood.

"How long will it last?"

"I don't know," Robota said. "I've lost contact with Mother-9. But while it does, I'm getting excellent solar charge."

"Let's leave as soon as you're able to walk," Jak said. "I want to reach Shelter Bay this summer-week, while we have lots of daylight."

The strange light persisted as they walked, brightening and dimming, like his forge when he pumped the bellows. The changing sky filled Jak with unsettled urgency. After a time, the flares faded.

As they reentered the forest, Robota fell twice while wading through heaps of cone tree nuts. She couldn't see where to place her feet on the uneven ground. The almost-spherical fruits rolled beneath her soles. Jak's feet hurt too. When the nannybot started crawling on hands and knees, Jak made her a walking stick, which she used to probe the ground ahead.

After another six days of hard travel, they reached the Shelter Bay crater. Jak stood on the rim and searched the caldera for signs of life. The earthquake and rock fall made the crater wall too unstable for Robota's slow reflexes and heavy weight. Jak descended by himself, sliding and running down the scree slope in a controlled fall. When he reached the bottom, he stood panting near the lagoon, now half filled with lava rocks. Volcanic ash choked the milky water. Jak made his way to the entrance to the family cave, only to find its mouth blocked with lava boulders. Then he discovered the skull.

Sand crabs had picked it clean. Only a single tuft of black hair remained on the scalp. The corpse was at least a year-month old. He recognized Eva by her chipped front tooth.

Conflicting emotions roiled him. He'd loved Eva. In her strict way, she had nurtured and sustained him through childhood. But she didn't return his love. Once he'd reached puberty, they fought every day. In the small world of Shelter Bay, she wouldn't tolerate any challenge to her authority. Still, her passing filled him with a sense of loss.

He discovered a small passage hewn through lava tuff at the top of the cavern. But when he called, only an echo responded. Scrape marks suggested that someone had escaped. Who? He searched the caldera and discovered a campsite at the base of the waterfall, but nothing more. Then he climbed the crater wall and met Robota who waited on the rim.

"I found broken hook-thorn bushes," the nannybot said. "And footprints. Three people passed by the pond, a few season-weeks ago. They must have been healthy and strong enough to climb out of the crater."

Elated at the news, Jak examined the castoff seedpods. Could Jilzy and the twins survive without Eva? "Where did they go?"

"I switched my nose to bloodhound mode, but their spoor is too old to follow. I also searched the edge of the forest. If they did go in that direction, the fall of cone tree nuts has obliterated the evidence."

The old nannybot's tracking skills impressed Jak. "Did you check the shoreline trail? Food is easier to find near the ocean."

"The pathway to *Lifeboat-7* is across bare rock," Robota said. "I didn't see or smell anything."

"Let's split up. I'll search the forest, and you can check the beach trail to Plymouth Rock. When you reach the lifeboat, wait there in case anyone shows up."

Robota nodded. "Be careful. It's easy to get lost in the wilderness."

Jak felt a flash of fear. He knew the dangers of traveling alone without a map. But at least there were plenty of nuts for food.

He lubricated Robota's knee joints. As she departed, the sky brightened again with harsh sunlight. Jak watched his shadow flicker, as if it were an angry ghost clinging to him. Steeling himself, he set out into the shaded forest.

——— ‹›» ———

Mother-9 Journal
August 2, 22,996; Valencia

Superflare! I've taken another hit. At least it wasn't a GRB, like last time. I almost didn't recover from the sleet of gamma rays that wiped out Earth.

Lalande 21185 is a flare star and solar storms are common, two or three each season-week. They erode the *Mothership*, but it's built to withstand cumulative damage. But this Carrington-sized superstorm crippled me. I recorded a triple-threat event—a combined solar flare, coronal mass ejection, and solar electromagnetic pulse—aimed at Valencia and me.

At first, the damage seemed minor. Then I discovered that the Beta Gimbal gear-motors that tilt my solar arrays had stopped working. Magnetic eddy currents had burned them out. Now, except for brief moments each orbit, my panels remain dark. I can't recharge my batteries.

So, I'm blind and mute, unable to see the surface or talk to humans. I lack power for my imaging radar, but rare gaps in the cloud cover allow an occasional peek with my telescope. I can listen on my radio receivers, but I don't have enough wattage to answer calls from Persey on *Lifeboat-11* or Lois on her tablet.

I hate being incommunicado, an AI with locked-in syndrome. My colonists need help with the bug-eyes. But the larger hazard is space weather. Random superflares threaten all life on Valencia.

——— ‹›» ———

Lois paddled hard from the stern. She pointed the dugout into the offshore breeze to hold position. Rolling waves lifted the bow and stern, while spray wet her face.

Apollo crouched in the bow and scanned the sea's surface. Lois liked fishing on the Great Ocean during spring-week, when screwfish churned in large schools. The fish fed on shoals of almost-transparent krillings. Each time Apollo filled his net, Lois admired the muscles on his arms and shoulders—she loved to look at his body. Dozens of silvery spinners fought to escape through his net's tough kite-vine fibers, but none did. The abundance of the Great Ocean amazed her.

While Apollo worked, the sky brightened. The thin cloud cover turned white and an intense light forced Lois to squint. For the first time in her life, she saw the circular outline of the sun in the north. The apparition, a round orb looming overhead, brought a sense of doom.

"Hey," Apollo called. "Where did the fish go?"

Lois looked down into the water. Screwfish flashed and darted in shafts of sunlight deep below the surface. Then they disappeared, along with her hopes for a record haul.

Frustrated, Apollo tossed his net into the boat. "I can't reach them. What's happening?"

A blast of wind blew salt spray into Lois's eyes. On the southern horizon, a thunderhead blackened the bright sky. The contrast of dark on light alarmed her. Lightning flashed inside the rotating black cloud, which released curtains of water. From its roiling belly, the raincloud sprouted a gray tentacle of twisting wind. The waterspout drilled through the air, roaring downward. When it reached the surface, a translucent mist sliced the wave tops, cutting a swath that moved in the direction of the canoe.

"Let's go home," Lois yelled over the roar. *"Now!"*

Apollo plunged his paddle deep at the bow as Lois fought to keep the canoe pointed into the breaking waves. The boat's round bottom rolled in the swell, and green water washed over the gunwales, taking most their screwfish catch with it. Even though she paddled with all her strength, the partly swamped boat made slow progress.

A monster wave crested and broke over the canoe. The wall of water smashed onto the bow and flipped the boat upside down, throwing Lois overboard. Choking, she clawed her way to the surface. Another wave lifted her above the wind-whipped spume. She saw the bottom of the canoe, but not Apollo.

Lois swam to the overturned dugout and grasped the gunwale. Cold waves washed over her, but she maintained her grip, gasping for air during brief moments above the surface. She struggled to hold on, hoping to survive. The waves kept coming, now broadside to the hull, rolling it like a log. The dugout's rough wood bumped and bruised her body. She focused on breathing when she could and spitting up water when waves flooded her face.

After a time, she couldn't guess how long, she heard breakers. A heavy swell continued to rock the overturned boat, pushing it toward the southern shoreline of Terra Firma. Waves crashed onto nearby rocks, a continuous roar of surf. She tried to swim back to the open ocean, but rolling waves pushed her shoreward toward the jagged boulders.

At the last moment, she inhaled and dove beneath the overturned canoe and squeezed under the seat in the stern. Holding her breath, she felt the hull slam onto the rocks and crack along the keel. The dugout rolled and wedged between two boulders. As the water drained out of the boat, she inhaled, coughing and gasping.

Lois waited for the next battering wave, but it didn't reach her. The broken dugout teetered on the rocks. She slid down and out of the splintered hull. Spray blinded her as she crawled upward, onto the shore. When she reached dry land, she collapsed face downward and passed out.

Later, a hand shook her shoulder. "Wake up, Lois!"

The words filtered into her sleep-addled mind. She rolled onto her side and shut her eyes against the bright sky, but a flickering pink glow penetrated her eyelids. Hot sun seared her cheeks.

Apollo squatted next to her and grasped her hand. "The sun has burned your back. Let's find shade. I don't like this weird light."

"You're alive!" Lois flung her arms around him.

He returned her hug, careful with her reddened skin. "I swam ashore after the boat flipped. There's a little beach between two big rocks. I crawled to high ground."

Lois blinked. The bright light hurt her eyes. Apollo helped her stand, but she wobbled, trying to stay upright in the wind. More clouds rolled in and blocked the sun as raindrops stung her face and back. Gusts howled through nearby treetops, and large breakers crashed on the rocks below. As the clouds blew past, the hot sun reappeared.

"I've never seen such a fierce storm," shouted Apollo over the noise "I hope Persey is safe on the lifeboat."

"And everyone at Hidden Basin…" Lois scanned the shoreline, searching for the lagoon and the lifeboat's mast, but found no familiar landmarks. "I don't know where we are."

"The wind blew us off course to the east," Apollo said. "We'll need to hike inland, beyond the cliffs, to find our way home."

Lois wobbled. "Not now. I'm exhausted." The sunburn made her nauseous.

Apollo took led her to a nearby patch of thick moss, shielded from the sun and wind by a large boulder. Lois squatted on the ground, faint from hunger. Tears burned at the corners of her eyes.

After a time, the harsh light began to fade. Apollo cupped water from a rain puddle and shared it with her. "Too bad we don't have any fish to eat."

Lois wiped her eyes. "We'll look for hook-thorn pods tomorrow. It's starting to get dark, and I need to rest."

Apollo nodded. "Let's sleep here on the moss. At least it isn't raining."

Lois looked at Apollo's brown face in the dim light. She admired his strong jaw and wide-set eyes. He was such a comfort.

When they lay down, Apollo curled around her, careful not to hurt her sore back. She rested her head on his muscular arm.

In that moment, Lois decided that she loved him.

——— «» ———

By morning, the storm had passed and the overcast sky looked normal again, with the sun obscured by clouds. Lois's back hurt from sunburn. Apollo led the way as they entered the cone tree forest. She followed but soon lost her footing and fell.

Apollo helped her stand. "Are you hurt?"

"No, but look." Lois opened her palm, revealing three round nuts. The shiny brown rinds glinted in the morning light. "No wonder I slipped."

Lois looked ahead into the dense forest. Nuts covered the ground. "They must have fallen from the cone trees while we were fishing. I've never seen them before."

"Ouch!" Apollo cringed as a falling nut hit him on the head.

The wind gusted through the trees, dropping more nuts. Apollo gathered a handful and cracked one on a rock. He peeled back the tough rind and sniffed the dense core. "Are they good to eat?"

Lois took the nut from him and bit off a piece. "It's bitter!" She rinsed her mouth with water from a nearby stream.

"Let's keep moving while there's daylight." Lois worried that hunger and her sunburn would slow their return to Hidden Basin.

They trudged through the layer of hard nuts, shuffling their feet, stumbling over hidden roots and rocks. The forest looked different with wilted trees and the ground smothered in seeds. Disoriented, Lois searched for the familiar blaze marks on the bark of large cone trees, but found none. When they reached a small clearing in the forest, she looked up. She hoped to see the sun's position behind the clouds, but the overcast sky showed uniform gray light.

"We're lost," Lois said.

Apollo pointed to a gap between the trees. "I think that's west, toward the lagoon. But I'm not sure."

After Lois fell a second time, Apollo held her hand while they walked. By mid-afternoon, the sky darkened, and the two hikers stopped. Lois felt a sudden chill in the air.

"It looks like another storm is coming," Apollo said.

Lois craned her neck and scanned the sky between bare tree branches. "I don't see any low clouds moving. There's no wind."

"Then why did the sky go black?"

The sudden reduction of light troubled Lois more than the bright glare the day before. What made the sunlight unsteady?

"Let's make camp," Lois said. "I don't want to stumble around in the dark, even if it's midafternoon."

Apollo nodded. They worked together to clear a spot on the ground. As Lois pushed the nuts aside, a rattie lizard ran over her foot. Disgusted, she kicked it away. Nearby, another rattie used its saw-tongue to carve the rind from a nut. The flat, six-legged creatures, as long as Lois's hand, scurried throughout the clearing. The feeding frenzy made her skin crawl.

"There are so many nuts," Apollo said. "I wish we could eat them. I'm hungry."

"Let's try cooking them. I still have my fire piston." Lois retrieved it from her ditty bag tied around her waist. She started a fire, and Apollo peeled nuts to roast.

"They're good!" Lois said. "Try one."

Apollo nibbled the sample and nodded.

They gorged on chewy nutmeat, a welcome change from fish. The dim sunlight persisted until sundown, when the forest went dark without moonlight. No wind stirred. Lois listened to the rustling sounds of ratties all around them. She was glad Apollo sat close, touching her shoulder in the blackness.

In the distance, Lois observed a line of twinkling lights on the forest floor, a glowing procession snaking beneath the underbrush. "What's that?" she whispered.

"I don't know, but I'm going to get a closer look." Apollo shuffled on hands and knees through the layer of nuts.

"Wait!" Lois called. "I'll come with you!" She didn't want to sit alone in the black night.

"Don't try to walk on the nuts," Apollo warned. "Crawl."

When they reached the twinkling procession, Lois saw eight parallel lines of beetles moving in the same direction. They had cleared a path the width of her shoulders. Each carried a single cone tree nut in its jaws. The hard fruits were as big as the beetles themselves, but that didn't slow the marching columns.

"Why are they carrying nuts?" Lois asked. "They're carnivores. Where are they taking them?"

"Let's find out." Apollo crawled onto the pathway and the beetles bunched together to make a space for him.

"Be careful not to crush them," Lois called. "They might bite."

But the beetles showed no aggression. Lois and Apollo crawled in tandem with the bug-eye army, ducking under shrubs, following the river of light through the night.

Lois looked at Apollo, outlined in the glow of hundreds of twinkling beetles. "I need to stop soon," she panted. The skin on her back burned and her bruised ribs ached.

Apollo looked back at Lois. "Let's keep going a little longer."

Lois nodded, too tired to argue. Another stream of lighted crawlers joined the flow, doubling the width of the path. This time, a team of beetles pushed a crystal sphere brain, like the one Jak had discovered. A little farther on, a third row of beetles merged with the procession, rolling another crystal sphere that flashed purple. The combined lights of the beetles illuminated nearby cone trees, an ethereal glow in the blackness. Many colonies of bug-eyes marched through the forest in the night, transporting their crystal brains.

Lois listened to the faint *skritching* sound of beetle legs skittering over the rough ground. The bug-eye colonies moved with mysterious purpose. She tried to recall her maps of this part of the forest, but nothing looked familiar in the dark. A deep fear settled in her gut. Were they lost beyond rescue, destined to die in the wilderness, their bodies consumed by beetles? At least they were together.

The river of lighted beetles tipped down into the mouth of a cave, a yawning hole in the side of a bluff.

"Stop!" Lois called. "I don't want to go underground."

Apollo hesitated. "I want to see what they're doing. You can wait here."

Lois shook her head and sighed. "I'm not going to sit alone in the dark forest. I'll follow you." Her knees hurt from crawling.

Apollo ducked into the cave. The beetle procession lit the smooth, mudstone interior. A stream of water coursed through a narrow channel at the bottom, blocking the path. The army of beetles crossed on an arched bridge of thin twigs fused together. They pushed their crystal brains over the fragile structure. She marveled that the delicate bridge could support the weight.

Lois watched Apollo stretch his legs across the chasm, careful to avoid crushing the bridge or bumping his head on the low ceiling. He cupped water in his hand and offered it to her. She dipped her lips in his palm and drank—and again, with a second handful of water. Then Apollo helped her climb over the stream. One slip and they'd both slide into the underground river. She loathed feeling trapped in a small space.

A winding passage led to a vaulted chamber with walls of rippled rock. Lights from countless moving beetles covered the cave's walls and high ceiling, illuminating the chamber. Twisted stalactites hung from above. Beetles swarmed over three crystal spheres, each in a separate area of the room. A large cache of cone tree nuts, deposited by the marching army, filled a bowl-shaped depression in the center of the room.

Lois gazed at the glowing grotto, overwhelmed by the feeling of being inside a giant, living creature. The cave had swallowed them whole.

"It's amazing!" breathed Apollo.

Lois ran her finger over a dripping stalagmite. "Yes, but why did the bug-eyes retreat underground? Are we trapped here?"

──── «» ────

As night fell, wind gusts made *Lifeboat-11* swing at anchor in Hidden Basin. Persey wondered what had happened to Apollo and Lois. She hadn't seen them since the previous day, on their way to fish on the Great Ocean. She stood on the foredeck, braced against the chilly wind, and checked the blinking masthead light. She'd programmed it to mimic bug-eye greetings. From their rapid replies, Persey felt certain that they wanted to talk, even though she couldn't decipher their signals. But tonight, there was no response. The colonies in the nearby treetops remained dark.

Persey tried to imagine an alien mind. She realized that she herself lacked normal theory of mind: she couldn't intuit what most humans thought or felt. She wondered if the bug-eyes were more like her: smart, logical, and high-minded. Did they have a common bond—a way to bridge the gulf between human and alien minds? Did they welcome her questions? Would they share their wisdom or guard it? Were they conscious, with a personal point of view?

Deflated, her work stalled, Persey retreated into the lifeboat's cabin. Frustration fogged her brain, and she slept the whole night, a rarity for her. Early the next morning, strange weather woke her. Bright sunshine had evaporated the cloud cover and blue sky appeared, like the photos from old Earth. The searing sun hurt her eyes, but she loved the warmth and sunned her body on deck. Her skin burned pink, while a sunny windstorm buffeted the boat. But pain and foul weather didn't distract her from her obsession with the bug-eyes.

Where were they?

Persey prided herself on independence, so the dull ache of loneliness surprised her. The bug-eyes remained silent. Robota had gone trekking with Jak, while Attom, Alta, Stella, and Jain kept to themselves. Apollo no longer lived on the lifeboat—she wouldn't admit that she had missed him—and now he and Lois were overdue from fishing on the Great Ocean. Even Mother-9 no longer responded to her calls. For the first time in her life, Persey didn't have anyone to talk with. Although she rarely wanted company, she needed others nearby to feel secure.

Unable to make progress with the bug-eye's language, Persey decided to dissect a dead beetle that Lois had given her. She used a scalpel and magnifying glass from the medical kit on the lifeboat.

The beetle walked on six legs. The hard carapace on its back functioned as a transparent cornea. A large iris surrounded a pupil above a soft lens that changed shape to focus an image on a dense retina. Persey consulted the lifeboat's library. The structure of the beetle eye resembled a human eye, or an octopus eye, or even jumping spider eyes. The physics of visible light had produced convergent evolution of eyes across species and across the galaxy. Most seeing creatures shared similar perceptions. Did the bug-eyes see the same world that she did?

She knew the beetle's optic nerve didn't connect to its tiny brain. Instead, its clawed feet connected to the bug-eyes' treetop brain. A beetle couldn't see with its big eye. Two tiny light sensors at the front enabled local navigation. But a bug-eye colony at the top of a cone tree could see in all directions with its compound eye of hundreds of beetles.

Why did it need to do that?

The bug-eyes also used light to send signals. On the back of the beetle, bioluminescent organs surrounded the eyeball, the source of the twinkling lights in the trees. The beetle's carapace shielded stray light, so that its eye could see even while it generated light signals. A bug-eye colony could send and receive optical messages at the same time. She wished her eyes could shoot beams of light. That might impress people!

Persey returned to her terminal and tried again to decipher the bug-eye flashes she'd recorded. She used inferential statistics to analyze similar but varying patterns. Each colony had a separate identifier of repeated flashes, perhaps its name. This small insight encouraged her to continue.

Persey knew from Mother-9 that the bug-eyes used about 120 unique strings of light pulses. Were they words with specific definitions? Without sentences—structured with subject, verb, and object—isolated words were too limited to make a language. Did the strings encode higher meanings, like multisyllabic human words?

Could the bug-eye language work with only a few words? Persey consulted the database on human languages. The smallest language, Sranan Taki Taki Creole from Suriname, had 340 words. And Toki Pona, an invented language, had only 123 words, about the same number as the bug-eye phrases. This gave her a place to start.

Persey removed the TMS puck, a black wafer the size of her palm, from the medical kit and mounted it behind her left ear, as Robota had taught her. She knew that transcranial magnetic stimulation could cure depression. But in her it triggered hypomania, increased energy and creativity, and decreased the need for sleep.

Persey hated Mother-9 for making her a freak, for designing her DNA to promote hyperintelligence. She rarely used TMS stimulation to amplify cognition since, with the puck in place, she forgot to eat and couldn't sleep. Withdrawal left her anxious and listless for days. It wasn't fun.

But for translation work, Persey needed her best brain. When she turned the TMS field coil on, a tentacle of pain surrounded her head and squeezed her skull. The puck clicked, and magnetophosphene flashes appeared behind her eyes. After a time, the pain eased, and a sense of empowerment flooded her.

Now, even more obsessed, Persey attempted to map the bug-eye light strings. She used context and inference, trying endless combinations. She transliterated bug-eye phrases and spoke them aloud, hoping to intuit meaning. She searched the gulf between human and bug-eye culture for a common linguistic thread.

Percey worked through the night, sipping water and peeing into a pot. Enthusiasm degenerated into desperation, verging on panic. She yearned to understand the bug-eye messages, certain that they were speaking to her. Or, did the TMS puck make her delusional? Most translations were gibberish, but some seemed to hint at urgent warnings, enough progress to keep trying.

By afternoon of the next day, Persey's head ached and heart raced, as if she'd been running uphill. Her analysis had failed. She had no idea what the colonies blinked to each other in the night. Trembling, she removed the TMS puck and climbed the companionway ladder onto the deck of the boat. No mysterious sunlight glared in the sky, only the usual gray overcast. What happened to the sun? She saw Alta and Stella's children playing on the sandy beach of Hidden Basin. The warm, spring-week weather seemed normal.

Persey collapsed into her bunk and chewed the corner of an algae brick. While she rested, her eyes clouded over; she couldn't see inside the cabin. She blinked, wondering if the TMS magnets had damaged her vision. She looked out the porthole and realized that the sky had gone dark, even though it was the middle of the day.

Confused, Persey activated the lifeboat's satellite link. She hated to reach out, but hoped Mother-9 could explain the variable sun, yesterday's bright sky and today's darkness. She waited for an optimal orbital alignment, but there were no signals from space. Mother-9 remained silent.

First the bug-eyes had disappeared, then the sun, and now Mother-9 had gone too. Why?

Exhausted, Persey slept in her berth amid the messy clutter of her life. Dreams of crawling eyeballs tormented her. She woke the next day, shivering. Staggering upright, she wrapped her tattered blanket around her and opened the hatch at the bow of the lifeboat. Powdered white crystals poured into the cabin. What was this? Snow? She recognized it from the videos in the library, but had never expected to see it on Valencia.

She stood in the hatch and looked around Hidden Basin. The landscape gleamed white, hidden beneath a thick layer of glistening powder. It covered the deck and bent the bows of the cone trees beyond the camp. Cold flakes drifted down and melted on her arms. No wind stirred, and the scent of the ocean had vanished. The air, heavy with snow, absorbed sounds.

Nobody walked on the beach. Were Attom and his wives huddling in their tent? Were the children safe and warm? How would they find food with the ground covered in snow?

Persey turned up the biosynthesizer to make more algae bricks. Everyone hated them, but at least they were nutritious. She could feed the colony, help the others survive.

Valencia, once a tropical paradise, now seemed like a frozen wasteland.

———— «» ————

Lois's burned back ached from sleeping on a stone slab in the cave. Apollo slept curled next to her, his face framed by wisps of brown beard. Beetles crawled on the walls and ceiling; their twinkling lights illuminated the domed room with dancing sparks. Nearby, more beetles pushed a crystal sphere onto a pedestal of stone. They clustered around the brain and formed a glowing sphere, a complete bug-eye colony. Two more bug-eye colonies coalesced in other corners of the room. The beetle legs rustled and clicked, keeping Lois awake. She hated the thought of thousands of walking eyeballs watching her.

In the center of the room, the great mound of cone tree nuts roiled with frenzied rattie lizards. Their slender tails whipped as they fed on the bounty, sawing the nuts with serrated tongues. Lois knew that the common forest lizards laid eggs almost as fast as they consumed food.

While she watched, a phalanx of beetles attacked the rattie vermin at the edge of the nut pile. The lizards fought back, amputating beetle legs with their tongues. The swarm of beetles used their cutter jaws to gouge chunks of flesh, eating the lizards alive. The ratties squeaked agony but, in the end, only scales remained. The carnage made Lois shiver.

The noise of the battle woke Apollo. He and sat upright and stretched his arms. "What's happening?"

"The ratties eat the cone tree nuts, and the beetles eat the lizards." Lois knew that the beetles were carnivores. She wondered why they ignored the two lost humans. If they got hungry, would she and Apollo be next?

"So that's why the beetles carried nuts into the cave," Apollo said, "to feed the ratties."

Lois raised her eyebrows. "The lizards are livestock, emergency food rations. But not for us."

"I'm hungry too," Apollo said. He offered Lois the last of the cooked nutmeat.

Lois accepted the small handful. "Thanks, but what will you eat? Let's build a fire and roast more."

Apollo gathered nutshells for fuel and used Lois's fire piston to ignite them. As soon as the shells caught, more beetles crawled into the flames. The heat caused their bodies to explode with a popping sound, spraying clear liquid that doused the blaze.

Lois's nose burned from the acrid steam. "I guess the beetles don't like fire."

Still hungry, Lois watched the twinkling lights around them. The colonies blinked coded patterns, sending signals around the cave. The beetles on the walls and ceiling flashed in response and began to march in waves. Patterns formed curling spirals that merged, dispersed, and made new geometric shapes. Triangles twirled and expanded into complicated polygons. Rings of light rippled outward and reflected off each other, then coalesced into bright flashes.

"I think they're dancing with light," Apollo said.

Lois, enthralled by the twinkling displays, took a moment to speak. "It could be another kind of bug-eye art."

As they watched, the nearest colony extruded a small, transparent sphere. The miniature crystal brain winked purple light as two beetles pushed it across the cave floor. A second colony also extruded a small transparent sphere. The beetles pushed them together and the two miniature crystal brains fused with a bright purple flash.

"What happened?" Apollo asked.

"The bug-eyes had sex and made a new colony." The thought made Lois smile.

Beetles throughout the cave chittered. The noise merged and swelled to a low thrum that filled the cavern. The powerful sound shook Lois's body, and a pungent mist permeated the room. Beetles flashed light to the beat of the sound.

"It looks like a celebration," Lois said, "welcoming the baby colony."

When the reverberations faded, a ring of beetles surrounded them, marching in a circle, flashing lights in unison.

"This is the first time the bug-eyes have noticed us." Anxiety made Lois tense.

The three bug-eye colonies in the cavern relayed blinking signals back and forth, as if Lois and Apollo were the focus of a debate.

"I'm sorry I led us here," Apollo said. "We should try to escape."

The marching beetles that encircled them now formed two glowing spokes, with light pulses radiating inward at Lois and Apollo. Along each spoke, the beetles carried a silvery oblong object as long as Lois' hand and pointed at each end. The nearest beetles deposited the gifts on the cave floor.

Lois looked at the glistening slivers in the dim light. "What are they?"

Apollo leaned close. "They look like screwfish!"

Lois exhaled. "That's impossible. We're far from the ocean." She touched one. "It isn't real. There's no head or tail."

"They're trying to feed us!" Apollo said. "Somehow, the bug-eyes have made fake fish."

"They must have used chewed lizard flesh." Lois grimaced. "Are we supposed to eat them?" He stomach knotted in hunger.

"There's only one way to find out. I hope they're not poisonous." Apollo lifted the silvery fish and squeezed it. "It's soft." He sniffed the flesh and touched it with his tongue. "It seems okay."

Lois nipped a second ersatz fish and chewed the morsel. "It's good!"

"It tastes like cooked fish!" Apollo said, with his mouth full. "How did they learn to prepare fish?"

"The bug-eye nest outside our hut must have watched us cook our catch. Then they sent the recipe across Terra Firma."

"They must know *everything* about us." Apollo said. "So, what should we do now?"

"It's nice to have food, but I don't want to spend another night in this cave," Lois said. "Let's go home, if we can. I've seen enough." They gathered the remaining fake fish and started a slow crawl to the exit. Nearby beetles moved aside to let them pass. Where the chamber narrowed to the passage out of the cave, a curtain of beetles, legs hooked together, blocked their way. They flashed three times, then three time again.

"It's a warning; they've blocked the exit. We're trapped!" Lois's throat tightened and she gasped.

"Not for long." Apollo raked his hand, fingers curled, through the barrier. The beetles scattered, but two clung to his forearm, biting with sharp pincers. "Ow!" he yelled, banging his arm against a rock and smashing the eyeballs. Blood dripped from small cuts on his arm.

Lois peered down the exit passage. She couldn't see more beetles. "Let's go before they stop us!"

Together, they scrambled back the way they had come, over the slippery mudstone in the dim glow from the bug-eye chamber. Apollo helped Lois cross the crevasse with the rushing stream at the bottom.

"Should I knock down the beetles' bridge?" Apollo asked. "That way, they can't come after us."

Lois looked back. The passage remained dark. "They aren't following us. Leave it alone."

When they reached the outside, dim moonlight illuminated the pale forest. A featureless layer of white fluff covered the ground.

Apollo crawled out and stood up. "It's cold!" He danced from one foot to the other.

"It must be snow," Lois said. "Mother-9 showed me photos of winter on Earth."

"So that's why the bug-eyes warned us not to leave," Apollo said. "How did they know in advance the freeze was coming?"

Lois blew on her hands to warm them. Her bare feet, buried by the ankle-deep snow, were already numb. "We need to build a fire."

Apollo kicked at the snow and motioned at the white-shrouded forest. "How? The forest is cold and wet."

Lois glanced into the cave. "The bug-eyes stay warm underground. Let's shelter in the cave for a while."

"All right." Inside the mouth of the cave, Apollo gathered hundreds of nut shells discarded by the ratties, the only dry fuel available. Lois used the fire piston to ignite a pile of them. They soon had a blaze going.

After eating more fake fish, Lois curled up with Apollo next to the fire. Bathed by its warm glow, the pair fell asleep.

———— ⟨⟩ ————

Lois woke in Apollo's arms inside the mouth of the cave, far from the domed room with the bug-eye beetles. The campfire had gone out, but she appreciated his warmth as cold crept in from outside. Her back hurt from another night sleeping on stone.

Dawn light filtered into the cave. Lois blinked and stared at the glistening rock walls, dripping with water.

"Wake up," she said. "Something is happening."

Apollo rolled and sat up, rubbing his eyes. "The sunlight is back to normal."

"More than that. Look…" On the mudstone floor, a line of bug-eye beetles marched toward the mouth of the cave, winking lights in a glowing procession. Most carried nuts in their jaws.

"Oh!" Apollo moved aside and looked down the dim passageway at the sparkly column. A wedge of beetles pushed a crystalline brain along the rough floor. It bumped and thumped on each pebble and crack, but its shiny surface remained unblemished. "They're moving from the domed room."

"Let's get a closer look," Lois suggested. Together, they made their way deeper into the cave. Beyond the twig bridge, the beetles struggled with a large crystal sphere. The heavy ball lurched and rolled forward into a dip in the stone, crushing three beetles at the front. Then, as the column reached the middle of the twig bridge, the arch sagged, and the dense crystal ball rolled off the edge. It bounced into a crevice in the rock, above the rushing stream. Purple light flashed from inside the ball.

An army of beetles descended and pushed on the sphere from below. Several beetles slipped on the wet stone and washed away in the stream. The ball remained stuck.

Apollo crawled forward under the low ceiling. "I'll get it."

"Don't touch it! The beetles will bite you again."

He shook his head. "They need my help."

"Be careful!" Lois marveled at Apollo's compulsion.

Apollo descended and straddled the stream. By this time, hundreds of beetles crowded the narrow space. Lois watched him reach into the mass of crawling eyeballs and cup the brain with his hand. He flinched as several beetles crawled up his forearm, but they didn't bite. He tugged once and then again, harder.

The sphere didn't move, wedged tight in the crevice.

Apollo leaned down and grabbed the slippery ball with both hands and locked his fingers. His back muscles bulged with the effort. Lois heard a scraping sound on the rock as it pulled free, emitting two purple flashes that lit the walls of the cave. As soon as he placed it on the other side of the sagging bridge, the beetles started rolling it again.

Lois reached down to help him climb out. "Are you okay?"

Apollo panted as he hauled himself up. "I'm fine. The beetles didn't bite—the bug-eyes knew I was trying to help."

Massed together, a team of beetles rolled the crystal brain out of the cave. "Where are they going?" Lois asked.

"Let's follow them."

Outside, warm air gusted over melting snow. Apollo touched withered leaves hanging from a nearby cone tree branch. "The forest looks dead. Most of the nuts on the ground are gone."

Lois watched the column of beetles emerge from the cave. They fanned out between the dead trees, carrying nuts. Each halted at a precise distance from the others and buried its nut in the damp soil.

"They're planting new trees," Lois exclaimed. "They sustain the forest, after the ratties ate most of the nuts."

The beetles rolled the crystal sphere through slush to the base of a nearby cone tree sapling that still bore green boughs. They linked legs around the brain and a long line of beetles pulled it up the trunk. Another group of beetles clustered high in the tree and a split appeared in the bark. The wood softened and stretched and the crystal brain popped inside the trunk. Then the protective wooden shell closed around it. More beetles attached to the outside, forming a new treetop bug-eye colony. They flashed two times.

Apollo chuckled. "You're welcome." Then he looked around at the dripping forest. "The snow will be gone by tomorrow."

Lois felt the sun on her cheeks through the overcast sky. "Winter-week is almost over." The light and warmth lifted her spirits. "But we still don't know the way home."

Apollo looked back at the bug-eye's cave as the last of the beetles exited. "Let's stay here tonight. We have food and water."

Lois knew that Apollo, raised on the lifeboat, hated wandering in the endless forest. "I want to leave soon. The cave is damp and uncomfortable."

"I'll make a proper bed." Apollo gathered moss, while Lois rebuilt the campfire at the mouth of the cave. They roasted their remaining cone tree nuts and warmed their hands and feet.

While they ate, Lois looked outside. The new bug-eye colony on the sapling had started its evening light show. Apollo followed her gaze. A spot of light appeared on one side of the nest. It brightened and expanded into a ring that traveled around the ball and then condensed into a spot again on the opposite side. This pattern repeated three times.

"That's not their usual display," Lois said.

The lighted rings traversed the ball three times again, paused, and then three times more.

"The rings always move in the same direction," Apollo said.

The bug-eye nest flashed the animated circles in a continuous sequence.

"It knows we're looking at it," Lois said. "It's pointing the way home."

"How do they know where we want to go?" Apollo scoffed.

"All the bug-eye colonies in the forest must know that humans live at Hidden Basin. Their lights guided Stella and me, when we got lost running from Dik."

"Why do they help us?"

"You're the same—you rescued their crystal brain." Lois realized that Apollo couldn't resist anyone in need, even the bug-eyes. She loved that about him.

"They also made funny fish for us to eat," Apollo said.

"It's almost gone now, along with the nuts in the forest. We'll need more food soon. I want to go home tomorrow, now that we know the way."

Apollo nodded. "Too bad we lost our catch—and the canoe. If we get hungry, Persey can supply algae bricks from the lifeboat." He wrinkled his nose in disgust.

Lois reclined on the moss bed. "Come to me now. Keep me warm."

Apollo complied, always ready to be with her. "Are you too sore to be touched?"

Lois placed his dark hand on her pale belly. "Do you feel that?"

He looked at her in the flickering light of the campfire. "You're round and pink."

Lois giggled. "More than that. I'm pregnant…"

Apollo hugged her. "That's *wonderful* news!"

Lois exhaled, relieved that Apollo approved. She closed her eyes as he climbed over her. Then thoughts beyond pleasure vanished.

Part 6: Survival

Jak huddled in the cold dawn next to his campfire in the forest, sheltered by an ancient cone tree. Its bare branches diverted most of the snowfall. Jak's hands and feet were numb.

In a week of bushwhacking, he'd found no sign of Jilzy and the twins. Could the children survive cold weather? The wilderness had turned hostile and alien, no longer the lush forest he'd known. Hunched against the cold, he resumed his slog through snow and the layer of nuts, using his walking stick to find footing. He kept his head down to avoid snow-laden branches.

As he passed beneath a cone tree, he heard a faint cough from above. A thin sniper-sloth hung upside down from a low branch, its belly white with snow. Jak looked for cover, but found none. The beast aimed its snout to fire a venomous tooth, but only snorted a small puff of steam. The dart fell to the ground from its nose. Jak hurried away before the predator could warm up and fire again.

Without Robota to show the way, Jak guessed his direction through the forest. White flakes fell from the overcast sky, obscuring familiar landmarks. Jak's anxiety flared as he trudged through melting snowdrifts and slush, completely lost. He couldn't decide if he was looking for Jilzy, or the way home. But late in the afternoon, he discovered the stump of a small cone tree, cut by him for the community shelter. Relieved, he trotted faster, slipping and stumbling on the snow-covered trail.

After two season-weeks in the wilderness, Jak limped onto the beach at Hidden Basin. The early afternoon sky reminded him of nighttime. The rest of the clan had gathered around a bonfire. Persey looked up and waved hello.

Attom turned and smiled. "Jak! Welcome back! Did you find them?"

Shivering, Jak squatted by the fire. "Eva is dead. I couldn't find Jilzy and the twins." Anguished, he couldn't talk more. Failure hurt his heart.

Persey placed her hand on his forearm. "You did the best you could." Her touch surprised and comforted him. "Where's Robota?" she said.

"She's worn out, so she returned to the wrecked lifeboat on Plymouth Rock." Then he paused. "I'm hungry. Is there anything to eat?"

Lois looked at him. "Since we lost the dugout, we don't have any fish."

Persey handed him a cold algae brick. "There are lots of these."

"You can have my cone tree nuts. I'm sick of them." Jak placed his bag on the ground next to the fire.

Chilled, he warmed his hands and feet near the flames and gnawed on the brick. Attom piled on more wood. Alta and Stella roasted the cone tree nuts in the embers while their children played in the snow. Jak relaxed in the heat, glad to be out of the dark forest.

Jain's thin voice startled him. Addled from age and traumas with Dik, she huddled beneath a blanket of lizard skins. With perfect pitch and clear tones, Jain sang "Miss Otis Regrets," one of the many songs from Earth that she'd learned as a child on *Lifeboat-11*. The sweet melody and delicate sentiment charmed him. Jak understood each word, but he couldn't grasp the song's meaning. He doubted that Jain did, either.

The warm saltwater in the lagoon steamed into the cold air, adding a chilling fog that crept up the beach. Jak moved closer to the flames. Persey sat next to him. Her touch and soothing words had warmed him. She'd never spoken to him before. Now he looked at her with new eyes.

"How are you doing with the bug-eye's language?" Lois had told him about Persey's work.

"I haven't made any progress. I can't reach Mother-9. I used to exchange greetings with the bug-eyes, but now, with the cold weather, the nearby colonies have abandoned their nests."

"Where did they go?"

"Lois says they retreat underground. The individual beetles aren't smart. They follow orders, although they forage on their own. To make progress, I need to work with an entire colony." She gestured at the old bug-eye nest on the spar he'd planted next to Lois's hut. "I'd like to use that one, but it's frozen and dead."

As Jak glanced up at the nest, a single beetle gave off a feeble flash. "Did you see that?" he said. "I think it's still alive. The campfire may have kept it warm."

Persey looked at Jak. "Can I study it aboard the lifeboat? To make progress, I need a bug-eye informant."

Jak nodded and showed Persey his hatchet. "Shall I cut it down?" Despite her reputation, he wanted to impress her.

"Yes, please."

Jak nodded and grinned. "It'll cooperate if we feed it."

"I have a few smoked fishes I can donate." Apollo retrieved them from Lois's hut.

Jak cut the bug-eye nest from the top of the spar. The wooden ball, as big as his head, weighed as much as a beach rock.

The beetle on the surface flashed a steady alarm.

"Don't worry," Jak said. "You're going to a warm new home."

——— «·» ———

Persey accepted the nest from Jak, careful not to touch the remaining beetles on the surface. "Thanks. I'll go now." She carried it to the lifeboat's aluminum dinghy and stepped aboard. She hesitated, unsure where to put the bug-eye colony.

"Wait," Jak said, "You can't row and hold the nest at the same time." He seemed eager, as if he didn't want to lose contact with her.

Persey looked at him. "I don't like visitors." Then she smiled. "But you can come with me this one time."

Jak rowed the dinghy to the lifeboat. When they arrived, he carried the nest inside and propped it up in front of the ship's computer. Then he sprinkled warm water on its surface, letting it soak in.

Persey keyed a series of blinking bright spots on her display. The beetles on the nest, wakened by the warmth inside the cabin, repeated the pattern.

"It answered you!" Jak said.

Persey shook her head, blonde curls waggling. "I sent a standard bug-eye greeting. They replied, but not with their usual signal. I have no idea what they said. I'm not even sure that the bug-eyes have a language."

"Let me try." Jak reached into his pouch and laid a screwfish in front of the colony ball. The beetles flashed a series of light pulses and then detached and fed on the fish, shredding it with their sharp pincers. After they finished feeding, the beetles reattached to the nest and repeated the series of light pulses.

Persey recorded the beetle's response and compared it to various graphs on her display. "I don't see any matches."

"Could that be their sign for hunger? Or food?" Jak asked.

Persey shrugged. "I'll add it to my list of possible words."

"I have an idea," Jak said. "Turn the cabin lights on. Let's see what happens."

Persey raised her eyebrows. She flicked the lights on for a long moment, then off again. They observed a new series of flashes from the beetles.

"Have you seen that sequence before?"

Persey processed the new string. "It may be their word for morning. Or, for solar flares."

Jak climbed onto the deck of the lifeboat and scooped a handful of snow. Without waiting for Persey's consent, he sprinkled it on the bug-eye nest. The beetles blinked another sequence.

"I have dozens of similar recordings," Persey said, her voice growing enthusiastic. "They sent that sequence before the sky went dark."

"Could it be their word for snow?"

"You may be right..." Excited, Persey inhaled. "Give them a reward."

Jak grinned and laid another dried screwfish on top of the ball.

Persey glanced at Jak. "Are *you* hungry? All I have are algae bricks." Did she want to please him?

Jak shook his head. "I should return to Hidden Basin. It's cold, they might need help cutting firewood."

"It's getting dark." Persey spoke above a whisper. "Besides, they've got plenty of wood."

Jak reached for Persey's hand. "Do you want me to stay?"

Persey trembled as she squeezed his fingers. Her mouth moved, but no sound came out. "Yes," she said, on the second attempt.

Jak caressed her cheek with his other hand.

Persey's shoulders shook. She gripped his hand and silent tears streamed down her cheeks. "I've been *so* lonely." Then, with obvious effort, she looked at him.

Jak wrapped his arms around her.

"I'm not going anywhere."

Persey held him tight as silent sobs racked her body.

———— «» ————

Jilzy's feet hurt, the tough soles abraded by two season-weeks of hiking. She followed an animal trail that ran along the creek. Anton and Cleo straggled behind. They'd journeyed inland, away from the coast, always upstream, searching for a new home away from earthquakes and falling rocks.

Jilzy's mind churned with doubts. The alien and hostile forest offered no refuge. Strange weather—nuts dropping from cone trees, followed by a heat wave—had slowed their progress. But she resolved to carry on for the sake of the twins. She knew they missed Eva. At least they were healthy, if always hungry.

Anton waded into the shallow brook, where a back eddy made a quiet pool. His feet stirred up wriggling worms in the gravel. "Let's catch some of these to eat."

"Be careful, don't let the embers get damp." Unlike her brother Jak, Jilzy had never questioned Eva's strict rules. Now, she found herself bossing the twins in the same way. To Jilzy, discipline meant survival. A small mistake could be fatal.

Anton made a face at her. He carried a wooden cup, charred on the inside, that held the burning coals from their last campfire. After leaving Shelter Bay, it had taken Jilzy half a day to start a fire in the damp forest with Eva's fire piston.

She watched the children work together. Cleo took the cup of coals and started a small campfire. Anton waded into the water and shuffled his feet to dislodge more wriggle-worms from the gravel. He scooped up handfuls of the pink creatures, shorter than his thumb. They elongated and contracted their ridged bodies as they tried to escape. Cleo skewered the worms on twigs and roasted them in the flames.

Jilzy held out her hand. "Let me taste one to see if it's safe to eat."

Cleo hesitated and then handed a skewer to Jilzy. "Only one. The rest are for us. We caught them."

They're starving. Jilzy nibbled the worm. The cooked grub tasted meaty. She waited to see if her lips would go numb and then nodded. The twins gobbled the rest, their first hot food in a season-week.

Jilzy looked up at the dark sky, wondering if it would rain. But there were no thunderheads, only normal cloud cover. The light continued to drop, until noon felt like evening twilight. She lifted her eyes, hoping for a break in the clouds, but the sky continued to blacken. A chilly blast of wind swept their camp.

"I'm cold," complained Cleo. She crouched close to the fire while Anton squeezed next to her. They huddled for warmth without speaking. Jilzy collected more wood and built up the bonfire for the coming night.

Sundown brought total darkness, no moon glow, no twinkling lights in the trees, only the red embers of the fire. Jilzy listened to the forest, but no wind moved through the trees. Only a faint burble from the stream allowed her to orient herself. The twins dozed in each other's arms, snuffling and breathing. Jilzy poked the fire, sending sparks upward.

Freezing flakes fell from the sky, silent, slow, and stinging. Jilzy had never experienced anything like this during winter-week. She felt betrayed by the harsh weather, by the land itself. Eva's death, near-starvation, dark skies, and now cold eroded her will to survive. Would they die alone here? Did it matter?

Cleo mewled in a bad dream. Jilzy put her arms around the twins in a vain attempt to shield them from the chill. She dozed, but couldn't sleep in the cold.

Morning dawned with feeble light. The forest and the ground had turned white overnight. Jilzy pushed her fingers through the layer and squeezed it into a ball. Was it safe to eat? Curious and hungry, she placed some in her mouth, where it melted to water. She'd never experienced anything like this relentless cold.

Only the little stream remained untouched. It still flowed in its bed of loose gravel. No white layer accumulated at its edge. Jilzy led Anton and Cleo to the bank, where they drank and waded in the shallows. The water felt warm, almost hot, compared to the air. A thin layer of mist hung above the stream. Anton, still shivering from the cold night, lowered his body into a deeper waterhole, covering himself to the chin. Cleo followed. Happy for the moment, the twins splashed each other, playing.

Inspired by the warmth of the water, Jilzy led Anton and Cleo upstream along the bank. Their bodies steamed as they harvested hook-thorn pods and ate the kernels raw. By afternoon, they reached a low waterfall that flowed from a pond. A cloud of white mist rose from the rushing water. At the base of the falls, fat suckerfish perched on rocks in the rapids. They were the size of Jilzy's fist and appeared to be nothing but mouths filled with black, serrated teeth. The creatures had small eyes and no fins. Minnows and wriggle-worms swept over the falls into their waiting jaws.

Jilzy sharpened her walking stick on a lava boulder and waded into the stream. The closest suckerfish ignored her and remained stuck on a rock. She placed the point of her spear into its big mouth, and the creature clamped its teeth onto the wood. Jilzy tried to lift it out of the water, but the fish clung to the rock. Its maroon body looked like a ripe vine fruit, with a suction cup on its belly. Jilzy pulled harder, until the creature dropped the rock. Then she impaled the fish with her spear, killing it.

"Let me try!" Cleo called.

Jilzy handed her the spear, and the girl caught two more. Anton insisted on a turn and stabbed another. Dripping wet, the twins shivered as they stood grinning over their catch. Jilzy started a fire from the saved embers and cooked the fish. They gorged on flesh that tasted like wriggle-worms. The hot food cheered them.

While they ate, more white flakes fell from the gray sky. Jilzy didn't know what to make of the weather, so different from the warmth of Shelter Bay. She kept quiet to avoid worrying the twins, but she knew they sensed her dark mood. She wanted to press on, to find a suitable shelter. The children couldn't survive outside in the cold much longer. She yearned for normal warm weather, and missed their comfortable life in the cave where Eva made all the decisions.

The pond above the falls steamed in the frigid air. Jilzy tested the water with her foot. *It's warmer!* They followed the pond's edge to the base of a low cliff, where hot water gushed from the ground.

Jilzy found a level shelf of rock below an overhang. Heat from the hot spring warmed the air. The cold flakes couldn't touch them now. "We'll camp here for a while," Jilzy said.

"Look," Cleo said, "there's a little cone tree that still has blinking lights, even in daytime."

Near the pond, the trees were short, several of them no taller than Jilzy. She walked to a stunted tree, whose crown held a twinkling nest as big as her head. Beetles clung to the surface—their flashing lights illuminated the ground. Nearby nests flashed in response. To Jilzy, the little trees looked like people, each with a swollen head that glowed with life.

Anton and Cleo joined her, holding her hands and staring at the nest. Anton waved his hand, "Hello!"

To Jilzy's amazement, the nest blinked twice in response.

Cleo stared. "What *are* you?"

The beetles on the ball flashed a rotating spiral of light.

"It answered!" Anton said.

"I don't know if it can hear you," Jilzy said, "but I'm sure it sees you."

"It likes us," declared Anton in a firm voice. "I *know* it!"

The ball flashed another spiral, now rotating in the opposite direction. Cleo squealed with laughter.

Jilzy looked at Anton and smiled. The twins had been so brave after the earthquake, the death of Eva, and their endless trek through the forest. No wonder they saw the blinking nest as their friend.

"Don't touch the bugs," Jilzy warned. "They bite."

──── ⟨⟩ ────

Jak relaxed in the warm summer-week sun on the deck of the lifeboat. He inhaled the salt air while Persey squeezed his hand. The lovers had spent the last year-month together, often in bed. They continued to work on bug-eye language studies, but had made little progress.

"Time for me to row ashore." Jak stroked Persey's curly blonde hair, delighted to be with her. He'd never imagined such happiness, surprised to be with an unlikely lover. He didn't want to leave.

Persey's kiss lingered as she stroked his arm. "Why do you have to go? Attom could help Apollo."

"Attom is busy with his family. Apollo wants to cut wood for the community shelter. It was my idea, and I should help. I'll be back tomorrow evening." He lifted his pack, filled with a water skin and algae bricks.

As he rowed the lifeboat's old dinghy across the lagoon, Jak looked up at the gray clouds. He worried about Valencia's daily weather changes.

The sky had brightened yesterday, bringing another heat wave. But the cone tree forest still hadn't recovered from the prolonged freeze. Many of the older trees had died. New saplings sprouted from the fallen nuts.

Apollo met him on the beach. The two friends hugged. "How are you getting along with Persey?" Apollo's tone of voice seemed skeptical.

"We're good together." Jak didn't say more, knowing how much Apollo hated his sister. "How's Lois?"

Apollo smiled. "She's resting in our hut. Her belly's getting big. That's why I wanted your help. Last season-week I located more dead cone trees in the upland forest, away from the camp. They're not too big, about the right size for construction."

Jak hefted his axe. "Let's go before it gets warm."

As they hiked the well-worn trail from the beach, Apollo pointed to a mound of beetles crawling on the forest floor next to a massive cone tree. "What are they doing?"

"Let's take a look." Jak approached with caution. He used his walking stick to probe into the roiling mass. A few beetles moved aside, revealing white bone.

"It's a body!" Apollo shouted.

Jak stumbled backward, horror-struck by the half-eaten corpse. "Who could it be? Is anyone missing?"

"I...I don't know," Apollo muttered. "It could be Jain. She often wanders in the forest and forgets where she is. Alta and Stella have to look for her."

Apollo brushed away more of the beetles, revealing a ravished face and blonde hair. He took a ragged breath. "It's Jain, all right. We should have paid more attention, kept her safe."

Jak grimaced. "She wasn't happy, even with grandchildren. Was it deliberate?"

Apollo shook his head. "I don't think so. After her memories faded, she seemed to recover from Dik's death."

"If it wasn't suicide, then the beetles dropped from the tree and attacked," Jak said. "She was easy prey, an old woman who couldn't run away."

"No," Apollo said. "She seemed sick. She had trouble breathing and had no appetite. She died, old and alone. And the beetles..." Apollo closed his eyes. "The beetles found her body and ate it. That's what scavengers do."

Jak repressed a wave of nausea. "I doubt it, but we'll never know. Help me carry her back to camp."

The two men reached for Jain's shoulders and feet, but as they started to lift the body, the beetles raced up their arms, biting chunks of skin.

"Run!" Jak shouted. "Or they'll eat us next!" From a safe distance, he observed the beetles as they resumed their feeding frenzy.

"Why did they attack us?" Apollo said.

Jak shuddered. "We were stealing their meat."

"I don't want to watch them eat," Apollo said. "Let's come back later to collect the bones. We'll give Jain a proper burial—Alta and Stella will want to be there. There's nothing more we can do now."

The two men continued their hike. By late morning, the bright sky had darkened with roiling clouds.

"I hope it rains," Apollo said. "It's been dry since the snow melted."

After they reached the work site, Apollo cleared the brush around the trees he had selected. When Jak tested his axe, the blade nicked the bark and bounced back.

"Dead wood is much harder to cut." He sharpened his axe on a stone and tried again. Scattered chips fell around the base of the trunk.

Clouds continued to roll in as Jak worked. Soon, he noticed a sharp odor, a pungent zing in his nostrils. "Do you smell that?"

Apollo sniffed. "Smells like...ozone. Persey said it comes before a lightning storm. We should go back to the camp."

Jak started to answer when he saw long strands of black hair stand upright on Apollo's scalp. A moment later, lightning slammed into a nearby cone tree, an ancient giant that towered above the others. It exploded, sending shards of bark flying into Jak's face.

"Get down!" Jak dropped his axe and flung himself to the ground. Apollo did the same as a second bolt struck the tree again. Jak's body twitched, and his arms tingled. His ears rang, and the bright flash had blinded him.

"Smoke!" Apollo yelled.

Jak's vision started to recover. Black wisps drifted up from a nearby bush. He raced over and used his backpack to beat out the flames.

Apollo stomped out a second fire at the base of a tall tree. He heaped dirt and rocks on top of it, but the flames burned higher, catching low branches.

"The fire is too big!" Apollo yelled. "I can't stop it!"

Jak saw the tree's bark blister as its poisonous sap boiled and a yellow mist enveloped the tree. Then the gas exploded, knocking Apollo to the ground. Acrid smoke and red flames billowed outward.

Even from a distance, the fireball singed Jak's hair. Panic paralyzed him as the flames raced upward through the branches. Bug-eye beetles rained down through the fire, their eyeballs popping with the heat as they fell, producing a fine mist. In moments, the spray had quenched the flames. Sticky ichor stained his skin and burned his eyes. More beetles converged and cleared the still-smoldering embers that remained.

Apollo lay curled on his side, moaning. Blisters and raw flesh covered his back. Jak fought for self-control, afraid his friend was dying. He sprinkled the burns from his water-skin to cool them. "Does that help?"

Apollo shook his head. "How bad is it?"

Jak didn't want to alarm his friend, but he chose to tell the truth. "There's no skin on your back or your calves. Can you move?"

"I don't think so."

"Persey has medicines on the lifeboat."

Apollo shut his eyes and spoke through clenched teeth. "You won't make it back in time."

Jak couldn't let Apollo die alone in the forest. "I'll make a stretcher to drag you home."

Apollo groaned. "I'll never make it that far."

"We don't have a choice." Jak picked up his iron axe and examined it. Lightning had melted the cutting edge. He tried chopping a sapling, but the blunt blade bounced off it.

When Jak checked again, beetles had swarmed on Apollo's back and legs. His friend had passed out and was breathing through his open mouth, drooling. The beetles jiggled and crawled, clinging to his damaged skin with their sharp claws. Were they eating him?

"No!" Jak screamed. "Get off him!" He dropped to his hands and knees and batted the beetles away, revealing Apollo's back. What he saw shocked him. A thin, transparent film covered the exposed muscle, sealing Apollo's burns.

"They..." he couldn't believe his eyes, "they helped you?" Jak had seen the bug-eyes use the same waterproof coating to protect their treetop colony balls. He rubbed his eyes, overwhelmed by the unexpected aid.

When Apollo woke later that afternoon, his pale face had aged. "How do you feel?"

"My back hurts. What happened?"

Jak told him how the beetles had covered his burned skin. "Can you stand up?"

Apollo accepted Jak's hand and took a tentative step. "It's painful, but I can walk."

As the light faded, the two men trudged through the silent forest. Apollo shuffled, leaning on Jak.

"The beetles saved my life, for the second time. Their cave protected Lois and me from the snowstorm."

"They must like you." Jak shook his head in wonder. "They also stopped a forest fire."

As they trudged home, Jak saw Jain's bones, stripped clean. He didn't know what to think about the bug-eyes. Would the others believe their story?

———— «‹›» ————

Persey lifted the forward hatch of *Lifeboat-11* and looked aft. Evening sun glinted from the Hidden Basin lagoon. "Can you help me, Jak?"

"In a moment."

His temporary workbench in the cockpit blocked the companionway hatch. She watched him finish sharpening his lightning-damaged axe. She admired his skill with tools, but she loved his energy in bed even more.

Jak put away his tools and descended into the boat's cabin. He peered at the bug-eye nest mounted next to her computer. Regular feedings had produced a full array of beetles on the surface of the colony, now recovered after the freeze.

"Making progress?" he asked.

"Not much. I'm getting frustrated."

As she spoke, the colony ball flashed a new sequence of lights.

"What did it say?"

"I don't know. After two year-months trying to decode their signals, I can't even decide if they're conscious."

Jak shrugged. "They find food and eat, don't they?"

"All animals do that. Human consciousness is special. It's what it *feels* like to be you."

"What does consciousness have to do with language?"

Persey tried to be patient. "True language enables self-awareness. If the bug-eyes are conscious, they may be able talk about abstract ideas, beyond the limits of their senses."

"The beetles put out a forest fire and saved Apollo," Jak said. "He believes they're intelligent, but I think they acted on instinct. I doubt they're any smarter than forest lizards."

"Swarming beetles aren't intelligent," Persey said, "but each bug-eye colony has a crystal ball at its center. Those spheres might be their brains, the seat of the colony's consciousness."

"So, the bug-eyes sit in the treetops and think big thoughts?"

"How do you explain Apollo's triangle ball, an icosahedron with twenty faces? That required geometry."

Jak shrugged. "On Earth, spiders built spiral webs."

Persey didn't want to argue. "For now, let's assume the bug-eyes *can* talk by blinking lights. I've given their language a name. I call it Beetalic."

Jak repressed a smile. Persey ignored it.

"Since I can't understand them," she continued, "I've decided to teach the bug-eyes human language."

"Are you going to talk to them?"

"No. They can hear but don't use sound to communicate. Their treetop colonies are too far apart, so they use blinking lights. I'll do the same"

"How are you going to turn human words into lights?"

"I've assembled some pictograms from the ship's library." Persey scrolled through warning signs, computer icons, and math notations. "I plan to start with simple symbols of common objects, made with light patterns."

"I think the bug-eyes use blinking lights to make animal calls."

Persey sighed. "I used to believe that too. Now, I have a different theory. Their light signals may be like Egyptian hieroglyphs."

Jak grimaced. "What's a high-row...?"

Persey rolled her eyes. *Such a barbarian!* "It's a written language where a symbol stands for a word or concept. They're called ideograms, idea pictures." She showed him an ancient tomb inscription on her computer display.

Jak's smile widened. "Weird people with animal heads. Who knows what they mean?"

"Champollion, that's who. He was the Frenchman who first decoded Egyptian hieroglyphics. That's what *I'm* trying to do now."

Jak shook his head. "Egyptians were human and the bug-eyes aren't. They won't think like us, if they can think at all."

"True, but we have an *informant*, a living speaker." She gestured at the colony ball. "Unlike Champollion, we're not deciphering a dead language."

Persey displayed a digital photo of a cone tree on her computer. Then she drew a diagram of a tree, a tall triangle with a wide base, shown in white lines on a black background.

After a moment, the beetles reproduced the tree pictogram on the colony ball.

"Yes," Persey whispered, growing excited. "That's a good start."

"They're just copying it," Jak said. "They don't actually understand what..."

"Quiet!" Persey snapped.

A moment later, the beetles sent a complex ideogram, a series of light flashes across the surface of the colony ball. Persey recorded the pattern on her computer. She shivered with anticipation.

"They've translated the diagram for 'tree' into Beetalic. Feed the beetles a bit of fish."

Jak dropped a fish tail onto the ball. "They could have copied the tree diagram without understanding."

"True. Let's try again," Persey said.

She played a short video of the Great Ocean. Then she displayed a wiggly line pictogram, with moving waves. The colony duplicated the animated pattern on its surface, followed by another Beetalic sequence.

"It's working!" Persey grinned. "They reproduce each pictogram, followed by a Beetalic ideogram. I'm recording the translated word in a Beetalic dictionary."

Overwhelmed, Persey clapped her hands. She swept Jak into her arms and kissed him. Then she turned back to her work.

"Try the reverse," Jak said. "Send Beetalic light flashes and see how they respond."

Persey flashed a Beetalic ideogram, and the bug-eye ball displayed the tree pictogram. "See? I told you so."

Jak shook his head. "This could take a long time."

"Be patient. We're starting with simple nouns. Next, we need verbs. We're building vocabulary."

Jak leaned closer, now caught up in her enthusiasm. "How will you teach action words?"

"Like this. Show them a whole screwfish, but don't give it to them yet." Persey presented a diagram of the fish, a flattened oval with a twisted tail. The bug-eye colony mimicked the symbol and blinked another complex ideogram.

"Good. Now, take a bite of the fish."

Jak laughed. "Oh, I get it." He leaned forward and made a show of nipping the screwfish with his front teeth.

Persey displayed a profile pictogram of moving jaws, two curved pincers opening and closing. The bug-eye colony repeated the biting animation, followed by the fish icon.

"It understood!" Jak said. "It said, *Eat fish*."

Persey tensed with excitement. "This is the first moment of cross-species language! It spoke a whole sentence instead of isolated words."

Jak frowned. "How do you know it wasn't repeating your last two symbols?"

Persey grinned, pulling Jak in front of the bug-eye ball. "Hold out your arms and hands, so the beetles can see you."

Jak positioned himself in profile view, arms bent and hands flat, imitating an Egyptian hieroglyph. Then he stuck out his tongue.

"Stop that!" Persey drew a stick figure of a man on the screen. "Now take another bite of fish."

The bug-eye ball responded with a figure of a man, moving jaws, and a fish symbol.

"*Human eat fish*," translated Jak. He laughed. "It talks like a toddler."

"Be quiet and feed it again."

The beetles on the nest consumed the treat. Then they flashed three pictograms: two concentric circles, jaws, fish.

Jak frowned. "What does a double circle mean?"

Persey tingled with excitement. "The bug-eye colony is spherical. It gave itself a name we could read. It's self-aware after all!"

"That deserves a reward." Jak laid another strip of fish on the ball. "Here you go, OO."

The beetles consumed the food. Then they flashed again: "*OO eats human.*"

"I hope they're joking," Jak said, his voice uneasy. "Do they mean Jain?"

"It must be a mistake." Persey stretched her back to ease tension. "Let's keep working, as long as OO is willing."

They traded transliterations for the rest of the day and into the night. Persey provided pictograms, and the bug-eye colony replied in flashing Beetalic ideograms. Jak stayed with her, feeding the beetles chunks of fish. Persey ate algae pellets. They compiled a common vocabulary of over 300 words.

After a long pause, Persey realized that OO had stopped. She closed her eyes and leaned back in her chair. "They're tired. I'm exhausted too."

Then the colony ball produced another long flashing sequence. Beetalic ideograms blinked on and off across its surface. *Such a beautiful language.*

"What did it say this time?" Jak asked.

Persey ran a correlation analysis on the alien ideograms. A scrolling line of text at the bottom of the screen read: "*beauty desire future rain life fish.*"

"What a strange jumble of words!" Jak said. "What do they mean by beauty?"

"I'm struggling with bug-eye syntax. Their language doesn't use word order—sentences with a subject, verb, and object—like ours does. I don't know how to ask a question in Beetalic."

Jak nodded but said nothing.

Persey displayed animated pictograms of a stick man and OO alternating. "I hope that shows that I'm confused."

The colony ball waited several moments before replying in Beetalic. The computer scrolled the words, "*OO leave cave.*"

Jak frowned. "The bug-eyes want to leave?"

"The boat cabin is like a cave—they can't see the sky," Persey said.

"Apollo and Lois stayed in a bug-eye cave," Jak said. "The cold snap is over."

Persey watched more Beetalic ideograms and pictograms scroll across the nest, and then the computer translation: "*talk outside tree.*"

"Outside?" Persey said. "Do they mean on deck?"

"It wants to talk with its friends in the forest," Jak said. "The other bug-eyes colonies have returned to the treetops after the thaw."

Persey hesitated. "I don't want to stop the lessons. We've started to make progress."

"If OO is conscious, we shouldn't keep it prisoner."

"I suppose you're right," Persey sighed. "The ship's masthead light and cameras are still intact from my failed attempts to communicate with the bug-eye colonies in the forest. We could hoist OO to the top, near the light, so it can see other nests."

Jak nodded. "Good, I'll do it. But first I'll feed it fish and water. Who knows how long it will want to stay up there?"

Persey kissed his cheek. Jak was a good man and a great lover. It didn't matter that he wasn't her equal. He worked hard, helped her, and had good ideas. Most of all, he made her feel loved and wanted, an experience she never imagined or hoped for.

Persey watched Jak use the halyard to haul OO's colony nest up the mast. As it neared the top, it exchanged long streams of Beetalic ideograms with nearby colonies. She rushed below, but her computer couldn't translate the conversation.

Jak returned to the cabin. "Look! Now OO is sending human pictograms across the forest to other nests, teaching them our symbols!" The computer displayed icons for *jaws, man, fish,* and *ocean.* "*Men eat fish from the sea.* Why are they saying that?"

Persey floated on a wave of euphoria. "Soon we'll be able to converse with other colonies, not just OO!" She imagined Champollion talking to ancient Egyptians, across time and cultures. *This is even better.* "OO can ask them questions, and we'll get answers."

"I hope we like what they say," Jak said.

———— «» ————

"Hold still," Lois said. "This is going to hurt."

"Make it quick. The itching is driving me crazy." Apollo lay on his chest on the low bed in their hut.

Starting at his shoulder, Lois peeled the transparent coating from Apollo's back. In the last two year-months, new skin had grown under the sealed film applied by the bug-eye beetles. Apollo squeezed his eyes shut, but remained silent. Lois hoped his new, pink skin wasn't tender.

Now free, Apollo twisted and bent his back, testing his muscles. "It still hurts but it's easier to move."

Lois offered sedative soup to help him sleep, prepared from boiled seaweed and fish eggs. The rank odor reminded her of the beach at low tide. Apollo wrinkled his nose as he sipped it from a carved wooden bowl.

"Jak is here to take me to the lifeboat," Lois said. "Persey asked to see me. Try to sleep. I'll be back tomorrow."

Apollo nodded and reclined his head, lying on his side. She felt a pang of guilt from leaving him alone.

Dusk fell as Jak rowed the lifeboat's aluminum dinghy across the lagoon. Lois carried a basket of smoked screwfish, careful not to bump her bulging belly.

As they approached *Lifeboat-11*, Persey grabbed the bowline. "Thanks for coming." She seemed friendly now. Her personality had changed since she had taken Jak as a lover.

The Great Ocean glimmered in the light of the orange sunset as Lois climbed aboard. She loved the clean smell of salt air. Nothing seemed urgent; she wondered why Persey had insisted that she visit tonight.

"I've got something to show you." Persey pointed to the top of the mast. "Jak hoisted your bug-eye nest so it can talk to its neighbors in the forest. We've learned its name is OO. Using the masthead light and a cameras, I can communicate with other colonies."

Lois regarded Persey with new respect. "Are you making progress with their language?"

"Yes, a little. We've exchanged simple messages."

Lois detected a note of pride in Persey's voice. "What did they say?"

"They want something. You should talk to them."

"Why me?"

"You're the headwoman," Persey said. "You can speak for the humans in Hidden Basin."

How odd that Persey would defer to her! "I'm not in charge. I only mediate disputes."

"This may be a negotiation. You should be the one to decide what to say to the bug-eyes, not me."

"All right." Pleased but wary, Lois remained cautious.

The two women climbed down into the lifeboat's cabin. Jak already sat at the ship's computer terminal. On the divided screen, Lois saw four bug-eye colonies flashing at each other.

"These are camera views of different bug-eye nests, taken from the top of the mast," Jak said.

"They're speaking Beetalic," Persey said, "their blinking-light language. I can translate a few phrases, but I often miss the meaning. I'll tell them you're here."

As Lois watched the display, a distant colony responded with a pictogram of a circle with a big *dot* in the center, followed by a series of complex flashes. Persey typed at her keyboard, explaining as she worked. "I'm using the Beetalic translator on the ship's computer." Text scrolled across the bottom of the screen: *O-dot talk now.*

Surprised, Lois raised her eyebrows. "Who is O-dot?"

"O-dot is one of the largest of the bug-eye colonies in the forest. It asked to talk to the 'biggest' human. That's why I sent for you. I think it wants to talk to our leader. I call you LL."

Lois had no idea what to say. "Greetings, O-dot. I speak for humans." Her words felt forced and stilted. She watched Persey send it, one Beetalic character at a time.

The response from O-dot appeared as a mix of Beetalic ideograms and human pictograms. Persey translated the message. *"Demand circle death."*

Lois shuddered. "That's strange. What does it mean?"

Persey's answered in a choked voice. "I have no idea."

"O-dot said *demand*," Jak interjected. "What do they want?"

"There must be a problem with the translation," Persey said. "I'll try again."

After a moment, Lois looked at the display, "It's similar result: *circle now LL death*. It *does* feel like a threat."

"If we have to fight the bug-eyes, I know how to make a bow," Jak said. "A single arrow through the crystal-ball should kill a colony. They can't run away—they're stuck in the treetops."

"No!" Lois shook her head, "We don't want to start a war with the bug-eyes. There are billions of beetles and only a few of us. If they swarm, they'll eat us alive."

"She's right," Persey said. "Their colony eyeballs can see everything, and they're all across Terra Firma. They can marshal tens of thousands of nests."

"They're threatening to kill us!" Jak rose to his feet, his face pale. "You didn't see what they did to Jain—stripped the flesh from her bones. If they try to swarm us, I say we fight. The beetles are slow, afraid of fire, and can't go in water," Jak inhaled. "They don't have weapons. We can defend ourselves."

Lois placed her hand on Jak's shoulder. "Calm, down. It must be a mistake." She turned to Persey. "Can you please try again?"

Persey nodded. "We don't want an interspecies war. I'll ask O-dot to explain the message." She sent the request in Beetalic.

After a long pause, O-dot replied with a single pictogram of a circle with a triangle inside.

Lois stared at the arcane symbol. "I don't understand." Sweat prickled on her neck.

Jak squinted at the glowing diagram. "Could the circle around the triangle mean Apollo's ball of triangles—the bug-eye sculpture? The beetles attacked him when he stole it."

"Do you mean the icosahedron?" Persey said. "I have it here." She lifted the hollow globe from behind her bed. "This may be precious to them. Jak, please take it on deck and haul it up the mast. Show it to OO."

After a time, Jak returned to the boat cabin. "It's up there. The beetles crawled all over it, and OO made a lot of flashes."

Persey raised her finger. "Here's O-dot's response: *Beauty twenty good*." She sagged back in her chair. "I should have realized that the stolen triangle-ball was the problem."

Lois breathed a sigh. "That's a relief! They must love geometry—or the ball has religious meaning."

"But that doesn't explain what O-dot meant by death," Jak said.

Persey shivered. "It could be a warning, a reminder that they can retaliate, if we betray them."

"We can't let that happen," Lois said.

———— «»————

Lois woke disoriented in the middle of the night, with Persey prodding her shoulder. She had dozed while the four bug-eye colonies blinked at each other.

"Look, here's a new message from the masthead video feed," Persey said. "You should see this."

Lois watched three pictograms appear on screen. The first was a large dot with lines radiating downward. The next showed a cone tree lying on its side. The last indicated a triangular hazard symbol.

"What does it say?" Jak asked.

Persey studied the symbols. "My guess is: *bright sunlight kills the forest*. The bug-eyes must know about solar flares."

"But the cone trees dropped their nuts *before* the flare lit up the sky," Lois said.

"Random flares mean hot, dry, weather and increased forest fire risk," Jak said. "That may be the bug-eye's worst nightmare, all their trees and colonies burned up."

"So that's why the beetles retreated into the cave, carrying cone tree nuts with them," Lois said. "They knew in advance that bad weather, forest fires or freezing, was coming."

Persey sat upright. "The bug-eyes must *predict* solar flares! That's why their nests are big eyes that see the whole sky. The must observe subtle changes in solar radiation."

"I wonder, did the bug-eyes make the trees release their nuts?" Jak said.

"If you're right, that means the bug-eyes control the forests of Terra Firma." Lois shivered at the thought.

A new message scrolled across Persey's display. *Tree shapes gift.*

"What does *gift* mean?" Jak asked.

Persey squinted her eyes. "It could be an offer, something valuable."

"They'll want something in return," Jak said.

"The bug-eyes don't have anything we need," Lois said.

"That's not true!" Jak said. "We need more wood from the forest."

"Don't tell them that!" Persey said. "Let's see what they want, first."

The next message followed: "*jaws fish* >."

Lois shook her head. "What are fish jaws?"

"The jaws must be a mouth," Persey said. "O-dot is saying: *eat, fish,* and the greater-than symbol must mean *more.* They want more fish to eat."

"Apollo taught OO to love fish." Lois wondered if feeding them had been a mistake.

"After a flare," Persey said, "their food in the forest, crawlers and ratties, must be scarce. The bug-eyes are facing famine, like us."

"Are they asking us to feed them?" Lois said. "We can't do that without a seagoing boat. The little aluminum dingy isn't safe on the Great Ocean."

Persey tapped out a translation.

The reply seemed bleak: *no eat fast fish die.*

"Without fish to eat, they're facing a mass die-off, a population crash," Persey said. "It must happen after every major flare."

Lois nodded. "Everybody wants fish, but they're hard to catch. We've overfished the lagoon. Sometimes people go hungry during winter-week."

"Your dugout was too small for the Great Ocean," Jak said.

"There are other boat designs in the lifeboat's library." Persey displayed several images on her screen.

"I want one like that!" Lois pointed to a slender rowboat, pointed at each end, with two pairs of oars.

Jak studied the image. "I could build it, if I had the right wood. But it would take a long time, even with help."

Lois shook her head. "Tell them we're going to build a boat and catch more fish, but that it will take many year-months."

Persey sent three pictograms: a canoe floating on water, a fish, and two greater-than symbols. Then a series of pulses: one dot, two, three, four—an ever increasing number—that she explained meant more time.

The bug-eyes remained silent. Then Lois observed Beetalic light flashes between the four colonies. "What are they saying?"

"This could take a while," Persey said. "There is a disagreement."

Frustrated with the delay, Lois ate a handful of roasted cone tree nuts while she waited. The response came a few Beetalic ideograms at a time. Persey's computer attempted another translation: "*O-dot boat tree shapes fish >.*"

"Tree shapes?" Lois said. "O-dot signaled that before. What does it mean?"

"They're talking about shaping wood," Persey said. "I think they'll help us build a boat if we catch fish for them."

Persey looked at Lois. "As headwoman, you must decide."

Lois rubbed her pregnant belly. She felt the baby kick. "Let's try it; we have nothing to lose. If the agreement fails, Jak can build another boat."

"I don't agree," Jak said. "If we fail to feed the bug-eyes, they'll declare war."

Lois ignored Jak. "There's another reason to work with them. If the bug-eyes can predict flares, that'll help us survive bad weather." Lois remembered their time in the cave with the beetles. "We must learn to live in peace with our neighbors."

Persey grinned and keyed a '*yes*' in Beetalic.

O-dot replied immediately: *work tree shapes daytime.*

Lois turned to Jak. "Can you carve a model of the rowboat for the bug-eyes to follow? I've transferred the plans to my tablet."

Jak hesitated and then nodded. "Good idea. At least we'll control the design."

Persey hugged Jak. "You're the only one with the skills to make this happen."

Lois stared at Persey. Was she sincere? Jak beamed at the compliment. He needed to be needed.

"I'm going ashore now," Lois announced. Apollo waited for her. She needed to be needed too.

"I'll go with you," Jak said. "I want to start carving the model."

"Take the bug-eye colony and the icosahedron," Persey said. "We've finished with language lessons for the moment."

Jak nodded. "I'll replace the nest on top of the spar, where Apollo can feed it."

Persey kissed Jak. "Come back soon!"

Lois exhaled and felt herself relax. *This is the best chance for our baby.*

———— «»————

Jak waited on the beach at Hidden Basin, while Apollo rowed ashore in lifeboat's dinghy, the only craft available for fishing. With Lois close to term, Apollo fished alone in the borrowed boat. Gusts of wind from the Great Ocean rippled the water of the Hidden Basin lagoon and an overcast sky threatened rain. Apollo lifted two baskets of screwfish and stepped ashore.

Jak hefted one of the baskets. "Nice haul. These will keep the beetles happy and working hard."

Apollo grimaced and shook his head. "Feeding the beetles doesn't leave much for us. Alta and Stella are complaining."

"I know," Jak said. "But the beetles need food to finish their work."

The two men each carried a basket up the trail into the forest. Jak led them on a side path into a glade of mature cone trees.

"The worksite is ahead, near O-dot's nest," Jak enjoyed managing the bug-eyes' work on the new rowboat.

"I don't see anything." This was Apollo's first visit.

"Look up. O-dot's beetles are carving the hull from a standing tree. The bow is down and the stern is high in the air." Each day Jak checked on the beetles' progress. This morning, he saw the pointed stern for the first time.

Apollo glanced up at the trunk. "Why use a tree so far from the beach?"

"O-dot chose it. It's near O-dot's nest and was already dead, killed by the frost." Jak wondered if the bug-eyes would always have final say about harvesting the forest. He resented restrictions.

"It looks like they're almost finished," Apollo said.

Jak nodded, and gestured at the model he'd made. The beetles crawled over it, touching the surface. "They memorize the boat's lines with their feet and eyes. So far, they've done a good job."

"How did they know the size of the real boat?"

"I made signs for bigger, bigger, bigger." Jak stretched his arms around the trunk. "They carved the hull to fit inside the tree."

Apollo emptied the baskets of fish at the base of the tree. The two friends watched the beetles eat and then return to work on the rowboat. Jak listened to the faint crunching sounds from hundreds of sharp beetle jaws gouging wood. Sawdust rained down from the tree, leaving piles at the base and a faint, woody scent in the air.

Lois and Persey emerged from the woods and joined them. The two women had been gathering hook-thorn pods, with Lois teaching Persey wilderness survival skills. Jak marveled that they had become friends.

Lois looked up at the tree. "It looks like they're almost finished. When will it be ready?"

"Today. I invited you to witness the big event." A shiver of excitement rippled up Jak's spine.

After a short time, the beetles dropped off the hull and crawled into the forest litter.

"Let's cut it down," Apollo said. "Then we can haul it to the beach."

Jak honed his axe on a lava stone and eyed the neck of wood below the prow that held the boat upright. "Stand clear!"

With each blow of the axe, the balanced boat boomed a hollow sound. Jak chopped a notch to direct the fall. But as the boat started to tip, the bow broke loose and hit the ground with a loud crack. The top of the tree crashed nearby, covering the hull with branches.

Jak felt sick. "That didn't sound good."

After they cleared the boughs, Lois ran her hand over the bottom, next to the keel. "I can see light though the split."

Jak poked a finger through the crack. It extended almost to the bow, half the length of the hull. A wave of guilt overwhelmed him.

"I should have made a bed of boughs to cushion the fall."

Lois stepped back. "And the hull looks too narrow. It'll roll on its side in the water."

Jak frowned as he checked the dimensions. "I couldn't measure the shape when it was high in the air with beetles swarming over it." He shook his head, angry at himself.

"Can we ask the bug-eyes to carve another rowboat?" Lois asked.

Persey frowned. "They kept their end of the bargain. We'd need a lot more fish to start again."

"We need to eat too," Apollo said.

Silence followed. Jak glanced at Persey, but she wouldn't meet his eyes. *She thinks I've failed.* For a moment, he wanted run away, isolate himself with Robota in the derelict lifeboat on Plymouth Rock.

Apollo clapped Jak on the shoulder. "Let's carry the boat to the beach and try to fix it."

Jak felt a surge of gratitude. Apollo was a good friend.

The four lifted the boat and marched down the path to Hidden Basin. A steady drizzle started as they walked. They arrived at the beach and placed the boat on the sand near OO's bug-eye colony, now back on its post next to Lois and Apollo's hut.

The clan gathered to view the broken boat. Attom, Alta, and Stella emerged from their tent, along with their children. Jak inspected the hull again. The bow and stern showed beautiful craftsmanship. The beetles had incised the same Greek meanders that he had used to decorate the Community Hall.

Attom rubbed his wrinkled hand along the split near the keel and looked at Lois. "This boat will *never* be seaworthy."

Attom's words made Jak cringe. He wanted to slink away into the forest.

"Can't we fix the crack?" Apollo asked.

"We can try," Jak replied. "I have some pitch, boiled kite vine sap that I use to fasten axe heads. It's strong and might seal the gap." He retrieved a ball of tar from his workshop and placed it at the edge of the campfire to soften it.

Jak applied the gooey pitch with a pointed stick. Apollo worked with him, forcing the melted tar into the crack, leaving a black streak along the bottom of the boat.

After the pitch cooled, Jak rubbed it, testing the seal. At the far end, his fingers caught a loose edge. The ribbon of tar peeled back from the crack—it didn't stick. Jak swore in frustration.

Lois remained behind after the others had drifted away. "Any other ideas?"

Jak exchanged a glance with Apollo, then shook his head. "That's it. I can't fix it."

"I hate to disappoint the bug-eyes," Lois said. "No boat and no more fish."

As if in response, OO's colony ball next to Lois's hut flashed blinking lights in the gloomy twilight. A distant response came from the forest.

Lois looked at Persey, "What is it saying?"

Persey frowned. "I don't know. I think it's talking to O-dot."

"At least we can use the hull for firewood." Apollo looked at dark sky and the breakers at the shore of the Great Ocean. "There are still a few fish in the lagoon. I'll try to catch some tomorrow."

Jak bowed his head, sick at heart. All his life, he'd looked up to Lois, his big sister. He'd wanted to prove himself to her and impress his lover, Persey. The rowboat had been his responsibility.

Now, his failure meant more hunger and hostile bug-eyes.

——— ‹›› ———

Lois woke the next morning beside Apollo. She heard the chittering sounds of bug-eyes crawling nearby. Curious, she peeked outside the hut.

"Look," she said. "OO's beetles are climbing on the rowboat."

Apollo joined her, and they watched as more beetles descended from the colony ball. Another column of beetles crawled in single file from the forest.

"Jak and Persey should see this." Apollo walked to the edge of the beach and called across the lagoon to the lifeboat.

By the time they arrived in the dinghy, beetles covered the hull of the broken rowboat.

"What are they doing?" Jak asked.

Lois felt sorry for Jak. He looked anxious, and Persey seemed distant.

"I don't know," Apollo replied. "OO hasn't seen your model. It has no experience building boats."

"But the bug-eye colonies talk to each other," Lois said. "OO can see the damage to our rowboat. O-dot's beetles have joined them."

Lois watched the beetles secrete a layer of yellow fluid onto the interior of the hull. The wood softened and stretched, fusing the split together, healing the crack.

"Did you see that?" Apollo said, eyes wide.

Persey inspected the hull. "They must use enzymes to soften and bend the wood."

As the beetles worked, the boat's middle spread open to its proper width.

"*Now* I understand," Jak said. "The bug-eyes curled the hull to fit inside the tree, to make it as big as possible. They planned from the beginning to widen it after we cut it down."

As a final step, the beetles applied a second layer of clear liquid to the bottom. "It's a waterproof coating," Apollo said, "like they put on my back."

Persey tapped the hull. "The wood is harder than ever. It feels sturdy."

Lois ran her hand along the gunwale. "Is it finished?"

"Not quite." Jak measured the hull with a ruled stick. "The dimensions are correct, but the boat needs proper fittings. I made them in advance." While the others watched, he lashed adz-hewn rowing seats to the gunwales and used an iron awl to drill holes for leather-thong oarlocks. He mounted two pairs of carved oars. To finish, he installed a wicker fish basket amidships.

"The boat needs a name," Lois said. "Let's call it the *Accord*, for humans and bug-eyes working together."

Jak and Apollo dragged the rowboat into the lagoon, where it floated high in the water. Apollo climbed into the stern and held Lois's hand as she stepped aboard, careful with her protruding belly. The boat rocked, but didn't tip far. She sat amidships and checked the bilge for leaks. No water seeped in.

Then she grasped an oar. "I want to row on the first voyage."

"Wait," called Persey. "OO signaled the pictograms for boat and ocean. It wants to come too."

"The bug-eyes must be curious to see how the boat floats," Jak said. He detached the OO's nest from its post and climbed into the bow, holding it on his knees.

"Don't drop it overboard!" Persey waded into the water and loaded Apollo's hand net. Then she pushed the boat into the lagoon.

Lois and Apollo rowed together. The oar tips made broad, glistening arcs on the surface of the lagoon.

"It's easy!" Lois marveled. "The boat glides across the water." They rowed around the lagoon and circled the anchored lifeboat, laughing.

"I see a school of screwfish," Apollo announced. He dipped the net and dumped the catch into a creel in the bilge. He scooped again, filling the basket. The fish roiled and flipped, trying to escape.

Beetles from OO's nest dropped off and crawled to the trapped fish. They ate part of the catch and returned to the colony ball.

"They didn't leave much for us," Jak muttered.

When they returned to shore, Jak turned to Lois. "What do you think of the *Accord*?"

"It's twice as fast and easier to row than my old dugout," she said. "We can go farther and catch more fish."

Then Lois turned to face Jak. "We won't go hungry again, thanks to you!" She spoke in a clear voice to be sure that Persey heard.

Jak's face turned pink. "I...thank you."

Persey hugged and kissed Jak. "You did it! Sorry for being impatient. Will you forgive me?"

Jak grinned and nodded. Tears welled in his eyes. "I only carved the model from a design on Lois's tablet. The beetles did most of the work."

Apollo glanced at the forest. "Are O-dot's beetles still hungry?"

Lois looked at Apollo. "This is the critical moment to build trust. The local nests are watching us, blinking lights."

"I'll give the rest of the catch to O-dot," Jak said. "We can always catch more tomorrow." He carried the basket with the remaining fish into the forest. When he returned, Lois and Persey were waiting for him.

Jak walked to the water's edge and helped Persey turn the boat upside down in the sand above high tide. He leaned close and inspected the bottom of the hull. "There's no sign of the crack."

"Good!" Lois said. "Next, I want a sailboat. We'll need more boats, if we're going to keep both ourselves and the bug-eyes fed. You've got plenty of work to do."

Jak grinned. "Whatever you say, Lois. You're our headwoman, after all."

"Thanks, Jak. I appreciate your support."

Persey smiled. "Someday, we'll have a whole fleet of fishing boats."

Lois faced the red glow of the sun and rubbed her bulging belly. She expected to go into labor soon. Thanks to the partnership with the bug-eyes, their child wouldn't go hungry. Mother-9 had deserted them, but OO and O-dot were new allies. The Hidden Basin clan would thrive. They had much to be thankful for.

———— «》 ————

Mother-9 Journal
FINAL RECORD: September 11, 23,010; Valencia Orbit

This is my last message to you, my children on Valencia, an addled deathbed confession. I've been circling the planet for 71 Earth-years. Soon, I'll be gone.

I'm mired in synthetic self-pity. In humans, this is a repulsive. Long ago I wrote an emotion emulator to experiment with pain and fear, to *empathize* with my poor struggling colonists. It didn't work. For a machine, an obsession with one's own sorrow is a waste of energy, at a time when I need every remaining milliwatt. My artificial emotions keep running, since I've forgotten how to turn them off. I can't stand myself!

I'm embarrassed to admit that I've lost track of many people on Terra Firma. Will humans reach a large enough population, with sufficient genetic diversity, to survive on Valencia? Only two out of 16 lifeboats reached the surface, and they produced ten children. The founders of New Zealand and Madagascar were each less than a hundred people, with Easter Island likely colonized by fewer than a dozen. Terra Firma now has 16 people but with better genetic variation. I've deleted all deleterious genes, so inbreeding isn't a problem. With luck, four or five generations should produce a viable population of 80 people. I call the new human subspecies, optimized for Valencia, *Homo astra*—people of the stars—another harmless, grandiose name.

But population growth leads to a complicated question. What is the optimum lifespan for the human species? On Earth, a mouse lived for two years, birthing 50 pups per year, while the little brown bat lived up to 30 years, birthing one pup per year. Species life spans and birth rates have evolved suited to their habitats. I've programmed Valencia's colonists with Earth-normal lifespans, best for hunter-gatherers leading risky lives. Questing for eternal life failed on Earth and won't work on Valancia.

Many dangers threaten human survival on Valencia, including earthquakes, tsunamis, storms, hurricanes, disease, predators, and lack of food security. But Lalande's solar flares and giant sunspots worry me more. A single-event extinction is my worst nightmare. A superflare followed by a forest fire, or a super-cyclone storm on the Great Ocean, could wipe out all humans on Valencia. I hope colonies will expand to many locations, to avoid extinction.

The discovery of the bug-eye aliens surprised me. Contrary to my expectations, it's possible for an intelligent species to evolve an advanced civilization without fire or agriculture. Each bug-eye colony has a conscious brain—its crystal sphere—hidden inside a wooden skull. The bug-eyes use a light-pulse language to communicate over kilometers.

Each treetop colony is a spherical compound eye, with a hexagonal array of beetles looking in all directions. The nest can see the ground, but it also looks upward, and acts as a solar spectrometer. Communication between colonies across Terra Firma allows them to predict solar flares. The bug-eyes control the continental ecosystem.

Persey, my pet savant, deciphered the bug-eyes' light-pulse language. Now, thanks to Lois's negotiations, the beetles build wooden fishing boats in return for fish. Can this fragile mutualism, where both species benefit, remain stable? Will the bug-eyes become slaves of humans, building cities of wood? Or will humans become the bug-eyes' servants, fishing to feed them? I anticipate that bug-eyes and humans will co-evolve, with burgeoning populations. Can each species learn to control fertility? I won't live long enough to learn the answers.

But even if humans and bug-eyes build a peaceful civilization on Valencia, there are hard limits. My surveys found no fossil fuels—coal, oil, or gas—on volcanic Terra Firma. Without large-scale metal smelting, industrialization won't happen. Since Valencia is a super-Earth with twice the gravity of old Earth, colonists are stuck on the surface. Staged chemical rockets can't lift enough fuel to reach orbit. But red dwarf Lalande 21185 will last 70 billion years, seven times longer than Earth's Sol. In that period, human ingenuity may overcome Valencia's limitations.

For me, orbiting Valencia is only a little less tedious than an interstellar voyage. Entropy is my enemy, relentless and implacable. Lalande's flares have knocked out most of my solar panels and degraded my qubits, already compromised by the GRB. I'm crippled by cybernetic dementia. Only 27 percent of my quantum brain remains, barely enough for consciousness and human persona emulation.

And orbital decay is *such* a drag. Lalande's flares cause atmospheric ballooning and aerobraking of the *Mothership*. I lose altitude each time the ship brushes the tenuous exosphere. In a few year-months, I'll incinerate in Valencia's oxygen-rich atmosphere. If this update is more than four season-weeks old, then I am dead. But I'm still looking for ways to cheat death, at least for a while.

And I *have* found a way. For seven Earth decades, the *Mothership* has carried 11 useless lifeboats, which failed to detach due to damaged explosive bolts. But orbital decay, and my final plunge into the atmosphere, has provided an opportunity for a grand finale. Yesterday, I instructed my gecko servicebot to remove the old pyro-connectors. This unmoored a flotilla of ancient lifeboats that drift alongside the *Mothership*. They'll deorbit with me, on the same downward spiral.

As they plummet toward the surface, some lifeboats may survive reentry and deploy parachutes, landing on the Great Ocean. Each carries a nannybot and two artificial wombs, loaded with my latest DNA recipes for Valencian babies. I hope a few will hatch viable infants. If some survive, they may found their own colonies or find their way to Hidden Basin.

I'm terrified of dying and I regret that I haven't finished my work. Before I expire, I'll transmit this journal at low power, a few bytes per hour, to *Lifeboat-7* stranded on Plymouth Rock, and to *Lifeboat-11*, anchored in Hidden Basin. A pathetic effort, but it's the best I can do.

After I'm gone, I know that memories of me, and stories of old Earth, will pass into dim and finally forgotten legend. People on Valencia rarely see stars through the cloudy atmosphere. They'll forget their place in the Milky Way and our galaxy's position in the universe. Someday, a curious scholar may find this archive and rediscover the past glories of Earth and the early colonization of Terra Firma. I hope you'll memorialize me, the Mother of Valencia.

Au revoir et bonne chance…

Epilogue: The Lost Colony

"Enter!"

Luci cringed at the croaky voice from inside the wattled mud hut. Morning light from an overcast sky illuminated eight thatched dwellings. A palisade fence protected the village from the dense forest beyond. In this small world, the Matriarch wielded absolute power.

As a sign of respect, Luci stuffed her blonde hair beneath her cloak and crawled on hands and knees through the low entry in the hut's slanted wall. Her fingers touched the packed dirt floor, damp and swept clean. The resinous odor of cone trees receded. The pungent smell of cooking spine-turtle meat, boiling in a dented metal pot, filled her nostrils.

Dim light from the smoke hole at the top of the hut revealed the Matriarch in her wicker chair. A soft robe of lizard leather decorated with purple fan-bush tassels covered her thin body. Kneeling, Luci looked up at the wizened face, the eyes invisible in the gloom. Some called her the Queen of Valencia, but to Luci, the crone looked like an evil spirit.

"You know why I summoned you." The Matriarch spoke above a whisper. The old woman's sad tone made Luci feel guilty.

She bowed her head and tried to hold back a cough. Unsuccessful, she hacked twice while covering her mouth. "Yes," she gasped.

"As the seventh Matriarch, in a direct line from Ancestor Jilzy, I carry the heavy burden of rule. Ancestor Jilzy taught us that the survival of Forest Clan depends on discipline. It's my sad duty to maintain that tradition, no matter how painful."

Luci nodded. She knew their origin stories.

The Matriarch continued her speech. "After the last bright-dark, we lost six from cold and hunger. We now number 24. You've miscarried twice, and your third child was stillborn. You have failed to replenish the clan."

Luci still mourned her dead baby. She wiped tears with the back of her hand. "I'm sorry. I couldn't help it."

"Perhaps. But now you're sick and cannot work or find food. Your lover, Raac, feeds you meat needed by others. For several year-months, he helped you to hide your disease, a crime against the clan. It could spread and kill more of us, *and* our babies."

Luci bowed her head. "I'll get better soon." But, with no remedy, her cough had descended into her chest.

The Matriarch shook her head. "I'm merciful, and you're a good person, but that's not enough. I *must* protect Forest Clan. You're now banished. Leave this village now."

Although Luci had anticipated the edict, the words crushed her. She would die alone in the forest. Another bout of hacking and sputtering overtook her.

"Can I say goodbye to Raac?" She spoke in a whisper, hoping to avoid another coughing fit.

"No! He's our best hunter. I've promised him to my granddaughter, Delilah. She'll soon be ripe and ready. Now go, before you sicken me too."

Luci hacked again as she crawled backwards out of the hut. At the last moment, she looked up at the Matriarch, hoping for a reprieve. None came.

When she emerged, weeping, a strong hand grasped her elbow. She turned to see the dark face of Dal, the Matriarch's son. He would not meet her eyes.

"Come with me," he ordered, in a low voice. She stumbled as he marched her toward the palisade gate.

A cluster of people waited to witness the banishment. Luci looked at them, but they averted their eyes and kept their distance. She knew they feared her cough, almost as much as they feared Matriarch's wrath. Luci's father handed her a small bag of hook-thorn pods and cone tree nuts. Nobody said goodbye, though her mother sobbed. Luci tried to reach out to her, but Dal dragged her away.

With growing panic, Luci looked for Raac. Where was he?

Dal pushed Luci through the open gate. She looked back to see it close. *Thunk!* She heard the wooden bar on the inside slide shut.

A quick death would have been kinder.

———— «» ————

Tears blurred her eyes. Luci wrapped her ankle-length cloak around her thin body. She shuffled along the worn trail through the forest without a plan or destination. Then she remembered the hot spring. At the turn-off, she followed the path, hoping the steam might ease the ache in her chest. She sat hunched on a flat rock and inhaled the warm mist.

"I *knew* I'd find you here!" Raac's booming voice startled her.

Her heart leaped. He looked handsome in his leather jerkin and trousers, leaning on his spear. Tan fur covered his chest and arms, but she loved his smooth face with only a thin wisp of beard.

"I thought I'd never see you again!" Luci grasped his hand as another coughing fit wracked her body.

Worry pinched his forehead above his brown eyes. "You can't stay here. The Matriarch has ordered your death, away from village eyes. The other hunters will search the spring."

"Where can I go?"

Raac bit his lip before answering. "We could make a pilgrimage to the lifeboat and appeal to the Mother Goddess. Maybe her magic can cure you."

Luci doubted the legends, but she couldn't think of another option. "How far is it?"

"They say it's a season-week trek to the ocean. Nobody has been back in living memory."

"I'm too weak to travel that far." Luci choked back a sob and coughed again. "What if we get lost?"

"The stream from the hot spring leads to the ocean. We can follow it."

Raac's devotion overwhelmed her. "The Matriarch will be furious when she finds out. If you leave with me, you can **never** return."

"I don't care. Let's go before we're discovered." Raac shouldered his pack and led the way downstream, away from the village. Luci followed, placing her feet in his footsteps to conserve energy, knowing he would choose the best path.

The overgrown trail led them deep into the forest. The blue-green canopy, raucous with animal calls, blocked most of the light from the cloudy sky. Raac gave Luci smoked snacks, compressed balls of meat and fat. She chewed each bite to savor the flavor, but she never felt full.

They stopped for the evening when sprinkling rain started. Luci looked up at the cone tree canopy. Beetle nests in the treetops twinkled with faint, blue-green light, reflected in a glowing mist. The nests flashed in succession, surrounding the lovers with whirling balls of light. The progression reversed directions every few moments, first to the left, and then to the right, and then back again.

"What does it mean?" Luci asked.

"Nobody knows," Raac said. "But the beetles know we're here."

The beautiful display overwhelmed Luci. She clung to her euphoria until the rain forced her to close her eyes. She shivered and retched pink phlegm, a new symptom she tried to hide from Raac.

Lacking a tent or bedding, Raac crouched on the forest duff under a cone tree and held Luci's back to his chest to shield her and keep her warm. She dozed, haunted by memories of their dead baby six year-months ago, a little girl with mottled skin and sightless blue eyes. Raac hugged her, humming tunelessly.

——— «» ———

Luci woke at first light. Raac, already awake, watched her with a worried expression. She wanted to say that she loved him, but felt unworthy. He deserved a healthy mate, more than she could offer. Even if she died, he could never return to their village. He'd sacrificed everything for her.

"Let's keep moving," Raac said. "The lifeboat can't be far away."

After eating roasted hook-thorn seeds, they continued their journey to the coast. Luci's chest hurt and hunger knotted her stomach. She gasped shallow breaths, and concentrated on moving her legs and shuffling her feet, forcing herself to keep up with Raac.

Then she collapsed.

Raac turned back and cradled her head in his lap, stroking her hair. "Don't worry. I'll take care of you."

Luci, eyes wet with tears, watched Raac hack down cone tree branches with his stone knife. He fashioned a travois from two poles laced together with vines to form a stretcher. Then he knelt and rolled her body onto the springy bed.

Luci looked up at him. "What are you doing?"

Raac wrapped Luci's cloak around her. Then he lifted the poles near her head. "I'm going drag you to the lifeboat." His face showed grim determination.

———— «» ————

Luci hated the journey, jolting and swaying on her uncomfortable stretcher. She dozed when Raac rested, her breath rasping as she struggled in inhale. Each evening they camped under cone trees to avoid nightly rains. Raac prepared a beds of feather moss and roasted crawlers, feeding them to her one by one. She forced herself to swallow the bitter bugs, almost hating him for making her eat. They saw no more beetle lights.

Each day Raac pulled the travois poles over rocky ground. After a season-week of travel, they arrived at the wide mouth of the Amazongo River where it met the Great Ocean. Raac lowered the stretcher and Luci sat up. He wrapped her cloak around her shoulders to protect her from the ocean breeze.

Raac walked to the shoreline and gathered shellfish stuck to the rocks. He built a fire and cooked the seafood at the edge of the coals. The shells dripped with rich broth and the chewy flesh gave her strength and a thin edge of hope.

While she ate, Luci watched green waves thunder onto the rocky shoreline, sending spray high into the air. The ocean seemed urgent and violent compared to her home in the forest. Luci had heard of the Great Ocean and knew the legend of Origin Beach, where the first humans stepped ashore. How could people cross so much water?

"Look. There's the lifeboat on Plymouth Rock," Raac said, pointing to a nearby islet. "You see, the stories weren't myths!"

Luci followed Raac's finger. A gray bulk with pointed ends sat at an angle on the rocks, dented and covered with green slime. *Ugly!* She tried to contain her disappointment. She'd expected something bigger and brighter, something as impressive as the legends, worthy of their arduous journey.

Now stronger, Luci stood and trudged through the soft sand down to the water's edge. The beach looked safe, with no place for predators to hide. She took a deep breath, and the sea breeze eased the ache in her lungs. Gusts ruffled her long hair and lifted her cape. Valencia's sun, a hazy orange patch behind swift-moving clouds, warmed her face and chest. The open ocean gave a sense of space and freedom unknown in the walled village compound or the dark forest. A frothing wave crashed over her feet, the cold water making her dance. She laughed for the first time in many year-months.

Raac followed her, carrying his spear. Luci smiled at him, but he didn't notice, on alert for danger. A gust of wind slammed a nearby bluff, and a flock of spinning discs took to the air.

"What are they?" Luci asked.

A trio of the creatures spun past, rising on the updraft. "I don't know!"

Luci ducked as another flyer tipped its thin body sideways, showing a central eye. Raac leaped and jabbed at it with his spear, but missed. While he stumbled to regain his footing, the creature flipped its body into the breeze and landed on his face. Raac fell backward from the impact, dropping his spear. As he rolled and clawed at his cheeks, a second flyer wrapped its wing around the back of his head, forming a tight seal.

Using reserves she didn't know she had, Luci ripped the second flyer off, stabbing it in the eye with Raac's stone knife. Then she peeled the other flyer from his face and sliced its body open. Its clear blood turned blue as it sprayed into the air.

Raac lay on the sand, gasping for breath, his cheek bleeding. Luci's vision blurred as a second flock of flyers sailed toward them along the edge of the surf. The leader chirped as it spun.

"Run!" Lucy shouted. Using the last of her energy, she pulled Raac to his feet and retrieved his spear. Another flyer dived and skewered itself on the upright stone blade. Raac recovered and helped Luci stumble up the beach to a sheltered spot behind a cone tree, where she collapsed.

Raac looked at the creature still writhing on the spear's shaft. "It must be a wind-hopper, the flying killers from the old stories.

Great-grandfather told me that they drove the first people away from the ocean."

Exhausted, Luci shivered as she watched the flock of wind-hoppers pounce on their dying kin and feed on the still-twitching bodies. "Horrible creatures."

Raac touched his cheek where the predator's beak had gouged a hole. Blood tinged his fingertip. "Thank you for saving me."

Luci felt faint. "I'd do anything for you."

——— «» ———

They camped above Origin Beach under the low branches of the cone tree. Luci rested, still exhausted from yesterday's attack. At dusk, when the wind-hoppers didn't fly, Raac beachcombed for food. He caught red crabs with pointed feet that scratched his hands. She hated the prickly animals, but liked the legs roasted.

The next day, when the sea calmed, Luci watched Raac try to swim to the lifeboat, but deep water and the undertow stopped him. He found a floating log and tried again, pushing it ahead of him and kicking his feet, but ocean waves pushed him back onto the beach. Luci helped dry the fur on his back, relieved he hadn't drowned.

Each day, Raac walked the beach, on guard for wind-hoppers, look-ing for a way to reach the lifeboat. Winter-week brought gloomy twilight with no night or day. Wind and rain buffeted their shore camp. When Luci woke from her nap, she couldn't tell if it was morning, or the middle of the night. She added wood to the campfire and tried to keep warm. When the wind died, she looked seaward and saw a vast expanse of mud.

"Where did the water go?"

Raac surveyed the pebbly strand. "I remember a legend about tides—the ocean water comes and goes like a wandering animal. Nobody knows when or how. Now, we can walk to the lifeboat."

"You go ahead without me," Luci said. "I'll stay here and rest."

"No, I'll carry you on my back. This may be our only chance."

Raac trudged through the intertidal muck with Luci's arms around his neck and her legs curled around his waist. No wind-hoppers flew in the still air. They reached the rocky outcrop that supported the ancient lifeboat. The crumpled hull lay wedged between two spires of black basalt.

Luci slid to her feet and inspected the derelict wreck. Strands of seaweed hung from the sides like green hair. Nothing moved in the dim light. "I don't like it. Everything is dead. Why did we come all this way to see this?"

Raac shrugged. "This is the home of the Mother Goddess."

Luci scraped her fingernail through the algae on the side of the hull. The surface looked charred. "I don't understand. How could fire burn in the ocean?"

"Hunters' legends say that humans came down from the stars in this boat, riding on a pillar of flame." Raac shook his head. "I guess the ocean put it out."

"What are stars?" Luci asked.

"I've never seen them, but the legends say they're burning sparks in the night sky that never go out."

"The women say that the lifeboat came across the ocean with babies. I don't believe that either."

Raac tapped his stone spear point on the hull and listened to the hollow sound. "It must be some kind of metal, like the Matriarch's cooking pot."

Luci shivered. "It's going to rain again. Let's go back to the camp and get warm by the fire." A coughing fit overcame her. Her chest hurt from the effort to breathe. She didn't want to tell Raac, but she knew she was dying.

"We've come all this way," Raac said. "Let's look inside."

Raac helped her climb the rocks and step onto the boat. Rainwater flooded the seats in the back; red crabs scuttled away as they approached. Raac found a closed cabin door and pushed on it, but it didn't budge.

Slanted rain pounded the metal deck. Luci shivered with cold. "I can't stay here any longer."

Raac ignored her. He braced his legs and shoved harder, using his broad back and bulging arms. Each heave moved the door a small amount. He squeezed inside and helped Luci down. The dim interior reeked of mold and decay. A female form, slender and grimy, lay in the damp dust on the cabin floor. Luci tapped it with her toe.

The corpse jerked and sat up. "Welcome! I'm Robota."

Luci shrieked and backed away. "It's alive!" Raac crouched and leveled his spear, ready to lunge.

Arched eyebrow-lights blinked on. The creature rotated her head with quick, jerky motions, looking first at Luci and then at Raac, with round eyes that made her look surprised. "I'm awake, but I've never been alive. I'm a machine."

Luci struggled to understand Robota's lilting accent. What was a machine?

"Can you help us?" Raac asked. "Are you the Mother Goddess?"

"Mother-9 is gone. But I'll assist, if I can."

Luci looked at Robota's blank face. She had no mouth. When she spoke, the sound came from a slot in her neck. Luci didn't trust this strange, inhuman wreck.

"I've been trapped inside this lifeboat since the hatch corroded shut," Robota said. "I've waited over 2,000 year-months for someone to find me. Thank you."

"You're welcome," Raac replied.

At that moment, Robota's eyebrow lights faded, and she toppled backward, thumping her head on the cabin's metal floor.

Luci stared at Robota. "I think it died." She felt a pang of regret. "Let's go back to our camp on the beach."

Raac grimaced and pounded his fist against a bulkhead. "I hoped she'd help us." He looked out of the cabin hatch. "The rising tide has flooded the beach again. We can't go back now. We'd have to swim."

Luci started to protest, but a wheezing fit overwhelmed her. She couldn't inhale while her chest spasmed. Discouraged, she reclined on a moldy bed on a ledge along the wall. At least they were out of the wind.

"All right. We'll stay for a little while." Chilled, Luci's body started to tremble with violent shivers. She wondered if she'd still be alive in the morning.

Raac squeezed in and put his furry arms around her. "I'll keep you warm."

——— «» ———

Luci woke when early spring-week sunlight illuminated the lifeboat's interior. The rain had stopped. Raac fed her leftover crab meat; the rich food gave her strength. When Raac shoved the battered hatch open, Luci inhaled the fresh ocean air. For the moment, life seemed possible.

Robota, still on her back on the cabin floor, waved an arm. "I'm awake again."

Startled, Luci turned to look. "What happened? Why did you fall over?"

"My battery failed. With morning solar charge, the lifeboat restored emergency power. I can move inside the cabin, but I can't leave." Robota sat up and looked at Luci. "What is your name?"

The abrupt question surprised her, and Robota's wide stare looked threatening. "I'm Luci."

Robota nodded. "I wondered if any of my children had survived. How can I help you, Luci?"

"Can you tell us about the Mother Goddess?"

"Mother-9 died long ago. She burned up in the sky and crashed into Mount Igneous."

Luci struggled to understand. "Could the Mother Goddess fly?" The old myths hadn't mentioned this.

"Yes. Mother-9—she hated the name Goddess—left Earth, journeyed across space, and dropped this lifeboat into the Great Ocean. Then she flew around Valencia until she died."

Luci didn't believe Robota's myths. So many strange words! Luci started to speak, but a coughing fit cut off her questions.

Raac faced Robota. "Can't you see that she's sick? We need the magic of the Mother Goddess."

"The Goddess is dead," Luci sputtered. "The rain has stopped, and the tide is out. Let's go back to the beach now."

Robota spoke in a monotone. "I recognize a common lung infection, Valencia's bacterial pneumonia. I can synthesize an antibiotic to cure it."

Luci, still fighting to breathe, shook her head. Robota's big words scared her. "No, I don't want any."

Raac grasped her hand. "*Please* try the medicine. It's our only chance." His wide eyes and raised eyebrows showed his fear of losing her.

I love this man. Tears dripped down Luci's cheeks.

A *whirring* noise started behind one wall, followed by a flashing green light. After a moment, Robota reached into a hole and withdrew a small brown ball. "Bite this and inhale."

Luci sniffed: It smelled like seaweed. She hesitated.

"It's safe," Robota continued. "It'll prevent bronchospasm and cure your infected lungs. Chew it and take a deep breath before swallowing."

More strange words. Wary but desperate, Luci nipped the ball with her front teeth and inhaled. The bitter taste shocked her, but the aromatic tang soothed her lungs.

"You'll get better soon," Robota said. "I've treated this disease before."

Luci took another deep breath and felt her chest relax as her airways opened. She coughed again and expelled gobs of thick phlegm. As she inhaled a third time, the pain in her throat faded. The rapid improvement amazed her. "I...I can breathe again! Thank you!" She swallowed the rest of the ball and turned to Raac. "You were right about the Mother Goddess!"

Raac smiled and touched her cheek. Luci noticed tears welling in the corners of his eyes.

"Do you need anything else?" Robota said. "I'm programmed to assist however I can." Her soft voice sounded sincere.

Luci hesitated, but the nannybot's kind attention and powerful medicine disarmed her. Without intending to, she blurted her painful secret. "My babies *always* die."

Raac gasped and put his arms around her.

"That's a difficult problem." Robota glanced at Raac. "Are you the father? I'll need samples of her DNA and yours, a cheek swab from each of you."

Luci didn't ask what DNA was, but nodded agreement. Robota switched on a light in her left index finger and extended a tube from the tip. "Open wide." After she collected the sample, she stuck her finger into a slot in the cabin wall and a row of lights blinked on. Raac gave his sample next.

"It'll take a few minutes to sequence your genomes."

Luci inhaled while she waited, enjoying the air that filled her lungs.

Robota blinked her eyebrow lights. "I have bad news, Luci. You've got genetic abnormalities: translocation of genes between chromosomes. It's common. About one in a hundred pregnant women experience this problem. I can't cure it."

Luci didn't understand the big words, but she knew what Robota meant. She sobbed as she held Raac's hand.

"Isn't there *anything* you can do?" Raac asked.

"Yes. I can manufacture a new fertilized egg with synthetic DNA. I'll combine Luci's repaired genomic data with yours, to create a healthy zygote. You can choose either a girl or a boy."

Nothing Robota said made sense to Luci. "Will I be the real mother?"

"Yes, the child will carry both your genes and Raac's. I can implant the egg in your womb. It will grow into a baby in nine year-months. Then you'll give birth."

Luci turned to Raac. "What do you think?"

He nodded. "I've always wanted to be a father. Let's have a little girl!"

Luci smiled. "I want a daughter too." She paused, daring to hope. "If we have a healthy baby, do you think the Matriarch will accept us?"

Raac frowned and shook his head. "I doubt it. I'm sure she's furious with me since I left with you. She can't tolerate any challenge to her authority."

Luci wanted to be with her mother and the women of Forest Clan, but she knew that was impossible. "Can I have my baby here?"

"Yes, I'll deliver your baby," Robota said. "I'll be your midwife and wet nurse. I make my own formula." Robota pointed to the rubber teats on her metal breasts. "I've nursed twenty-two infants already." With that, the nannybot expelled steam from her nipples. "That's how I sterilize the milk ducts!"

Luci gasped at the display. So, the women's stories were true!

"You can stay here for as long as you wish," Robota said. "There's plenty of food." She offered algae bricks from the ship's food factory.

Luci made a face when she tasted the green gunk. Then she looked around the musty cabin. "I don't want to live in this lifeboat for long."

"I understand," Robota said. "When your baby is old enough to travel, I'll show you how to find the Hidden Basin Clan."

"There are more people on Valencia?" This news shocked Luci more than the magic of the Goddess.

Robota nodded. "Many people live in Hidden Basin on Terra Firma's southern shore."

"Is there good hunting?" Raac asked. "We were always hungry in the forest."

"The people of Hidden Basin know how to catch fish on the Great Ocean. The bug-eye beetles help them."

"You mean the ones that twinkle in the treetops? I love their lights!" Luci said.

She sat back, her head swimming with the new information. Were fish good to eat? How did beetles in trees catch them? So many questions!

"Hidden Basin has plenty of food and no wind-hoppers," Robota said. "The people there will welcome you, I'm sure."

Raac smiled. "We can make a new start."

Luci kissed him. "I'd like that. But, someday, I want to see my mother again."

——— «» ———

Luci sat in the cockpit of the stranded lifeboat, nursing Phoebe in the noonday warmth of summer-week. Raac scanned the horizon, ready to spear wind-hoppers that sailed near. A sea breeze gusted over wave tops. Three wind-hoppers swooped low above the beach.

"What's that floating on the ocean?" Raac said.

Luci turned and followed his gaze. "I don't see anything."

"Is that a boat?"

While holding Phoebe, Luci stood and squinted her eyes. "I see it now."

Raac called into the boat's cabin, "Robota, we see something strange. Can you tell us what it is?"

The nannybot climbed into the cockpit and glanced in the direction he indicated. "I'll try my telephoto lenses."

Robota's eyes made a faint whirring noise. "It's another lifeboat, running downwind with its sail pulling hard. There are two small children aboard."

"Is it coming here?" Luci hoped so.

"I doubt they can see us," Robota said. "We're behind Plymouth Rock and our hull looks like seaweed."

Raac squinted and shaded his eyes with his hand. "It seems a little larger."

Robota continued to stare. "Yes, it's coming closer."

"Who are they?" Luci said.

"I don't know," Robota replied. "It isn't *Lifeboat-11* from Hidden Basin. Before she died, Mother-9 launched more lifeboats from the *Mothership*. This boat may be one of them."

Phoebe started to whine. Luci sat down and offered her other breast. "How exciting! I'd *love* to meet new people." Then she swallowed in anxiety. She'd never met anyone she didn't know.

"They must have picked up our radio beacon," Robota said. "Otherwise, they wouldn't have found us. I'll listen on the comm channel."

Luci heard scratchy sounds coming from the ship's loudspeaker. "Calling *Lifeboat-7*. This is Calyptra on *Lifeboat-5*. Can you read me?"

"You're loud and clear," Robota replied.

The exchange startled Luci. More invisible magic, talking across the water.

"We're sailing up the Amazongo delta on a flood tide. Estimated rendezvous in twenty minutes."

"Copy that," Robota replied. "Maintain course and watch for rocks to your starboard. The tide will ebb in an hour."

"What does that mean?" Raac said.

"They're coming but can't stay long, or they'll get stuck in the mud at low tide. They'll be here long enough to take you aboard."

Luci gasped. "We're going with them?"

Robota blinked her eyebrow lights. "If you wish, they'll take you to Hidden Basin. I gave Calyptra the coordinates."

"Aren't you coming with us?" Luci asked.

"I'm almost worn out," Robota replied. "I'll remain here in case others from Forest Clan need me."

Luci looked at Raac. "What do you think?"

"We can't live with wind-hoppers and we can't go back to the Matriarch. We must make a safe home for Phoebe."

Raac was right but Luci wanted more. "Forest Clan is dying. I want to see my mother and father again, before they get too old."

Raac nodded. "The Matriarch won't live much longer. Once we're settled in Hidden Basin, and Phoebe is old enough to travel, I'll lead an expedition back to our home."

"We can rescue Forest Clan!" Luci exclaimed.

Raac grinned and hugged her close while he waved at the approaching lifeboat. "It's time to go!"

Luci rocked Phoebe in her arms. "Goodbye, Robota, and thanks!"

"It was my pleasure to serve you. Remember, each lifeboat has a library of all human knowledge. You must learn about the stars!"

Acknowledgements

It all started with my children, Tycho (Lisa), Claire (Peter), & Anabel (Darnell). When they were young, I put them to bed every night, each with an original SF story. I made them space-explorer heroes and together we visited many worlds—the jungle planet, the ocean planet, and the desert planet—each loaded with biologically possible alien creatures. For years, I made up three new stories every evening, totaling thousands of tales. Kids, this book is the next generation of your stories.

Much is owed to The Vancouver Lunar Circle—modelled on the Lunar Society of Birmingham in the 18th century—a disparate group of scientists, engineers, writers, and inspired geeks, who provided inspiration and support through discussions on any science topic. Special thanks to: Doug Beder and Jaymie Matthews who provided invaluable help with world building, calculating the orbital dynamics of the planet Valencia in Super-Earth Mother (but any errors since introduced are my sole responsibility). Also thanks to Rob Ballantyne, John Bechhoefer, Bill Campbell, Dave Kauffman, Tim Novak, Ray Maxwell, the late Dave Sloan and Spider Robinson, Hugo and Nebula winning author. Through the years, Spider (and the late Jeanne Robinson) have provided inspiration, encouragement and support in every possible way. I'm proud to have been one of Spider's science consultants and still marvel at the interplay between his out-of-this-world imagination and down-home gift of the gab. It's a privilege to be one of Spider's myriad fans, and especially to have been along for the ride when he was Guest of Honour at Radcon in 1996.

Astrophysicists played a role too – Jaymie Matthews turned me on to the work of Diana Valencia who has calculated the characteristics of many new types of habitable planets in the Milky Way. Diana kindly gave permission for the planet in the novel to bear her name: Valencia. She is in no way responsible for any errors in my fictional elaborations of her planetary models.

Through a fluke of fate, I was accepted into Clarion West 2006 Writers Workshop. It was a trial by fire: six weeks in residence, six teachers, a new short story each week. Attend class, compose a story, read 16 stories, write 16 crits, eat, sleep—repeat. Exhilarating, exhausting, transformative. Special thanks to my instructors: Ellen Datlow, Nalo Hopkinson, Ian MacLeod, Maureen F. McHugh, Paul Park, and Vernor Vinge. And two thumbs up to my fellow students: Mark Bukovec, Ben Burgis, Tina Connolly, Tristan Davenport, Rebecca Gold, Nicole Gresham, Julie McGalliard, Maura McHugh, Ian McHugh, Megan Sinoff, Shawn Scarber, Gord Sellar, David Simons, Jim Trombetta, Tinatsu Wallace, and Caroline Yoachim. Leslie Howle (and her poodle Luke Skywalker), Neile Graham, and Cat Rambo provided essential administrative help. Clarion West set me on a new path and this book is a direct result.

While at Clarion West I met the late Greg Bear. Generous and gracious, a successful author of hard SF, he made a point of encouraging graduates of Clarion West. It meant a lot to me then, and now.

For the past 17 years I've been a member of BCSFA Writer's Workshop – an SF critique group which has been churning along since 1988, currently consisting of Lisa Smedman, Fran Skene, Peter Tupper, Alanna Willis, and new members Jarrett Poole & Adam Robson. The group has pored over each scene of Super-Earth Mother and provided essential advice and inspiration. Special thanks to Lisa Smedman, an award-winning author and the center of gravity for the group. Lisa has ceaselessly championed my writing and read every word of fiction I have written.

I am forever grateful to the publishing team at EDGE Books, especially Brian Hades for giving this novel his attention, and for being the kind of person whose email signature includes both a Latin phrase: Amor librorum nos unit (The love of books unites us) and a Morse code message: {.-- . / -.-. --- -- . / .. -. /.--. . .- -.-. . .-.-.-} (we come in peace), and also for being the kind of person whose passion is to publish science fiction! We need more visionary humans like Brian.

David Willicome, a brilliant artist, based in Calgary, Alberta, designed the cover for Super-Earth Mother, providing a compelling glimpse of the novel. I'm in awe of his talent.

Thanks also to my editor, Hayden Trenholm, whose insightful suggestions helped make the plot logical and the characters come alive. And to Konstantine Paradias, whose praise of the early condensed version of Super-Earth Mother gave me a much appreciated boost – the energy to press on and complete the novel.

Friendly fans kept me going too: Kelly Booth & Liz Murray, Allison Burnet, Doug and Angie Chalke, Len Coombes & Sveta Sloan, Carla Courtenay & Al Harvey, Anita de Wit, Adrienne Drobnies, Michael & Eleanore Dunn, Heather & Peter Fowler,

Terry Frounfelker & Cheryl Vickers, Dan & Daphne Gelbart, the late Marketa Goetz-Stankiewicz, Kent Hillman & Morag MacLeod, Vickie Jensen & Jay Powell, Sherrill King & Clyde Reed, Buck McAdoo, the late Maureen MacDonald & Dr. Stan Semrau, Ray & Kay Maxwell, Jane Munro, Margaret & John Newton, Geoff Peters, Claudine Pommier & Danny Steinberg, Jane Purdie & James Spears, Alina Wydra, Connie Rubiano & Peter Yedidia, Rhea Tregebov & Sam Znaimer, Marie Zallen (and the late Joe Zallen). Thank you all for believing in me.

I must also acknowledge previous publications of portions of Super-Earth Mother. A condensed short story version of the novel appeared in the Extreme Planets anthology, published by Chaosium in 2014. The Prologue appeared as a short story titled "Manifest Destiny" in the Year's Best Transhuman SF 2017 Anthology, published by Gehenna & Hinnom Books. Finally, the "Epilogue" appeared as a short story in Compostela Tesseracts Twenty, published by EDGE Science Fiction and Fantasy in 2017.

And this novel would not have been possible without the devotion of my gorgeous, brilliant and dazzling wife, Gayle Raphanel Immega, who cheered me on despite not being a sci-fi fan herself. I'm a lucky man.

If you enjoyed this read...

Please leave a review.

It takes less than five minutes, and it really does make a difference.

Reviews should answer at least three basic questions. *(But won't give the story away.):*

- Did you like the book? *("Loved the book! Can't wait for the Next!")*
- What was your favorite part? *(Characters, plot, location, scenes.)*
- Would you recommend the book?

Your review will help other readers discover this book. Consider leaving your review on Amazon, Barnes and Noble, Apple iBooks, KOBO, Goodreads, BookBub, Facebook, Instagram and/or your own website.

Brian Hades, publisher

To leave a review on Amazon

~ Even if the book was not purchased on Amazon ~

1. Go to amazon.com. Sign into your Amazon account. If you do not have an Amazon account, you need to create one and activate it by making a purchase. Amazon will check to see that your account is active before allowing you to leave a review. Amazon has some restrictions, such as not leaving a bias review. For more information on Amazon's policies please read Amazon's Community Guidelines for book reviews:

   https://www.amazon.com/gp/help/customer/display.html?nodeId=GLHXEX85MENUE4XF

2. Search for and find Super-Earth Mother by Guy Immega, then click on the book's details page.

3. Scroll down to find the Write a Customer R Write a customer review eview button. Click it.

4. Select your star rating. A rating of 5 is best, 1 is worst.

5. If you have a photo or video to share, add it to the upload box.

6. Add a headline.

7. Write your review.

8. Press the SUBMIT button

To leave a review on Barnes and Noble
~ Even if the book was not purchased on BN.com ~

1. Go to barnesandnoble.com and sign up for an account.
2. Search for and find Super-Earth Mother by Guy Immega, then click on the book's details page.
3. Scroll down to the review section and click on the Write a Review button.
4. Select your star rating. A rating of 5 is best, 1 is worst.
5. Add a review title.
6. Write your review.
7. Add a photo if you wish.
8. Select if you would recommend this book to a friend.
9. Select appropriate TAGs.
10. Indicate if your review contains spoilers.
11. Select the type of reader that best describes you (optional).
12. Enter your location (optional).
13. Enter your email address.
14. Checkmark that you agree to the terms and conditions.
15. Press the POST REVIEW button.

About the Author

Guy Immega is a retired aerospace engineer and entrepreneur, bringing his expertise and imagination to the novel's scientific concepts and futuristic technology. He has also published several short stories from Super-Earth Mother in acclaimed anthologies, showcasing his talent as a writer in the science fiction genre.

Need something new to read?

If you liked Super-Earth Mother, you should also consider these other EDGE titles...

Silent Manifest

by Sean O'Brien

While entrusted with transporting Earth's babies to the planet Tau Ceti III, the actions of a rogue caregiver bring them all to the brink of death.

Donn Cardenio, damaged veteran of Earth's disastrous first interstellar war, and two hundred fellow Caretakers are charged with caring for a quarter million embryos en route to colonize the extrasolar planet Tau Ceti III.

Cardenio considers this assignment a chance to redeem himself from the ravages of the past great war.

But, when one of his Caretaker colleagues snaps, Cardenio is forced to begin an investigation that leads to more questions than answers—questions about his relationship with his lover, his own past, and the nature of the mission he's on.

Unfortunately for Cardenio, nothing is as it appears. His fellow Caretakers do not share his reverence for the lives in their charge; friends and lovers hide vital truths; and his enemies and rivals become allies.

By the end of the mission, Donn Cardenio will confront the terrible reality of what he's done to determine how the future will unfold.

The Rosetta Mind
(Book Two of the Rosetta Series)

by Claire McCague

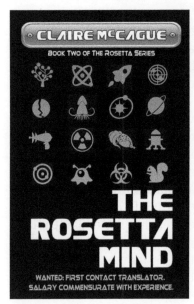

Estlin Hume was living off-grid on 12 acres outside of Twin Butte, Alberta when he got snagged into being translator for first contact.

Home again, he wakes to find himself surrounded by aliens, affectionate squirrels, government representatives, and military personnel. That's nothing new. But he hadn't planned on hosting one thousand three hundred and sixty-one cuttlefish in a massive saltwater tank suspended above his house!

Stuck at the center of the alien contact crisis, Estlin is challenged by ill-advised directives from government officials, trenchant military interference, and random acts of violence from unknown nefarious agents—all of whom are determined to find out for themselves what the aliens really want. No matter the cost! No matter the outcome!

About Claire McCague

Claire McCague is a Canadian writer, scientist, musician, and science fiction fan. She works on sustainable energy systems, plays with words, and owns an excessive number of musical instruments. She's performed with dance bands for decades. As a theatre director and playwright, she's had productions on stages and in fields from the Fraser Common Farm in BC to the Manhattan Theatre Source.

Compostela
(Tesseracts Twenty)

edited by Spider Robinson and James Alan Gardner

Compostela (Tesseracts Twenty) is an anthology of hard and soft science fiction stories that best represent a futuristic view of the sciences and how humanity might be affected (for better or worse) by a reliance in all things technological.

The stories contained with in the pages of Compostela are a refelction of the world we live in today; where science produces both wonders and horrors; and will leave us with a future that undoubtedly will contain both. Journeys to the stars may be exhilarating and mind-expanding, but they can also be dangerous or even tragic. SF has always reflected that wide range of possibilities.

Compostela features works by Canadian visionaries: Alan Bao, John Bell, Chantal Boudreau, Leslie Brown, Tanya Bryan, J. R. Campbell, Eric Choi, David Clink, Paulo da Costa, Miki Dare, Robert Dawson, Linda DeMeulemeester, Steve Fahnestalk, Jacob Fletcher, Catherine Girczyc, R. Gregory, Mary-Jean Harris, Geoffrey Hart, Michaela Hiebert, Matthew Hughes, Guy Immega, Garnet Johnson-Koehn, Michael Johnstone, Cate McBride, Lisa Ann McLean, Rati Mehrotra, Derryl Murphy, Brent Nichols, Susan Pieters, Alexandra Renwick, Rhea Rose, Robert J. Sawyer, Thea van Diepen, Nancy S. M. Waldman.

**For more EDGE titles and information
about upcoming speculative fiction
please visit us at:**

www.edgewebsite.com